Also by Irene Carr

Mary's Child
Chrissie's Children
Lovers Meeting
Love Child
Katy's Men

About the author

Irene Carr was born and brought up on the river in Monkwearmouth, Sunderland, in the 1930s. Her father and brother worked in shipyards in the North East and her mother was a Sunderland barmaid. She has written five previous novels: *Mary's Child, Chrissie's Children, Lovers Meeting, Love Child* and *Katy's Men.*

Emily

Irene Carr

CORONET BOOKS
Hodder & Stoughton

First published in Great Britain in 2001
by Hodder & Stoughton
First published in paperback in 2001
by Hodder & Stoughton
A division of Hodder Headline

A Cornet Paperback

10 9 8 7 6

A CIP catalogue record for this book is available from the British Library

ISBN 978 0 340 75085 8

Printed and bound in the UK by
CPI Mackays, Chatham ME5 8TD

Hodder & Stoughton
A division of Hoddr Headline
338 Euston Road
London NW1 3BH

EMILY

Chapter One

The child wept from loss, bereft of her mother, frightened, bewildered and in shock. She was neat in a dress and coat that came down to the tops of her buttoned boots, a bonnet on her dark curls, secured by ribbons tied under her chin. She paused to catch her breath and the night noises closed in about her. The quay on which she stood, its cobbles gleaming damply with the mist coiling in from the sea, seemed empty save for her. The river lapped against the piles, and out in the darkness a ship slid away down-river on the ebb tide, headed out to sea. Its propeller churned in a steady *swish-swash*.

Mist lay on the child's face, its salt smell mixed with the salt taste of her tears. Only a single flaring gas jet lit the cobbled quay, and fog shrouded the towering cranes of the shipyards that lined the river and the tall chimneys, which added the tang of smoke to the sea air. The river's surface was black and oily and the child thought she was alone. A fog-horn sounded distantly and a steamer's siren blared, seemingly in reply. Their melancholy groans frightened the child anew and her tears fell faster.

The little girl was not alone. The watcher, hidden in a warehouse doorway, had shrunk away when, only minutes before, she had seen murder committed. She had heard the woman call her child, had looked on in horror as the killers struck and ran from the scene. But she had not stirred.

Florence Hartley was little more than a child herself. Her guardian had tried to put her to work on the streets, but she had run away from him and hidden. Her dress was dark and so long it covered her feet, which were bare – she needed to move quietly. Her shoes and everything she owned, with her savings, were in one small bag. Her shawl was black and swathed about her so only her eyes showed. Florence tried to listen through the child's crying for the footfall of her pursuer, Felix Ogden, who she knew was hunting her.

The thieves were still running. Jaikie Nash, a skinny rat of a man, growled, 'What did you shove her in for, Maggie? We'd got the bags.' He carried one – a worn leather suitcase bearing the initials M. F.

'She was trying to stop me getting the rings off her! You should have got a tighter grip of her. I just gave her a push when I'd got them' the woman snarled. In one hand she clutched a handbag while the other gripped her child, another little girl, of a size with the one left weeping on the quay. This one had a dirty face, though, and a runny nose.

Maggie slowed to a walk, breathless, and Jaikie followed suit, but his head was turned to look back the way they had come. 'We've got to get away from here,' he warned. 'That bairn back there will be a witness.'

'Will she hell!' Maggie scoffed. 'Don't be bloody daft! She's no older than Tishy here, and *she* can just about tell you her name.'

'Ah!' Jaikie acknowledged the truth of that with a nod. 'But we've got to get well away. There'll be a lot o' trouble over this. They'll stretch your neck if they catch us and it'll be ten years' hard labour for me.'

'*My* neck!' Maggie glared at him. 'You were in it as much as me!'

'Only for the snatching. I never wanted her drowned.'

'Nor me! I told you, it was an accident. She tried to fight so I gave her a nudge.' Maggie's eyes narrowed, threatening. 'You try to drop me in it and we'll hang together.'

'Don't talk like that!' Jaikie scowled. 'And we've got to get off the streets wi' this lot.' He shook the case. 'It weighs heavy – should be rich pickings. We'll get what we want out of it then toss the rest away. The same goes for that handbag.'

Maggie nodded. 'We'll kip at Sammy's tonight instead

of some doss-house. I'll keep him talking while you slide in wi' the bags. He'll be three parts drunk by this time.'

'He won't be the only one before the night's out.' Jaikie licked his lips.

Florence watched from the darkness, nerves on edge, as the child wailed. She prayed the little girl would shut up or wander away, prayed that that plaintive cry would not bring Felix Ogden down on her. Florence was the orphaned daughter of Ogden's sister, and her parents had been vastly different from him, but when they had died Ogden had claimed her as her next-of-kin. At six years old she had been too young to object and there had been no one to speak up for her. Now, she knew, he would be searching the dark streets and alleys with his gold-headed walking-cane. He had often thrashed her with it, but never again, she swore. She wondered if she should run or wait. What if—

She held her breath, quivering with fear as she saw the thickset figure appear in the dim yellow fog-wreathed light. The child stopped crying and Florence could hear the hiss of the gas jet, the clump of boots on the cobbles. Now she could see him, a man with a beard, in a workman's rough jacket, trousers and cap. There was no walking-cane. It was not Felix Ogden but Bert Jackson.

Florence almost collapsed with relief but stayed still and silent, watched and listened. She knew Bert and his wife, Ada. He was a nightwatchman at Ballantyne's shipyard. They lived only a few doors away from the rooms she had shared with Ogden, his slatternly wife and daughters, who were to school Florence in their trade on the streets. But not now, not ever. Florence liked Ada, who would not speak to the Ogdens but had a kind word for her. Ada did not know how Ogden treated Florence, who would not tell her for fear of him, would not speak out to Bert now.

She saw Bert stoop over the child and heard him say, 'Are you lost, little lass? Where's your mammy?' He looked around him, then he turned back to the little girl and asked, 'What's your name, eh? Tell me your name, that's a clever little lass.' The child whispered something Florence could not hear but Bert said, 'Emily. That's a nice name.'

Florence thought, That's not right. Her mother said—

But Bert was going on, 'Now, what's your other name? Emily what?' The child stared up at him, mute. He fingered the cloth of her coat. 'You're nicely dressed, mind.' That was true – even in the feeble light Florence could see its neat fit. Bert said, 'Well . . .' He glanced about him again, this time as if seeking inspiration. Eventually he said, 'Well, Emily, you'd better come home with me. I haven't time to hunt about for your mammy. I have to get back to work.'

He took her hand and led her off the quay, through a narrow alley, then past the mouth of a cul-de-sac. At the end were the lighted windows of a public house. A rumble of talk, singing and drunken shouting filtered out to them.

Emily, frightened again, pressed against Bert. He lifted her and said reassuringly, 'There, there, Emily. That's only the fellers in the Clipper. They're a wild lot in there but there's not one would hurt you.' That comforted her as they went on, Emily in his arms now.

Bert's home consisted of two rooms on the top floor of a crowded tenement. He carried Emily up the narrow wooden stairs, the only light coming from an occasional window, and she clung to him in the gloom. He pushed open the door at the top and entered the room beyond. 'Here y'are, Ada. I've brought you a little lass that's lost her mammy.'

It was both kitchen and sitting room, furnished with a small table, two upright chairs pushed under it, and two battered old armchairs on a scrap of worn carpet before the fire. The grate shone with blackleading and the flames made the room cosy. A fly-specked, cracked mirror hung over the mantelpiece, which was crowded with a clock and little ornaments, while a coloured portrait of Queen Victoria and Prince Albert hung from a nail on one wall. Ada Jackson was just forty but white-haired; this past year tragedy had aged her. She wore a dark brown dress down to her buttoned boots, with a white pinny and a woollen shawl about her shoulders. She sat in one of the armchairs and stretched out her arms to take the child Bert handed to her. 'She says her name's Emily,' he told his wife. 'Doesn't know owt else. How old d'ye think she is?'

Ada appraised the child and saw solemn grey eyes under dark hair. 'I'd say two years old, not more, maybe less.' She cuddled the child to her. 'Emily, eh? Well, you're a bonny little lass.'

Bert said, 'I'd forgotten my bait so I nipped out o' the yard to come back here to fetch it, and there she was, all by herself on the quay and crying her eyes out.' As a nightwatchman his 'bait', a newspaper-wrapped packet of sandwiches, would feed him through the night.

Ada looked up at him. 'And you didn't see her mother?'

'Neither sight nor sound of her.'

'I wonder if the bairn was abandoned?' Ada suggested.

Bert pursed his lips. 'I doubt it. She's been well cared-for. Just look at her.'

'Aye,' Ada agreed, but then said, 'Just the same, you hear o' cases . . .' She trailed off and sat smiling thoughtfully at the child.

Bert had found his sandwiches and shoved the bundle into the pocket of his patched old jacket. 'I'll take her over to the police station in the morning.'

Ada's head snapped up. 'You'll do no such thing! If she's just lost then there'll be a bit in the paper about her mam and dad looking for her. But if she was abandoned you know what'll happen to her. It'll be the orphanage.'

'I suppose so. But what'll we do with her, then?' Bert said unhappily.

'Nothing tonight,' said Ada, her arms tightening about the child. 'We'll wait and see if anybody's looking for her.

And we'll have a think about it. Now, you get yourself back to work afore you get the sack.'

She listened until the clatter of his boots on the stairs had died away. She sat with the child for a while, talking to her and crooning. Then, after a glance at the cheap clock on the mantelpiece, she made her a little supper of sweet tea and bread thinly spread with jam. The little girl ate hungrily and soon her face was smeared with jam instead of tears. Ada wiped it clean. 'That's better,' she said.

In the bedroom next door there was a double bed and a chest of drawers. She fashioned a makeshift cot by emptying the bottom drawer of its few clothes and lining it with a blanket. As she undressed the child, Ada noted that she was clean and that the clothes were handmade; none bore a maker's label. They look a bit foreign to me, thought Ada. Through it all the child watched her, but her eyelids were drooping. She was tired. Ada laid her in the cot and hummed softly until, after a minute or two, little Emily was sound asleep.

Ada stood up, watching her. 'I reckon you were sent,' she said softly. 'Aye, that's it. You were sent.'

As Bert left the house he saw a prowling figure slinking in the shadows and made out that it was Felix Ogden. His cap was pulled down low on his brow and he carried the gold-handled cane he flaunted. Bert muttered to himself, 'I wonder what he's up to? No good, I'll lay odds on that.'

He and Ogden passed with only a nod, Felix not meeting Bert's cold stare, and went their separate ways. Bert carried on to Ballantyne's yard, grateful that his absence had not been noticed.

The thieves crossed the river Wear by the ferry, to the east end of Sunderland. Sammy's boarding-house was near-derelict, built on piles at the riverside and stretching out over it. The front door opened on to a dark, cobbled alley. Sammy Blenkinsop sat at a table inside the front door, his feet stretched out to the fire, a bottle of gin and a half-empty tumbler at his elbow. His moon face rested on two wobbly chins and his paunch stretched tight his greasy black suit. An oil-lamp swung above the table from a hook in the ceiling. 'I'll not have that bloody gas in here, too dangerous!' Sammy would insist.

Maggie Nash entered first, Tishy still clinging to her skirts. She launched herself at Sammy, wrapped her arms around him and buried his head in her meagre bosom. 'Now then, Sammy! Have ye got a bed for us tonight?'

'Aye.' His voice was muffled, and his hand fumbled at her legs through her skirts. 'There's one out ower the watter at the back. The feller in there will be out in a minute.'

'There's a grand lad ye are.' Maggie held him as Jaikie slipped by, carrying the suitcase and the handbag. He waited for her out of sight of Sammy past the turn of the rickety stairs.

A minute later Maggie joined him, shaking out her skirts and carrying the oil lamp Sammy had given to her. The three started up the stairs but then had to press to one side to allow a stocky young man past on his way down. The previous resident of their room, he carried a sailor's sea-bag slung over one shoulder. 'What cheer, Fred,' Jaikie said with false heartiness, and Maggie smirked. The young man eyed them coldly and gave only a curt grunt as acknowledgement.

They found the room at the back of the house with its door open. There was nothing in it but a bed with a soiled mattress, blankets, pillows and a chamber pot. Maggie looked it over with some satisfaction: this was better than a doss-house or a doorway. There was no glass in the window but Sammy had nailed wooden boards over the frame to keep out riverborne burglars, though there was precious little to steal. One board had been broken and Maggie peered out through the narrow slit. The water of the river lapped beneath her where it ran under the house, washing around the barnacled and weed-clothed piles. Maggie drew the ragged curtains and turned back into the room. 'Now let's see what we got,' she said, as Jaikie scraped a match and lit the lamp.

'Aye. Let's have a look at them rings.'

Maggie held out her left hand. On her third finger was a thin gold band and another ring with a small diamond. Another finger was encircled by a gold signet ring. Jaikie peered at them inexpertly and muttered dubiously, 'They might be worth a few bob, I suppose.' He turned his attention elsewhere. 'It's money I'm after now, though.'

Maggie opened the handbag and emptied its contents on to the bed: a scrap of handkerchief, hairpins – she pounced on the purse. 'Aha!' She shook its contents on to her palm. There was small change in copper and silver . . . and ten gold sovereigns.

'Gi' me that!' Jaikie's fingers snapped around her wrist. Maggie clenched her fist over the coins, but he held her fast and she yielded to his strength. He picked out all of the sovereigns and a little of the rest. 'What about the case?'

Beneath neatly folded clothes they found a tin box. It held a marriage certificate but neither could read it and they set it aside. There were several photographs, of a young man, a woman and a little girl, sometimes singly, sometimes in posed little groups, a packet of letters tied with ribbon. Impatiently Jaikie riffled the edges then tossed them on to the bed. 'Nowt there.' He moved towards the door. 'I'm away for a drink. You can get rid of this lot.'

Maggie was sorting through the clothes. She did not look round as she said, 'I'll have these for me and Tishy. They're all good stuff.'

Jaikie shrugged. 'Suit yourself. They're no good to me,' he said, and left the room.

Maggie held up a child's dress, embroidered and trimmed with lace. 'Look at that, Tishy.' Her little daughter was sitting on the bed, thumb in her mouth, watching incuriously. Now Maggie stood her on the floor and held up the dress against her. 'Fits perfect. We'll have them old things off you.' She stripped off Tishy's clothes and dressed her again from the contents of the case. Then Maggie took off her own clothes, threw them with Tishy's out of the slit in the window boardings to drift away on the tide. The new dress fitted her, although it was a little loose over her flat bosom.

She preened herself for a moment, then remembered Jaikie's instruction. She thrust the purse with what was left of the money into the top of her dress, scooped up the oddments from the bed and returned them to the handbag. She rolled the tin box in the remaining clothes, put the bundle into the case and fastened it. Then she dropped both case and bag out of the window into the water where they sank. Maggie knew that on this part of the river they would be exposed at the next low tide, but she didn't care; the tide was just starting to flow and the shore beneath her would not show for eight or ten hours. By then she would be a long way off.

She climbed on to the bed with Tishy, pulled the blankets over them and blew out the light.

After Bert had taken the child away, Florence waited in her hiding place. She stayed there until he had returned alone, on his way back to Ballantyne's yard, and then she waited longer, eyes and ears alert, but Ogden did not come. Eventually, keeping in the shadows of the black-dark back-streets, she made her way to Monkwearmouth station. There she took out the money she had hoarded from her cleaning work and other odd jobs, bought a ticket and took a train, which crossed the river by the bridge, hissing and clanking, into the central station. From there she went to Durham and boarded the express to London. Ogden would not find her there and she was never coming back.

Jaikie returned to the house after midnight. Sammy still sat at the table with his glass but the bottle was empty and he was snoring. Jaikie had bought another bottle and was smoking a cigar. He shook Sammy, 'Wake up ye drunken ould sot!' but failed to wake him. He dragged another chair up to the table, dropped down into it, and took a swig from his bottle. 'Don't you want a nip?' he asked. But Sammy slept on. Jaikie peered around him and muttered, 'Need a light for the stairs.' He went to the cupboard behind Sammy's chair where the store of lamps was kept. He found one and filled it with oil, spilling some on the floor and the table, then hunted fruitlessly in his pockets for a match. He decided to light it from the lamp that hung from the ceiling. He lifted it down, stumbled and the lamp fell on to the table. The glass smashed, and the oil he had spilt caught fire. In seconds the table and the floor were alight. Sammy woke up as flames licked at his ankles. He leaped up yelling. Jaikie had made for the front door. However, Sammy, befuddled with drink and sleep, ran for the stairs. He had just rounded the first turn when he slipped, struck his head on the wall and lost consciousness.

✳   ✳   ✳

In the bedroom Maggie woke up, coughing on acrid fumes and blind in the smoke-filled darkness. She rolled out of bed, dragging the screeching Tishy with her, and fumbled her way along the wall until she found the door. She yanked it open then screamed as the fire roared in. Tishy clung to her mother as she blundered towards the window, choking in the smoke. Maggie beat feebly on the wooden bars but the fumes overcame her. She slid to the floor, where Tishy already lay silent.

The house was a brick shell, its internal walls of lath and plaster, and it burned like a torch. The flames were only extinguished when the inside of the house collapsed, mostly into the river, leaving just the outside walls. Jaikie, stunned and fearful, staggered away. In the morning he caught the first train to Durham, on his way south.

On the afternoon of the following day Nathaniel Franklin, owner of the Franklin Shipping Line and Franklin's Shipyard, was called upon to identify the bodies. He drove to the mortuary in his carriage, which was pulled by a pair of greys. It was open because the day was fine, but Nathaniel took no pleasure in the sunlight.

He was met by a grave-faced policeman, an Inspector Edmundson: Nathaniel Franklin was a figure of some standing in the town and county. 'Good day, sir.'

'Good day to you, Inspector.' Nathaniel was as tall as the policeman and had once been powerful, but the last few years had aged him and his once dark hair was now flecked with white. 'Where do we go?' he asked.

Edmundson led him to an office where a long table was spread with a white cloth. The Inspector said, 'This was a very bad fire. By an awful coincidence it occurred a year to the day after the Victoria Hall disaster.' On that occasion two thousand children had attended a show there and over a thousand had sat in the gallery. It had been advertised that presents were to be handed out on the ground floor at the end, and towards the close of the show the children in the gallery streamed down the stairs. The first failed to open the door, which opened inward, and were crushed against it by those coming behind. A hundred and eighty-three children died.

'Last night's tragedy was not on the same scale but appalling nevertheless,' Edmundson went on. 'There were no survivors. Eight people perished, six men, one woman and a little girl. We asked you to come here because we found these items.' He gestured at the table. 'They were in the river among the ruins of the house when the low tide exposed them.'

He paused and Nathaniel stepped up to the table. He nodded at the suitcase, stained and torn now, with its initials: M. F. 'That was my daughter's – Marie Franklin, as she was before she married.' There was the handbag, also battered and discoloured, a leather purse and a handful of small change inside it.

The purse was badly charred and Edmundson said, 'I can't explain why the suitcase and handbag escaped burning, except that the building may have collapsed under them, letting them fall into the river before they were consumed by the flames.'

Franklin bit his lip as he looked at the clothing that had come from the case. It was damp and soiled.

The Inspector said softly, 'There are no labels on the clothes. Only embroidered initials: M.L.'

Franklin nodded. 'She made all her clothes. It was her hobby. Leigh was her married name.' The tin box was open and the marriage certificate and photographs were marked by damp, but still intact. He stooped over the table to peer at them all. 'Yes,' he said. He sank into a chair. He was silent for a time, then said, 'May I see them now?'

Edmundson did not answer and said instead, 'We were surprised to find a lady like your daughter in a place like that, a cheap boarding-house?'

'We parted just over two years ago,' Nathaniel said heavily. 'I think now that I must bear part of the blame for that. I told her the man she wished to marry was unsuitable – he was an American actor – so she eloped with him. She wrote once, not giving an address, and I didn't hear from her again until just three weeks ago. Then I had a letter from her in America, to tell me she was widowed and coming home – with her daughter, my granddaughter. I sent a cable to say I wanted her and the child to come to me but there was no reply. I think she had already set out. And she might have been unsure of her welcome, afraid to face me. She was probably tired after a long journey and had little money so sought shelter in the only place she could afford.'

Poor devil! Edmundson thought. He agreed, 'Yes, there was little money.'

Nathaniel stood up. 'May I see them now?'

The Inspector hesitated. 'If you wish. However . . .' he paused to choose his words '. . . we're sure they felt no pain, that they asphyxiated on the smoke before the flames reached them. Immersion in the river when the house collapsed saved them from some of the worst, but there are no . . . recognisable features. If you know of a birthmark or similar . . . ?' He let the question hang. When Nathaniel shook his head, Edmundson finished, 'Otherwise I think we can accept a positive identification without you undergoing a harrowing experience for no purpose.'

But Nathaniel said only, 'If you please.'

Edmundson saw that he was determined and led the way into the cold room, lifted the covering sheets and heard Nathaniel's sharp intake of breath. However, he gazed steadily at the bodies of the woman and child, and noted the rings on the woman's fingers. He said hoarsely, 'The rings – I recognise the signet, which I gave her. I suppose the others came from her late husband.'

Edmundson replaced the sheet.

He conducted Nathaniel off the premises. A sergeant was watching the rich man's departure and remarked, 'He looks like he's seen a ghost.'

Edmundson replied grimly, 'He has to live with one.'

*　*　*

Nathaniel sat stiffly erect in his carriage behind the greys as it bore him back to his big house on the outskirts of the town. Before long it swung into the long driveway, past the gatekeeper standing at the door of his lodge, finger to his cap. Nathaniel thought numbly, He's looking old, due to retire in a few years and he's earned his pension. Nathaniel felt old himself now. His thoughts ran on, his mind recoiling from the afternoon's ordeal. His house-keeper, Mrs Lumley, had given notice because she was sixty-five and he would have to pay her a pension, too. He would also have to engage a replacement. But such thoughts were only automatic, the machine running on without the driver.

As the gatekeeper was left behind, Nathaniel called to his coachman, 'Let me down here.' When he was standing on the gravel of the drive, he said, 'I want to walk and I won't need you any more today.'

'Thank ye, sir.' The coachman drove on, to be back in his cottage early and telling his wife, 'The old feller's looking like death. God knows what he saw at the mortuary.'

Nathaniel walked through the woods that surrounded his house. It was cool in the trees and the wind from the sea rustled the leaves as he strode along. He came to a clearing where a swing hung from a bough and a treehouse was built in the lower branches. He sat down on a log as if his legs had given way. His daughter had played here as a child and he could picture her now. Franklin's wife had died when the child was young so he had brought up Marie on his own. They had been very close. He gave way to his grief and buried his face in his hands.

Emily played happily before the fire in Ada Jackson's kitchen. The woman was kneading dough in a bowl on the table and glancing at the child from time to time. When Bert came in, yawning, from the bedroom, she told him, 'I'll make your supper and sandwiches in a minute. You just sit there with our Emily.'

Bert corrected her, 'She's not *our* Emily.' But he sat in the chair near the child and grinned at her.

Ada made no reply but smiled to herself.

In the days that followed Ada found the little girl would answer to her name, turning her head when Ada called, 'Emily!' But when questioned, 'Where's your mammy?' she returned a blank stare or burst into tears. Ada concluded, 'Something's frightened the little lamb.' And: 'I don't think she's two years old. More likely about eighteen months.'

Emily woke at night, wailing and crying, 'Mamma!' When Ada took her up from the drawer in which she lay, the child clung to her. Ada took her into her own bed, cuddling and soothing her, her heart full of love for the foundling she had made her own. Soon the child would sleep again.

* * *

The body of the woman drowned by Jaikie and Maggie Nash was battered beyond recognition by the screw of a steamer passing downriver. Then it was washed out to sea by some vagary of tide or current and never recovered.

Chapter Two

FRIDAY 23 JUNE 1884. MONKWEARMOUTH.

'All week and never a murmur from anybody.' Ada was cutting slices from a freshly baked loaf to make thick sandwiches for Bert's bait. He was soon to start his shift at the shipyard. 'Nobody's asked after her, said there was a bairn missing, nothing,' Ada continued. She glanced sideways at Emily, who was standing on tiptoe to peer out of the window. 'She was abandoned. It stands to reason.'

Bert was eating a supper of bacon pieces — cheaper than rashers — and fried bread. 'Well, aye, it looks as though—'

'O' course she was!' Ada insisted. She waved the bread-knife at him. 'And it's a good job you never took her to the pollis like you were going to, because that bairn would ha' wound up in the orphanage and you wouldn't want that on your conscience, would you?'

Bert had to agree. 'Aye, that's true.' He drank dark brown tea from a china mug and looked at the clock on the mantelpiece. 'I'll have to get down to the yard. I don't want to be late after that ticking-off I got last week. Somebody saw me out o' the yard and reported me. I reckon it was probably that Felix Ogden but he'd never admit it. I was warned it would be the sack if I gave any more trouble.' He pushed back his chair, stood up and called, 'I'm off to work, Emily.'

The child had been engrossed in the world outside. Ada had not taken her out since Bert had brought her in or told anyone else of her presence. Now Emily turned from watching the children playing in the street below, the gulls flying among the tendrils of smoke rising from thousands of chimneys. She was an affectionate child, thin-faced and solemn, and came to wind her arms around the neck of the stooping Bert and kiss his stubbled cheek.

Ada went with Bert as he made for the door. She said softly, 'She's a little love and I believe she was sent.'

Bert stared at her. 'What d'ye mean?'

'The night you brought her home, it was just a year from the night we lost our bairn.' Their only child, a girl of eight, had perished in the Victoria Hall disaster. Bert flinched at the memory, had remembered the anniversary only too well when he found Emily. 'Now Emily comes, no one with her or asking after her, so I think she was sent for us. We have to keep her. She's ours.'

'We can't!' Bert protested.

'Don't you want to keep her?' Ada demanded fiercely.

Bert turned to look back at Emily. It was only seconds since he had felt her soft kiss on his cheek. He could only give one answer: 'Aye.'

'And we *will* keep her, because she's ours!' Ada's grip on his arm was painful.

'People will be asking where she came from,' Bert pointed out.

'Not where we're going because they don't know us there.'

'Going?' Bert blinked at her, startled. 'Where are we going?'

'I've found some rooms across the river. The rent here is paid up and when the rentman came today I told him we were leaving. When you finish work tomorrow morning you can borrow a barrow and we'll shift out tomorrow night.'

'Why not during the day?'

'Because I don't want the folks in here seeing Emily and talking about her. Remember the orphanage.'

Bert did. He had come from there. His eyes on Emily, he said, 'I know where I can get a barrow, and where I can hide it handy till I want it here.'

'And when we've moved you can get a job at the Franklin shipyard,' Ada told him. 'I hear they're wanting men.'

'The barrow's at the front door,' Bert said, low-voiced. It was one in the morning, the streets were deserted and the tenement silent, its crowded residents sleeping. Bert made no sound as he entered the kitchen; he had taken off his boots to work in his stockinged feet. Ada followed his example and helped him carry the heavier items of furniture like the bed and chest of drawers.

The street lay empty under a quarter-moon, sufficient for Bert to see to lash the furniture on to the barrow but inside the house only the pale rectangles of the windows lit their work. Each toiled up and down the stairs with arms full of smaller items. They spoke only in whispers and when all else was gone they took the bottom drawer, which held the sleeping Emily. Ada lifted the child out and Bert carried the drawer down. Ada followed with Emily in her arms. They passed through the house like wraiths. At one turn of the stairs Ada missed her footing in the near darkness and stumbled. Emily's eyes opened and she peered up at Ada. Then she closed her eyes again.

Out in the street once more, they put on their boots and set off. Bert pushed the barrow and Ada walked by his side with Emily in her arms. As they crossed the bridge over the Wear to the south shore, Ada looked down at the river filled with shipping, either on the stocks, at the fitting-out quays or moored to buoys out in the stream and waiting to get alongside to discharge their cargoes. All were silent and still.

Ada was sad to leave some good neighbours, but she was pleased to be getting away from Felix Ogden. Nothing good came out of that family, she thought, except that lass, Florence, and she was a Hartley. Now I think of it, I've not seen owt of that lass these last few days. It wouldn't surprise me if she's run off.

Now she was feeling a sense of adventure. Eyes gleaming with excitement, she said, 'We're starting all over again, Bert! You'll be getting a new job, we're getting a new place to live and we have a new little lass!'

Her eagerness was infectious and the phlegmatic Bert grinned and peeped inside the hood of the blanket at Emily. 'She's right bonny. And she seems happy with us.'

Ada sniffed. 'O' course she is. She's got a good life to look forward to.' Then she remembered the circumstances of her own times, the poverty and hunger, and amended, 'Better than that orphanage, anyway. With us she'll have a chance to get on.'

So they went on to their new life.

It was a month later, nearing the end of July, when Clarice Carver urged waspishly, 'This is your chance to get on!' She circled around the twelve-year-old boy, her long skirts sweeping the floor. She was a thin woman, in black save for a high white lace collar. Her pointed face held sharp little teeth and her eyes had a hungry glitter. Bradley, her son, in a black knickerbocker suit and tie, was tall and handsome save for a sullen curl of the lip. Clarice noted that and rebuked him: 'You can get rid of that pout and put a smile on your face. If your uncle Nathaniel sees you with that expression he'll not take you on.'

'I can get a position somewhere else.' Bradley shrugged.

'A position! Like your father, I suppose,' his mother jeered.

The boy flushed. 'Don't talk about my father like that!'

Henry Carver, Clarice's husband, had been a shipyard draughtsman, clever at his job but unambitious, given to drink and violent in his cups. He had been killed in a bar fight when Bradley was small. Clarice had chafed at his lowly position and small salary. They had lived in some comfort because of the dowry she had brought with her from the Franklin estate when she married but she envied Nathaniel, her brother, because as the only son he had inherited the majority of the estate. Now she snapped, 'Your father could have made something of himself but he didn't try. He was satisfied with a job! You can get a job, but if Nathaniel takes you on there's a chance you could be his heir. That lass of his is dead, and her daughter with her, so Nathaniel is the last of the line except for you. When he goes, the Franklin Line and the Franklin yard could come to you. So if you don't want to be a clerk, working for somebody else for a pittance all your life, you'll do as I say.'

Bradley took in what his mother had said. Then he twisted his lips into a smirk. His mother nodded approvingly, 'That's better.' She pinned on her wide-brimmed black hat and pulled down its veil. She said, 'Think of the big house and the money, and the men saying, "Please, Mr Carver, thank you, Mr Carver." Now, come on.' She led him out to the waiting cab, its horse tossing its head at the flies buzzing around it.

It was a fine day with only the breath of a breeze off the sea. The men working in the shipyards were sweating and the Carvers were warm in their best clothes. The cab swung away from the neat little cottage in Fulwell – 'One of the nicest parts of the town, don't you think?' Clarice would say – and headed towards the bridge over the river to the south shore then on to Nathaniel Franklin's house. Eventually the car drove through imposing gates, up a drive and came to a stop outside a large house. Clarice and Bradley got out, paid the driver and went up the steps to the front door. As she entered the hall Clarice took off her black gloves and pushed back her veil. She greeted her brother, 'I wrote that note to you when I heard the awful news but did not call because I did not wish to intrude on your sorrow.'

'I quite understand,' replied Nathaniel, 'and appreciate your concern.' He had recovered from his immediate grief though he would mourn in silence for a long time. He was interested in little now, and when he went to his office he stared out of the window at the ships in the river while his managers did the work.

But now, with natural courtesy, he ushered his sister and her son into the drawing room for tea. He smiled at Clarice; she was empty-headed but he had always tried to care for her because she was his sister. He had guessed that there must be a reason for her visit, apart from the expression of sympathy.

He engaged in small-talk with her until Clarice said, 'Bradley will be thirteen soon and his school reports have been excellent, so good, in fact, that his headmaster said he may leave and embark on a profession.' He had also said Bradley was a bully who had injured a number of boys, one so badly that he had been taken to hospital. Bradley had been lucky to escape expulsion. Clarice said nothing of this.

Nathaniel murmured his congratulations. He thought he knew what was coming but was only partly right.

'I wondered, dear brother, if you could find a place for Bradley.'

Nathaniel glanced at the boy, who sat straight in his chair, cap in hand, and who smiled back at him. Nathaniel thought the boy might well be clever like his father, and that he deserved a chance. 'I should think so,' he said.

Clarice clapped her hands in delight. 'Oh, thank you, Nathaniel! I'm sure you will not regret it.'

'Thank you, sir,' Bradley echoed.

Clarice changed the subject now that she had what she wanted and enthused over her garden and her little house. She emphasised how happy she was there. After some minutes she reached for the tea pot again. 'More tea, Nathaniel?'

'No, thank you.'

Clarice poured for herself and sipped. 'A lovely pot of tea. Really, Mrs Lumley runs your house like clockwork. You would be lost without her.'

'I will be soon,' Nathaniel said ruefully.

Clarice feigned puzzlement: 'I beg your pardon?'

'She's given notice, retiring.'

'Good heavens!' Clarice shook her head. 'Have you engaged a replacement?'

'Not yet . . . I've done nothing because—' He broke off, and waved his hand helplessly.

'Of course. I quite understand. At a time like this . . .' Clarice sat silent for some time. Then she leaned forward. 'If you wish, I will take up those duties for you. I am grateful for your offer to Bradley and in any case I want to help all I can when you have such sorrow. Please do not refuse me.'

Nathaniel was touched. She was offering to make such a sacrifice for him – she had just said that she was happy where she was and had no desire to move. Yet to keep house for him she would have to live here. However, there was no doubt that she would be able to run the house. She had grown up here after all. And if she took it over he would be rid of the task of appointing someone else.

'I would be grateful if you would do that,' Franklin said.

Clarice smiled bravely. 'I will try my best to make you comfortable, brother.'

On the way back to the little cottage in Fulwell – riding in Nathaniel's carriage at his insistence – Bradley glanced at his mother. 'That lady you talked to yesterday, she told you Uncle Nathaniel's housekeeper was leaving him.'

Clarice shot him a sharp look. She saw, with relief, that the coachman had not heard his remark, but hissed, 'Shut your mouth!'

Her son obeyed, and stared into a future in which Nathaniel Franklin had retired and Bradley Carver had taken over the running of the Franklin Line and the shipyard. People might patronise him now as a poor boy, but when he came into his own he would make them pay.

'*Look out!*' A man shouted, but Florence Hartley had already hoisted up her skirts and now leaped away from the edge of the kerb. She was just in time to avoid the London mud, a thick amalgam of dirt, horse manure and urine, thrown up from the wheels of a passing carriage. Others on the crowded pavement were not so quick and cursed as they were spattered with it. Florence had seen the carriage rattling up behind her because she still kept a constant watch around her, although it was a week since she had fled from Felix Ogden to the capital, a week since she had seen murder done on the quay in Monkwearmouth. She had left Ogden and his cane over three hundred miles away in the north but it would be weeks before she lost her fear completely.

She could hardly believe she was free! The size, noise and crowds of the city awed and exhilarated her at the same time. She was alone in the world, had to work for every meal and a roof over her head, was without anyone to care for her, but she was out of Ogden's shadow and could *live*. Within an hour of stepping off the train at King's Cross station, she had found a room, and a job the next day. It was poorly paid, menial work, as a washer-up in a restaurant kitchen, but she was determined to improve herself and become a waitress or an assistant cook.

Florence turned into a narrow alley and entered the restaurant by the back door, which was flanked by two dustbins. She was early for work today for a special reason. She hung up her coat and pulled on her apron, watching the door that led from the kitchen to the dining room. A few minutes later Harry Browning, a young waiter, handsome in his black jacket and bow-tie, shouldered through it with a tray loaded high with dirty crockery. He set it down by the sink with a bang. Florence approached him respectfully because he was a rank or two above her in the pecking order. However, he had been disarmingly friendly from when they had met and would come to chat with her when business was slack. He greeted her now: 'Hello, Flo! You're early.'

'Hello, Mr Browning.' Florence delved in the pocket of her apron. 'I've got the letter I was asking you about.' She had written to a friend in Monkwearmouth, Nancy Bell, a girl she had known for years and trusted. She held out the envelope to him. 'It's already stamped. Will you post it as you said, please?' He lived in lodgings in Ealing and had promised to put it in a pillar-box there. He had also agreed that Florence's friend could write to her care of his address. He had done so because he was intrigued by and attracted to this mysterious young girl with the wide eyes and soft mouth.

'Course I can.' He slipped the letter into his pocket. 'I'll post it tonight on my way home.' He grinned sheepishly. 'I can't help wondering what it's all about, though.'

Florence hesitated only briefly. She liked his smile, his patent honesty and gentleness. 'I'll tell you about it, if you like.'

She told him that afternoon, when they had a few minutes to spare, the lunch trade finished and tea not started. Harry listened to her halting tale with growing anger. When he finished he said indignantly, 'This chap Ogden seems a real bad lot. If I get hold of him—'

He stopped for Florence had laid a hand on his arm. 'Please! I don't want you to get into any trouble. If I thought you would I wouldn't have asked you to post the letter for me. You probably think I'm worrying too much, but I've been afraid of him for so long. I just want to be sure he can't trace me.'

Harry grasped her hand in his. 'You can be sure of me. I won't let on where you are to anyone.' He was determined on that. Then he asked, 'Do you fancy a stroll in Hyde Park on Sunday?'

'No!' Florence replied quickly, and saw the hurt on his face. She had not had an invitation like this before: Felix Ogden had kept young men well clear of her, saving her for his trade. She had refused Harry automatically for fear of Ogden's wrath. But, of course, he didn't rule her now. She swallowed her fear and said, 'I'm sorry. I meant yes. Yes, I'd like that.'

'I don't know what *you*'d like, but *I* would like to see you doing something about these crocks!' The head chef, short, tubby, moustachioed and bristling, had bustled up behind them. Hurriedly Florence dumped the plates in the sink. The chef went on, eyeing Harry now, 'And you ought to be looking after your customers, young feller,' and Harry made off. Chef grinned to himself. Not much wrong with those two, he thought.

'Are you washing up, pet?' Ada Jackson laughed as she dried the dishes, watching Emily out of the open window as she did so. It was a week now since the Jacksons had moved into their new rooms on the south side of the river. Little Emily had looked about her with bewilderment when she woke on the first morning to strange quarters yet again, but already she had settled down. These rooms were on the ground floor and Emily, playing outside the open window, was barely a yard away from Ada.

Ada had put her out in the yard with a bowl filled with water and some old tin cups. Emily was splashing cheerfully. The clothes she had been wearing when Bert found her had been washed and put away and she was now in new clothes bought for her by Ada. They were wet, and dirty from the yard, but Ada did not care.

Bert came to stand at her side and she told him, 'We'll have her birthday on the first of May next year.'

'That was our Charlotte's birthday,' said Bert. Charlotte was their child, lost in the Victoria Hall disaster.

'Aye. It's all falling into place,' Ada agreed.

'What do you mean?'

Ada stated what was obvious to her: 'That she was sent, o' course.'

Bert was not sure about that, but he said, 'She seems happy enough.'

'Aye,' said Ada. 'As long as she's happy, that's all that matters.'

Chapter Three

'You'll be the man of the house while I'm away.' Richard Walsh grinned down at his son and eight-year-old David tried to return the smile but the corners of his mouth drooped. His father had been home for just two weeks after spending six months away at sea and it broke David's heart to see him go again.

'Aye, Dad.'

'Be a good lad and help your mother.'

'Aye, Dad. I will.' He couldn't say any more because he was choking. He looked to his mother for help but Molly Walsh's own lips were working. Two of the girls, younger than David and not fully realising what was happening, clung to her skirts, thumbs in their mouths. She held the youngest, a baby, in her arms. Now she said, 'Take care, love. I wish you didn't have to go.' He would be away for

35

three months, six months or a year. It would all depend on what cargoes they found.

'It might be the last time I go deep sea.' Richard tried to cheer her. 'It's my third berth as mate. There's a good chance I might get command of a little coaster next and then I'll be home nearly every week.'

'It can't come too soon for me. I want you home for good, my love.'

'Aye, but I have to go now.' Richard kissed them all one last time then gently pulled away from his wife's embrace. He lifted his big white canvas sea-bag, heavy with his bedding, spare clothing and boots, and slung it over his shoulder. He had one last word for David: 'I'm depending on you.'

'Aye, Dad.' David watched through a mist of tears as his father strode away. Richard's ship, an ocean-going tramp steamer called the *Alice Ross*, sailed with the tide two hours later.

Bert Jackson saw her slip downriver from his perch high on the wooden staging around the half-built hull of a ship in the Franklin yard where he now worked. He peered at her, through a fine drizzle driving in from the sea on the wind, with a degree of yearning: he had been a seaman once, which was not unusual in this town. Then he shrugged; he had given up the sea over ten years ago and he was happy at home with Ada – and Emily. He smiled at the thought of her. There was a blessing, now!

He was still smiling as he started heading for the ship's stern. It was then that his foot slipped and he fell, screaming as he plummeted forty feet to the timber and steel plates below. The other men close by had heard his shout above the hammering all around them, and rushed to his aid. They lifted him tenderly and when he had been sent off to the hospital they told each other, 'He's lucky to be alive,' but later they added, 'He'll not be much good for owt after this.'

When the fractures healed Bert was left with a bad limp and there was no work for him in a shipyard. Clancy, sharp-featured and sharp-eyed, the manager of the Franklin yard, was a strict disciplinarian but a good-hearted man. He arranged a meeting in the bar of the Palace Hotel with Wainwright, broad and red-faced, the land agent who ran Nathaniel Franklin's estate. He had grown up on it, starting as a garden boy and working his way up through the ranks. When they were seated, with a glass of Scotch each and a soda siphon between them, Clancy asked, 'I wondered if you could find a billet for a man I've had to lay off. He had an accident that left him with a bad limp. He can get about but a shipyard isn't the place for him now. He was only a labourer but he was a seaman and a good worker, sober, honest, responsible. He's married with a young daughter.'

'Snap!' Wainwright gave his booming laugh. 'Your problem is the answer to mine. The gatekeeper up at the house is retiring at the end of the month. I've been looking for a replacement and I've had a few after the job, but I don't want a drunk and the sober ones were wanting nothing but free lodging. Send — what's his name?'

'Bert Jackson.'

'Send him up to my office. If I like the look of him I'll take him on.'

'I'm obliged to you.'

Wainwright grinned, 'You can top 'em up again, then.'

Ada saw Bert off to the appointment, inspecting him in his navy blue serge suit. It hung looser than it had: since his fall he had lost weight through worry. Those days if a man could no longer work he had to depend on the scrapings of parish relief or charity, and his family with him. Ada saw the looseness of the suit, but she said nothing and brushed it vigorously. Emily, a white pinny over her brown dress, pink-cheeked, dark-eyed and hair hanging glossy down her back, followed her and asked, 'What have you got your suit on for, Daddy? It isn't Sunday.'

On Sunday they always walked to the cemetery where Ada laid flowers on the grave of her first-born. 'Your sister,' Ada would say, with a tear. Emily was used to the weekly pilgrimage, the few minutes of silent vigil as all three stood at the graveside. Solemnly she mourned the 'sister' she had never known. Afterwards Ada would hold her in a tight embrace as if afraid she would lose Emily too.

'He has to see a gentleman about a job,' Ada said.

'Aren't you going to work at the yard any more, then?'

Bert shook his head and Ada snapped, 'Keep still!' as she straightened his tie.

'I had to give it up. Can't go labouring in the yard with a bad leg like mine,' he said.

'You never put your suit on when you worked in the yard, Dad.'

'I won't wear it at this job, either.' He grinned at her, then glanced at Ada and muttered, 'If I get it.'

'O' course you will,' she answered brusquely, but her lips twitched with anxiety.

'O' course you will,' echoed Emily, with trusting confidence. But she persisted, 'But why are you wearing your suit now?'

'He'll have a better chance of getting the job if he goes to see this gentleman in his suit.' Ada peered down to see that Bert had polished his boots, and nodded. She took a deep breath. 'Well, now, you're ready. Off you go.'

Bert glanced at the clock on the mantelpiece. 'It's a bit early.'

'Better early than late. If you get there with time to spare you can walk round the block. Besides, you've got to allow for getting there – you don't walk as fast as you used to.'

'Aye, that's true.' Bert moved towards the door, one leg swinging stiffly. 'I don't know how he'll take the bad leg.'

'That Mr Clancy said it wouldn't matter,' Ada assured him. 'Now get away and don't you worry.' But her hands were twisting in her apron. 'Good luck.'

She picked up Emily, followed Bert to the front door and watched him limp off up the street. Then she kissed the child and prayed silently. Both she and Bert were afraid: if he failed to find work of some sort then the workhouse loomed.

Within the hour Bert returned. Ada heard the rapid dot-and-carry-one of his limping stride and realised he was running as well as he could. She started towards the kitchen door but he burst in and shouted, 'We've got it!' He swept her into his arms and waltzed her round the kitchen table while Emily laughed and danced after them.

This time they moved in the light of day with the neighbours gathering to wish them well, and a cart from the Franklin estate to carry their few sticks of furniture. Ada and Emily cried to be leaving their friends but cheered up when they were out on the road on top of the cart. Emily twisted and turned on Ada's knee, a battered old doll in her arms, not wanting to miss any of the sights along the way. She patted the horse's broad brown rump and craned to peer at the traffic in the high street and Fawcett Street where the big shops were, until Ada said, laughing, 'For God's sake, lass, sit still!'

'Is it all yours, Daddy?' Emily asked, when they came to the Franklin estate, which was surrounded by a high stone wall.

The lodge stood just inside the gates, in a plot of land hedged about as a garden, with flowers growing in the front and vegetables at the rear. Emily had no recollection of living anywhere except the two downstairs rooms with another family occupying the rooms above, and only a cobbled street at the front, a yard and back lane behind. The gatekeeper's lodge stood in splendid isolation.

'Aye, it's all ours.' Bert grinned. 'You'll have plenty of room to play here.'

But Ada looked around at the wooded estate inside its encircling wall, the farmland all about, and asked Bert, 'Will the bairn be all right, playing in these woods all by herself?'

Bert laughed. 'Course she will! Didn't Franklin's own bairn play here? What harm could come to her?'

Each day Emily set off for the village school, walking the half-mile down the country roads. She was quick to learn, a good scholar, and made friends among the children of the village, happy with the only parents she had ever known. In the winter evenings she was content to play with her toys, read a book beside the coal fire in the lodge, or play dominoes with Bert while Ada looked on as she sewed. They were happy through that winter as the wind howled and rain lashed the windows, or snow and frost painted them white.

But not all was perfect. One bitterly cold morning Nathaniel Franklin's carriage swung in at the gates and stopped outside the lodge. Bert stood at the open gates and Ada was sweeping the front path, Emily at her side carrying her doll. Clarice Carver lowered the carriage window and called to Ada, 'I need your help at the house this evening. We have a lot of people coming to dinner and I'd like you to help serve.'

Ada was about to reply, but Bert was quicker: 'She won't be able to do anything of that sort. Sorry, ma'am.'

Clarice gasped, outraged. 'Are you refusing to obey my orders?'

'No, ma'am. I'm just saying she can't do it because she has a house and a family of her own to care for and she wasn't hired to work at the big house. I was taken on to be gatekeeper here and I'm grateful to Mr Franklin, but there my duties – and hers – end.'

Clarice was flushed with anger, and well aware that the coachman and the footman were listening impassively to this exchange. 'I will report this to Mr Franklin and we'll see what he has to say.' And to the coachman: 'Drive on!'

'Yes, ma'am,' answered Bert, and put a finger to his cap as the carriage rolled on up the gravelled drive towards the house.

'She was cross,' Emily whispered.

'Aye,' said Bert.

Ada watched the carriage go, biting her lip, then turned on Bert: 'You shouldn't have talked to her like that. And I could have gone up there and helped out, fitted it in.'

Bert was unmoved. 'I wasn't rude and I only spoke the truth. The old man took me on, not her, and it was to be gatekeeper. You aren't working for her. I've been up to the house a few times to talk to him about the job and I've seen and heard her. I don't like the way she talks to them servants, as if they were nothing and she was the fine lady. She doesn't do it when the old man's around, she's too fly, but when he isn't . . .' He came to put his arm around Ada and squeezed her gently. 'I won't have her sort talking to you that way.'

That brought a smile briefly to Ada's lips but she said unhappily, 'What if she complains to old Franklin?'

'Let her,' said Bert confidently. 'We'll get a fair crack o' the whip from him.'

'People like that should be whipped!' Clarice stormed into Nathaniel Franklin's study, a room off the hall, where he sat in an old leather armchair before a coal fire. He lowered his newspaper to stare at her, startled. 'Good God! What's the matter?'

'That — that gatekeeper, Jackson. He has just been extremely insolent.'

Nathaniel frowned. 'You surprise me. I've always found him polite.'

'Well, he probably thinks he has to be polite to you.' Clarice sniffed.

'Um.' Nathaniel refused to be provoked into anger without just cause. 'What did he say exactly?'

That word 'exactly' gave Clarice pause. She realised she dared not paraphrase because her brother might well check her statement against that of the gatekeeper — and possibly the coachman. Of course, they would all stick together! So she repeated the conversation word for word. Nathaniel listened, then was silent for a moment, thinking. He looked his sister in the eye. 'Well, he spoke no more than the truth. They weren't hired to work in the house. But I'm surprised he refused to let Ada work. I'd have thought they would have liked to make a shilling or two extra. I wonder why he turned down the chance?'

This was not going the way Clarice had thought. She did not want Nathaniel making enquiries as to why Jackson had refused. Even less did she want him extending that kind of enquiry to the other servants. She knew they were hostile to her and did not care so long as she could dictate to them — and there was no chance of Nathaniel finding out. She managed to smile. 'I expect he was just a bit fed up about something. It's nothing to make a fuss over. We've done without Ada's help before so we will again.' She turned to the door. 'And that reminds me — I must talk to Cook about the dinner tonight.' She bustled out.

Nathaniel wondered about the truth behind the little storm that had just blown over. He suspected his sister might have been at fault: he remembered similar outbursts when they were children. However, under her the house ran like clockwork and that was enough to satisfy him now. And her son, his nephew, young Bradley . . . Nathaniel tossed aside the newspaper and strode out into the hall, calling for his carriage.

He was driven down to the shipyard, walked into the manager's office and asked, 'Where's young Bradley?'

Clancy stood up from his swivel chair. 'He's out heating rivets this week.'

'How's he getting on?'

'Very well,' Clancy said. 'He's quick to learn and forgets nothing. In fact, he's an outstanding lad, and I'm not saying that because he's your nephew.'

Nathaniel was pleased. 'I'll go and have a word with him.'

After he had gone, Clancy murmured, 'And I'm not saying he's good because he might be my boss one of these days, either. He'd get on anyway, without the push from the old man.'

Nathaniel had soon divined that Clarice wanted him to name Bradley as his heir and didn't think she could be criticised for that: she was a mother looking out for her son. And Nathaniel did not care, so long as the boy proved a good man. He was kin, after all – Nathaniel's only kin now.

He walked down the yard to where the hull of a part-completed ship stood ringed by staging. The men working in the yard made way for the 'Old Man', nudged each other as he passed and muttered, 'He's looking ould now.' Out there on the riverbank Nathaniel felt the full force of the wind whistling in from the sea smelling of salt, and was glad of his thick overcoat. He paused for a moment, staring up at the staging, then picked out his nephew. Bradley Carver was stooped beside a brazier filled with glowing coals.

Nathaniel climbed the ladder to stand on the staging.

For a minute Bradley was unaware of his presence and he watched his nephew at his work. At eighteen he was tall and handsome, with blond hair and pale blue eyes. He was heating rivets in the brazier until they glowed white hot, then picking them out with a pair of tongs and passing them to the catcher boy with the riveting team above. They inserted them into the holes in the ship's plating and beat down the ends with hammers to hold the plates in place. He was working well, Nathaniel was pleased to see. He himself had set out the programme for Bradley's training: 'I want him to do every job in the yard and the shipping office.' The boy had been at it for five years now, and Nathaniel was pleased with him, although Bradley still had a long way to go before he could take over the running of the shipyard and the Franklin Line.

Nathaniel raised his voice to be heard above the wind and the pounding of the hammers: 'Hello!'

Bradley turned, his cheeks glowing from the heat of the brazier. The old jacket and trousers he wore for working in the yard were pockmarked with holes, burnt in by sparks. For a split second his face was expressionless, then he smiled. 'Hello, sir.'

'Enjoying yourself?'

'It's warmer than working on the quay.' He had worked out on the edge of the quay all the previous month, sometimes in sleet or snow.

Nathaniel laughed, then said, 'I want you to do a spell in the drawing office, starting next week. How does that suit you?'

'That will be fine with me, sir.'

A little later, Nathaniel left him, descended the ladder and returned to his carriage. For the thousandth time, he thought that the boy was pleasant and could not be faulted in his work, but . . . there was something not quite right about young Bradley Carver. He seemed always too ready to please. Then he told himself he was trying to find fault because he had no son of his own to follow him . . . no daughter either, now. He should be glad that the boy was turning out so well.

When Bradley had turned back to his work after his uncle left, his smile slipped away. It appeared only when he needed it. He was determined to inherit the yard and the line and would do whatever it took to ensure that he did.

A voice jeered behind him, 'So the boss has been to see his pet!' It was Marley, who was also heating rivets further along the staging.

Bradley was holding the tongs in the fire, gripping a rivet among the coals. Now he whipped it out and thrust it, glowing red hot, into Marley's face. He leaped back from the heat of it but Bradley followed him until Marley was backed into a corner with nothing behind him but a drop to the yard far below. He gasped out, eyes wide and fixed on the red steel pulsing heat just in front of his face, 'For Christ's sake! Are you trying to kill me?' The rivet was scorching Marley's nose.

'You'll keep your trap shut and give me a wide berth from now on. Yes?' Bradley growled.

'Aye!' Marley teetered on the edge of the staging and Bradley held him there for a few seconds more as Marley repeated, 'Aye! Aye! Just give over! Aye!' Finally the rivet was withdrawn and Bradley walked back to his brazier.

Marley wiped his sweating face and stumbled away on shaking legs, avoiding the eyes of the grinning men. Nobody liked a big-mouth, but they were wary of Bradley, too, and not only because he was the boss's nephew. He had established that it was dangerous to trifle with him.

It was springtime and Bradley, booted and spurred, was in the stables. 'Saddle up Samson for me,' he told the groom.

'Begging your pardon, sir, but the master won't let anyone ride Samson but himself,' the groom replied. 'He says the horse is too dangerous, likes to buck all of a sudden. Will you take Juliet instead, sir?'

'Juliet's a rocking horse. Just do as you're told and saddle Samson. He won't throw *me*.'

'Sir, the master—'

'Never mind the master! He won't know anything about it. Now, do as you're told!' His glare silenced the old man and he obeyed.

Bradley found the horse frisky but no more than that, and after a while he relaxed. He could handle Samson. They cantered out of the trees into a clearing, where a swing bearing a little girl soared up past Samson's nose.

He reared and Bradley lost his grip on the reins and had to cling to the horse's neck. Moments later he held the reins again and had regained his seat.

The child was laughing at him. 'What are you sniggering at?' He urged Samson forward until the horse was alongside the swing and looked down on her. Emily flinched. 'Who the hell are you and what are you doing here, eh? Climbed over the wall, did you? Bloody village brats – you think you can go where you like! I've a mind to flog you!'

He lifted his whip but the blow never fell because a hand seized Samson's head and turned him away. He pranced again but Bert held him. 'What the hell d'you think you're doing, Jackson? Let go!' Bradley demanded.

But Bert would not. 'I'm doing you a good turn, Mr Carver. If you try to use that whip on me I'll have you out o' that saddle and on your back. And if you'd laid a hand on that bairn o' mine you'd ha' been up in court after I'd finished wi' you. And the old man wouldn't be able to save you from that, even if he wanted to, which I doubt.'

Mention of Nathaniel brought Bradley up short. He knew how his uncle would react if this came to his attention. He lowered the whip. 'I didn't know the – the child was yours.'

'She's been living in the lodge all winter. But I don't suppose you noticed her.' Bert released the horse's head and Bradley rode away.

Bert picked up Emily and held her close. 'There now, there. You're all right now, bonny lass.'

When he told Ada what had happened her lips tightened with anger. 'What a mercy you were there. Here, give her to me.'

Bert passed Emily to her but warned the child, 'You keep away from that house,' then added reassuringly, 'There now, you don't need to fret about that Mr Carver. He won't bother you again.' But he was wrong.

Bradley galloped recklessly back to the stables. In the yard he hauled on the reins and brought the horse to a skidding halt. The worried groom grabbed Samson's bridle and asked, 'Everything all right, sir?'

'*Aye!*' Bradley shouted, and jumped down. 'Of course I'm all right. Any fool can ride him.' He threw the reins at the old man and strode away to the house. Seconds later he marched into his mother's parlour where she was making up her housekeeping accounts. 'That man Jackson, the gatekeeper, he ought to be sacked.'

Clarice Carver looked up from her books. 'What has he done now?'

'I caught his brat using the swing in the woods, in the clearing where old Franklin sits. I ticked her off and Jackson threatened me. Insolence!'

Clarice pursed her lips. 'You're right. I've noticed it before. He and his family were a most unsuitable appointment. The whole tribe should be turned out of there.'

'Then let's talk to the old man.' Bradley's eyes gleamed at the thought of revenge. 'Tell him to get rid of them.'

Clarice was more cautious: 'No. If we complain to him he'll ask all manner of questions and no doubt Jackson will tell him a different tale.'

'So we let him get away with it?' Bradley scowled.

'For the time being.' Clarice smiled malevolently. 'But Nathaniel is growing old. Your time will come.'

Bradley Carver nodded sullenly. Later he thought over his actions coldly. He knew he had been high-handed and that he was unpopular with the servants. He also realised that if Nathaniel found out he might decide his nephew was not a suitable heir. Bradley decided that that must not be allowed to happen. He would change his attitude – for now. When he inherited he would settle the score – or sooner if an opportunity arose.

Florence Browning set breakfast before her young husband of one week and kissed the top of his head. 'There you are. Get that inside you.' Then she squeaked and jumped away from his hand. 'No, you don't!' She circled the kitchen table with its oilcloth cover and sat in her own place opposite him.

Harry grinned across at her, 'I'll get you next time.' Then, when she pulled a face at him, he asked, 'Who's the letter from?'

'Nancy Bell.'

His brows lifted. 'She writes regular as clockwork.'

'Every month.' Florence slit open the envelope with a kitchen knife and scanned the pages inside.

Harry watched her and saw her smile slip away and the corners of her mouth turn down. He knew what that meant: news of Felix Ogden. The smile returned. Florence looked up and passed him the letter. 'Nancy's fine. She says Ogden's as bad as ever, giving those lasses of his a terrible life. She keeps out of his way. Like me. I'm never going back.' She smiled across the table at him. 'I've got all I want here.'

Florence remembered vividly the night she had run away; every detail was clear of the murder, the child left alone, and her own flight through the dark back-streets.

'It's a letter from Dad!' David Walsh snatched it up from where it had fallen inside the front door of the little cottage. Richard wrote to his family two or three times a week, but he was only able to post his letters when his ship, the *Alice Ross*, was in port so one envelope might hold ten or twenty sheets of paper. Delivery was subject to the vagaries of the post, whether from Naples, Port Said or Singapore. It was not unusual for his family to have no word from him for a month or two then receive three or four letters.

This time they had waited only a week since they had opened a packet of letters and here was another. It was only when his wife looked more closely at the envelope that she realised the copperplate handwriting was not his. She opened it sitting on a chair in the kitchen, David at her shoulder and the two girls kneeling either side of her.

It had been written by the captain of the *Alice Ross* and told her that a typhoon had struck when they were three days out of Singapore. The big seas had swept over the deck and men had been washed overboard.

'Why are you crying, Mam?' David asked, frightened.

Richard's widow tried to hold them all in her arms.

Chapter Four

JANUARY 1894, MONKWEARMOUTH.

'I want you here with me.' David's mother put her arm round him and smiled at her son. They were in the kitchen of the little cottage and his two sisters played in a corner, while rain lashed the windows and a clothes-horse hung with damp washing hid the fire. 'You've grown these last five years.' They stood eye to eye now. 'You're thirteen and you're going to be as tall as your father.' Her smile slipped at the thought of her husband, lost at sea on the other side of the world. Fear clutched at Molly's heart, and she said, 'I know you want to take your father's place and provide for us, and I love you for that, but I don't want you to go to sea.'

'But, Mam—'

David stopped as Molly held up a hand. She went on, 'You've done well at school and your headmaster has found you a job in the office at Buchanan's yard. It isn't much of a wage to start with but you'll have the chance to get on and it's regular work.'

'I'll hate it in an office, Mam,' David protested, 'I know I will. Why can't I go to sea like my dad?'

Molly shook her head. 'I never liked him sailing off for weeks or months at a time. It was always my hope that he'd find a job ashore. If he had, he would have been alive now.'

'Men get killed in the shipyards, Mam,' David pointed out.

'Not in the office.' In a tone that David knew was final, she said, 'I won't be left alone with the two lasses. You take this job, work hard, and come home to me every night. I'm sure you'll soon get to like it and you'll be glad you listened to me.' She knew of boys who had talked of going to sea but had settled for a life ashore. She could have married one, but Richard Walsh had always been the one for her.

David sighed. 'Aye, all right, Mam.'

He stuck at the office job for six months, in a dark blue suit and stiff collar, making tea, filling the inkwells and running errands for his seniors. For the most part they were good to him and he made friends. They noted that he worked hard and well and was always ready to take on any task. But David was trying to squeeze into a mould for which he was unfitted. From the office window near his desk he could see the river, with the sea beyond, and became increasingly miserable as the days lengthened into summer. He watched the ships steam downriver, headed for the sea, and in his lunch-break he walked on the quays, looked longingly at the ships moored there and talked to the men aboard them.

On a warm night in June he rose from his bed, dressed and crept downstairs with his boots in one hand. In the other was a sack holding spare clothing, bread and cheese and a bottle of water. He had planned this carefully. He left a note on the kitchen table: 'Dearest Mother, I have gone to sea. I will send some of my pay like Dad did. Your loving son, David.'

He looked back once from the corner of the street, dry-eyed because regret and sorrow were overlaid with excitement. Then he turned away from home and family and set off into the dark streets until he came to the river. There, he climbed the wall to enter the huge shipyard, with its network of railway lines, glinting in the light of a quarter-moon, and trucks, loaded with coal. He looked about him for the ship he wanted and soon saw her, the *Cliveden* of the Franklin Line, lying under the coaling staithes, the chutes down which the coal would rumble to fall into the belly of the ship.

The night before he had asked one of her crew when she would sail. The seaman had been chewing tobacco. Before he answered, he spat out a stream of juice then said, 'We'll be hauling up to the staithes tonight and coaling first thing in the morning.' He grinned at David in his suit, stiff collar and tie. 'Are you coming to give us a hand?'

'No fear.' David played up to the joke. 'My ma

wouldn't like it if I got coal on this shirt.' They both laughed, David a shade guiltily at the thought of his mother.

Now he stole to the foot of the gangway that led up from the quay to the *Cliveden*'s deck.

On deck no one stirred so he took a deep breath and tiptoed up the gangway. Once on the ship he crossed to the deeper shadow under the bridge and paused again. He was about to move on when a door opened in the upperworks right alongside him. A man stepped out over the coaming and stood peering about him for long seconds. Taken by surprise, David froze and held his breath. The open door partially hid him but the man was only a yard away and David saw he was the seaman he had spoken to yesterday. The other sailors had called him Toddy. Now he turned back without seeing David, and the door closed behind him.

David let out his breath in a shuddering sigh. He knew he had been close to being returned to his home to become the butt of jokes in the office. That would have been humiliating and he was more determined than ever to succeed in his venture. He sidled along the deck to where the ship's lifeboats hung in their davits. He climbed up to one, loosened the canvas cover, crawled inside then slid out a hand to tighten the lashings again. He settled down in the bottom of the boat but knew he was too wide awake to sleep.

The coaling woke him, the first wagonload thundering down the chute to crash into the hold. Through the slit between the canvas cover and the boat he could see that it was a fine morning, but the ship was enveloped in a cloud of coal dust. It filtered in under the cover to coat the inside of the boat and David. He sat, cramped, cold and miserable, but still without regret.

Finally *Cliveden*'s holds were full, and she was hauled away from the staithes by tugs to be towed downriver. After a time David felt the tremor through the ship as her engines turned over, and not long after that he sensed a different motion and knew she was at sea. He had done it!

He celebrated by eating his sandwiches and drinking some of his water. Soon after this he got cramp and straightened up so that his head pushed up the cover of the lifeboat. It was his bad luck that just then the cook had come to the galley door to throw some slops over the side. 'There's something moving in the boat here!' he bawled up to the bridge.

Minutes later the canvas cover was unlashed, a head under a cloth cap peered in and a voice said, 'Bloody hell!'

'Hello, Toddy,' David answered.

Toddy stared at him, as another, harsher voice yelled, 'What the hell's going on, Toddy?'

'We've got a stowaway, sir.'

'Aw! For God's *sake*! Hook him out!'

'Right y'are, sir!' Toddy gripped David's collar and dragged him out of the boat to stand on the deck. 'Up there.' Toddy shoved the boy at the ladder and David climbed up to the open bridge. The owner of the harsh voice stood outside the wheelhouse, a battered bowler hat crammed on to his bullet head. He was little taller than David, wiry and fierce, with a jutting, pointed beard.

'I'm the Captain, Charlie Daggett,' he barked 'You call me "sir". What are you doing aboard my ship?'

David swallowed. It didn't seem a very good answer now but he gave it anyway: 'I want to be a sailor.' Then he added hastily, 'Sir.'

'Sailor?' Daggett looked him over, from tangled hair to dirty boots, covered in coal dust from head to foot. 'You look more like a stoker to me! And why pick on my ship? D'ye think it's some sort o' charity for waifs and strays?'

'I knew you were going foreign and you were short of hands,' David answered.

Daggett stared and Toddy put in, 'He got talking to me. I told him we were bound for the Med and needing hands because those two Dutch fellers got drunk and arrested.'

Daggett's glare shifted back to David, 'Why d'ye want to go foreign?'

'Because there wouldn't be much chance for you to put me ashore, sir, like you could if this was a coaster.'

'Bloody impudence!' Daggett exploded. 'Picking your passage like you were a fare-paying passenger! But you're not. I need a couple of hands, true enough, but sailormen, not a snotty-nosed bairn! You haven't got bad weather gear or owt else but what you stand up in and I'll have to fit you out. You're all loss and no profit.' He glowered in silence for a while, and then demanded, 'Well, your name's got to go in the log. What is it?'

'David Walsh, sir. Sir, can I say—'

'No, you can't!' Daggett bellowed, then cocked his head on one side and asked, 'What's your father's name?'

'Richard Walsh, sir.'

'He died out foreign.'

'Yes, sir. Washed overboard, sir.'

'Aye, you've got the look of him,' Daggett muttered. 'I can see it now. He was a good man.' He was silent again, scowling over the bow. David opened his mouth to speak but saw Toddy shaking his head warningly and held his tongue. Daggett turned back to him and said, 'Right, I'll rate you cabin-boy in the ship's books. The boy I've got knows enough now to serve as ordinary seaman and he's a bloody awful cabin-boy anyway.' And to Toddy, 'Find him a bunk and some gear – and see he cleans himself up. He's making my deck dirty.'

'Thank you, sir!' David burst out, face glowing.

'You won't thank me later,' Daggett growled. But he was grinning now.

So David started on his great adventure.

Emily, too, went adventuring that summer. One fine morning she heard Ada say, 'There they go,' and ran to stand at her adoptive mother's side at the window of the lodge. Bert stood outside at the open gates, a finger to his cap as the carriage rolled by, carrying Nathaniel Franklin, his sister and her son. Clarice had suggested that the family should go to London for the Season and

Nathaniel had agreed because his doctor had told him to go south for a change.

'Here's another one – and another,' said Ada, as two more carriages, this time hired cabs, swung out of the gates. These held most of the servants, who were also going to the house in London. An advance party had departed some days ago to prepare it for its new tenants.

'That little body, Mrs Huckaby, is housekeeper while they're away.' Ada laughed, 'It'll keep her busy but she likes that.' Only a small skeleton staff remained: the Jacksons in the lodge, the housekeeper, a maid and one footman in the big house.

'Like you, Mam,' said Emily, teasing but truthful.

'Don't be cheeky,' Ada smacked her bottom affectionately, 'or I'll tell your dad.' Emily smiled because that threat did not frighten her. 'We'll be busy now,' Ada went on. 'You can help me put this place straight and start the dinner.'

They worked happily together for an hour or more until Ada slid the pie they had made into the oven and closed its door, which gleamed with blacklead. 'That's all we can do for now. You go out and have a wander.' With that she settled into a chair outside the front door. There she could do her knitting and bask in the sunlight while Bert pottered in the front garden. She smiled up at Emily. 'We're done for the day and you've been wanting to get out.'

Emily had been casting longing glances at the windows as she helped Ada with the household chores. She was just twelve years old now, all arms and legs in her brown dress and white pinny, though these were old, washed thin and patched. Her best clothes, like her boots, were kept for school; she went barefoot in this summer weather. Emily did not care; she was used to it and remembered nothing better. 'Thanks, Mam,' she said, and skipped off into the trees. She made for the clearing where she would find the swing and tree-house, but did not continue on her usual path through the wood, which kept her out of sight of the house. Instead, as the family were away, she came out of the trees and headed up the long sweep of the drive. She stopped short when she rounded a bend in the drive and saw the big house. The sunlight lay warm on the old red brickwork and glinted from the scores of windows. The massive front door stood wide at the top of the steps and all the windows were thrown open, curtains fluttering on the breeze.

Emily had not seen the house like this before; she saw it only rarely anyway, heeding the warning Bert had issued years before: 'You keep away from that house!' But that had been because of Clarice Carver and her son, Bradley. The family were not at home now, and the house fascinated Emily. She walked on, keeping to the grass verge because the gravel of the drive hurt her bare feet, until she came to the steps leading up to the front door. She hesitated for some time at the foot. Then she climbed slowly up to the porch, enjoying the coolness of the stone under her feet. At first the interior of the house seemed hidden in semi-darkness, but then her eyes became accustomed to the gloom and she could see the long hall stretching away before her.

There was a stand holding umbrellas and walking-sticks, a dark wooden settle against one wall and a grandfather clock facing it. Carpet stretched away between borders of gleaming polished floor to a grand staircase that lifted gracefully to the landing above. The walls were hung with portraits of stern-faced men and beautiful but lifeless women. Emily could smell polish and flowers – there were vases on little tables – but she could see no one and could hear nothing except the slow ticking of the clock as its pendulum swung to and fro. She ventured in.

There were doors to right and left, tall doors twice the height of the ones in the gatekeeper's lodge, and those on the left were double – wide enough to let in a carriage, thought Emily. One stood ajar. She tiptoed across to it, edged around it – and stopped again, awed. She stood at the entrance to a room that stretched the entire length of that wing of the house. It was wide and high with glittering glass chandeliers suspended from the ornate ceiling. There were two huge fireplaces on either side of the room, though they were empty now, and at the end was a stage. Spindle-legged, straight-backed chairs lined the walls, covered with white dust-sheets. The floor was polished to a mirror shine and Emily felt it glassy under her feet as she walked quietly across it to the stage on which stood a piano.

She sidled round the shrouded instrument. She knew it was a grand piano – she had seen pictures of them in books. She stood behind it, facing the doors by which she had entered, and lifted the edge of the sheet high above her with both hands so the piano was fully revealed. Its dark wood had a lustrous glow and Emily gasped in awe at its magnificence. She held up the sheet with one hand and fingered the keys.

A shriek made her snatch back her hand and drop the sheet. A little woman stood in the doorway, a hand to her mouth, eyes wide. 'God Almighty! You frightened the life out o' me! I thought it was a ghost when I came in and saw that sheet standing up flapping at me and the music playing!'

Emily recognised Mrs Huckaby, who sometimes paused at the lodge to pass the time of day. She was a brisk wisp of a woman, birdlike, in her black dress and white apron, her hair in a bun under a starched white cap. Her movements belied her age, which showed in the lines and veins on her face and hands. She was holding a cloth and a feather duster on a long cane, and scurried across the expanse of gleaming floor. 'You're from the gatekeeper's lodge, Ada's bairn, aren't you? I've not seen much of you because Bert keeps you and Ada away from the house. He doesn't like that Mrs Carver, and I don't blame him. You've got to be careful with her.' She stood at the edge of the stage and peered up at Emily, her eyes sharp but kindly too. 'So, what are you doing here?'

'I was out for a walk and saw the door open,' Emily explained.

'And curiosity got the better of you.' Mrs Huckaby

nodded. 'I can't blame a young lass for that. My late husband used to say, "Your curiosity will be the death o' you!" But I lasted him out by a lot o' years. Mind, he was lost at sea or else he might ha' buried me first.' She nodded again vigorously, then looked about her. 'I'm giving the place a bit of a blow through and a dust. There's no harm in you looking around now. Mr Franklin, Mrs Carver and that son of hers are away to London. Bradley was a bit high and mighty and bad-tempered when he was younger, but he's quite the gentleman now.' She set to with the dusting, flicking with the feathers at the ornamental coving on the ceiling.

'Can I help?' Emily asked.

Mrs Huckaby peered at her doubtfully, then said, 'That Ada will have learnt you properly, I'm sure, so, aye, here you are,' and she handed the cloth to Emily. 'Anything you can reach that's not covered, give it a wipe.'

They worked busily, Mrs Huckaby humming like a bee as she bustled about. Then still awestruck by the space and beauty of the room, Emily said, 'It's very grand, isn't it?'

Mrs Huckaby chuckled. 'Aye, even now, when it's empty. But you should see it on an evening when there's a ball, with the fires glowing and the lights blazing down, the ladies and gentlemen dressed in all their finery and jewellery, waltzing around the floor.' She saw Emily staring and said, 'Here, I'll show you.' She whisked away a dust-sheet that had covered a painting hung above the stage. It was a blaze of colour. The artist had painted the ballroom from a viewpoint at its entrance and it was alive with people. An orchestra played on the stage, dancers swirled and circled the floor while onlookers lined the sides and grouped around the fireplaces. But all that was background to the central figure: a dark-haired, dark-eyed young woman dressed in a ballgown of glowing silk, standing poised and smiling at the artist.

Emily stared round-eyed, taking in the scene, but most of all . . .

Mrs Huckaby sighed. 'It's years now since we had a dance. That was the last.'

'She's lovely. Who is she?' Emily whispered.

'Marie Franklin, as she was then. Mr Franklin's daughter. It wasn't long after the picture was done that she ran off with as actor to America. It nearly broke the old man's heart, though there was some of us thought he'd brought it on himself, that he'd been too harsh with her. He should ha' seen she was set on the young feller. Anyway, when her husband died in America she came home but she and her bairn were both killed when Sammy Blenkinsop's boarding-house burned down.'

'Oh, no!' Emily gasped.

'Aye, that was a terrible day.' Mrs Huckaby shuddered. 'Sammy's place burned like a torch and everybody in there was lost. The master was never the same after that. He hardly spoke a word for weeks. He came back that day and was out in the woods for hours, then he sat in here looking at that picture. It was gone midnight afore he left it and went up to his bed – and that hadn't been slept in next morning. This room has never been used since. He still comes in here sometimes, sits and looks at the picture, but he never brings anybody else in.'

Emily, still transfixed, blinked away tears. 'Oh, that's sad.' She had a strange feeling that she had seen this young woman before, but could not recall where.

Now Mrs Huckaby stirred. 'Ah, well, that was ten years ago. You'd ha' been only one or two years old then.' She draped the dust-sheet over the picture again and the spell was broken. 'This'll never do. We've got to get on.' She went back to her dusting and Emily joined her, but she was quieter now, appalled by the fate of Marie Franklin.

They worked together for the rest of the morning and soon Emily's mood lightened and she joined in with Mrs Huckaby's humming. At one point they were busy in the study with its big desk, leather chairs and shelves of books. Then there were the pictures, all of ships.

'There's an awful lot of them,' Emily said.

'Oh, aye,' Mrs Huckaby agreed. 'That's how the old man made his money that paid for this place. He built ships and bought ships, they sailed all over the world and every time one came home he was a bit richer.'

'All over the world,' breathed Emily. What a wonderful way to live. Here was romance! Not slaving in service to clean and polish someone else's house but living in your own like this. Not working as someone's skivvy or in an office but sending ships to the four points of the compass.

They spent the last hour in the kitchen, preparing lunch and dinner for the staff. Emily met the rest at the table. Mrs Huckaby introduced her: 'This is Ada's lass. She's a little treasure.' In the evening, Emily went home happy with an invitation to return.

That summer she spent many days in the big house, helping when she could or just wandering through the rooms, taking in all the pictures and furnishings, so different from those in the gatekeeper's lodge. And as she moved through this different world she often thought of Marie Franklin. Sometimes she slipped into the ballroom and climbed on to a chair. Then, cautiously, she would unveil the picture and study the smiling girl, who looked so happy yet was so sad. And steadily her childish resolution grew: she would save her money and some day buy ships.

'There's your money, lad. You've earned it and you've got the makings of a seafaring man.' Captain Daggett handed the coins to David.

He took them. 'Thank you, sir.' He had scrubbed decks, cleaned cutlery, polished brasswork, made up bunks for the Captain and the other officers, and acted as assistant cook in the galley, besides serving the officers' meals in the saloon. The work he had found hardest was drawing water from over the side to wash the decks, heaving it up bucketful by bucketful on the end of a line. Every night he had fallen into his bunk dead beat, but was always the first to turn out for duty.

Now Daggett asked, 'D'ye still want to be a sailor?'

'Yes, sir.'

Daggett grinned at him. 'You come up to the shipping office when I'm signing on the crew for the next voyage and I'll have a berth for you.'

As he trudged home David whistled and sang, his belongings in an old sack slung over one shoulder. He had sent money home from Marseille or, rather, Daggett had done it for him, and now he had more in his pocket. He pushed open the door of the cottage. It seemed smaller now, but he felt a catch in his throat as he entered. His mother stood ironing in the kitchen and his sisters played by the fire. It was as if he had never been away. When they saw him they ran at him, crying, 'David!' They kissed and hugged him, and then, like every sailorman, he dug out of his sack the presents he had brought them from foreign parts. He smiled at his mother and said, 'I have a week at home before I sign on again at the shipping office on Tuesday. Captain Daggett wants me.' He said it with pride.

Molly Walsh accepted the inevitable. 'Is that your gear in that old sack?' When he nodded sheepishly she said, 'I've got your dad's sea-bag in the cupboard. You can have that.'

For a week David luxuriated in being spoilt by his mother and the two girls, but then he set off again for sea. Molly watched him go and knew that she had lost her little boy. He had gone from her into a man's world and would return only to visit. She prayed that the sea would not take him as it had his father.

*　　*　　*

The girl in the shabby coat and threadbare dress knocked at the door of the farmhouse. Digby Gamblin opened it to her. She was not reassured by the sight of him: he was thin, heavily moustached and looked hostile; his collarless shirt was dirty and open at the neck to show a grubby vest; his braces dangled. But she was hungry so she asked, 'Have you got any jobs you want doing, please? I'm out of work.'

Gamblin looked her over: small, frightened, pale, young. 'How old are you?'

'Eighteen, mister.'

'Where's your family?'

'They're both dead,' and hoping for his pity, 'I haven't anyone.'

Gamblin thought that that was a point in her favour. 'Why did you lose your last job?' She was silent, pale face flooding with blood now, but he pressed her harshly: 'What did you get up to?'

'The master – his wife came on us when he thought she was out,' she whispered, looking down at her feet in cracked boots. 'He said I'd led him on but I hadn't – I hadn't! She said I had to go.'

Gamblin thought that would do. 'Well, you can't work the farm because you're not big enough, but I expect my missus can find you something. Come in.'

She hesitated for a moment, but that mention of 'my missus' reassured her, as Gamblin had meant it to. She entered as he held the door wide. Then it slammed behind her and he turned the key. The girl tried to fight but a blow and his threats stilled her. Afterwards he threw a few coppers at her, then sent her on her way. 'No use you complaining. I've got people will swear I was with them all today and you'll be branded a liar,' he said, with the confidence of one who had done it before.

He would again.

Chapter Five

SUMMER 1897. SUNDERLAND.

'Blast you! Get out of my way!' The words remained unspoken but Bradley Carver bawled them in his mind as he swung the horse's head with a savage tug on the reins. He was a tall, strongly built handsome man now and had just emerged from the open gates of the Franklin house. He had almost been unseated when his mount checked and swerved aside, whisking past the small girl meandering in the middle of the road – which was usually safe, in those far-off days of little traffic. She shrieked in fright and Bradley fought his rage as he battled with his dancing horse. He had learnt to control his savage temper, reckoning that if word of an outburst reached the ears of Nathaniel Franklin his inheritance might be in peril. Controlling his passion was another matter.

For a moment Bradley had thought that that was the

Jackson girl because he had just passed the gatekeeper's lodge. Then he realised this child was younger and doubtless one of the village children. He settled in the saddle again and rode on.

He was the image of a young gentleman now with his hair neatly trimmed by a good barber, his jacket and breeches well cut by a London tailor. He had studied the part and acted it to perfection, aided by Nathaniel Franklin's money. The old man paid him a generous salary but Bradley could always use more, and looked forward to the day when all of it would be his.

As he trotted on down the road on his morning ride he thought of the 'Jackson brat'. Over the years he had seen her as one of the score of children of the estate workers when they assembled at the house for a party. Bradley had helped Nathaniel to entertain them and managed to be pleasant, though he had no time for them. The Jackson girl had just been one of many, but he had often glimpsed her when he was passing the lodge and noted that she had grown, was now a gawky fourteen, her hair still down her back and still wearing a white pinny over her brown dress. She would drop a curtsy as he and Nathaniel drove by in the carriage. He remembered the day, years ago, when Emily had startled Samson and Bert had sent him packing. It was a long way in the past, but now he thought grimly of revenge on the Jacksons.

Over the years Emily had taken care that he should not see her. She, too, remembered that day with Samson. As time slipped by she, like the others, had been won over by the change in Bradley Carver. Nevertheless, she followed the code laid down by Bert. Her visits to the house and Mrs Huckaby ceased when the family returned from London, though they resumed on later occasions when they were all away. Bradley was as distant from her as she was from him, so he had not realised that she was leaving childhood behind.

Bradley returned to the house and changed into a sober business suit and starched collar. He was seated at the table when Nathaniel entered the breakfast room and rose to greet the old man, 'Good morning, Uncle.'

Nathaniel returned the greeting and waved him back into his seat. 'You know Wainwright is leaving at the end of the month.'

'Yes,' agreed Bradley. 'A pity, because he's a good man.' He knew the old man thought so. The agent, who managed the Franklin estate, was retiring.

'The chap who was going to take over the job has turned it down now,' Nathaniel went on. He waved the letter. 'He says his wife doesn't want to move because of her mother so now we need to start looking again for a replacement.' He smiled at his nephew. 'D'you think you can see to that?'

Bradley knew the response required and did not hesitate. 'I should hope so.'

Nathaniel nodded approvingly. 'Good man.' He thought that Bradley, at twenty-six, was almost fit to take over all the running of the Franklin affairs. His opinion of his nephew had steadily improved over the years. He had heard it said occasionally that the young man had a bad temper but had put that down to the jealousy of others. It was no bad thing that Bradley could stick up for himself in the shipyard. At one time Nathaniel had felt that the servants did not like Bradley, but that was in the past. The most important endorsements came from the managers of the shipyard and the Franklin Line, who testified to Bradley's diligence and ability.

These days, Nathaniel spent little time at his office. Instead he read and walked a good deal but his energy and drive had begun to desert him when his daughter ran away, had gone altogether when she died. He tried not to brood but still visited the clearing in the woods, which held so many memories. He passed the ballroom without entering – most of the time. But on the anniversary of the awful deaths of his daughter and granddaughter he would shut himself in there and stare at the portrait of the smiling girl.

The next day, when Bradley rode out, he headed for a farm a mile or so away, on the outskirts of Sunderland. The man he wanted was emerging from the house as he arrived and they met in the yard. Carver sat straight in his saddle and wrinkled his nose at the smell from a steaming midden close by. 'My God, Gamblin, how can you stand to live next door to a stink like that?' he said, disgusted.

Digby Gamblin owned three farms and this was one of them. He was in his thirties, thin and wearing rough tweeds, muddy boots and leather gaiters. His face was cadaverous, with sideburns and a full moustache over big yellow teeth. He smirked up at Bradley, 'It's part o' my living, sir. Ye know what they say, "Where there's muck, there's money."'

Bradley smiled, tight-lipped. 'That's what I came to talk to you about. Do you still want that job as agent to my uncle?'

Gamblin's smirk disappeared. He hungered for the job, would do anything to get it. While he made a comfortable living from his farms, the salary as agent for Nathaniel would double his income. 'You told me a month back that the old man would do all the choosing for that job and you wouldn't lift a finger to help me get it.'

'That's true,' Bradley admitted cheerfully. He had not wanted to risk antagonising the old man, who had already decided on the successor to Wainwright.

'I suppose you want more money,' Gamblin scowled.

'I do.' Bradley's grin widened.

'Aye, that's what I thought,' said Gamblin bitterly. 'How much?'

'You'll have to double your offer.'

'*Double*! You want a hundred quid—'

Bradley cut in maliciously, 'Guineas.'

'*Guineas*! That's another fiver on top!' He fumed while Bradley smiled down at him. Then Gamblin gave in. 'All right, but you'll put my name forward and I'll have a chance of getting the job?'

'I'll do better than that. I guarantee you'll get it.'

Gamblin stared, jaw loose, then grinned triumphantly. 'That's marvellous!' Then he caught Bradley's hard eye on him and added hurriedly, 'Sir.' Bradley turned his horse. As he rode away he called over his shoulder, 'Just have the money ready tomorrow, in cash.'

'It'll be waiting for you, sir.'

Just over a week later Gamblin was standing outside the gatekeeper's lodge with Wainwright, holding the reins of the ponies they were riding around the estate. There's a choice young piece, standing there with her feet bare, he thought. I wonder what the rest of her looks like. Outwardly he smiled paternally at Emily, then returned his gaze to Bert Jackson. She thought he seemed a friendly man, though she did not like him as much as that Wainwright.

The cheerful, red-faced Wainwright was saying now, 'This is Mr Gamblin, the new agent. I'm retiring at the end of the month.'

They knew this already, had heard it on the servants' grapevine.

The Jacksons had been waiting with curiosity to see the new man and listened as Gamblin said jovially, 'I don't propose making any changes here. Everything seems to run like clockwork.'

That was reassuring. Later, as they watched him ride away at Wainwright's side, Ada said, 'He looks a pleasant feller. Funny he isn't married, though.'

Bert reserved judgement: 'We'll see how he behaves.' However, he did not see how any harm could come to them from Gamblin; he was just the agent and Nathaniel employed Bert.

'Can I go out now?' Emily asked. 'It's a beautiful day.'

'Take your book and get along with you,' Ada smiled at her. Emily had stolen away all this summer to read. Now she tucked the book, *Great Expectations*, under her arm and set off, still barefoot in the summer's heat. She took a circular route through the woods as usual, so that she would not be seen from the big house. At the clearing, she climbed up the dangling rope-ladder into the tree-house and settled down with her book. The story of the poor boy translated into the world of the wealthy fascinated her.

Back at the gatekeeper's lodge, Bert doffed his cap at the cab, which was carrying a man he had seen before at the house. As it rumbled by, Captain Charlie Daggett poked his bullet head with its pointed beard out of the window. 'What cheer, Bert!' he bellowed.

Bert grinned and waved as the cab rolled on up the drive with a crunch of gravel and disappeared from sight. 'Charlie Daggett on his way up to report to the old man,' he said to Ada. 'Franklin likes to see all his captains when they're in port. I haven't seen the young feller before, though.'

'Now then, Davy,' said Daggett as he got down from the cab at the front door of the house, 'you wait here. It'll depend on the old man, o' course, but I reckon he'll give me a couple o' rums and a half-hour to hear my report on the voyage, then send me off.'

'Aye, sir,' said David Walsh, now a seasoned ordinary seaman of sixteen. He was a head taller than Daggett now, all arms and legs but broadening out and shaving three or four times a week — when he was in port. Now he was dressed in his best, and only, suit with its narrow trousers and a high tight white collar. His boots shone and his mop of black hair had been watered into place but was already springing free. His mother had inspected her son critically but proudly and found no fault. Now he stood by the cab and watched as Daggett climbed the steps to the front door and was admitted by a maid.

David gazed about him, awed and curious at the sight of the great house set in its acres of woodland and lawns. He strolled back and forth for a few minutes but the house stared back at him with blank windows and the cabbie was dozing on his seat. David grew bored and wished he had brought a book. He wrestled his pocket-watch out of his waistcoat pocket and noted the time. He still had twenty minutes to wait for Daggett. He decided to explore.

He found the clearing only by chance. He paused at its edge, noticing the swing moving gently on the breeze, and the house built among the branches. He crossed to the swing, sat on it and grinned as it creaked beneath his weight. If Toddy and the fellers aboard the *Cliveden* could see him now, how they would pull his leg!

Inside the tree-house, Emily heard movement below and froze. Then the swing stopped creaking and she saw the top of the rope-ladder tighten as someone set his weight on it. They were climbing! She drew further back into the house and pulled up her legs, partly to make herself small, partly to be ready to escape or defend herself. Suddenly a head showed in the entrance and she kicked out. Her bare foot just missed the face that gaped in at her.

David ducked and called, 'Here, steady on! I didn't know anybody was up here!'

Emily's heart was beating fast. 'Are you from the house?' She asked.

'No. I'm here with my skipper, Charlie Daggett. Old Franklin sent for him and he's in the house now. I got bored, just hanging about. Look here, are you going to kick me?'

Emily hesitated. Then she answered, 'No.'

David's black thatch lifted above the top of the rope-ladder and he grinned at her. 'Hello.' He peered in at the young girl before him, seeing wide grey eyes, and long, dark hair falling down her back.

'Hello,' she replied. And doubting, 'Are you a sailor?'

'O' course I am,' David replied indignantly.

Emily peered at his hands where he gripped the top of the rope ladder: 'You aren't tattooed.'

'That doesn't matter. I could get tattooed if I wanted to, but my mam said I shouldn't. My dad never did. Said he saw no point in it.' Then he asked, 'Are you in service here?'

'No. My father's the gatekeeper.'

'Ah! So you'll be in service in the house one day.' It was a natural assumption.

But Emily was annoyed. She voiced the dream of a fourteen-year-old: 'No, I won't! I'm going to save up to buy ships and send them all over the world.'

David stared, then laughed. 'Don't be daft! Lasses don't own ships!'

'I will!' Incensed, she went on, 'I bet you're only a cabin-boy on the ferry.'

'I am not!' At that instant the rung of the rope-ladder broke beneath his weight – it had hung there for nearly twenty years – and he fell to the ground below.

Emily gasped in horror and within seconds she had slid down the ladder to kneel at his side. 'Are you hurt?' she asked anxiously.

David sat up and wiggled his toes and fingers. 'No, I'm fine. Worse things happen at sea.'

'A fine sailor you are, falling out of a tree,' Emily teased.

He grinned sheepishly. 'That wasn't my fault. Your rigging needs setting up again.'

Emily sat down beside him. 'Is your father a sailor, too, then?'

'He was, but he was lost at sea when I was little.'

'Oh! I'm sorry.' Emily sounded distressed.

David was touched, and embarrassed. 'Well, it was a

long time ago.' And he didn't want to be reminded of it. The memory still hurt. He jumped to his feet. 'Come on, I'll give you a swing.'

Emily took her seat, laughing, and David stood behind and shoved as he had for his sisters. Soon she was swooping and soaring, propelled by his muscular arms, and both of them were laughing.

'What the 'ell d'ye think you're doing, Davy?' Charlie Daggett bellowed. He stood at the edge of the clearing, a respectful half-pace behind Nathaniel Franklin. 'Excuse me, sir,' he apologised to Nathaniel. He stalked across to where David had halted the swing and Emily watched him warily. His voice was thick with suppressed outrage when he said to David, 'I told Mr Franklin, "I've brought this bright lad up for you to see" so when I came out to the cab he comes with me and you aren't there! The cabbie says he woke up twenty minutes ago just in time to see you clearing off!' David knew Charlie was getting into his stride, about to give him a dressing-down he would remember for a long time, and steeled himself for it.

But Nathaniel Franklin stepped in. He had followed the sound of laughter, which he recalled all too vividly in this place. He had seen the young girl on the swing, had glimpsed her sometimes when passing the gatekeeper's lodge and she reminded him of . . . He said, 'Hold on, Captain Daggett,' then asked, 'You're the Jacksons' girl, aren't you?'

'Yes, sir,' she replied, thinking that Bert would be

having something to say to her about this, somewhat on the lines of Charlie's outburst. 'Emily Jackson, sir.'

'Are you in the habit of playing here?' Nathaniel was smiling.

That did not reassure Emily but she admitted, 'Yes, sir. I climb up into the tree-house and read. I've left a book up there now, sir.'

Nathaniel recalled that Marie had liked to read up there. 'That's all right,' he said. 'You use it, and if anyone tries to turn you out refer them to me.'

Emily could not believe her luck. 'Thank you, sir.'

Nathaniel turned to David: 'What brought you out here?'

'I was bored, sir. I hadn't anything to read, nothing to do. I didn't mean to cause any trouble.'

Nathaniel grinned. 'Captain Daggett tells me you're the brightest lad he's ever had aboard, that he's thinking of rating you able seaman as soon as you're old enough. He reckons that will be when you're seventeen.' And as David stared, stunned, he added, 'Did you know that?'

'No, sir.'

'Well, you do now. But that is information, not a promise. If you start fooling around you won't get the promotion. Any man serving on one of my ships will get the rank and pay he deserves, no more and no less. Now this is between us. You don't brag about it in the fo'c'sle. Understood?'

'Yes, sir.'

* * *

As they drove off in the cab, Charlie grumbled, 'You're a lucky young devil to get off like that. His daughter used to play on that swing. Up at the house they say that every now and again he goes there just to sit. It's like a private place to him, a chapel. And that Jackson lass, she was lucky too.'

'Yes, sir,' David replied meekly. He was going to be rated able seaman when he was seventeen! He had already forgotten the girl.

Emily also knew she was lucky. Nathaniel Franklin always came to the annual servants' ball and the Christmas party for the children of the estate and the village, but Bert had once said, 'I reckon he doesn't know one o' these bairns from another. Our Emily might be anyone's as far as he's concerned. But he means well.'

Now Emily ran home and blurted out excitedly, 'Mr Franklin found me in the tree-house with Davy and said I could play or read there whenever I like!'

'Who is this Davy? What were the two of you up to?' Ada asked, suspicious.

'He's a sailor—' Emily began.

'A *sailor*! You were with a *sailor*?' Ada was horrified.

'I was a sailor when I courted you,' Bert put in mildly.

'That was different.' Ada did not try to explain why it was, but listened as Emily recounted her meeting with the boy. At the end she said, 'So he was only a lad and there because Mr Franklin thinks a lot of him,' and seemed mollified.

'Yes.'

'I told you I saw him in the cab with Charlie Daggett. He looked a decent lad to me,' Bert said.

Ada fired a final shot: 'You can't tell with sailors.' Bert was not sure if it had been aimed at him but decided not to pursue it. So did Ada. She said, hopefully, 'It sounds as though you've made a friend in old Mr Franklin.'

Bert disagreed, 'Not a friend. He was good to you today but don't try to take advantage. Be careful. I think he's a good man, but these rich people easily forget about the likes of us, too busy with their own affairs.'

But Emily looked forward dreamily to blissful days of reading in the tree-house with nobody to deny her. She hardly gave another thought to the young sailor, except to recall with irritation that he had scoffed, 'Lasses don't own ships!' He had entered her life briefly then passed out of it. He would probably be off to sea the next day and she was unlikely to see him again.

Two weeks later Dr Willoughby told Nathaniel Franklin, 'You can put your clothes on now.'

He sat down behind his desk as Nathaniel pulled on vest and shirt, buttoned his waistcoat and shrugged into his jacket. He sat down opposite the doctor and asked, 'So, can you give me a bottle for this cough?'

'I will.' Then the doctor looked up from his notes.

'You're sixty-five now. You were hale and hearty at fifty, but you've been in my hands too often in recent years. The last two winters you've been a virtual invalid.'

'Nonsense!' Nathaniel straightened in the chair. 'I've had a few colds, touch of bronchitis—'

'It's no good, Nathaniel,' Willoughby interrupted his old friend gently. 'I have it all here.' He tapped the notes. 'Coughs, colds, bronchitis three times, and last winter it was pneumonia. That was bad.' He knew the reason for the deterioration and that Nathaniel did too, but neither mentioned the death of Marie and her daughter.

The old man sat in silence for a minute, accepting what Willoughby had said. 'So, what is the treatment?' he asked.

The doctor was ready with his answer because he had thought about this for some time. 'You need to get away from here for the winter, away from the cold winds, the sleet, snow, rain and fogs. I suggest you try the South of France. Go out now, come back in April, and do that every year.'

'I'm not a bird to fly south in the autumn,' Nathaniel protested irascibly. 'You seem to forget I'm running two large businesses. A lot of people depend on me.'

'All the more reason for you to go, or they may have to manage without you permanently before next spring.' Willoughby leant forward over his desk. 'You have very good managers and that nephew of yours, Bradley Carver – you told me not so long ago that he would soon be able to run your affairs. Give him his chance now.' He laid a hand on Franklin's shoulder. 'Take my advice, Nathaniel, please.'

Later Franklin admitted to himself that his managers were running their companies anyway, and left early in September for St Raphael in the South of France. Another week's illness had left him with a racking cough. He had told Bradley that he was to oversee the shipyard, the line and the estate. 'You've got good managers in the yard and the Franklin Line, and Gamblin seems to keep the estate ticking over. You have my confidence. If you want my advice telegraph me or come over.'

Exulting inside, Bradley said gravely, 'I'm overwhelmed by your trust in me, sir. I'll try not to let you down.'

He and Clarice flanked the grey-faced, frail old man as he walked down the steps from the front door to the waiting carriage. His luggage had gone on ahead to the villa where he was to spend the winter months. The house servants lined the steps, except for Jenkins, a footman who was to accompany him as valet. The estate workers, the gardeners, farmers, their workmen and their families, headed by Digby Gamblin, stood around the carriage at a respectful distance. Only Emily was missing.

'Where's that lass got to? I told her we should come and see the old boy off,' Bert hissed.

'She said she'd meet us here, then ran off before I could stop her,' Ada whispered back.

The old man had reached the carriage and turned to look back at them all. That was when Emily wriggled through the group and pressed a bunch of flowers into Nathaniel's hand. 'I hope you're soon well again, sir.' She backed off into the crowd, blushing.

Startled, Nathaniel stared after her for a moment then smiled. 'Thank you.' He remembered her, the Jackson girl, Emily. He took the flowers into the carriage and waved one last time. Then he was gone.

The servants scattered, into the house or back to their duties on the estate. Clarice walked inside, her head high, knowing that now she was truly mistress of this mansion. Now they would all need to mind their Ps and Qs. She would stand for no insolence from such as the gatekeeper, Jackson.

Gamblin sidled over to stand by Bradley Carver. 'He doesn't look good to me. To tell you the truth, I doubt if he'll be back.'

Bradley shrugged. 'If he is, it won't be for six months.' That gave him ample time to settle some old scores. And if Nathaniel did return, Bradley would manufacture a story to clear himself. 'There's something I want you to do but I don't want to be involved . . .'

The Jacksons sat down at the table in the kitchen of the lodge for their midday meal. Ada had berated Emily for being late at the ceremony of Nathaniel Franklin's departure, but had praised her presentation of the flowers: 'That was a kind thought. I think he was pleased.'

'Taken aback, more like,' Bert grumbled.

'Well, it's done now,' Ada said comfortably. And: 'Hello, here's that Mr Gamblin.' He cast a shadow where he sat on his pony outside the window.

Bert rose from the table. 'I wonder what he wants.'

Ada and Emily went with him and stood behind him as he opened the door. Gamblin saluted Ada with his whip, putting it to his cap, but his face beneath it was long. 'Good day to you, ma'am. And you, Jackson, Miss Jackson.'

Bert scented trouble. 'What can I do for you, Mr Gamblin?'

'I wish I could do something for you, Mr Jackson, but I can't. I have my orders and I have to carry them out. I want you out of the lodge by this time next week. You're sacked.'

The Jacksons stood in stunned silence, taking this in, with all its implications. Then Bert asked, 'Who gave you these orders? Carver?' Gamblin shook his head.

'I can't believe it of Mr Franklin,' Ada wailed.

Bert was bewildered. 'Couldn't be anyone else. But why? Is there any reason?'

Gamblin sighed. 'Well, he's getting on and he's been poorly. Maybe he's senile. But I tell you what I can do, I'll lend you a cart from the Home Farm to move your furniture for you. I'm only sorry I can't do more.'

They watched as he turned his pony and rode away up the drive. Bert walked back into the kitchen and slumped into his chair. 'We won't have a roof over our heads and I'll never get another job at my age.' He buried his face in his hands.

Ada sat beside him, her arm about his shoulders in a vain attempt to comfort him. 'We've got a little bit saved up. We'll find a couple of rooms somewhere in the town.'

Bert's voice came muffled and despairing: 'And when that's spent we'll be turned out. It'll be the workhouse for us.'

Emily looked at the two people she loved most in all the world and knew she would have to care for them now. She also knew that she would remember Nathaniel Franklin with bitterness for the rest of her days.

And as Gamblin rode back up to the house to report to Bradley Carver he reminded himself that he had not finished with the Jacksons yet. He licked his lips in anticipation.

Chapter Six

Autumn 1897. Sunderland.

'I said I couldn't help you but I've been thinking and looking about.' Gamblin had returned on the eve of the Jacksons' departure. He sat on his pony outside the door of the lodge again and this time he was smiling.

Bert could not raise a smile in response. He had got over the initial shock of being turned out of home and employment, but was still despondent. He seemed to have aged overnight. Now he asked dully, 'What does that mean?'

'It means I've found work for your lass with a decent couple who work a farm not far from here. She'll earn her keep and twelve shillings a month so she'll be able to send a few shillings home to you. That is, if she wants the job.' He looked quizzically at Emily, standing beside Bert.

'Oh, yes! I'd like that!' she replied eagerly. Emily turned

to Ada. 'I'll be able to come and see you sometimes – I think.' She looked hopefully at Gamblin.

'One afternoon a month,' he said magnanimously.

'You see?' Emily turned back to Ada. 'So you'll let me go?'

Ada glanced at Bert, the corners of her mouth drooping. 'I knew you'd have to go out to work some time soon, lass, but I hoped you'd still be living at home. What do you say, Bert?'

'I can't afford to keep her any longer.' His voice broke. 'She'll be better off there than with us.'

Ada wept then and Emily put a comforting arm around her. 'I'd like to take that job, Mr Gamblin,' she said. 'When do I start?'

Gamblin wanted to savour a future pleasure. 'You can help your parents to get settled where they're going. Let me have the address and I'll tell Mr Swindell – that's the name of your master – to pick up you and your baggage in his cart a week from today.'

'Thank you, sir.' Emily was grateful to him because she would be helping Ada and Bert.

'I'm glad I was able to be of assistance to you all.' Gamblin touched his cap to Ada and trotted away on his pony.

The cart came from the Home Farm, driven by one of the labourers. He greeted them awkwardly, 'Sorry to hear about you leaving. I can't understand the old man acting like this.' He helped them load their furniture, then drove them into Sunderland, to the two upstairs rooms Bert had found in a terrace on the south side of the Wear, close to the river and the shipyards. There was a kitchen and a bedroom, both opening off a landing. The bedroom looked out on the cobbled street and the kitchen was over the yard with its coalhouses — one for upstairs and one for down — washhouse and lavatory.

Emily thought the place dirty, smoky and noisy after the space and quiet of the countryside, and it was crowded with people who were strangers to her, calling to each other across the street. She could not remember her early days as a child in the town, ten years ago, and now it was a foreign land. In the first hour, though, Ada was befriended by the woman in the rooms below. Bridget Cassidy was short and stout, red-faced, grey-haired and cheerful. She bustled out of her kitchen on the ground floor and said, 'I'll make all of you a cup o' tea. My Sid is out at work but you'll see him tonight.'

Over that week Emily worked with Ada and Bert to clean the rooms, wash the windows and install the furniture, but soon it was time for her to go. 'Here's a cart now!' she called from where she stood at the window overlooking the street. It was pulled by a shaggy, tired-looking horse whose driver sat on one of the shafts, reins in one hand, whip in the other. He was short and stocky, dull-faced, in an old jacket and trousers, dirty leather leggings and boots. He halted the cart below Emily as she leant out of the window to wave. 'Mr Swindell?'

He peered up at her vacantly. 'Aye. You the lass for the farm?'

'Yes, I am. I'll fetch my box.'

'Aye.' He waited impassively.

'He seems a nice man,' she said to Ada trying to console her.

Bert had been sitting dejectedly by the fire, but now he rose and went to where Emily's tin box stood near the kitchen door. He lifted it to his shoulder, grunting with the effort, though it held nothing but her clothes and they were pathetically few: two dresses for work, petticoats and drawers. She was dressed in her best for the journey, the light blue cotton dress that had been new that summer and the navy blue woollen coat bought second-hand the previous winter, though it was small for her now. 'I'll carry your box down, lass. At least I can do that,' he said.

In the event both he and Ada went downstairs with her. Bert loaded the box on to the cart while Swindell watched apathetically. 'Well, I'm off to make my fortune. Wish me luck,' Emily said brightly. She kissed Ada, whose lined face ran with tears, and hugged Bert. 'Cheer up, Dad. Things will be easier for you now I have a job.'

'It breaks my heart to see you go,' Ada cried.

And Bert said, 'I'll try to put a brave face on it, but I always wanted to do better than this for you. I'm beginning to think that all those years ago I shouldn't have—' He stopped as Ada gripped his arm, her fingers biting into his flesh.

Puzzled, Emily asked, 'Shouldn't have what, Dad?'

Ada answered for him: 'Nothing. He's always on to me about how he shouldn't have come ashore, should have

96

stayed at sea. If he had he'd probably have drowned by now.'

Bert wiped his eyes. 'Aye, that's all it was.'

Swindell shifted impatiently. 'I've got to get back for the milking.'

'Yes, sir. I'm sorry,' Emily climbed up on to the cart and sat on her box. Swindell shook the reins, the horse stepped forward and the cart pulled away, creaking. Emily was half turned to look back at her parents, smiling, until the cart rounded the next corner. They were clinging to each other, but oddly, it seemed that Ada was now supporting Bert. At last Emily could cry, and big tears ran down her cheeks.

The farm was far outside the town, beyond Fulwell Mill, and the journey seemed to go on for ever. Swindell maintained a morose silence throughout. When Emily's tears dried she endeavoured to be polite and asked, 'I hope you and Mrs Swindell are both well, sir.'

'Aye.' He was equally monosyllabic when Emily commented on the weather. After that she was as silent as he.

Finally the cart wheeled into a farmyard and halted facing a house, whose windows were grubby, the curtains drab; some of the panes were broken. A few hens scratched in the dirt of the yard, which was pockmarked with pools of dirty water. A herd of cows stood outside a shed in a pen that was inches deep in mud. A woman was with them, shooing in the last stragglers. She had kilted her skirts up to her knees and her boots were shapeless lumps of mud and manure. 'Send that lass in with her box and you get on wi' milking these cows!' she screeched.

'Don't give me orders or you'll get the back o' my hand!' Swindell bawled back. But he got down from the cart and lifted the box. Emily had descended into the dirt of the yard and he shoved it into her arms, saying curtly, 'In ye go,' then slouched off to the cowshed.

His wife made for the house, calling to Emily, 'Come away in! There's work to do.'

Emily followed her, struggling with the box, into a stone-floored kitchen with a grubby black oven and fireplace, and a stained wooden table. Mrs Swindell kicked off her boots at the door and shoved her feet into slippers but the precaution appeared wasted because the floor was already covered in mud. She led Emily up narrow, winding stairs to an attic room with a narrow bed, and a chest of drawers on which stood a china bowl and jug. 'When you want a wash you come and get some water from the pump. But now get them fancy things off and your work clothes on. He'll be wanting his dinner when he's done milking and you can give me a hand in the kitchen.'

Emily changed, shivering in the early-evening chill. She discovered that the bed was unstable, its legs too near its centre, so if she sat on one end the other rose like a seesaw. The chest of drawers was dirty inside. She wrinkled her nose and decided to leave her clothes in her box. Unpacking could wait until she had scrubbed the chest.

When she ran downstairs Mrs Swindell was sitting by

the fire smoking a blackened clay pipe. 'Peel that lot and then clean this floor,' she said. Emily peeled the potatoes, fetching water from the pump in the yard, and then got down on her knees with a scrubbing brush, a rock-hard lump of soap and a cloth. It seemed to her that the floor had not been cleaned for some time, but she laboured until the woman grumbled, 'Aye, that's good enough.'

Emily sat back on her heels in relief, tired and hungry. 'Tell him his dinner's ready,' Mrs Swindell said, 'and take your bucket and brush with you.' So Emily carried bucket and scrubbing brush out to the cowshed. Night had fallen and she had to pick her way between the puddles to cross the yard.

Swindell had just finished milking and grunted, 'Here y'are. Next door in the dairy.' Emily trailed after him into a small building next door to the cowshed. 'Clean this floor,' Swindell said. He struck a match and lit a stub of candle stuck in the neck of a bottle. He handed this to Emily and said, 'Now ye can see what you're doing,' then left her. Emily had to get down on her aching knees again to scrub the floor of the dairy, sliding the bottle along with her to give her light.

When she had finished she was exhausted. She stumbled across the dark yard, splashing through the puddles she could not see, and pushed open the farmhouse door. Her employers were sitting at either side of the fireplace, Mrs Swindell smoking, her husband snoring in his chair. Mrs Swindell shouted, 'Take those dirty shoes off! Your dinner's on top of the oven.'

Emily did as she was told, and found a plate of thin stew with potatoes. She ate some of it, but was too tired to finish. 'May I go to bed now, please?' she asked.

'Aye, get yourself away.' Mrs Swindell sucked at the pipe. 'You've got a full day tomorrow. There's a candle on the mantelpiece you can take to light your way but don't keep it burning too long – they cost money. I've put a clock in your room and it's set for six. I want you up then to fetch us hot water and to cook the breakfast.'

'All right.' Emily did not care; she was too tired.

'You call me ma'am,' Mrs Swindell snapped.

'Yes, ma'am.' Emily fetched her jug from her little room, filled it with water at the pump then said, 'Goodnight, ma'am. Goodnight, sir,' then dragged herself up the narrow, winding stairs again. The clock stood on the chest of drawers, ticking busily. Emily undressed, washed and crawled into bed, remembering not to sit on the end. She blew out the candle, too tired to bemoan her change in fortune or to worry about tomorrow.

At the Franklin mansion, Bradley Carver, heir apparent to the Franklin fortune, and Clarice, his mother, sat in the drawing room. They had eaten a leisurely dinner of five courses, served in the dining room by the maids and supervised by Porteous, the butler. Both had dressed for dinner, Bradley in evening dress with starched shirt front, Clarice in a silk gown. She sipped coffee while Bradley swirled brandy in a balloon-shaped glass. Clarice glanced around the room to make sure that all the servants had gone before she said, 'I saw a new man in the gatekeeper's lodge today. What happened to the Jacksons?'

Bradley savoured his revenge. 'That was Darnley. I told Gamblin to throw out the Jacksons.'

Clarice smiled. 'Good. I never liked that man. He could be insolent. Where have they gone?'

Bradley grinned comfortably. 'Don't know, don't care. We're rid of them, that's all that matters.'

Clarice nodded approval. 'It's good to be able to set this place to rights. If only we had the ordering of it all of the time, rather than just the winter months.'

'And all of the money,' Bradley added.

Clarice's eyes gleamed. 'Nathaniel did not look well. You may come into your inheritance sooner than you think. It's fortunate that that daughter of his ran away.'

Bradley agreed. 'And never came back – her and her brat.'

Emily woke at six the next day, shaken out of sleep by the insistent clanging of the alarm clock. She crawled out of bed, poured water from the jug into the bowl and washed, shivering at the chill. Then she ran downstairs and set to work, stoking up the fire and then cooking breakfast. She drew jugs of hot water from the kettle singing on the fire, and carried them upstairs to the Swindells. They were still snoring until her knock woke them and Mrs Swindell croaked, 'Put them on the dresser.'

Later, on Mrs Swindell's orders, Emily washed the curtains and was hanging them out to dry on a line at the back of the house when a voice called from the road nearby, 'Hello! You've got a good day for drying them.'

Emily took the clothes pegs out of her mouth to reply, 'Hello. Yes, it's beautiful.' And it was, with a clear blue sky and scattered clouds shredded by the wind. She saw before her a sandy-haired youth two or three years older than herself, in jacket, breeches and leggings. He was seated on a cart loaded with cabbages.

He grinned at her. 'Have you just moved in? Some relation of the Swindells?'

'No, I just work here. I came yesterday.'

'I thought so. I drive past here every day and I haven't seen you before.' His brows lifted. 'How do you like it?'

Emily hesitated, looked around to confirm that the Swindells were out of earshot, then admitted, 'It's pretty hard.'

He said drily, 'I'll bet it is. I know them.'

Emily went back to pegging but asked, 'Do you work around here?'

He jerked his head, indicating the way he had come. 'I work for my dad, that's on Foster's farm — I'm Billy Foster.'

'You're a farmer, then.'

'I wish I was.' He added ruefully, 'There's no chance of that. Vince, my older brother, he'll inherit the farm and he's married. It won't stretch to a living for two of us. I'd like to farm but I'll have to manage a farm for somebody else, and jobs like that are hard to come by.'

Emily glanced warily over her shoulder at the house. 'I have to get back, but I hope you find the job you want.'

'Thank you.' Then he called after her, 'What's your name?'

'Emily Jackson.'

Emily returned to the house and her labours somewhat cheered. As the day wore on she churned butter in the dairy until her arms ached, cleaned windows, prepared meals and scrubbed out the dairy again. At dinner that night, Mrs Swindell said to her, 'Washing day tomorrow. I'll have all the sheets done.'

Then Swindell made his claim: 'I'm going to be wanting her out in the field wi' me afore long. I have fences to mend and she can help me wi' that.'

'When I'm finished wi' her in here,' insisted his wife.

Emily staggered up to bed, leaving them arguing over her.

The next day as Emily started work, Bert was leaving Ada in their new home and setting out for the pit heap. He took a coal rake and a sack. 'You're too old for that! We'll manage without you going to the tip,' Ada protested.

'If we keep on spending our little bit o' savings we'll wind up with nothing before long,' Bert insisted. 'If I can keep us in coal for the fire that'll be one expense less.'

'What about those pains in your belly you've been

complaining of? You'd do better to go to the doctor, not the tip,' Ada said.

'That was just a bit of indigestion,' Bert replied, although he knew it was worse than that. 'I'm off.'

The heap, or the tip, was two or three miles away, a litter of stone shed by the colliery after most of the coal had been taken from it. Like others in need, Bert raked over it for the coal that remained. He had to keep a wary eye open for the guardians of the heap, who kicked stones down on the men grubbing in the shale below, but by midday he had filled the sack.

He started for home, with the sack slung over his shoulder, and the pain hit him, a red-hot knife in his belly. He moaned but limped on, bent nearly double. He would not let Ada down again, would not be beaten by this sack of coal. He had turned the corner into the street, was in sight of home, when the pain wrenched a cry of agony from him and he collapsed. The neighbours carried him and the coal to Ada then fetched a doctor but he was too late. Bert's appendix had burst, and he was dead.

All Ada could say was, 'Send for my bonny lass,' but she wrote the letter herself, with a shaking hand.

Emily received it the next day. In tears she asked Mrs Swindell, 'Can I go to the funeral, please, ma'am?'

Her employer agreed reluctantly, 'Aye, I suppose so.'

An hour later Emily left, wearing her best blue dress, and walked down the long, dusty road into Sunderland. She found Ada sitting in the kitchen behind curtains closed in mourning, surrounded by Bridget Cassidy and other kindly neighbours, who had been strangers just a few days ago. 'Come here, bonny lass!' Ada cried, and threw her arms around Emily. She wept for Bert all over again, and Emily joined her. Then she became concerned for Emily: 'Are they feeding you all right? Are they working you too hard? Have you got a room to yourself, a bed of your own?' Emily answered her cheerfully, lying so that she would not worry.

Digby Gamblin rode his pony into the farmyard and jumped down. Mrs Swindell came to the kitchen door to greet him but he looked beyond her, ordering impatiently, 'Make yourself scarce for a while – get out in the fields with Swindell. Where's the new lass?' He had waited long enough.

'Gone to her father's funeral,' she explained, reaching for her coat and boots.

'*What?*'

She flinched before his anger. 'We had to let her go for that. We didn't know you'd be coming today.'

Gamblin let out a string of obscenities, then climbed back on to his pony. 'Let me know as soon as she's back. You know what to do if you want to stay on here. Otherwise you're out. Is that understood?'

'Aye,' she was quick to answer. The Swindells would be penniless and homeless if he turned them out so they did as he ordered. 'We'll see to it, Mr Gamblin.'

'You'd better.' And he spurred the pony out of the yard.

Emily made most of the funeral arrangements and stood by Ada at the graveside. Afterwards she served tea and ham sandwiches to all the mourners, their neighbours. When, at last, they had gone, she knelt by Ada's chair and said gently, 'Mam, I have to go back now.'

Ada stroked her soft brown hair and sighed. 'I know, my love, but at least I know you're happy there and Bert will rest easy.'

Emily felt a twinge of conscience, but said only, 'I'll be in to see you at the end of the month and I'll fetch you ten shillings out of my pay.'

'Bless you, but don't leave yourself short,' Ada said.

Emily walked back to the farm and arrived in the early evening, just in time to scrub out the dairy. They had not made a meal for her so she had only a crust of bread and a cup of tea, but she was too tired and unhappy to eat. Now that she was alone she realised that she would never see Bert again, had no one in the world now but Ada, her mother. She wept for him, for all of them, and did not hear Swindell drive out in the pony and trap, or his return later, his visit to Gamblin completed.

The following day Emily was at work early in the morning, but that afternoon the Swindells dressed in their best clothes. As the farmer brought the pony and trap round to the front door his wife told Emily, 'You can stay here.'

'Yes, ma'am. What do you want me to do?'

'Nothing. Just stay in the house.' She hesitated, then added, avoiding Emily's gaze, 'Go back to bed, if you like.' She pulled black gloves on to her reddened hands as she hurried out.

In relief Emily sagged against the table. She had been up since six and knew exactly how to make use of her time now. She took down the hip bath, which hung on the wall outside the kitchen, and set it in front of the fire. Then she poured in a big panful of hot water and luxuriated in it. Afterwards she dressed in clean underclothes but laid her dress on the chair in her room. She slid into bed and closed her eyes. Sleep, blessed sleep . . .

The bed shifted under her and Emily woke in fear. She opened her eyes to see Digby Gamblin sitting there. He was naked to the waist and was now pulling down his breeches. 'I've been waiting for this for a long time.' He grinned at her. Emily recoiled from him and screamed, but Gamblin only laughed. 'Shout as much as you like! Nobody will hear you.'

Emily remembered Mrs Swindell's furtive manner and realised now that the woman had known that this was to happen and had been too ashamed to face her. Fear and anger gave her strength. As Gamblin reached out a hand towards her she kicked out to free herself from the blankets and caught him, sending him rocking away from her. She rolled out of the bed. As she did so her end of it lifted behind her and Gamblin crashed to the floor, the bedding on top of him and his breeches around his ankles.

Emily grabbed her clothes from the chair, her shoes from beneath it and ran, Gamblin's bellows of rage echoing after her. His pony was tethered to a post in the yard, and Emily raced past it and on towards the road. When she could no longer hear him she slowed to a walk, gasping for breath. She realised then that she was still barefoot and in her shift. She glanced up and down the road, saw with relief that it was empty, and pulled on her dress, stockings and shoes. In doing so she discovered that the bundle she had snatched from the chair had also included a shirt and waistcoat.

She would not take them back, that was certain. As she hesitated, wondering what to do with them, she saw a cart approaching down the road. She was ready to run again but then she saw that it was Billy Foster, the farmer's son, on his way into Sunderland. She waited until he came up to her and pulled up the horse.

He grinned. 'Got an afternoon off?'

'No.' At the sight of his friendly face Emily burst into tears.

Billy jumped down from the cart and put his arm round her. 'Here, steady on. What's the matter? Don't cry.' He offered her his handkerchief. 'It's fairly clean.' Emily wiped her eyes and told her story. 'That devil Gamblin!' Billy exploded. 'He owns that farm and the Swindells work it for him. We've heard rumours about him and young girls with no one to protect them! The girl's always alone so it's her word against his, and he always has a friend who'll say he was somewhere else at the time. But I've a mind to go back and settle him once and for all!'

'No! Please!' Emily held on to his arm. 'It's over now and I just want to put it out of my mind. Only——' She broke off.

Billy prompted her, 'Only what?'

'I picked up these when I ran out. They were with my dress and I didn't realise.' Emily held up the shirt and waistcoat.

Billy grinned, 'Serves him right.'

'But what shall I do with them?'

Billy took them from her. 'I'll give them to him – when I get back from the town.' He was about to throw them on to the cart when he said, 'Hello! What have we got here?' He fumbled in one of the waistcoat pockets and took out a leather purse. He opened it and whistled. 'Phew! Two sovereigns, silver and copper.' And then: 'You aren't going to go back to the farm?' Emily shuddered. 'So do they owe you any wages?'

'They do. I worked four days – just,' Emily said ruefully.

'Well, it's Gamblin's farm so you were really working for him.'

'I suppose so.'

'How much was he paying you?'

'He said I'd get twelve shillings a month,' Emily said sadly; she needed that money.

'So for four days you're due . . .' Billy struggled with mental arithmetic.

Emily supplied the answer: 'Eighteen pence.'

'Right,' Billy agreed. He counted out a shilling and sixpence from the purse and gave them to her. 'There you are. I'll tell him I took them to settle his outstanding debt.'

Emily clutched the coins – money for Ada. 'Thank you.' Then Billy asked, awkwardly because he did not want to embarrass her, 'What about your – your other things?'

Emily blushed. 'They're still in my box in my room.'

'I'll ask Mrs Swindell for them. Where can I find you?'

Emily told him the address then glanced at the cart. 'Are you going into the town?'

'Aye. Do you want a ride?'

Emily rode into Sunderland seated on a cushion of folded meal sacks on the front of the cart. Billy kept up a cheerful conversation all the way, and finally halted the cart at a greengrocer's shop in the Newcastle Road just on the edge of the town. 'I'm delivering these potatoes here.' He jerked his head at the sacks ranged behind him. 'Can you walk now?'

'Yes, thank you.' Emily climbed down, grateful for the ride. 'I hope you find that manager's job one day.'

'One day,' he said ruefully.

Emily walked on into the town, but gradually her pace slowed. She had to go home, there was nowhere else, but that meant facing Ada and telling her she had left her job. She would not return empty-handed because, thanks to Billy, she had money. A shilling would buy a pound of ham and six eggs so they would not starve, but there would be explanations and Ada would be upset.

At the busy Wheatsheaf junction Emily hesitated. Five roads met there, so carts, trams, carriages and pedestrians swarmed. All were hurrying, except for the little knots of off-shift shipyard workers and pitmen: Monkwearmouth colliery was close by. Emily wondered if she should go straight on past the public house and across the bridge to the south side of the river and home. Eventually she turned left down Roker Avenue. Maybe she could find work in Monkwearmouth.

Chapter Seven

Emily walked down Roker Avenue with open-top trams grinding by, each pulled by a pair of horses. Her dreams of caring for Ada and Bert lay in ashes. She knew it was not her fault but she was haunted by failure. She was without employment and unable to keep herself, let alone support Ada. She had only a few hours to find work before she crept miserably home to tell her mother the bad news.

She passed the Salvation Army Citadel and soon afterwards came to a looming fortress of a factory building. A crowd of some forty or fifty women and girls stood against the factory wall. They all wore coarse canvas aprons and each had a sharp-looking knife hanging from a belt of twine. They were watching the passers-by and making cheerful comments about them. They called out to one young dandy with an incipient moustache, three-inch-high starched collar and walking-cane: 'Look, lasses, he's got a 'tache now!'

'No, he hasn't!'

'Aye, he has!'

'No! That's a mark from when he drank his cocoa!' That was a small, slender girl, with a cloud of blonde hair, two or three years older than Emily. She laughed as the young man blushed and hurried away.

'You're a card, Lily!' one woman called.

Lily took a few dancing steps. Then her gaze shifted to Emily: 'Here, see this one! She's carrying her bed around with her!'

Emily looked down at herself, then up at the girl. 'What do you mean?'

Lily danced round her. 'I mean this,' she explained, and picked straw from the back of Emily's dress. 'You're covered with it.'

Emily hitched her skirt round: she had picked up straw from sitting on the meal sacks.

'Where did you pick up that lot?' Lily asked.

'A farm lad gave me a ride on his cart,' Emily said.

'Ooh!' Lily winked at the crowd behind her. 'You went for a ride with a farm lad! You're a little goer, aren't you?'

'No!' Emily's cheeks flamed. 'He was just being a good friend. I'd lost my job and hadn't any money so he brought me into the town to find work.'

Lily decided this girl was not fair game after all. 'Sorry, pet. What sort o' work do you want? In service?'

'Yes – no,' Emily floundered.

Lily stiffened. 'Nothing wrong wi' service. I have a young feller and he's in service out Hylton way.'

'I meant I'll do anything,' Emily explained. Then, seeing that this girl now seemed sympathetic, she said, 'I've got to get work. I've a widowed mother to support.'

'Oh!' Lily understood that because she also had a widowed mother. She asked one of the older women, 'D'ye think Craggie will take another lass on?'

The other shrugged. 'Mebbe. We're busy enough now.'

Lily explained, 'We've got a lot of orders at the moment so we're working three shifts a day. We're the two-till-ten shift, waiting to go on at two o'clock. It's eight hours of hard labour,' she said, 'but the ropery lasses – that's us – are a grand lot to work with.'

Emily seized on the opportunity. 'Will you show me where to find Mr Craggie, please?'

'Mr Cragg!' Lily laughed. 'We call him Craggie, but don't you call him that or you'll be out as quick as you got in.' She linked her arm through Emily's. 'Come on, I'll take you round to ask him for a job.'

They walked round the corner to the factory entrance, where a man stood, pocket watch in hand. He was short and barrel-chested, bearded, in a blue serge suit with collar and tie, and a fierce glare. Lily whispered, 'That's him.'

As they came up he glanced at the watch. 'You've got another five minutes afore you start.'

'Aye, I know, Mr Cragg.' Lily was respectful now. 'But I've got a good lass here, quick with her fingers and strong in her back, and she's needing a job. Will you take her on, please?' And she pushed Emily forward.

Cragg looked her up and down, with a dispassionate stare. 'No.'

Emily was about to turn away but Lily held her. 'I thought you were looking for lasses with all these orders you've got.'

Cragg nodded. 'Aye, but I'm wanting lasses that know what they're doing. I never saw this one before in my life.'

'Ah! But she's willing and a quick learner. A pair o' hands is a pair o' hands, and that's what you might be wishing for when it gets to nine o'clock tonight and you're behind. And I'm needing just such a pair, as well you know.'

'Um.' Craggie looked at Emily again. 'She doesn't look all that strong to me but – will you look after her?'

'Aye, I will that, Mr Cragg,' Lily assured him.

'Right, you can start by getting her fitted out. Name?'

That last was directed at Emily. 'Emily Jackson,' she said.

'Thank you, Mr Cragg,' said Lily, and urged Emily away. Minutes later she was dressed like Lily in a canvas apron complete with knife, and borrowed clogs padded out with canvas so her feet would not slide about in them.

Emily worked the full eight-hour shift, and was exhausted when it ended at ten. The company made ropes and she laboured with Lily in the shop where the process started and the huge bales of sisal fibres were teased out by machine. If left unsupervised for a second they would snarl up and have to be cut free. The noise from the pounding steam engines that powered the machines hammered at Emily's ears. She soon found that speech was impossible and she had to resort to trying to lip-read like the other girls, who were expert. With growing weariness came the fear that she might be caught in the massive machinery or get the sack for not working hard enough; she knew she was slower than Lily, who helped her again and again.

At ten Emily walked out dragging her feet. Lily came to take her arm again and console her: 'I bet you're whacked, but that's because you're new. You'll get used to it.' She sounded confident.

'I'm not so sure,' Emily said. 'I could have slept on my feet like a horse this last hour.'

Lily laughed. 'There you are! You're joking about it already. Now, I live around here but you come from ower the watter. You can get the tram back home but that's the long way round and it costs twopence. All the lasses from the other side of the river use the ferry. It's quicker and it's only a ha'penny. Follow that lot — they're off to catch it now.' She gave Emily a shove towards a hurrying group of girls and called after her, 'I'll see you tomorrow! Good-night!'

'Goodnight and thank you,' Emily replied, and ran after the others.

She caught the ferry and paid her halfpenny for the crossing, then trudged the last half-mile to Ada's two rooms. As she climbed the stairs wearily Ada came out of the kitchen to stand at the head of them, peering down into the darkness. 'Who's that?'

Emily replied, 'It's me, Mam, Emily.'

'What are you doing here?' Ada scented trouble. 'Why aren't you at work?'

Emily came to stand by her. 'I've left, Mam.'

'But you've been there no time! You didn't get the sack?'

'No, Mam.'

'Well, then?' Ada waited as Emily tried to find words to describe what had happened to her.

'There was this man . . .' she began.

Ada took her arm and pulled her into the kitchen. She sat down in her old armchair and Emily knelt beside her, Ada's arm around her shoulders. Ada peered down at the girl, who was avoiding her gaze. 'You've done nothing you're ashamed of?'

'No, Mam.'

'But somebody else has.' She gripped Emily's wrist, painfully. 'Tell me.'

Emily told the truth, haltingly but leaving nothing out.

Ada sighed. 'That Billy Foster sounds as though he has his head screwed on the right way. I think he told the truth when he said Gamblin would have somebody to swear he never touched you. There's nowt we can do, but you've nothing to be ashamed of, and you got paid for the work you did. That's some consolation. It's a pity you've lost the job but I wouldn't have you going near that place again. We'll manage somehow.'

'I've got another job.' And Emily told her about the work at the ropery.

Ada bit her lip. 'You're young to be working at that, Emily. It's hard.'

'I'm earning more money than I did on the farm, and there's a girl there who helps me.' She told Ada about Lily and the other girls and her shift that day.

Later, in bed, Emily lay awake for a time, reliving the events of the day, taking pride in her work at the ropery, shuddering at the memory of the half-naked Gamblin. She told herself that she had to forget him, would not be bothered by him again, and finally she slept.

Emily worked at the ropery for two months, at first on the shift from two until ten and later, when the number of orders eased, a nine-hour day shift. Each morning she hurried to the ferry, shivering in the cold wind as autumn gave way to winter. She met up with Lily and the other women and girls at the ropery gates, where Lily was dancing or stamping her feet to keep warm.

One evening in early December Emily stayed talking with Lily at the end of the shift. When she set out to catch the next ferry the other girls had already left. As she walked down Church Street, which was dark and deserted, a hand suddenly clapped over her mouth and another clamped itself around her waist. She was pulled into the darkness and her attacker threw her to the ground. She could not see his face but knew Gamblin's voice as soon as he spoke. 'I caught sight o' you going into the ropery this morning. Couldn't believe my luck. You won't get away this time.' His weight pinned her to the ground and his free hand fumbled at her clothing.

'*Get out, you!*' a voice shrieked above them. Startled, Gamblin turned and the blow aimed at his head landed on his shoulder, but he yelled in pain. Then he was up and running. Lily stooped over Emily. 'Are you all right, bonny lass?'

Emily pushed herself up, holding on to the wall. She felt sick but smiled tremulously at Lily. 'I'm fine.' Then she burst into tears. Lily held her and soothed her until she quietened. 'Thank you,' Emily said. 'I was so frightened. I was never so glad to see anyone as when you came.'

'It was a bit of luck,' Lily said. 'I was just setting off for home when I remembered I wanted to ask you if you'd like to come round to my mam's for your tea on Sunday. I chased after you to ask and saw that feller grab you. Did you know him?'

'It was a man called Gamblin,' Emily said, and she told her story to Lily. 'If I complained he'd find somebody to swear he was somewhere else tonight.'

'I got one in on him but I wish I'd had another chance,' Lily said. She held up one of her clogs: 'I hit him with this. I missed his head but I'll bet he has a bruise to show for it tomorrow.' She stooped to put on the clog then said, 'Come on, I'll walk with you as far as the ferry.'

They walked arm in arm and in silence, Emily lost in

her thoughts. Eventually Emily said sadly, 'I'll have to give up the ropery and get right away. He knows I work there now and he'll watch out for me, follow me home, find out where I live and lie in wait for me again. I'll have to get another job.'

'It's not that bad!' Lily protested. 'Me and the other lasses'll take it in turns to watch out for you and give him what-for.'

'I know you would.' Emily was silent again. After a little while she added, 'I've been thinking about another job for some time now. Don't think I'm putting on airs, but I don't want to stay at the ropery for ever. I want to get on in the world. I don't know how I'll do it but I'll have to start by trying some different jobs. It'll be a way of learning.' She turned anxiously to Lily. 'You'll still be my friend, won't you?'

'O' course I will.' Lily squeezed her arm. 'Always. So where are you going to look for work?'

'Oh, somewhere in the town.' But then Gamblin might find her again. 'No, better in Newcastle or a place right out of here where he won't find me.'

Lily said thoughtfully, 'What about Hylton? Jimmy, the lad I'm walking out with — remember, I told you about him — he's a groom in a big house that way. He works for some people called Wilkinson and Mr Wilkinson is something high up in Newcastle. Jimmy was saying last Saturday that they were looking for a lass to start in the kitchen. Eight pound a year and all found. That's good money for a scullery-maid but the family are open-handed.

Mind, Jimmy says you have to work for it, but that won't frighten you. I'd take the job myself but my mam's not too well and can't manage at home on her own.'

Hylton was far outside the town and Emily thought that Gamblin would never find her there. She could send Ada ten shillings every month out of her pay. She could learn to cook, how to be a housekeeper or – she shied away from her ridiculous dream. 'I'd like to try that,' she said.

'You go out there on Saturday afternoon. Better than that, I'll go with you and get Jimmy to put in a word for you.'

Then they parted and Emily waved to Lily from the ferry as it pulled away from the steps. She had not mentioned her dream of owning ships or whirling round a ballroom floor like the girl in the portrait at the Franklin house. But one day . . .

Chapter Eight

'A summer ball, lasses. The mistress tells me she wants one for her daughters. That's work for all of us, but mainly you in here.' Aitkyne, the Wilkinsons' long-faced Scottish butler, had come into the kitchen with the news.

Mrs Bellamy, the plump, red-faced cook, threw up her hands in despair. 'We'll never cope! God knows, it's difficult enough to get by from one day to the next! And now a summer ball! What are we paid for all this? Coppers!'

Emily, a lissom, curvy young woman now, though still only in her mid-teens, looked up from where she was weighing flour for a pie. She smiled, unconcerned, though she knew she would have her share of the extra cooking. In spite of her tender age she had been assistant to Mrs Bellamy for two months now. The cook had reported to the mistress of the house that 'Emily learns quicker than anybody I've ever had in my kitchen and forgets nothing, ma'am. Whatever I give her to do is finished on time, or sooner, and just as it should be. I know she's just turned sixteen but I'll be glad to have her as assistant cook.'

Emily had also got to know Mrs Bellamy: no matter how she complained the food served at the ball would be just as the mistress asked. 'I think it will be lovely to see all the ladies in their dresses, and the dancing,' she said.

'Aye, a lassie like you might feel that way, but when you get to our age you'll feel different,' Aitkyne said gloomily. Then he changed the subject: 'I gave the post to the master but there was one for you, Emily.'

'Thank you.' Emily took it and put it in the pocket of her apron. It was her weekly letter from Ada.

'And there's another one for Jimmy. Will you give it to him when you see him?' Aitkyne went on.

'Aye, I'll do that.' Emily took it and perched it on the mantelpiece over the big black kitchen range. Breakfast was over now, and it was time to start preparing lunch and dinner. She worked quickly, economically, thinking ahead. She could smile now at her ambition to own ships, but she held on to her dream as a light at the end of a tunnel of hard work. However, now she was only too well aware of the economic facts of life: she could never save enough money to buy a ship.

But she could be proud that in just two years she had more than doubled her income to eighteen pounds a year. It had been earned: she would never forget the early months of scrubbing, with soda, the pans that were soot-blackened from cooking on the fire, scrubbing until her hands were raw to the point of bleeding, of falling asleep as she tried to write her weekly letter to her mother, by the light of a guttering candle in the little attic room she shared with one of the housemaids. After that initiation her present conditions seemed luxurious, with a room of her own and cooking with Mrs Bellamy.

And now there was Alastair.

Through the partially steamed window, Emily spotted a figure crossing the stableyard. She snatched the letter from the mantelpiece, ran to the kitchen door and called, 'Jimmy!'

Lily's lad came striding over to her, a fresh-faced young man with an easy grin. 'Now then, Emily, what is it?'

'A letter for you,' and she gave it to him.

Jimmy glanced at it. 'From my uncle in South Africa. He writes about once every six months. See the stamp?'

Emily had seen one before and heard about the uncle, too, but pretended she had not because she knew Jimmy was proud of his distant relative. She peered at the envelope and exclaimed, 'My! A letter from all that way! Is he with the Army?' The British Army were fighting against the Boers.

'With it but not in it,' Jimmy replied. 'He went out there years and years ago, jumped ship when he got to Durban and got a job ashore. He's driving wagons for the Army's supply train now. I'll tell you what he has to say when I've read it.' Then he snatched back the letter and stuffed it hastily into the pocket of his breeches. 'Look out! Here comes the boss! I'd better be off.'

His boss was the head groom, who was just turning the corner of the house. Emily watched Jimmy go, and loitered in case she caught a glimpse of Alastair Wilkinson on his way to the stables. She told herself she was being silly because they dared not acknowledge each other. That would have meant instant dismissal and separation from Alastair. They both agreed they did not want that because they were in love. It would be different in a year's time when Alastair came down from university. He would be able to earn a living then and they would declare their love to the world. For the present, however, they had to be satisfied with snatched kisses. 'Nobody must know,' Alastair had insisted. So Emily had not even told Ada.

She waited a full minute but the son of the house, tall, fair and handsome, did not appear. She sighed and returned to her work.

'That took you long enough,' Mrs Bellamy complained. 'I saw Jimmy go off ten minutes ago.' That was an exaggeration, but Emily only smiled.

The preparations for the summer ball went forward. Mrs Wilkinson called the cook for frequent meetings after which Mrs Bellamy would wail, 'Wait till you hear what she wants now! You'll never believe it!' Emily did, though, because this was not the first ball for which she had helped with the cooking.

On an evening in July she toiled in the heat of the kitchen while the sound of dance music drifted in through the open windows. It was late, the buffet served and eaten, when Mrs Bellamy wiped the sweat from her brow and sighed with relief. 'We can put our feet up for a while and have a nice cup of tea.'

Emily pushed back a damp tendril of soft brown hair. 'Will it be all right if I go to watch the dancing for a few minutes, please?'

'Aye, you go on. I was expecting you to ask.' The cook patted her shoulder. 'You've earned a rest, anyway.'

Emily left the kitchen, and enjoyed the feel of the cool night air on her skin as she made her way round the side of the house. At one point she had to make a tactful diversion through the undergrowth to avoid being seen by a group of young men, who were drinking and laughing. Then she came to the front lawn where a marquee had been erected because there was no ballroom in the house. She crept round it until she found a gap in the canvas and pressed her eye to it. The ball was in full swing, the orchestra playing on the stage at one end and the dancers circling on the floor. Emily's foot tapped in time to the music. Then she froze.

Alastair Wilkinson was dancing towards her, a girl in his arms. He was smiling down at her and she was gazing adoringly up at him. Emily recognised that look of Alastair's, had seen it when he had directed it at her, with his hands on her waist. Now they were caressing the back of this strange girl, who was evidently no stranger to Alastair for her fingers were playing with the hair on his neck. They passed within feet of Emily and whirled on.

She stayed there, the picture of the two lovers burned into her mind.

The music had stopped and started again before she stirred. Then she turned her back on the marquee and the dancing, and set out for the kitchen. She was forced to divert again to avoid the young men and had almost passed them when she realised that Alastair was now among them. She stopped in her tracks when one called out, 'I saw you dancing with the Rochester girl, Alastair. Lucky dog!'

Another said, 'I think she's fallen for you, old boy. But what about the little bit of indoor entertainment you were telling us about, the young Venus who cooks your dinner – and maybe warms your bed for all we know?' This witticism brought a roar of laughter.

'As a gentleman I may say nothing,' Alastair responded. When they groaned, he added, 'But I could!' More hoots of laughter followed.

Emily put her hands over her ears and hurried to get away from them, seething with hurt and anger. When she entered the kitchen, the tears were still wet on her cheeks but she had ceased crying. There was work to be done. The table was loaded with desserts ready to be served, though that was work for the maids.

Two minutes later someone shouldered aside one of the young bucks surrounding Alastair Wilkinson. As he staggered Emily walked through the gap and slammed a bowl of blancmange into Alastair's face. While he spluttered and blinked through it, she scraped a handful from his shirt front and smeared it into his face again. Then she turned and walked away.

One of the young men said weakly, 'I say!' The others stared open-mouthed.

'What happened to you?' Mrs Bellamy asked.

Emily rinsed her hands and dried them. She said only, 'I don't want to talk about it, but you'll hear soon enough.' Now she just wanted to hide, but she carried on with her work. At the end of the evening as she helped to clean the kitchen she expected a summons, which did not come. She went to her bed dead tired but was unable to sleep. Thoughts of how Alastair had treated her were mixed with worry as to how she would find another job, how she would support Ada. She knew she would be sacked with a poor reference, if she got one at all, so she would be lucky to get another job in service. But she would not apologise.

The morning indeed brought a summons, but not from the mistress. Aitkyne was trying unsuccessfully to solve a mystery, interrogating every one of the staff: 'That Marjorie Jenkins says she saw Master Alastair come in from the garden smothered in blancmange and run upstairs.' Marjorie was a young housemaid. Then the butler asked, 'Do you know what happened?' No one could help him and Emily would not.

After breakfast he appeared with the post and handed a letter to Emily. 'Your usual,' he said.

But it was not. The writing on the envelope was not Ada's. It came from a neighbour who told her that Ada was poorly. The doctor had seen her and said she was delirious. She was calling for Emily.

She showed the letter to Mrs Bellamy and later, as soon as she could gain an audience, to the mistress. Mrs Wilkinson said, with reluctant generosity, 'It's come at a most unfortunate time — we're hosting a luncheon party and a dinner later this week — but you must go to your mother at once, of course. One of the grooms can take you in the trap.'

Emily packed her tin box, worrying all the time about Ada, and Jimmy carried it down the servants' back stairs. She bade farewell to Mrs Bellamy and the rest of the staff in the kitchen as she passed through. 'God only knows how I'll manage without you!' the cook wailed. 'And what are you taking your box for? You'll only be away a few days.'

Emily knew that she was not coming back, was certain that, sooner or later, Aitkyne's mystery would be solved and she would be sacked. Besides, she had a foreboding . . .

She was walking across the stableyard to where Jimmy sat waiting in the trap when Alastair Wilkinson snapped, 'Just a minute!' Emily stopped and turned. She saw that he had been waiting in the stable, but had now stepped into the sunlight. 'Come here,' he called.

After two years in service, Emily moved instinctively to obey, but then she stayed still. 'No,' she said.

Alastair's lips tightened. He glanced at Jimmy, who was watching curiously, and strode over to stand within a yard of Emily. He lowered his voice and said, 'Did you go mad last night? If that was your idea of a joke it wasn't funny! But I haven't told my mother, and I won't, if you apologise.' He waited, magnanimous.

'I won't say I'm sorry because it wouldn't be true,' Emily answered.

'You made me look a fool in front of my friends last night,' Alastair said angrily.

'It was your turn,' Emily replied.

'What do you mean?' He was nonplussed.

' "You were dancing with the Rochester girl, you lucky dog, Alastair," ' Emily quoted to him. As his face fell she went on, ' "But she isn't the young Venus who's keeping your bed warm." '

'You were listening! Eavesdroppers hear no good of themselves.'

'I didn't want to hear what I did.' It had caused her pain. 'But I'm glad now.' Because she had avoided heart-break.

'So you thought you'd take out your spite on me!' he ground out. 'Well, you'll regret it. Just you wait, you little bitch, I'll make your life a misery!' He spun on his heel and stalked off.

Emily stood still for a minute, swallowing her anger and sorrow. Then Jimmy called, 'Are you all right, lass?'

Emily turned, walked over to him and smiled. 'I'm fine.' She climbed into the trap and he drove off on the way to Sunderland, Emily sitting straight-backed by his side. She acknowledged that she had been lucky. Alastair would have used her then made her life a misery. She had just found out sooner than he had intended.

'She's dropped off,' whispered Bridget Cassidy. 'I think we should let her sleep.'

Ada lay, pale and ill, in bed, and Emily had found the neighbour sitting knitting beside her. Now she learned that Mrs Cassidy was one of a succession keeping watch on her mother and attending to her needs. Peering over spectacles tied together with black thread, Bridget said, 'We all come in for an hour or two every day so she's never alone for long.' She gathered up her knitting and stuck the needles into the ball of wool. 'I'll get back now and make my man's tea, but if you want anybody to come in while you do a bit o' shopping, you just have to say.' Then, lowering her voice, 'She'll be glad to see you. She's been asking for you.'

Emily hung her coat on the hook on the kitchen door and unpacked her box. The fire needed making up and the coal bucket was empty. She peeped into the front room and saw that Ada was still asleep so she went downstairs to the coalhouse. When she came back she looked into the front room again, and saw Ada stirring. Her eyes opened and she stared blankly for a moment at the smiling Emily, then smiled back. 'There you are, my bonny lass.'

They held each other and Ada cried a little from weakness. Then she said worriedly, 'You'd better not stay too long. You don't want to lose that good job.'

'Don't worry. I'm not going back there because I'm getting another job close to you,' Emily said soothingly.

'You don't need to worry about me,' Ada assured her. 'I can look after myself.'

'I'm sure you can, but I just want to be at home again till you're properly better.' In fact Emily knew that Ada was not well enough to care for herself: the house was not as clean as Ada usually kept it. Later that day the doctor came, a young man, taking the stairs two at a time. After examining Ada he talked to Emily in the kitchen: 'The fever hit her badly, but I think you being here will help a great deal in her recovery. She's shaken off the worst now but she's very weak. Your company and rest, that's what she needs.' And then he was gone, down the stairs and into his waiting trap.

Emily wrote a letter of resignation to Mrs Wilkinson, took it to the post, and went to shop in the nearby high street. While she was out Mrs Cassidy came in to sit with Ada. On Emily's return Bridget said to her, low-voiced, in the kitchen: 'When she was dilairious she kept on and on about you: "Fetch my bonny lass! Emily was meant. Emily was sent to us." I wonder what she was trying to say?'

Emily was baffled. 'Are you sure that's what she said?'

'Oh, aye.' Bridget nodded emphatically. 'A few of us heard her say it. We all took notice because it seemed a funny thing to say.'

Emily had no answer to that and decided to ask Ada later. She cleaned, cooked, fed Ada and talked cheerfully to her, then settled her down for the night. Just before she blew out the candle, she asked, 'When you were so poorly you said, "Emily was meant, Emily was sent." What did you mean?'

Suddenly Ada was alert. 'I meant the Good Lord sent you. What else?'

Emily was not convinced but Ada was becoming agitated so she whispered, 'Oh, aye, what else? Now you can get some sleep.'

Early the next morning, Emily took the ferry across the river and sought out Lily. She found her friend standing outside the ropery, as usual, waiting to go on shift. 'Is there any work going, Lily?'

'What happened to your place at the Wilkinsons'? You were doing well there.'

Emily told her, quietly, about Alastair, and Ada's illness. 'So one way or another, I'm finished with the Wilkinsons. But what about work?'

Lily pulled a face. 'Not here, pet. The orders are right down and there's been a lot o' lasses laid off.' She saw the disappointment on Emily's face and added quickly, 'But I'll see if anybody knows of anything.' She consulted with the other girls who offered several suggestions, with more hope than confidence. Emily scribbled them all down on a scrap of paper with a stub of pencil she had borrowed from one of the older women – it was normally used for writing out illegal betting slips. Then the owner of the pencil said doubtfully, 'There's always Rafe Ramsden. He's wanting help again, down at the Clipper.'

Lily grimaced. 'That's not surprising.' As Emily made

to write down the name, she went on, 'You wouldn't like that. It's a pub down by the river. There's a fight in there every night and them that goes to work there don't last long.'

'Aye, and that Rafe Ramsden frightens the life out o' them,' said the woman with the pencil.

Emily set out determinedly, clutching her slip of paper. Two hours later she had trudged the length and breadth of Monkwearmouth. She was still determined but still without work, and there were no more names on the paper to visit. She hesitated at the bottom of Church Street for some time, mindful of Lily's warning, but finally she told herself that she had to find work and beggars could not be choosers. She walked on again apprehensively.

She found the Clipper in a cul-de-sac hard by the river and slotted into a row of terraced houses. Although she had passed it with Bert Jackson when he had found her on the quay all those years ago, it rang no bell of memory.

She could see only one door to the pub; it was brass-handled and bore a sign that read 'Bar'. A low growl of noise came from behind it. Emily took a deep breath and went in. She found herself at the head of a short flight of steps, and as it was midday the pub was crowded with workmen from the shipyards and seamen from ships in the river. The ceiling was low and the room smoke-filled. She hesitated, looking down at the men below her. The noise faded and she realised she was the focus of a hundred eyes.

A voice broke it: 'You're not allowed in here, lass.' Its owner faced Emily across the polished counter. He was short, broad, powerful, the ugliest man she had ever seen: simian, low-browed and pockmarked, with hard eyes under bushy black brows. She saw surprise and temper there, but also . . . amusement? He lifted a hand with fingers like bananas and pointed at the door behind Emily: 'Out.'

But Emily was desperate for work. She stood her ground. 'I'm looking for a gentleman called Ramsden, sir.'

The silence was broken, this time with a gale of laughter. 'There y'are Rafe, ye're a gentleman at last!' bellowed a bearded sailor.

'And a "sir"! It'll be Lord Rafe next!' a boilermaker boomed.

Rafe eyed them with grim tolerance, then said, 'I don't know what you want, lassie, but if you defy me all you'll get is trouble. Now do as you're told, get out, and whatever you want to see me about you can do it in the Bottle and Jug round the corner.'

Emily obeyed. She had taken the villainous-looking man for a barman, not the publican and had unwittingly made him the butt for jokes from the men in the bar. He was not likely to take her on now. Did she want him to? At first sight of him she had quailed, but there had been that hint of humour. And she needed work.

Outside in the street Emily saw a narrow, cobbled alley that ran down the side of the pub. She entered it and found two doors, one with a sign, 'Sitting Room' the other 'Bottle and Jug'. The second opened on to a room that was little bigger than a cupboard. It held a scrubbed wooden table, a bench that would seat three or four and a small bar. Two old women sat at the table, shawls around their shoulders and glasses of stout in front of them. 'Come in, lass. Just ring the bell on the bar,' one said.

'Thank you,' Emily replied. She reached out to tap the plunger on the brass bell, but a big hand covered it.

'All right, give me time. I've got customers to serve besides you. Now, what do you want?' Rafe Ramsden asked gruffly.

'I heard you needed help in the bar.' Emily tried to sound more confident than she felt.

'I do. Are you asking for the job?'

'Yes, Mr Ramsden.'

'Where have you worked before?'

'I was two years with Mrs Wilkinson — that was in a big house out Hylton way. I was assistant cook.'

Rafe was not impressed. 'There's no cooking needed here. I sell beer, wines and spirits. Fellers bring their bait in here to eat with a pint, but I don't bother wi' grub.'

'I have served at table.' A white lie: she had only done so on two occasions when there was a shortage of staff.

'That's no use here either. How old are you, anyway?'

'Nineteen,' lied Emily. She felt the blood rise to her face as he stared at her.

'I reckon a year or two less than that,' he said, and pushed back from the bar, ending the interview. 'It would be a waste of time taking you on. You'd never last the course and you've no experience. So what's the point?'

It was a rhetorical question but Emily, stung and

disappointed, answered it: 'But you need help in here and you're likely to go on needing it because everybody says you frighten the life out of all the people you get in here. But you don't frighten me.' That was not true but she would never admit it.

She turned to the door and saw that the two old women had been listening wide-eyed.

'Wait a bit!' Rafe's voice cracked behind her. Emily stopped, her hand on the door, head turned to look back. She thought she saw that hint of humour in Rafe's eyes again before he scowled and said, 'I'll give you a week's trial.'

'Th – thank you,' Emily stammered, taken aback.

Rafe laughed harshly, 'We'll see if you thank me later – if you last the week.'

Emily could have given up before that week was out. The warnings she had received about the Clipper had been exaggerated, but not much. There was a fight at least once a week, indeed she witnessed one that first night when she had only been working behind the bar for a few hours. Voices were raised, cursing, above the usual drone and other voices fell silent. Emily, hauling on the handle of the beer engine, saw fists flying, and Rafe, standing beside her, grabbed a mallet from behind him and vaulted over the bar. He cleaved through the crowd, elbowing them aside, to reach the two men swinging wildly at each other. He shoved them apart with a hand spread flat on the chest of each. 'Give over and get out, or I'll brain the pair o' ye!' He raised the mallet and the adversaries hustled their way out into the street.

Rafe returned to his place behind the bar and found that Emily was still serving beer. 'Weren't you scared then?'

Emily tried to be laconic. 'Not very.' She was glad that the glasses on the tray she held under the pump were steady, but she was as surprised by that as Rafe seemed.

As the week went on that apparent self-possession became real. In the course of an evening she had to go out among the men several times to collect empty glasses. The first time she set out apprehensively, but soon realised that while the men were rough with each other, they did not molest her and refrained from swearing in her hearing. When she returned to the bar, Rafe said drily, 'Their bark's worse than their bite – as far as you're concerned, anyway.'

Most of the work in the bar was done by Rafe while Emily had to serve the customers in the Sitting Room and the Bottle and Jug. Next to the Sitting Room Emily discovered a big storeroom, which was virtually empty except for a few crates of bottled beer. She thought it a waste of space but Rafe said flatly, 'I can't put anybody in there and there's room enough as it is for the customers I've got.' In short, he was making all the money he needed.

The customers in the Bottle and Jug were usually old women drinking glasses of stout, or port and lemon, and sometimes a small boy or girl, with a penny in one hand and a jug in the other, came in for their father's supper beer. The Sitting Room was filled with shipyard foremen, senior clerks and other men with business on the riverside. Conversation was muted in there and the customers drank spirits rather than beer. As Rafe had said, no food was served except what the drinkers brought in. Young bloods on a night out would grill kippers or sausages on a casually cleaned shovel perched on the fire, or heat up their ale by plunging a red-hot poker into it.

Bar or Sitting Room, Emily was conscious of the men's admiring eyes on her, but Rafe said gruffly, 'No need to worry about us looking, lass. You can't expect any other. You're well worth looking at and that's all we want to do, Emily, just look.' She blushed, but believed him, and went about her business with more confidence. She was also easier in her mind about Ada, thankfully on her way back to health.

At the end of that first week Rafe asked, 'Well, d'ye want to stay on?'

Emily did not. She wanted to be like the Rochester girl who had charmed Alastair Wilkinson or, better still, like the girl in the picture at the Franklin house. She wanted to dance at a ball in a silk dress — she still cherished that bright though impossible vision of sending her own ships across the seas. If she had told Rafe about it, he would have hooted with laughter, and while she worked at the Clipper, or the ropery, she would do none of these things. She had thought of learning to type and qualify that way for a better job but she knew she would not realise her ambitions as an office clerk.

But then . . . She would not make her fortune working at the Clipper, but all day long she was among men who built ships, sailed them, had business with them or even owned shares in them . . .

Emily smiled at Rafe. 'Yes, please,' she said.

Chapter Nine

WINTER 1899. MONKWEARMOUTH.

'It's two topcoats warmer the night.' The drinker used the local phrase for milder weather – feeling as if one wore two overcoats.

'Aye. It's been fine all day.'

Emily listened to the men as they talked in the evening after the day's work was done. They were glad of the unseasonably high temperatures, accustomed to working on the ships or the quays in the biting wind.

Besides getting to know all the men who came in, Emily studied the old women and children who used the Bottle and Jug, and there was Sadie Theakstone, too, a wiry little woman in her thirties. She was a young widow who lived next door to the Clipper and scratched a living for herself and her two children by baking bread and pies. She came into the Bottle and Jug in the quiet of the afternoon, when her eldest son, home from school, could look after the shop. She and Emily liked to share that quiet hour. Sadie herself had been a barmaid before she married and was a source of useful tips. So was Ada, fully recovered for some months now and feeding advice to Emily daily, 'You watch out for the fellers in that pub. The sailors are the worst. Here today and gone tomorrow . . .'

Now Emily was flushed with heat as she worked behind the bar at the end of a busy Saturday night. Rafe had been silent and abstracted all day but now he said, 'Stay and have a drink with me tonight.' When she glanced at him, startled and wary, he added, 'I don't want to drink on my own, but the one woman for me died ten years ago this night.'

Emily saw the sadness in his eyes. 'Oh, I'm so sorry,' she said.

'No call for you to be sorry, lass.' They had just finished clearing up after the last customer had staggered out into the street. Behind the bar there was a kitchen and a private living room and Rafe led the way in, slumped down in an old armchair and said, 'Get me a Scotch, Emily, there's a good lass, a big one, and whatever you want.' She obeyed, set the whisky in front of him and sat in the opposite chair with a small whisky and water for herself.

Rafe swallowed half of his at a gulp, then sat staring morosely ahead. He did not try to make conversation but Emily, thinking it might help him to talk about his loss, probed gently, 'Had you been married long?'

'Aye. No.' He shook his head. 'A year. Not long if you look at it one way, but it was a year more than I ever expected.' He looked at Emily. 'I'm an ugly bastard, I know that. I never knew my mother or father, was brought up in an orphanage, and for as long as I can remember I was called an ugly bastard.'

'Oh, Rafe!' Emily touched his hand. 'That's cruel.'

'That's life.' He shrugged. 'But by the time I was thirty I deserved it. The Navy had thrown me out for fighting and striking a petty officer. I'd done time for assault and battery – that was because of fellers who miscalled me and I half killed them. I could write a list. Then Biddy came along and there'd never been anybody like her. She'd take my head in her hands and smile and kiss me. And she married me.' He emptied his glass and pushed it at Emily. She filled it again, returned to her seat and waited.

It was some minutes before Rafe went on, 'We'd been married just over a year when she died having our babby. That's the worst part. I keep thinking I killed her.'

'No, Rafe.'

He groaned. 'Aye, I know the argument, that these things happen and I shouldn't blame myself, but I still feel the guilt as well as the sorrow. I can put it out o' my mind for the rest of each year, but about this time it haunts me.'

'Not Biddy,' said Emily gently. 'I'm sure she loved you.'

'That she did,' Rafe said simply, 'and I lost her.' His glass was empty again and he pushed it towards Emily, who silently refilled it. As she set it down before him, he said, 'You'd better get yourself home.'

'No.' Emily did not want to leave him. 'Tell me about Biddy.'

He stared at her, surprised, then slowly harked back: 'She was dark, always smiling, little – I used to lift her wi' one o' these.' He looked at his hands, spread broad on the table. And then he went on to talk hesitantly of the love that had come to him late and was torn from him too soon. Emily listened and sat very still, except when she filled his glass again and again.

It was past midnight when he fell asleep with his head on his arms. Emily fetched his overcoat from where it hung behind the kitchen door and spread it over him. Then she walked home alone through the dark, silent streets. The ferry had long since stopped running and she had to cross the river by the bridge. She paused there to peer down at the ships crowded below, marked by riding lights, their reflections shivering on the black water. There was beauty in it, her heart ached and she wept for Rafe.

The next day, Rafe said only, 'Thanks, lass,' and neither of them referred to the incident again but from that time Rafe treated her as an equal, even asking her advice or opinion, though he still made up his own mind.

Emily had noticed that the Sitting Room clientele was sparse and irregular. The foremen, managers and business-men would come in some lunchtimes but not others. When she mentioned this to Rafe he said dismissively, 'They only come in here if all they want is a drink. They go up into the town for a meal.'

'Couldn't we sell them something to eat?' Emily asked.

Rafe's brows shot up. 'We've enough to do as it is. Let's have some glasses washed.' Neither was he interested in her tentative suggestion – again – that the storeroom be put to use: he was content to jog along as he always had, and Emily settled into a hard-working but peaceful niche. Until one night a month later.

It's her! After two years! And riper for the waiting! Digby Gamblin put up a hand as if to stroke his full moustache but in fact to cover his face. By chance he had stepped into the Sitting Room of the Clipper, and stopped dead in his tracks. Emily had worked at the Clipper for six months now, and came through from the bar with a whisk of skirts to serve four ships' chandlers sitting at one of the round tables with wrought-iron legs. Intent on them and with her back to the door, she did not see the stranger enter.

The men at the table greeted her cheerfully, 'Good evening, Emily.'

'Hello, gentlemen. What can I get you?' She took their orders.

Gamblin's lips twisted in a travesty of a smile, then he turned away quickly and left the pub. From the corner of her eye, Emily saw the door open and close and glanced round but was too late to see the man who had come and gone.

When the Clipper had closed and Emily had finished clearing up, she put on her coat and called to Rafe, 'All done! Goodnight!'

He was eating his supper in the kitchen behind the bar. 'Goodnight, Emily!'

She hurried through the darkened bar and let herself out. The cul-de-sac was dark without the lights from the pub, but this did not disturb her — she had often walked this stretch alone. As usual the last ferry had sailed so she would have to take a tram across the bridge to get home. Emily made for the street at the mouth of the alley where a gas lamp burned, but before she could reach it a figure stepped out from the darkness close to the wall, a hand fastened on her throat and another whipped around her slender waist, dragging her backwards and trying to throw her down.

She knew at once who it was, remembered his rank smell of sweat and cheap cigars, his foul breath. Gamblin had tracked her down again. Emily struggled and fought, flailing her arms and kicking out. She could not scream because of his grip on her throat. She could hear the desperate scraping of her buttoned boots on the cobbles, the whisper of her threshing skirts. Then her head was whirling and she saw flashing lights as consciousness slipped away.

Suddenly feet were pounding down the alley and a deep voice said, 'What the hell!' A long arm reached out, grabbed Gamblin by the collar and yanked him clear of Emily. She staggered and fell against the wall then started to slip down it. Her saviour saw her collapse and let go of Gamblin, who seized his opportunity and ran. The other man swore and pulled Emily to her feet. 'Steady now. You're all right. Here, let's get out in the light.' He half carried her, easily though Emily's legs were wobbly under her, to the gas lamp. So far she had seen only his tall figure in silhouette, smelt the salt and coal-smoke that hung about him. Now she realised that her head did not reach to his shoulder, and that he wore a dark blue reefer jacket with brass buttons, the uniform of a ship's officer. But he was young for an officer — she judged him to be only a year or two older than herself.

David Walsh looked down at her. A pretty girl, he thought, and there was something about her . . . Had he seen her somewhere before? He frowned, but failed to recognise the leggy and skinny schoolgirl on a swing in the young woman he now supported. 'I'm David Walsh,' he said. 'I heard a scuffling sound as I passed here and wondered what was going on . . . I take it that feller was pressing his unwanted attentions on you.'

Emily knew that Gamblin had been intent on rape but she said only, 'Yes.' Her neck felt sore and her voice was a croak. She was frightened both by Gamblin's attack and by everyone now, including this stranger. She pushed herself away from him.

'Are you sure you're well?' David asked.

'It's just my throat where he tried to choke me,' Emily said shakily.

'We'll have to get the police on to him. Do you know him, by any chance?'

'I think so, but there's no point in telling the police.' Emily explained that Gamblin would have a friend to prove him innocent.

'I shouldn't have let him get away.'

'But you did it to save me from falling,' Emily remonstrated. 'I'm grateful for your help, but now I must go.'

'Where do you live? I'll keep you company on the way home.'

'There's no need for that.' Now that Emily was in the lit street she felt safe, but still wary of this stranger. He towered over her, head and shoulders taller, broad-chested and long-legged, and she knew the strength of him.

David censured mildly, 'You shouldn't be walking unescorted in places like that at this time of night.'

Emily knew that now. But she would not be lectured to by this youth. 'Thank you for your advice, sir, but it isn't needed,' she said, then turned and walked away.

But David followed her: 'I'll see you safe home.'

'I can find my own way, thank you.'

He did not answer but strode alongside her and they climbed the rise of Church Street together. Reaching the top, Emily saw the last tram on the point of leaving. She had just time to catch it if she ran. She took to her heels and leaped on, but on the platform she looked back to see him standing in the road. Relenting, she waved and cried, 'Thank you! Goodnight!' He grinned and lifted a hand in salute, then she turned, entered the tram and sank grate-fully into a seat. She paid her penny to the conductor and it was when she held out her hand for the ticket that she found she was shaking.

Emily was grateful for the chance to sit still, hands clasped in her lap to hide their tremor. By the time she reached home and kissed Ada she had regained control of herself. She said nothing of the attack she had suffered, but that night she went over it again and again, shuddering at the memory. Also, she decided she had been ungrateful: she could have accepted the young man's offer to accompany her. If he had not come to the rescue . . . she owed him an apology – if she ever saw him again.

The next day Emily had her chance to apologise. She was serving in the bar in the lunch hour when Rafe came in from the Sitting Room carrying a tray of dirty glasses. He called, 'Customers in the room, Emily! One Navy rum and half a pint o' beer.'

'Right you are!' She gave the riveter she was serving his change from a threepenny piece, poured a glass of bitter and the treacly rum then whisked through to the Sitting Room. She was confronted by a short man with a pointed beard, who wore a brown serge suit that was shiny with age and carried a battered bowler hat. At his shoulder, dwarfing him, stood the young giant of the previous evening, in his blue reefer jacket with the gleaming brass buttons.

The small man glared at her fiercely but said, 'Thank ye, miss.' He paid with a half-crown and Emily went to fetch his change. She was flustered, had not anticipated meeting the young man again, let alone so soon. And she was bothered by a stirring of memory. There was something about the little man, his ferocity and his beard, but she could not place him.

Then Rafe turned from pulling pints to say, 'Tell Charlie I'll be in for a crack with him as soon as I get a minute.'

'Charlie?' Emily queried. Was that the young man's name?

'Charlie Daggett – Captain Daggett, the feller with the beard.'

'Oh!' Emily remembered now: Captain Daggett, a clearing in the woods on the Franklin estate, a boy pushing her on a swing then being upbraided by the fierce little man who had called him Davy. She smiled, no longer flustered but in command of herself. She remembered the boy and he had not daunted her like this young officer. She presented the change to Daggett and said, 'Rafe will be in to see you as soon as he can.'

'Aye,' said Daggett, scowling. 'He's here now. Come to make sure I pay up, bloody tightwad.'

Rafe appeared at Emily's side. 'You've not drowned yet, then.'

The men shook hands and Daggett guffawed. 'Not yet.' He jerked his head at the tall young man beside him. 'D'ye remember this young feller, Rafe? He ran away to sea, had the cheek to stow away aboard my ship and I gave him a job as cabin boy. Now he's a second mate. Davy Walsh.'

'You're not *his* second mate?' Rafe shook David's hand.

David grinned. 'Not yet.' He was watching Emily, biding his time.

'He's dressed up in a monkey suit because he's been out

foreign,' Daggett said, 'in some ship that carries passengers so all the officers have to be in the company's uniform. Very fancy.' He dug an elbow into David's ribs.

Emily thought, Out foreign! So that's why he's so brown.

'I take it you got home safely last night, miss?' David said.

'I did, thank you, sir. I'm grateful to you.' Emily replied politely.

Daggett looked from one to the other, and Rafe's brows lifted. 'What's all this?' he asked. 'Are you two keeping company?' His tone was light, amused, but his eyes were watchful.

Emily felt the colour rushing to her face again and she said quickly, 'No!' and explained, 'This gentleman came to my assistance last night when I was attacked outside here.'

Rafe demanded, 'What's all this?' When Emily told him what had happened, he growled, 'I should have seen you on the road. I'll sort this out later.'

Embarrassed now, Emily excused herself: 'They'll be wanting to be served in the other bar,' and hurried away. But from time to time she had to visit the Sitting Room to serve a customer in there and caught some of the conversation between the three men. Once she heard David say, 'I'm in uniform because it's all I've got at the moment. My trunk with all my other gear has still not arrived. It had better come soon because I'll be off again before long.'

'They don't give you much leave, then,' Rafe said.

'They do, but there's a vacant berth for a first mate and the owners have told me it's mine if I want it. I can't turn down a chance like that.'

And all the time Emily knew his eyes were on her with a puzzled look in them. When he and Daggett were on the point of leaving, he smiled down at her and asked, 'Have we met before?'

Emily pictured him pushing her on the swing at the Franklin house, but also recalled his amusement when she had told him of her dream: 'Don't be daft. Lasses don't own ships!' She had learned that that was true but it had not given him the right to patronise her. Then perversity, or annoyance that he had not remembered her as she had him, made her say, 'I don't know. Have we?' Then she smiled and went about her business.

He shook his tousled dark head, then strode long-legged after the terrier-like figure of Daggett.

In the comparative quiet of the afternoon Rafe came to Emily and said, 'Young Walsh said you know who it was last night, but you can't prove it. If you see him again, you point him out to me.'

'I don't want you to get into trouble,' Emily protested.

'I don't want you in any trouble, either,' Rafe retorted. 'If he comes in here, you point him out.'

It was an order, and Emily met his glare. She knew she had nothing to fear from this man and said meekly, 'Aye, Rafe.'

On the next Saturday night Emily was working in the bar. It was crowded, the men standing almost shoulder to shoulder under a cloud of tobacco smoke. She caught just a glimpse of one man in particular and drew in her breath sharply. Rafe was beside her at the time and said quickly, 'Seen him?'

Emily nodded, not looking at the man skulking at the rear of the crowd with his cap pulled down over his eyes, although she could feel his gaze burning into her. 'He's behind Freddie Thornton, the one in the cap pulled down so you can hardly see his face. That's Gamblin.'

Rafe leaped over the bar and pushed his way through the press. He shoved Freddie Thornton aside, grabbed Gamblin by his collar and yanked the cap from his head. 'Let's have a look at you.' Rafe held him, squirming, with one hand, and lifted him so that his toes tapped on the sawdust-covered floor.

'What the hell's the matter wi' you? You're strangling me!' Gamblin protested, choking.

'Like you did wi' that lass the other night.' Rafe saw him flinch.

'I can prove I wasn't there,' Gamblin was quick to claim.

'Shut it before I belt you,' Rafe told him contemptuously. 'I know all about that. Get out of this place and don't come in again. If I see you around here I'll tell these fellers what you were up to with that lass. They'll probably hang you from a lamp-post.'

Gamblin's narrowed eyes hunted about the room. He could see the ranked faces peering at him curiously. He knew what their reaction would be if they thought he had attacked Emily, and the sweat started on his face.

Rafe ran him to the door and shoved him out into the street, then watched him hurry away, stumbling on the cobbles and rubbing at his neck. Rafe returned to the bar. 'You won't have any more trouble with that feller,' he told Emily.

And Emily believed him.

Emily's life returned to normal, a whirl of work interspersed with slack periods, which she filled with odd jobs like washing curtains. Rafe had never bothered and was nonplussed when she washed, ironed and rehung them. He was taken aback when some of the customers in the Sitting Room commented that it looked brighter. 'You were right to clean those curtains,' he said, grinning. 'You'll be running the place next!'

'God forbid,' Emily replied.

A week later she recalled those words. Early one morning she arrived at the Clipper and found the pub open but Rafe sitting in his armchair in the kitchen behind the bar, hunched over a roaring fire. 'I feel bad, Emily lass. I c-can't get b-bloody warm,' he said weakly.

She felt his brow and found it burning, wrapped him in blankets and dashed to the street door. She saw a small boy passing, blue-faced and shivering in just a jersey in the cold. Emily sent him running to fetch a doctor: 'I'll give you a ha'penny when you get back.'

The doctor was an elderly, grey-haired man, and arrived in a trap pulled by a grey-muzzled pony. He moved deliberately but was swift in diagnosing a fever. 'Put him to bed and keep him there. I'll give you something to bring the temperature down but he must rest.' So Emily put Rafe to bed while he tried, through chattering teeth, to give her instructions on how to run the Clipper. She left him alone briefly to put on his nightshirt, and ran down to wrap a shelf hot from the oven in a scrap of old blanket. When she returned she thrust it into the bed to keep Rafe warm.

Then she stood back to survey him anxiously. 'I'll be up later to see to you,' she said, then ran downstairs to open up the bar and the Sitting Room. She lit a fire in both, and minutes later when they were drawing well she was busy serving coffee, sometimes with rum, to men on their way to work. That first rush of business was hard work even when Rafe was there but without him she was run off her feet. By nine in the morning, when the pub had almost emptied, she knew she could not run the Clipper on her own, and she had come up with a possible solution.

Emily tapped on the wall with Rafe's mallet, the traditional method of communication with Sadie Theakstone's little shop. Sadie would know a cry for help when she heard it.

Emily was not disappointed: Sadie came hurrying in, her face flushed from the heat of her fire. 'I came as quick as I could, but I was lifting a tray of pies out of the oven. What's the matter, love?'

'Rafe's poorly. I've had the doctor to him and he's been ordered to bed. I opened up for the men going to work but I hardly had time draw breath. I can't manage this place on my own.'

'Why, of course you can't, love.' Sadie was sympathetic. 'You'll have to get some help in.'

'That's why I knocked you. You used to be a barmaid, so you know the ropes. Will you come in?'

Sadie said doubtfully, 'I'd like to help, aye, but I've got my little shop there and my customers. I don't want to turn them away.'

'I don't want you to. Put a sign in your window: "Pies and bread on sale in the the Clipper Bottle and Jug." You keep what you get for them from your customers. Any you sell to Rafe's customers you share the profit with him. And I'll pay you a barmaid's wages.'

Sadie took only a second to see the advantage to her in this: 'Right, then. I'll put the sign up, get a clean apron and bring in my stuff.'

She proved a little rusty at serving behind the bar, but she was willing and soon picked it up again. Between them she and Emily handled the midday trade successfully.

When Emily carried a bowl of soup upstairs to Rafe for his lunch, she told him what she had done. Before his illness he would have argued, but now he was apathetic. 'It sounds a funny arrangement, but if all the fellers got served, in the bar and the Sitting Room, I suppose it's all right – temporary like.'

Emily had her own ideas about 'temporary' but said nothing. Sufficient unto the day . . .

Emily made a hasty visit to Ada, leaving Sadie to look

after the pub. She explained the situation to her mother, and added, 'He can't be left on his own overnight.'

'Aye, he's been good to you,' Ada agreed.

So Emily packed a change of clothing and returned to the Clipper. That night she slept, when she could, on the armchair in the kitchen and visited Rafe every hour. When he ran with sweat she changed his bedding and nightshirt, and cooled his brow with a damp cloth. Just before dawn he sank into a quiet sleep. The doctor came later that morning and when he had examined his patient, he said to Emily, 'You've done very well. His temperature's down, almost back to normal.'

Within a week Rafe was up and about, and a week after that he was back at work. 'That doctor said I might easily have snuffed it if it hadn't been for you looking after me,' he told Emily.

She blushed. 'Oh, you'd have managed without me.'

But Rafe said, seriously, 'No, I wouldn't and I won't forget it.' When it came to the 'temporary' arrangement, he would have ended it, but for Emily. 'Look at the profit we made out of selling the pies in here,' she said. 'We've built up custom for them in just these two weeks. We can't stop now. We should buy them from Sadie and keep on selling them in here.' Presented with the figures, Rafe could not argue, and although Sadie went back to her shop she was happy to have a big customer like the Clipper. And Rafe doubled Emily's wages: 'You've put that much on the profits.'

Emily wondered if, after all, her dream of wealth and

owning ships might come true through the Clipper. She read everything about ships that she could get her hands on, newspapers and books. She listened to the conversations of the businessmen in the Sitting Room and began to learn something of their lives, and of the ships that sailed from this port to Russia, China, America and Australia. In their turn the men were willing to explain things to her that she did not understand and found, as Rafe had, that she was quick to learn.

She had become fond of Rafe and he of her, though there was no question of love: Emily was wary after her bitter experience with Alastair, and Rafe would never find another Biddy.

Digby Gamblin went about his work on the Franklin estate, taking his orders from Bradley Carver, even when Nathaniel returned from the South of France to spend the summer months of each year at home. Gamblin treated Bradley with respect, because he was the heir apparent to the Franklin fortune and because he had an uneasy feeling that he might be a dangerous man.

For a long time, Bradley Carver had been spending the occasional weekend in London. On his first departure he had told his mother, 'I need a change.'

'I'll come with you,' Clarice offered brightly.

Bradley turned her down flat, 'No, you won't.'

One evening in the Strand he caught the eye of a young girl nervously plying her trade for the first time and went with her to her room. She told him, 'I haven't done this before but I've been out of a job for three weeks and the rent is due.'

Bradley smiled reassuringly. 'I'll pay your rent and a bit besides.' That brought a tentative smile to her lips, but when he left her she was bruised, bleeding and whimpering.

Chapter Ten

APRIL 1904. MONKWEARMOUTH.

'By, you're a bonny lass!' The big blacksmith clamped a strong arm around Emily's waist and hugged her. No one could have argued with his description: at twenty-one, the pretty girl of a year or two earlier had blossomed into a beauty.

Emily had never seen him before in the Clipper but one of the men who had entered with him said, 'Let her alone, Joe, you'll frighten the lass.' She was not frightened, saw only good-humour in the face looming over her. He was a young man, broad-shouldered and strong, with a shock of hair under the cap on the back of his head.

Then Rafe shoved between them, grabbed Joe by the collar and dragged him away. 'Let go, man! We're only having a bit o' fun!' he protested, laughing, and thrust Rafe away. At any other time Rafe would have kept his feet, but now he tripped over the dog that had come in with the rat-catcher. The mongrel terrier yelped and scurried out of the way, but Rafe fell backwards awkwardly and his head struck the brass rail along the foot of the bar with a sickening thud.

Joe lumbered forward. 'Hey, man! I'm sorry. I was just trying to get you off my neck. Here, I'll give you a hand up.' He stooped over Rafe, concerned now. 'Are you all right, man?'

Emily pushed past Joe and fell on her knees beside Rafe. She shook him gently but there was no response. She bent over him, but could feel no breath from his open mouth. She touched his neck, but no pulse beat there. 'Fetch a doctor!' she cried.

But there was nothing a doctor could do. Rafe had died when he hit the rail. A policeman came too, and Emily told him, through her tears, 'It was an accident. Joe pushed him but it was only horseplay.'

However, Joe was arrested and led away, dazed and shocked, repeating, 'I never meant him any harm. God forgive me!'

Emily grieved for Rafe and worked furiously to keep the Clipper going. She moved into the pub, partly to save herself the time she spent travelling, but also so that it was not left empty, a prey to burglars at night. When she had a moment to spare she wondered what would become of her now. The new owner might have no use for her. Perhaps Lily could find her a job at the ropery. Emily had saved a little so she and Ada would not starve, but she did not want to see that eroded by a long period of unemployment.

One day Ezra Arkenstall came to the Clipper. He called in occasionally when he was in that part of the town on business. A man in his forties with a beard and wire-rimmed spectacles, he was a solicitor. He asked Emily, 'I would be grateful if you could come to my office at some time convenient to you. I am the executor of Mr Ramsden's will.'

'Will you keep an eye on the place while it's quiet this afternoon?' Emily asked Sadie. 'I have to go and see Mr Arkenstall about Rafe's will.'

'Ooh!' said Sadie, round-eyed. 'He must have left you something.'

Emily pulled a face. 'Maybe.' But she went hopefully to Arkenstall's office in the high street. An hour later she emerged in a daze, the solicitor's words echoing in her brain: 'Because of your loyalty and kindness to him, particularly when he was ill to the point of death, your patience and understanding . . .'

Rafe had left her the Clipper, lock, stock and barrel.

Now gratitude was added to Emily's sorrow at Rafe's death. This was a chance for her to move ahead, although owning ships and dancing in a ballroom were still a long way off. She reminded herself that she had not inherited a fortune, she just owned a dockside public house. But while she might be looking up at a long ladder, at least now she had her foot on the lowest rung.

She soon realised that Rafe had also left her the work. When she had got over the shock and was able to think straight, she decided to ask Sadie if she would come to work full time behind the bar. 'I'm thinking of selling meals in the Sitting Room,' she added, 'and you can still sell your pies in here, as we did before.'

Sadie jumped at the chance; for the first time in her life she saw financial security on the horizon. Her late husband, a labourer in the shipyards, had been unemployed for long periods. 'I'd like that. When do you want me to start?'

'Now!'

Emily was called to give evidence at Joe Kirby's trial and repeated her original statement that it had been a complete accident, sheer bad luck: 'Mr Ramsden would have shrugged it off. He was not a vindictive man.' As a result, Joe was sentenced only to six months' hard labour.

His young wife, who was no older than Emily, thanked her and wept tears of relief: 'God bless you! I hope you have all the luck in the world. I'll pray for you.'

Over the next months Emily remembered her words and concluded that the girl's prayers had not been heard: trouble brewed continually in the pub as the few bad characters who spent time there grasped that there was only a woman to run the place now. Fights became more frequent, and there were arguments over change, demands for drinks 'on tick'. Emily stood her ground, even intervened in the fights, but Sadie was afraid and Emily worried that she would lose her. She, too, was wearying of the battles. Then she heard that complaints had been made to the justices: there was a possibility that the Clipper's licence would not be renewed.

She was near to despair in November when a young

man walked into the bar. It was almost full and several of the troublemakers were there, including one of the leaders. Archie Fearon was a cocky tormentor, long and skinny with smarmed-back hair and a look-at-me smirk. He was arguing with Emily, jeering, 'Why can't you let me have a few drinks till payday? Is this pub going bloody broke?'

'I told you last night and I tell you again, no tick,' Emily replied wearily. Then she saw the muscular man at Fearon's side and recognised Joe Kirby. She smiled, pleased to see him. 'Hello, Joe, what can I get you? On the house.'

Archie Fearon seized on that: 'You can let me have one on the house an' all.' He looked round at his mates with a triumphant grin.

The grin slipped away when Joe seized the seat of his trousers, lifted him on to his toes and spun him round. With his other hand locked in Archie's hair, Joe marched him across the bar, up the steps and out of the door. He returned moments later licking the bruised knuckles of one hand. He looked at Archie's mates, still standing gaping at the bar, eying each one in turn, then said, 'He's not coming back. Do you want to go with him or will you behave yourselves?'

'They'll be all right without him,' Emily said quickly. As the buzz of conversation started up again, she pulled a beer for Joe and took it to a comparatively quiet spot at the end of the bar. 'I didn't know you were home, but I see your wife, Jane, every now and then in the street. She told me you were fine.'

'I'm better for being back with her,' Joe said wryly. 'They turned me out of Durham jail this morning. She told me if it hadn't been for you I could have gone down for life. The solicitor that took my case said the same.'

'I only told the truth.'

'Aye, but there's plenty that would ha' thought I should be put away for good over that. If one o' them had been the witness, then God help me. So I'm grateful. Now Jane tells me you've been having a bit of trouble with the likes of that feller I just turned out so I've come to ask you for a job. I'll pull pints, be pot-boy, sweep out, whatever you like. And I'll handle the fellers that are trying to put on you. Will you take me on?'

Emily didn't need to think about his offer – a powerful man around the place would solve her problems. 'I'll take you on,' she said.

So Joe Kirby took up his duties at the Clipper. He moved in with his wife, Jane, who also helped in the bar, and Emily could rest easier at night, no longer alone in the pub. In the first two weeks Joe dealt with two more bar-room bullies, and any others received the message. There was no more trouble – save for the usual fights between customers – and the Clipper kept its licence.

Emily was able to proceed with her plans. With Joe working behind the bar and Sadie cooking in the kitchen, Emily called in a local builder, showed him the storeroom next to the Sitting Room and asked, 'How much would you charge to knock these two rooms into one?' And then offered, 'I'll pay you weekly.'

He closed his notebook in which he was about to make his calculations and jammed it in his pocket. 'That's ridiculous. It's only big companies who pay like that.'

'Big companies sometimes go broke and don't pay at all,' said Emily. He winced because a company client of his had defaulted in that way. Emily knew it because it had been reported in the *Sunderland Daily Echo*. She added, 'And better a job paid by the week than no job at all.' She also knew he needed business because some of the men working for him had talked about it in the Clipper.

He admitted grudgingly, 'You know a thing or two.'

Emily soothed his pride: 'I know you do a good job. And I think we can do each other a good turn here.' She stopped there to let him think about it.

After a minute or so of lip-chewing, he took out his notebook again, made some calculations and named a figure.

Emily had to get a loan from the bank to cover the cost of furnishings, and the interest on that, plus the builder's fee, swallowed her profits for a while. However, two months later she was selling meals to a few of her regular customers in the bigger sitting room, and after six months she had a solid trade and was almost free of debt to the bank.

Lily came one day to say, 'By lass, you're doing well. Better than the ropery.'

'I had some good times there with you, Lily.'

'Aye, didn't we.'

Lily had called in several times over the years. She was

married to her Jimmy now – Emily had been a guest at the wedding – and they lived in a tied cottage on the Wilkinson estate where Jimmy still worked.

Emily asked, 'How's your mam?'

'Not strong, but she's better for having some grand-children.' They both laughed. Lily had two little girls now.

Emily told Ada of her success but nothing of her worries because the old woman would only have fretted. She was sixty now, although she looked older, and refused to leave her two rooms to live at the Clipper: 'The neighbours here have been very good to me and I know all of them. I'm not moving.'

Emily crossed by the ferry to visit her every day and every day she looked at the ships lying in the river, big and small, a thread of smoke rising from the funnel of each berthed vessel, a plume when it raised steam to get under way. These ships traded all over the globe or around the coast of Britain, carrying everything from coal to corn, tea to timber.

Emily had listened to the talk of the men in the Sitting Room of the Clipper, and knew of the money that was to be made. Nathaniel Franklin owned ships and his name was often mentioned. She hated the man for what he had done to her family in throwing them out of home and work, but acknowledged his success. There was a goal to aim for: a fortune like the Franklins'. She knew she would never be rich by working as a publican – but if she bought a ship? It was still just a dream.

Or was it?

Chapter Eleven

SUMMER 1905. MONKWEARMOUTH.

'My word, Emily! You've built up a grand trade in the last year or so.' Silas Worthy beamed at her. He was a plump little man in his forties with pendulous red cheeks. Always neatly dressed in a dark grey suit, he removed his bowler hat punctiliously as he entered the Sitting Room of the Clipper.

'Thank you.' Emily smiled at him. Numerous Monkwearmouth businessmen, or men with business in the town, managers, foremen, professionals and tradesmen, had found they no longer needed to cross the river Wear to eat at lunchtime and the Clipper was full then and had a steady evening trade. The bank manager had ruefully adjusted his valuation of the Clipper for mortgage purposes — upwards, while young men had come courting Emily. Some were still friends but none had touched her heart.

'Would you like your usual?' Emily asked. She knew Worthy liked the idea that he was one of a select band of regular customers. She also knew that he was a shipbroker. Months before he died, Rafe had told her, 'Worthy's an agent for buying and selling things, shares in ships, for example.'

Now Worthy chuckled jovially. 'Aye, that'll do fine.' He took his beer and found a seat at a table. There he exchanged smiles and nods with other men of business already gathered around other tables, eating or waiting for food.

Emily brought him his meal, slipping light-footed between the tables. As she served the steak and kidney pie she murmured, 'I'd like to talk business with you sometime, Mr Worthy.'

He looked startled for a moment. 'Business? With me?' He wondered what sort of business he and a publican might have in common. Then he recalled this was a very successful publican, despite her sex and youth. 'I'm always glad to help a lady, but what business would that be?'

'I want to buy a share in a ship,' Emily said quietly, so that only he could hear.

Worthy smiled widely. 'Well, well! Yes, indeed. I can assist you with that. Don't worry your pretty little head. You know me: Worthy by name and worthy by nature.' He laughed at his jest. 'I look forward to seeing you in my office.' They fixed a day and a time, then Emily left him and he began to eat. You've got something to think about here, lad! he thought.

*　　*　　*

On the day that Emily was due to call at the office near the river, Worthy rubbed his plump hands gleefully. 'We've got a new client coming in today and I'm reckoning to make a bit of money out of her,' he told his secretary.

She looked up from her seat at the typewriter, a plain little woman in a dowdy brown dress, with her hair pulled back tightly into a bun and an embittered expression. 'Who's that, then?'

'A young lass come into some money. Emily Jackson.'

Cora Worthy sat back in her chair and folded her arms. 'Her that has the Clipper now?'

'That's right.' Worthy's eyebrows lifted. 'You know about her?'

'Oh, aye.' Cora nodded. 'Like I know about you.'

She was ten years older than he. Worthy had married Cora for money – her dowry – and squandered it on get-rich-quick schemes. Cora had soon detected the weakness of his character and put her foot down at such waste. Now she dominated him, which was his good fortune because she had the head for business that he lacked. Her father had been a successful shipbroker and she had learned while she worked for him, so it was due to her that Worthy had achieved some little success. When she cracked the whip, he jumped. But it did not make him fond of her.

Cora cracked it now: 'You'll not swindle that lass. I'll be listening and the wall between your room and mine is like paper. You know the people she's dealing with all day in that pub of hers. If you had any sense you'd see that if you clipped her the word would get round and nobody would do business with you.'

Worthy blustered, 'Don't order me about! Telling me what I can and can't do! I can—'

'*Shut up!*' Cora snapped at him and he stopped, gaping. Her tone was contemptuous. 'You'll do as I tell you or I walk out and leave you to stew in your own juice! You wouldn't last long without me.' It was true and Worthy's face showed he knew it. Cora ordered him, 'You'll treat this girl fair. We'll get a commission and some goodwill out of it.'

Minutes later Emily appeared at the office door, in a wide-brimmed felt hat and a smart tailored costume. Its skirt was short, skimming the tops of the buttoned boots that encased her ankles. Cora greeted her with a thin smile: 'Miss Jackson? Mr Worthy is expecting you. This way, please.' She opened the door for Emily and announced, 'Miss Jackson, sir.' Then, behind Emily's back, she shot a dagger-like glance at Worthy before she closed the door. She returned to her desk but did not type. Worthy could hear the silence in the outer office and knew she was keeping her word and listening to him.

Emily emerged as the owner of a sixty-fourth share in a small coastal tramp steamer, the *Highland Lass*.

She celebrated by walking into the town and buying a new dress at Binns' in Fawcett Street. On her way out of the shop she almost collided with a young man who jumped from one of the electric trams that now clanged its way about the town. He lifted his cap and apologised.

Then he looked again at the attractive young woman and said hesitantly, 'Emily?'

'Billy Foster!' Emily was delighted to meet him again. 'I've not seen you since you brought me into the Wheatsheaf on your cart. You did me a good turn that day.'

'I've heard about you from quite a few people.' She stared at him, surprised, so he explained, 'They were talking about this young lass, Emily Jackson, who runs the Clipper down by the river. I've thought of coming to see you because they say the grub's good.'

Emily laughed, 'So it's not me that's attracting you but the food!'

He grinned, 'Maybe it's both.'

'And what about you? Are you still working for your father on the farm?' Emily asked.

'No, there wasn't the work for both my brother and me. I've got a job managing a farm for a businessman from Newcastle. He bought it for a country place.'

'Oh.' Emily detected a lack of enthusiasm. 'Don't you like it?'

Billy shrugged, 'There's nothing to get my teeth into. It's a toy for him to play with at weekends and I'm virtually a labourer. Still,' the grin returned, 'I won't complain. At least I'm working, though I'm not paid enough to marry on.'

'You're courting?'

'I've got a girl – Polly Edwards. She's in service in a place at South Shields. We're both saving but we haven't got enough yet. One of these days, though . . .' He lifted his cap again. 'I've got to get on — work to do back at the farm. But I'll try to look in on you at the Clipper.'

'Do.' Then Emily called after him, 'And bring Polly if you can.'

As usual Nathaniel Franklin had come home from the South of France in early May. He was seventy-three now, slightly stooped, white-haired and his face lined. Towards the end of that summer he visited his nephew at the shipyard on the Monkwearmouth side of the river. He talked with both Bradley Carver and the manager, then strolled about the busy yard exchanging a word here and there with some of the older workers. The din and bustle washed around him and he savoured the memories it brought.

'Where shall we lunch?' he asked Bradley at noon.

'Sorry, sir, but I'll not be going out. There's too much to do,' his nephew replied.

Nathaniel was impressed. He could remember days when he, too, had eaten a hurried meal at his desk and worked into the night. 'As you wish.'

Bradley would have preferred to lunch at the Palace Hotel as he normally did but he wanted to impress his uncle with his diligence: he knew that Nathaniel could still leave his fortune to charity if Bradley offended him.

Nathaniel walked out of the yard. At the gate he met his manager again. 'I'm off to the Palace for lunch,' he told him.

'I usually go to the Clipper, these days. It's not grand like the hotel but it's close and the food is good. A lot of the shipping crowd get in there, foremen and managers, brokers and chandlers,' Clancy said.

Nathaniel liked the sound of that: they were his kind of people, and it would be a change form the Palace Hotel. 'Where is it?'

Clancy gave him directions and Nathaniel set out. He was somewhat disconcerted by the narrow, crowded streets of houses around it, the children running barefoot and sometimes almost naked in the summer's heat. He knew these streets, of course, had passed through them every day on his way to his yard or the offices of his shipping line, but had never expected to take a meal there.

He entered the Clipper's Sitting Room, surveyed it with a critical eye and saw that it was clean and bright, with a bar that shone with polish. There were comfortable chairs and he knew several of the customers who were sitting in them. When Nathaniel's gaze shifted towards the bar he started, shocked. For a moment he thought he saw his daughter there and the room rocked. Then it steadied, and he was looking at a young woman with soft brown hair and wide grey eyes. Indeed, there was a look of his daughter about her but only at first glance. Marie had been a beauty, as was this girl, but a brunette with dark eyes. And Marie had been dead these twenty years. He had seen her body – his mind shied away from that memory. He had quarrelled with her and she had run away, had died before he could make his peace with her. Dear God! Would his conscience never let him rest?

When Emily saw Nathaniel, her smile vanished. She had not seen him since the day he had first gone to France, when she had pressed a bunch of flowers on him, a day she would never forget. She left a customer staring after her and walked to meet him.

'Good day,' he said, and smiled.

Emily's face was set, but even now she was reluctant to wound this old man. 'You are not welcome in this house. I would be glad if you would leave,' she said quietly, so that only he could hear.

Nathaniel was bewildered. He had not recognised her as the child of eight years ago, in white pinny with hair hanging down her back. 'I don't understand,' he said. 'Why? What have I done?'

'You may have forgotten but I never will,' Emily said bitterly. 'I'm Emily Jackson and I am the daughter of the man who was the gatekeeper at your big house. You turned us out of the lodge, my family and myself, threw us out on to the streets. You drove off in your carriage to go to France and left orders for us to be evicted. My father is dead now and I believe that helped to put him in his grave. So please go. I won't have you here.'

Nathaniel put a hand to his head, dazed. Already shocked by thinking he had seen his daughter, now to have such a charge levelled against him! The room whirled around him and the girl's face floated up towards him before the room went black.

Emily reached out to catch him, and staggered under his weight. 'Help me to take him through to the back,' she gasped, as other customers ran to her aid. They carried Nathaniel into her private living room, and laid him on a couch set along one wall. An open door led to the busy kitchen where Sadie was working with two other girls. One was Jane Kirby, Joe's wife.

'Jane!' Emily called. 'Will you run up the street and fetch the doctor.'

Nathaniel was coming round. He blinked for a moment, disoriented, then said weakly, 'No doctor.' When he saw Emily hesitate, he repeated, 'I don't need a doctor. I'll be all right in a minute.'

Emily yielded. 'Never mind, Jane,' she said, and then, softly, to Nathaniel, 'Lie still and try to sip this.' She held a glass of brandy to his lips.

'I didn't know anything of this – this eviction,' he said weakly.

'Don't worry. It doesn't matter now,' Emily whispered. And to the other men who still clustered around them, 'I think we can manage now. I'm grateful for your help.' They drifted back to the Sitting Room and their lunch.

Nathaniel drank more of the brandy, and said, more strongly, 'It does matter. The first time I came home from France I noticed there was a new man in the gatekeeper's lodge. I asked my nephew where Jackson had gone. He said my agent had told him the man had left to better himself, and I thought no more about it.' His head fell back on the cushion. 'It's no wonder you hate me.'

'No!' Emily was firm about that. 'I don't now. I could hardly believe you would treat us so cruelly but the agent, Gamblin . . .' She cast her mind back over the years. 'I can't recall his exact words but he suggested that you had done it because you had not been well and because—' She stopped.

Nathaniel guessed what she had been about to say: 'And because I was getting old and senile. We'll soon see about that.' He started to push himself up from the couch.

Emily held him down. 'No, please lie still. I think you need to rest. I'm worried at the way you fainted.'

He knew he was not yet strong enough to rise and did as she said. 'Why should you worry about me?'

'Because I accused you and condemned you without letting you say a word in your own defence. I'm to blame for you lying here now.'

'No. Something else caused it.' He lay silent for a time, lost in his thoughts. Emily sat beside him and eventually he asked, 'Will you call a cab for me, please? I think I'm well enough now.'

When it came she went with him, ready to provide a steadying arm, but he walked confidently and climbed up into it. Then he turned to say, 'I have some business to attend to now, but I will call on you again – if I may?'

Emily smiled at him. 'You will be very welcome.' She watched the cab roll away, its iron-shod wheels noisy on the cobbles, and wondered if he had meant it when he said he would return. It was unlikely after the reception she had given him, she thought ruefully. And it had all been a mistake. She sighed, regretful, and went back to work.

Nathaniel went first to his shipyard and sought out Bradley Carver. 'I've just left a lady called Emily Jackson. Her family used to be in the gatekeeper's lodge. She told me Gamblin threw them out and implied it was on my orders.'

Bradley feigned outrage. 'Good God!'

'I want to see him. I'm going back to the house now,' Nathaniel said.

When Bradley was left alone he swore savagely then hurried from his office. He now owned a Humber motor-car, with its hood folded down and big carbide headlamps. He drove carefully at first but once clear of the town he let out the throttle. He knew where to look for Gamblin: the agent spent his afternoons on work at his own farm. Bradley found him in the yard, shovelling manure. 'Franklin wants to see you,' he said baldly. 'He's going to give you the sack.'

'*What?*' Gamblin gaped at him. 'Why?'

'For throwing out the Jacksons and letting them think it was his idea.'

'But you—'

'You keep your mouth shut. I told you I wasn't to be involved.'

'But I'm losing my job!' Gamblin protested.

'You'll lose more than that if you try to saddle me with the blame.' Gamblin saw the malevolence in Bradley's eyes before he swung the Humber round in a tight turn and accelerated away, spraying the agent with mud.

Bradley did not take any chances and made sure that he was present at the interview.

'You evicted my tenants, the Jacksons, and put a friend of yours in their place. You led them to believe it was on my orders. Have you anything to say?' Nathaniel asked Gamblin.

Bradley stood behind Nathaniel's chair, his gaze piercing.

'No, sir,' Gamblin muttered.

'I doubt if you will obtain a position of trust anywhere on this river. Now get out,' Nathaniel said.

As Gamblin rode away on his pony Bradley intercepted him. He slipped Gamblin a handful of sovereigns. 'What will you do now?'

'I'll get away from this place, probably start again up north of the Tyne. You heard what he said. There's nothing here for me now.' He glanced at the sovereigns as he thrust them into his pocket. 'That won't make up for losing my position.'

'It wasn't meant to. It was just to help you make a fresh start. And don't blame me for this. It was the Jackson girl who pointed the finger at you.' Bradley returned to the house. Some day he would go to see this girl. He, too, had a score to settle with her.

Nathaniel Franklin visited her the next day. Emily saw him enter and made a point of serving him herself. 'I took Gamblin, my agent, to task over your eviction. He did not deny his guilt so I gave him notice. All I can do now is apologise to you and your family, and to say that if there is any way I can make it up to you . . .?' He left the question hanging, ready to take out his wallet.

'It's all behind us now,' Emily said. 'How are you today?'

'Fine.' Nathaniel said, 'I've never fainted like that before, but—' He stopped, remembering the vision of his daughter.

Emily waited a moment, but when he did not go on she excused herself: 'I must get back to work.'

'Of course.'

She could not feel sorry for Gamblin. He had treated her and her family cruelly. As she hurried about her duties she told herself that he had deserved his dismissal. Then a thought came to her, which stopped her in her tracks. Later she went to speak to Nathaniel again. 'May I ask a favour?'

He stood up and extended a hand. 'Won't you sit down? Please?' And when she was seated opposite him, 'What can I do for you?'

'May I ask if you have appointed a new agent?'

'Not yet.'

'Then may I suggest a young man? His name is Billy Foster. I think you will find him keen and hardworking.'

Nathaniel took out his notebook and wrote down the name and address. 'I'll see him.' And then, smiling, 'Is he your young man?'

Emily laughed. 'No, but he did me a good turn.'

Soon afterwards Nathaniel left, and Emily did not see him for some days, but one evening Billy Foster walked into the Sitting Room with a pretty blonde girl on his arm. 'This is Polly.' He grinned. 'We've named the day, thanks to you.'

'What do you mean?' Emily was puzzled.

'You got me the job. Mr Franklin invited me to his place for an interview, questioned me on what I had done, my experience, then made me his agent. I've trebled my wages so I can afford to marry.'

'We're very grateful,' Polly broke in.

Emily blushed. 'I only repaid a debt.'

'Mebbe,' said Billy, 'but you repaid it with interest. So, if we can ever do anything for you, just say the word.'

When Nathaniel Franklin called in a few days later, Emily thanked him. 'It was kind of you to take on Billy Foster as your agent.'

Nathaniel smiled. 'I think I did well. He strikes me as a promising young man and he will do a good job of looking after the estate.' After he had eaten his lunch he asked as she passed, 'Would you care to join me now for a while?'

Emily glanced around the room. It was almost empty, the lunch trade over, and she knew that Joe, Sadie and the girls could manage without her. 'Thank you.' She sat across from him.

They chatted for ten minutes or so, though mainly he was curious as to what she had done after leaving the gatekeeper's lodge. She gave him a tactfully edited version of her adventures and trials, making light of the latter. She did not mention Gamblin's assaults but made him laugh with stories of the girls at the ropery.

After that he came two or three times each week, always at a quiet time, and they would talk for a while. It was in September that he said, 'I won't be in again for some time. I'm going to France again for the winter. Doctor's orders.' Then he told her of the villa he had bought in St Raphael on the Riviera and his life there. 'I have my books and a few friends I meet in the café each day, old chaps like myself.' Emily thought it sounded lonely, and as if he was trying to say something.

He finally came out with it: 'That day when I fainted in here, it was because I'd just had a shock. I came in at that door and saw a young woman I thought was my daughter. It was you, of course, though you only have a passing likeness to Marie. She was dark-haired, dark-eyed, and she died over twenty years ago.'

'Yes, I know. The fire in the boarding-house,' Emily said quietly.

Nathaniel sighed. 'I think it was my fault she was there. We had quarrelled – over the man she wanted to marry. I didn't think him suitable but I was wrong there because he seems to have been good to her. She had written to me from America, saying she was widowed and coming home with her child. I wrote back, saying she would be welcome and sending money, but both letters were returned later – she had left before they arrived. I found she had taken passage from New York in a tramp steamer bound for Bordeaux. From there she picked up another passage, again on a tramp, right into the Wear. She had little money, and she wasn't sure of what welcome she would have from me so she decided to spend the night in a cheap boarding-house, her and the child, my grandchild. So they died in the fire. I had to identify them. The bodies were . . . not recognisable, but there was their luggage, clothes, Marie's rings . . .' He closed his eyes briefly as if he could blot out the memory. 'Once in a while a stranger reminds me of her, though not as clearly as you did the other day.'

He was silent. He shed no tears because they had all fallen over the years and now he was dry-eyed, but Emily could see the grief carved into his face. She reached over to take his hand. 'You cannot hold yourself responsible. The fire, the fact that your daughter was short of money, they weren't your fault but accidents. As for your quarrelling, forbidding her to marry her young man, fathers do this every day, and probably quite rightly. I know if I had taken home a young man that my father didn't think would look after me properly, he would have put his foot down.'

Nathaniel stared at her, doubting. 'Do you really believe that?'

'I do,' said Emily firmly, and met his gaze with a straight one of her own.

But Franklin had lived too long with his guilt to shrug it off. He said, 'I'm grateful for your kindness.' He pulled his watch from his waistcoat pocket and opened its gold case. 'I must go now.' He rose. 'I've enjoyed our talks. Perhaps when I come home next summer we may start again.'

Emily saw him to the door and watched him walk off

up the cul-de-sac towards the street. She hoped he had taken heart from what she had said.

Florence Browning, née Hartley, who had fled from Monkwearmouth and Felix Ogden some twenty-two years ago, woke in her little house in Ealing to the sound of Harry's coughing. She climbed out of bed, shivering in the chill of the night, and said, 'I'll make you a cup of tea.' As she walked down the stairs she thought that if the cough did not stop soon she would take Harry to see the doctors, even if it meant he would lose a few hours' wages. Although they were far from rich, they were not poor and had almost paid for this little house. It helped that they had never had children, although they both regretted that, but they had been happy together. Now it was only when she received a letter from her friend Nancy Bell, that Florence thought of Felix Ogden and the terrible night when she had seen a woman murdered on the quay. She had resolved never to go back to Sunderland while Ogden was alive.

Tom Peterson was tall and broad, with ice-blue eyes under yellow hair that needed cutting, and with a young American's easy poise. That autumn he entertained his state's governor on his ranch in Colorado. It was a fairly informal occasion with just a score of them seated in the dining room around the long table, which gleamed while the silver and glasses sparkled in the light from a huge Venetian chandelier. Paintings hung on the walls but there were few portraits. It was not that kind of family.

Tom was telling the governor, 'My grandfather got out of Russia in 1848 – Peterson is an anglicised version of the family name. He farmed here for a while but then he moved into contracting for the railroads. I took over about five years back when my father retired. We still have family over there, around St Petersburg.'

The governor knew Tom had not just 'taken over': in those five years he had doubled the size of the Peterson fortune. At twenty-nine he was a millionaire several times over.

There was one picture that might have been called a portrait, though it was only two feet square. The governor commented on it: 'I take it they are kin of yours?'

'That's so.' Tom looked up at the picture of a young woman with a child, a small girl of possibly a year old, seated on her knee.

The governor said, 'And you value them.'

'I did.' Then Tom explained, sombrely, 'Marie was English and she married a cousin of mine, Vincent Leigh. That's their daughter on Marie's knee. Vincent paid for that picture to be painted when he first made some real money as an actor. He died soon after it was done and his widow and the child died in a fire in England.'

There were murmurs of consternation around the table and the governor said, 'I'm sorry, Tom. That's tough. I take it they were buried over there?'

'That's right. Marie was going home to her father. It seems they had a bust-up when she married Vincent. The old man got over that and wanted her back home but then she got caught in this fire. I still miss her and the little girl. I helped nurse her once, the kid, that is, when she got burned by a set of curling tongs. I was just a boy of six or seven years old and she was less than a year. I used to play with her. The burn must have hurt like hell but she never complained. She was a solemn little kid but every now and then she would give out with this big smile, real cute.'

'I think you were in love with her,' said a lady half-way down the table.

Tom grinned. 'As I recall, the only things I was in love with then were cookies.'

'Will you be going over there some day?' she enquired.

'One of these days, maybe, but not now. Too busy.'

Digby Gamblin locked the door of what had been his farmhouse for the last time. He had sold up and had bought another farm in Northumberland but found that no consolation. He had been driven out and that rankled.

'That flaming Jackson lass! She was the cause of this,' he muttered as he climbed up into his trap, and with Emily on his mind he laid his whip across the pony's flank. 'I'll see my day with her. She'll rue that she ever crossed me, damn her!' He laid the lash on the pony again and the trap raced out of the yard, bouncing and swaying.

Chapter Twelve

'The bloody woman's making a fortune!' Silas Worthy tossed the papers on to his desk and threw his pudgy body back in his chair.

Cora retrieved them and shuffled them into a tidy pile. 'I thought you'd like to see them. Emily Jackson's done very well since she first came to this office and you were thinking of defrauding her. She's doubled and redoubled her investment half a dozen times or more. She'll be looking for a ship of her own soon.'

Worthy scowled at her. 'Why should a young lass make money like that?'

'You mean when you can't?' His wife looked down at him. 'It's because Emily Jackson has business flair and a good head on her shoulders. If you had any sense you'd be glad she was making so much money.

You're her agent and she pays you commission on every deal she does. You should pray she becomes a millionaire, another Franklin.'

'That's another thing,' Worthy muttered. 'Franklin and her are as thick as thieves.' He stared down at his desk then looked up sharply as Cora moaned. She was leaning against the wall, a hand pressed to her side, her face twisted in pain. 'Here! What's the matter with you?' Worthy got up and came round his desk to her.

'It's just a turn, a touch of indigestion. I've had a lot of it lately,' Cora said, her teeth clenched against the pain. 'My age, I suppose. I'll be all right in a minute.'

Silas stood by helplessly. 'It doesn't look like indigestion to me.' He noticed suddenly that his wife had aged rapidly in the past few months. She was thinner too, gaunt, her eyes huge in her face. 'You look very poorly to me. You should see a doctor,' he said.

'I'm not seeing any doctor.' Cora shoved herself away from the wall, walked out to her own office and slumped in her chair. 'You leave me alone. I'll get over it.'

He shrugged. 'Please yourself. I'm going to lunch at the Clipper.' He took his bowler from the hatrack and made for the door.

Cora called after him, 'And mind you keep the right side of that Emily Jackson, because it will mean money for us. Her and Franklin are two of a kind.'

Worthy waved his hat in acknowledgement. He wondered if Cora would be able to keep up with the work of the office. It would be an infernal nuisance if she could not. But then again . . .

'You've done very well.' Nathaniel Franklin sat in the Clipper and smiled across the table at Emily. He had returned from France early, because of the mild spring, just a few days ago. 'I hear you're quite the shipowner now.'

'I have shares in several vessels. I've been lucky in the ones I bought.'

'Lucky?' Nathaniel said wryly. 'That's what they said about me when I had any success. When I lost money they said I'd made an error of judgement.' Then he grinned. 'Mind, I didn't do that often.'

Emily laughed. 'Neither have I!' She tapped the shining, polished wood of the table between them.

Nathaniel was still smiling but serious now when he went on, 'But what is it for? Are you planning on being the richest shipowner on the river? That isn't so important, you know. I found that out.'

Emily knew that he was referring to the loss of his daughter and grandchild. 'Nothing so grand.' She could not tell him of her dream of waltzing around a ballroom: she thought he would think her silly. Neither would she mention the other dream of sending ships, her ships, around the world. He did not boast of his wealth or achievements.

But he seemed to read her mind: 'So — what next? A

ship all of your own? That seems a logical step. Then you can do what you like with it, without considering the wishes of other shareholders.'

Emily hesitated. Then she admitted, 'I'm thinking about it, but it won't be for a little while yet.' She had already amassed the money to buy a ship but modesty forbade her to boast of it. She was prepared to risk all, but was waiting until she felt the time was right.

Nathaniel chuckled. 'You'll hoist your own flag one of these days: the Jackson Line.' Then he got up to go. He paused a moment to ask diffidently, 'Would you care to lunch with me at the house one day soon? Nothing formal or grand. Just myself and my sister.'

Emily was taken aback. Invited to lunch with Nathaniel Franklin? The daughter of his former gatekeeper? As a child she had been told to keep out of sight of the house. She was reluctant to accept, but Nathaniel pleaded, 'It would give me pleasure to show you the house and entertain you.'

Emily could not refuse him. 'Thank you, I will.'

'Splendid! Will I send my carriage for you?'

'That won't be necessary.' Or advisable, thought Emily, to be transported up to the house in his carriage, like some courtesan. That was how it might look to gossips. 'It will be more convenient to take a cab, in case I am delayed by business.'

Nathaniel guessed at her reasoning. 'Very well. I'll look forward to that.'

The following week Emily drove up to the Franklin

house. She got down from the cab and said to the driver, 'Will you call back for me at—' but Nathaniel interrupted.

He had hurried down the steps to meet her. 'No need for that. I'll turn out the pony and trap.' He paid and tipped the man, then asked Emily, 'Would you care to stroll around the grounds first? It's a beautiful day.'

'I'd love to,' Emily said. The sun blazed down from a cloudless sky, and she had put on a dress of pale flowered muslin, light as thistledown, and a wide-brimmed, beribboned straw hat. They visited the stables and the horses, then moved on through the formal gardens and into the green shadows under the trees. There, they talked of what Emily had been doing during the winter months while Nathaniel had been away. Emily guessed that he was unconsciously following a regular route, and this was confirmed when they came to a clearing she remembered where the tree-house was perched in the spreading boughs and the swing dangled beneath. Nathaniel stopped and said, 'I usually come this way. Marie, my daughter, used to play here.' He smiled at Emily. 'I seem to recall you doing the same thing.'

'I was naughty and you were kind.' She moved to the swing and sat on it, looking around. 'It's nice here. I think this must have been a happy place for her.'

'I'm glad.' Suddenly Nathaniel cocked his head to one side, listening. They both heard the sound of wheels crunching on the gravel and horses' hoofs. Nathaniel frowned. 'I wasn't expecting anyone. Bradley, my nephew, may join us but I wouldn't have thought he would be back from the office yet. Oh, well. If I'm wanted they'll know where to find me.'

That was borne out a minute later when a footman came hurrying through the trees to say breathlessly, 'Captain Walsh to see you, sir.'

'Captain Walsh! Good Lord! So he's back – thank you. I'll come.' He glanced apologetically at Emily. 'This is a young friend of mine who has been working east of Suez for some years. We wrote to each other now and then and I told him to come and see me as soon as he returned. If you will excuse me?'

'Of course.' Emily made to rise.

Nathaniel held up a hand. 'No need for you to stir. Stay and rest for a while.' He made off along the woodland path heading towards the house and Emily settled down again to swing idly back and forth.

David Walsh . . . The name was familiar. Then it came to her: he was the young ship's officer who had saved her from Digby Gamblin. She had been glad to see him then. But he had been critical and patronising, had lectured her on the dangers of walking out at night when she had been well aware of them but had had little choice. She had no great desire to meet him again.

Emily's thoughts returned to Nathaniel. He had loved his daughter, still mourned her, and the grandchild he had never seen. Emily wondered what Marie had really been like. Headstrong and determined, certainly, to leave her luxurious home to follow the poor man she loved.

Beautiful, too, from the ballroom portrait Emily had seen so many years ago . . .

She daydreamed for a while, her hat on her lap as she sat in the dappled shade. This grove, with the tree-house and swing, was a pleasant place. But then she remembered the confrontation she had had here with Bradley Carver, how he had terrified her until Bert came to her rescue. But by all accounts Bradley had grown out of adolescent bullying. Years ago Mrs Huckaby had said so and it had been confirmed by the talk Emily had heard in the Clipper; men had spoken of him with respect.

'Good day, ma'am.'

Emily jumped as a voice spoke behind her. She grabbed at the hat as it slid from her lap but knocked it flying across the clearing. 'Bother!'

A tall figure stepped from behind her. Flustered by his sudden appearance she jerked again, the swing collapsed and she fell to the ground with a bump. She lay winded for a few seconds, staring up at the branches waving above her head, then recovered herself and sat up, hastily pushing down her skirts. The tall man stooped over her. 'I'm sorry. Did I startle you? Let me help you up.' His big hands took hers and pulled her easily to her feet. He was grinning but his expression changed to surprise when he saw her properly. 'You're the girl from the Clipper,' he said. 'Here! And now I remember that I saw you in the tree-house when you were a schoolgirl!' He also remembered that the last time they met, when he had rescued her from Gamblin, they had been at odds.

Towering above Emily was David Walsh, but this was no longer the young second mate, still in his teens: this was a man of the world in his mid-twenties who had commanded his own vessel, confident and assured. 'It was a silly trick to creep up behind me and shout in my ear,' Emily snapped.

'I didn't creep and I didn't shout,' David said reasonably. 'The path came out behind you so I said: "Hello."' He pointed and Emily saw that another path did emerge from the trees as he said.

Now he picked up her hat and passed it to her. The crown was dented and the ribbons tangled, the brim smeared with moss. She was also aware that her hair had come down at the back — and her dress would surely be marked. She pushed at the loose tendrils while she strained round to see the back of her skirt. 'What do you want, anyway?' she asked tightly.

'Mr Franklin asked me to fetch you for lunch. He couldn't come himself because a boy brought a telegram for him, about one of his ships, and he had to answer it. He just said there was a lady here. I didn't know it was you.'

Emily read between the lines: he had not expected to find a barmaid. She looked up at him, saw now that he was sunburned, dark eyes fixed on her — curious? looking down on her? criticising her? Should she slap his face? Give him a tongue-lashing? The words were ready, boiling up inside her.

He pulled out a big white handkerchief. 'Maybe I can

clean the hat.' She let him take it from her and watched him smear the moss even further. He said, 'I'm sorry.'

Emily reclaimed it. 'I hear about marine disasters every day, Captain, but you are in a class of your own.'

He blinked at that but still grinned, which infuriated Emily as she tried again to see the back of her dress.

David offered without thinking, 'Would you like me to swab you down?'

Emily slapped his face. His hand flew to his jaw as she flitted across the clearing and into the trees. 'You bitch!' he shouted.

Emily heard that with satisfaction: she had punctured his massive self-confidence.

He was striding after her now, and soon caught up with her. They were together but with a yard at least between them when they reached the house. It might as well have been a mile.

In the hall Nathaniel met them with Clarice Carver and Bradley. Nathaniel performed the introductions and Clarice purred, 'Have you had an accident, my dear?'

'I'm afraid the swing collapsed under me.'

Nathaniel, concerned, apologised. 'I must see Foster and have it rigged again.'

'Is that necessary, Nathaniel? There are no children here now,' Clarice demurred.

'Yes, it is,' he answered shortly, and went on, 'Will you be so good as to assist Miss Jackson with her toilette? Lunch can wait.'

Clarice assented, and handed Emily over to her maid, a

cheerful girl. 'Oh, you've marked your dress and it's ever so pretty, but I'll soon get it clean.'

'The swing let me down when I fell back. Captain Walsh startled me,' Emily explained.

The maid giggled, 'He can startle me any time he fancies, begging your pardon, miss!'

That was probably the reason for David's self-confidence, Emily thought. He was used to silly girls falling for him. 'He does not attract me, and I did not ask for your opinion,' she replied icily.

'No, miss. I'm sorry.' The maid bent over her work on the dress, subdued.

Emily was ashamed. She had taken out her anger with David Walsh on this girl. It was not so long ago that she herself had been subject to the whims of an uncaring employer in the shape of Mrs Swindell. To make up for it Emily was profuse in her thanks when the work was done: 'That's wonderful! There's scarcely a mark to be seen. I'm so grateful. I will tell Mrs Carver of your kindness and skill.'

Emily went back to the luncheon party blaming David Walsh for her awkwardness. Throughout the meal she spoke to him only when he addressed her, which was rarely and then he was distant and polite. Nathaniel was aware of the coolness between them and bewildered by it but ignored it. Bradley filled the gaps in the conversation, attentive to Emily, smiling, nodding, questioning her about her shipping interests.

'You own shares in ships?' David put in, surprised.

Emily shot him a cool glance. 'Several. Are you seeking employment, Captain?'

The others laughed, assuming it was a joke, but David knew it was not. 'I will be looking for another ship but not for a while. And certainly not in a freezing climate,' he replied, with a grin.

Nathaniel explained, 'Captain Walsh has been commanding ships in the East.'

Emily thought that was where his deep tan came from. His hands spread on the white cloth looked almost black. She remembered the strength in them when he had lifted her and thought it was as well their fighting was verbal. He infuriated her, but this was Nathaniel's party and she would try not to spoil it.

Emily turned from David to Bradley: 'You handle more ships than I have shares, but don't you find it a fascinating business?'

'I do,' Bradley glanced at Nathaniel, 'though they are not my ships.'

'So what are your plans now, David?' Nathaniel asked.

'A long leave. I'm going to spend it in London and Buckinghamshire.'

'Why there? I know of the pleasures of the capital, but Buckinghamshire?' Nathaniel asked.

'I have an invitation.'

Emily forgot her resolution not to spoil the party, and smiled at David, 'From a lady? They say a sailor has a girl in every port.'

'The invitation was from her father.' His smile was still

in place but Emily saw that his lips had tightened and knew she had scored again.

Nathaniel put in quickly, 'But afterwards?'

David turned to him pointedly. 'Another ship, but one returning to a home port. I've had enough of the East for a while.'

After lunch Bradley said, 'My car is outside. I'm going back to my office and I can carry both of you into town.'

David said, 'Thanks, but I'll walk. It's a fine day,' but Emily accepted his offer.

As she and Bradley drove off, she glanced back once and saw Captain Walsh striding after them. The walk will do him good, she thought, and smiled to herself. The girl in Buckinghamshire was welcome to him.

Bradley smiled too. He had exchanged his first car for a new one, with deep leather bench seats and a single acetylene headlamp. 'She cost me six hundred but she's worth it,' he said. It was twice the price of a substantial house with five or six bedrooms. He went on, 'A pleasant lunch in interesting company.'

'Yes,' Emily agreed, because it had been interesting, and satisfying to score off David Walsh. But pleasant? She had not enjoyed herself.

Bradley thought Emily was a revelation. It was the first time he had seen her as a woman and he would have liked to let his eyes roam over her at will but he kept his gaze fixed on the road ahead.

They talked lightly as they drove and Emily found him attentive, courteous, a true gentleman. He finally set her down outside the Clipper. 'Good day to you, Miss Jackson.' He lifted his cap.

'Goodbye, Mr Carver.'

He watched her walk away, the lines of her body clear through the thin summer dress. He felt the lust rising in him, a hunger demanding to be fed. He could not wait to visit London, the huge metropolis where he was anonymous. He went hunting close to home that night and found a girl, hard-faced and confident from experience, but she learned anew.

David Walsh sat at the kitchen table while his mother and sisters chatted around the fire. He was writing a letter to Dulcie Smythe in the south: 'I will be with you in a day or two.' She was a débutante, slim and pretty, the only child of a wealthy man. David had met her on the ship bringing her home from the East Indies, where her father had interests. He was looking forward to meeting her again – especially after Emily Jackson.

'Bradley Carver?' Felix Ogden, a broad but paunchy fifty-year-old, was not liked in the tenement where he lived. His neighbours were poor but clean and tidy, while he was neither. They also knew that his money came from his daughters and disapproved. Now he seized his daughter Rhoda by the shoulder and swung her round to face him and the bright morning sunlight that streamed through the dirty windows with their dingy curtains. Rhoda winced as a shaft of light shone into her eyes. 'When?' he ground out.

'Last night.' Rhoda added, 'He stuffed the end o' my shawl into my mouth so I couldn't shout.'

Felix sucked in his breath and swore, 'Hell's flames!' He held the girl when she tried to turn away. 'Stand still!' He carried his walking-cane in one hand and she watched it warily: like the other girls she had felt the whip of it. With his other hand he turned her head this way and that between his thick fingers to examine her injuries. 'Are there any more?' he demanded.

'Aye.' She was in tears now.

'Let me see.' He made her strip, sucked in his breath again, then mouthed an obscenity. 'He'll suffer for this, I'll see to that. Now put your clothes on.'

'You can't do owt. He paid me anyway. Threw the money at me afterwards and said, "You won't need to work till that lot heals so keep your trap shut." I don't want to cross him.'

'I do. I'd like to see the bugger put in jail.'

Rhoda said wearily, 'It's only my word against his and they wouldn't believe me.'

'Ah! But that's not the end of it.'

'What d'ye mean?'

'He's going to pay. That's what I mean.' Felix picked up his bowler hat and walking-cane, tramped down the stairs of the tenement and out into the street. He walked down to the offices of the Franklin Line by the river and waited. He knew that if his man did not appear there he would probably be at the shipyard. But sure enough, an hour later at noon, he saw Bradley Carver emerge from the offices.

Felix hurried to intercept him. 'I want a word wi' you, Mr Carver.'

Bradley paused and looked Felix up and down, seeing the greasy tie, clean collar but grubby shirt, the gold watch-chain stretched across the cheap waistcoat of the loudly patterned serge suit, the walking-cane. Bradley raised his eyebrows. 'Yes?'

Felix came straight to the point: 'I'm the father of the lass you badly used last night.'

Bradley blinked, but replied, 'You've got the wrong man. I was at home last night.' His mother would confirm that. Clarice had asked him about the blood on his knuckles and he had told her to mind her own business.

Felix was not deterred. 'I knew you'd say that, reckon to get off because we can't prove it was you. But I can lay charges just the same and mud sticks. Maybe if it got talked about it would flush out one or two more to speak up against you.'

That was true, Bradley knew. There had been others. London was far enough away to be safe – but Newcastle? 'She was paid to hold her tongue,' he snapped.

'Not enough.' Felix thought he had a chance now: a few pounds was nothing to this toff.

'I see. So how much do you want to forget all this?' Bradley said grimly.

Felix pitched it as high as he dared. 'Twenty quid.'

Bradley laughed. 'Rubbish! For that money I could buy a witness who would swear to you attempting to blackmail me. How long do you think you would get?' He saw the flicker in Ogden's eyes and said flatly, 'I'll give you ten, but that's all. And you give me a note that you have been paid in full. Well?'

Felix pretended to hesitate but was delighted. Ten pounds! Many a man couldn't earn that in a month in the shipyards. 'Right, then. Let's have it.' He held out his hand.

'I'm not going to pay you here, for anyone to see,' Carver growled. 'Besides, I don't carry that amount of cash around. A gentleman doesn't need to.' A gentleman always charged his purchases and settled the bill when the account came in. 'I'll go to the bank this afternoon and pay you tonight, somewhere private, away from prying eyes. Go down past the Clipper to the river. It will be quiet enough there and we can do our business.' He pushed Ogden aside but paused to say, 'Don't forget the note.' Then he strode away.

Ogden grinned. You can have as many notes as you want because they won't stop me coming back again – and again, he thought. He looked forward to a rosy future with a regular income.

His family found him unusually pleasant for the rest of that day. He chuckled a great deal and sang snatches of songs. 'What's got into you that you're so cheerful?' his sullen wife asked.

'The ould bugger's hiding something,' his daughters muttered.

He was, of course, and was determined to go on hiding it. The less they knew the better, he thought. If they found out about the money they would whine for a share in it. They were happier as they were.

That night he walked down to the river, as jauntily as his fat bulk would allow, swinging his walking-cane. He passed the cul-de-sac that held the Clipper, the light from its windows gleaming on the cobbles outside, which were wet from a recent shower. He heard the rumble of the voices inside, and thought that on his way back he would call in there for a nip or two of gin in celebration. As he came out on to the quay he saw a ship, a tramp steamer, coming in between the piers. He did not know it but she was the *Ribbledale*, out of Bordeaux.

The quay was dark with only one gaslight and huge patches of shadow, deserted except for a lone figure standing by the water's edge. Ogden saw that it was Carver and waddled towards him.

The *Ribbledale* made fast to a buoy for the night. A tall young man stood on her deck looking out at the lights of the town. He knew this was Monkwearmouth but could not see the two figures standing on the quay. He had intended to wait until the morning but now he was impatient. He sought out the Captain on the bridge:

'Say, do you think one of your boys could set me ashore for an hour or two?'

Bradley Carver stood at the edge of the quay, breathing heavily. He saw the boat lowered from the ship to the river and looked down at the black water below him, slapping against the piles of the quay, then turned away. His boot knocked aside the walking-cane and he picked it up, broke it over his knee then threw it into the river after its owner. Walking away up the street he passed the entrance to the cul-de-sac and saw the lights of the Clipper but he carried on. He did not want to be seen around there tonight.

Some ten minutes later Emily saw a tall stranger enter the Sitting Room. He was a young man with yellow hair and ice-blue eyes, which roved slowly over the room, assessing the place and the people in there. Finally his gaze settled on Emily and he crossed the room, moving easily, to where she stood behind the bar. 'Good evening, ma'am. I'm Tom Peterson and I'm looking for a gentleman by the name of Nathaniel Franklin.'

Chapter Thirteen

APRIL 1907. MONKWEARMOUTH.

'You're looking for Mr Franklin?' Emily echoed. She was aware of his gaze on her, assessing, admiring. He wore light tweeds of a foreign cut.

'That's so. I believe he's well known in this neck of the woods.'

Emily blinked at the phrase: Neck of the woods? 'He's well known in this town, yes.' She recognised the stranger's accent as North American. A year ago she had served American sailors when their ship lay in the river. But what did he want with Nathaniel Franklin? 'Do you have business with him, sir?'

'Not business. It's something of a family matter.' Tom paused, wondering how much he should tell this girl – this very pretty girl. 'I take it he is still alive?'

'Oh, yes,' Emily answered quickly. 'What made you think he might not be?'

'I wrote to him some weeks back, saying I was coming to Europe and would like to call on him. I never got a reply so I guessed he may have died – he is quite an elderly gentleman, I believe – or he didn't want to see me.'

'That is not like Mr Franklin. I think if he did not want to receive you he would have said so.'

'Then you know him well.'

'We are acquainted.'

Tom was tired of fencing. 'Look, ma'am, I don't intend any harm to Mr Franklin. I have his address so I'll call on him tomorrow.'

He turned to leave but Emily said, 'Please, sir, you did say you were family?' This was a young American and Marie Franklin had run away with an American actor. 'Do I take it you are related to him through his daughter?'

Tom swung back to face her again. 'That's right. I was a cousin of her husband, Vincent Leigh. His mother and mine were sisters. And you seem to know more than I'd expect in an acquaintance. Maybe you can tell me how I can get to his place? Or is that a secret?'

Emily flushed. 'I respect Mr Franklin and would not direct any Tom, Dick or Harry to his house,' she replied coldly. 'But I can tell you that he will be in this room tomorrow in the early afternoon. If you are in any doubt as to your reception you might prefer to meet him here.'

'And if I don't?'

'Then you can go to the devil your own way,' Emily, pink-cheeked, replied.

Tom stared, then broke into a grin. 'You sure make yourself clear, ma'am.' Then he was serious. 'You're fond of him, to guard him this way.'

'He's had a great deal of unhappiness.'

'And you want to save him from any more.'

'If I can.'

Tom was silent a moment. Then he said, 'Well, I won't go to his house, wherever that is, and you can rest easy that I won't trouble the old boy. I'll call in here tomorrow. Then if he tells me to go to hell I'll have saved the cab fare. Goodnight, ma'am.'

'Thank you, sir. Goodnight.' Emily watched his broad back as he crossed to the door and was gone into the darkness. He was a determined young man, she thought. Handsome too. But she would not introduce him to Nathaniel Franklin without first asking the old man.

Tom Peterson found his boat where he had left it at the foot of a flight of stone steps slimy with weed. The seaman was seated on the thwart and resting on his oars but he, too, had been ashore: Tom smelt rum on the man's breath as he picked his way cautiously down the steps and clambered into the boat. But the seaman handled his craft deftly and laid it alongside the tramp steamer. Tom gave him a shilling, and the man grinned. 'Thank ye, sir.'

That night Tom slept aboard. In the morning he took

a cab to the Palace Hotel and booked into a room there. Then he walked over the bridge to the north side of the river and gazed, impressed, at the shipyards lining both banks and the ships lying to their buoys or moored alongside the quays. At the Clipper he exchanged greetings with Emily and said, 'I'd been told this was the biggest shipbuilding town in the world. Now I can believe it. I suppose Mr Franklin owns some of the ships I saw in the river.'

Emily smiled. 'I would think it likely.' She did not mention that she had shares in two of those he had seen, and in others at sea.

Looking around the Sitting Room he asked, 'Has your Mr Franklin showed yet?'

'Not yet,' replied Emily. It was only just noon and the first of the lunch trade was drifting in. 'Later.'

'Thank you.' He took a seat in a corner and watched the scene around him, the solid businessmen and foremen, the managers and brokers. And he watched the girl who seemed to be running the place. Certainly she was giving orders to the gorilla behind the bar – she called him Joe – and to the other girls. He waited an hour. Then he saw her cross the room to an elderly man with a shock of white hair, who had just entered and seated himself at a table. She stooped to speak to him. Tom saw the surprise on the old man's face and stood up. He crossed the room, nodded at Nathaniel and said, 'I'd like it fine if I could talk with you, Mr Franklin, but I'm ready to walk away if that's what you want. I won't force myself on you because

I reckon this lady would have my hide if I tried. I'm Tom Peterson, and Vincent Leigh was my cousin.'

'My daughter's husband!' Nathaniel exclaimed.

Tom nodded. 'Yes, sir. I knew Marie, though I was only a boy at the time. A fine lady.'

Nathaniel stood up and held out his hand. 'I'm pleased to meet you. And that is not just a pleasantry.' They shook hands and Nathaniel gestured to a chair. 'Will you join me?' As Emily moved away he asked, 'And you, my dear? Will you stay? I think Mr Peterson is about to tell us something of interest concerning my daughter and I think you would like to hear it. Perhaps one of your girls would fetch my whisky – and whatever Mr Peterson and yourself would like.'

They sat around the table, the buzz of conversation all around them, and Nathaniel asked, 'Why did you think you would be unwelcome? I can't believe Marie, or even Vincent, would paint me as an ogre.' His face clouded then and he added, 'Though, God knows, they had reason.'

'I wrote to you about a month ago when I was waiting for a passage from Bordeaux, sir, saying I would like to call on you, but never had a reply before I sailed.'

'That's easily explained,' said Nathaniel. 'I've just returned from France. I think your letter was forwarded there, but I came home early. It's doubtless lying there still – or it's on the way back to me now. So, may I ask what brings you here?'

Tom hesitated, then said awkwardly, 'I guess it's sort

of a pilgrimage. The first time I remember seeing Marie was when I was about seven years old. My mother was taken ill, and Marie came to nurse her and to look after me. For two whole weeks she *was* my mother, somebody I could cling to when I was scared Mother was going to die – and she came close to it. It was a hell of a shock when I heard Marie was dead and the little girl with her. I cried for days.'

Emily was touched by the way this strong, self-assured man could confess his emotions. She decided that that was a measure of his strength.

He continued, 'I always meant to come over to see where they lay and to pay my respects, but I was working hard.' He grinned self-consciously. 'Making my pile.' Then he sobered and went on, 'But just a month back I realised it was coming up to twenty-three years since they were killed, and I thought, If you're too busy to visit Marie and her daughter then you're too damned busy altogether. I found a tramp that was sailing from New York for Bordeaux – because I wanted to follow the route she took – and another from Bordeaux into this river.'

'And here you are,' finished Nathaniel. 'I will take you to see where they are buried tomorrow. Can I help you in any other way? Where are you staying?' And when Tom told him, Nathaniel insisted, 'You must come to me today.'

'Thank you . . . I would like to find out more as to how it happened. We had a letter from you but it did not give many details.'

'I was distraught at the time,' Nathaniel told him, 'so I could only write a brief note.'

'I can understand that, sir.' Tom was sympathetic. 'It must have been a terrible blow.'

The old man nodded. 'I knew Marie was coming home with her child . . .' He told Tom of the fire in Sammy's boarding-house and the bodies found.

Tom had sat still and attentive. Now he said gently, 'Thank you, sir.' He, like Emily, could see how reminiscence had upset the old man. 'Maybe we could talk of something else now? You said you had recently returned from abroad. Where in France would that be?'

'I have a little place on the coast outside St Raphael . . .' Nathaniel became more cheerful as he talked.

Eventually he left for home, saying to Tom, 'I will send my carriage to the Palace for you — about four?'

'Thank you, sir. I'll be ready.'

When Nathaniel had gone Tom approached Emily who had returned behind the bar. 'Excuse me, ma'am. May I ask a favour?'

'Of course,' Emily answered, wondering warily what it might be.

'I want to follow this trail to the end.' Tom was serious now. 'That means seeing this Sammy's boarding-house where they died, and maybe reading some accounts of what happened. I don't want to ask Mr Franklin because it obviously causes him pain to recall all these details. I wonder if you would help me?'

'In any way I can,' Emily said.

'May we meet at ten tomorrow?' he asked, and when Emily agreed, he smiled. 'Thank you, ma'am. I'll look forward to escorting you.' He left and Emily watched him go. Then she became aware that the two girls' eyes were on her. She felt a blush rising to her cheeks and hastily turned away, only to find herself staring into Joe's face. He said grimly, 'They've just pulled a feller's body out of the river.'

Rhoda identified the body of Felix Ogden, and at the inquest held in the Albion Hotel, the verdict was accidental death by drowning. Mrs Ogden and her other daughters wept but suspected nothing wrong with the verdict although they testified that, far from being depressed, the deceased had been unwontedly cheerful before his death. Rhoda thought that if somebody held you under until you drowned that was hardly an accident, but she held her tongue. She was the only one who knew that Felix had hoped to blackmail Bradley Carver, and she read his death as a warning. She would not attract Carver's rage by asserting, without proof, that he had murdered her father. If he came near her again she would run from him as if the devil was after her — and maybe he was.

Nancy Bell read the report of the inquest with satisfaction, as did many others. Then she bought a penny packet of writing-paper with envelopes from the shop on the corner.

She sat down at her kitchen table with its oilskin cloth, took the cork from her bottle of ink and dipped in the nib of her pen. She was pleased to be sending good news to her old friend: 'Dear Flo, Just a few lines to let you know that Felix Ogden was drowned last week. Good riddance if you ask me. Now you can come home.'

The next day Florence received the letter. Normally she would have ripped open the envelope eagerly, keen to read the news of Monkwearmouth from Nancy, but today she was not interested and stuffed it behind the clock on the mantelpiece, unopened. She did not take it down until the evening, and then only skimmed through it. The death of Felix Ogden left her unmoved: she had had enough of death and the threat of it. The only good news she wanted to hear was that Harry would be well again soon, but she knew that was impossible. She put the letter aside. They had been so happy. How would she manage without him?

Digby Gamblin pushed through the swing doors of the bar of the Grand Hotel, Newcastle. His gaze swept the room and alighted on a corpulent man who was rising from his chair to wave a fat, beringed hand. 'Over here, Digby, dear chap!' he called. Gamblin crossed to him and the pudgy fingers wrapped around his. 'What can I get you, old boy?'

'Whisky and soda, please, Lawrence.'

'That's my boy!' Lawrence snapped his fingers and a waiter came hurrying – this man was known as an open-handed tipper. Then Lawrence sank back into his chair. He beamed at Gamblin. 'So what have you been up to today?'

'Just knocking about on my land, y'know.'

They had met two weeks before when Lawrence had jogged Gamblin's elbow and spilt a teaspoonful of his beer. Lawrence had insisted on buying him another pint and they had fallen into conversation. Lawrence had soon suggested moving to the Grand: 'Rather more comfortable, old chap, and I've got a room there.' It turned out that he was an art-dealer and he had come north to buy a picture – or try to buy one.

'It's a Monet: *Gare St Lazare: Arrival of a train.*'

Gamblin said, 'Oh, aye.' He had never heard of Monet or the picture.

Lawrence laid a finger along the side of his nose. 'The owner doesn't know what it's worth. He's the son of one of these old families, never done a day's work but now he's running out of money. He wants a thousand for it but I knocked him down to nine hundred. The trouble is, I only have five hundred. In cash, that is. He insists on cash, won't take a cheque, and my money's all tied up in stock. *You* know what I mean: in the same way yours is in land. Pity. If I don't take it off him in the next couple of days he's talking of going down to London with it and bang goes my profit.'

'So how much is it worth?' Gamblin asked.

Lawrence became reverential. 'You can't really measure a work of art like this solely in terms of money. When people buy this kind of picture in London it's for the uplifting pleasure of looking at it day after day. That's why they pay three to four thousand.'

Gamblin swallowed. He had not prospered since he had left Sunderland. He licked his lips. 'Suppose I came in with you, sort of half-shares?'

Lawrence stared at him, impressed. 'I hadn't thought of that. I see you're a man with an eye for a business opportunity.' He hesitated, then said, 'Don't get the wrong idea. There's nothing illegal or immoral in this. If the chap can't be bothered to get a valuation from someone else, then that's his fault. That's business.'

'That's quite right,' Gamblin agreed. But he did not give a damn if the owner of the picture was swindled.

That conversation had taken place two days before. Now Lawrence said, 'Well, our man is in my room upstairs with the picture. Have you brought your share?'

Gamblin tapped his breast pocket where he had hidden the envelope with four hundred and fifty pounds in banknotes. He had mortgaged everything he had to raise it. Lawrence was more casual: he took a roll of notes from his pocket and tossed them across to Gamblin. 'Put those with yours.' He drained his glass and glanced at his watch. 'Better go up now. We don't want him walking out on us.'

Ten minutes later they were back in the bar. The languid young man had taken the money from Gamblin, counted it and departed. Now Gamblin carried the picture. It was some two feet square and showed a puffing engine pulling a train into a station. Gamblin thought it nice enough but he would not have given twopence for it. But that was not the point. It was the sum he could *sell* it for. Lawrence slapped his back, called for a bottle of champagne and paid for it. As they drank he said, 'Be at the station at ten tomorrow. We'll go to London and make the sale. I gave you the picture to bring down because you may as well take it with you tonight. I've got a hell of a lot of luggage as it is.'

Gamblin had intended to take the picture anyway, by force if necessary, but was gratified by the trust shown in him: 'Don't you worry. I'll be there.' He left as soon as the bottle was empty. Once outside he did not make for home but instead hurried to the station and caught the next train headed south. He slept sometimes in the rocking carriage, holding the painting on his lap, and climbed down from the train at King's Cross in the morning bleary-eyed and unshaven. He went straight to Sotheby's – and was told the painting was a worthless copy.

During the next few weeks he learnt from the police that he was not the first to be cheated: 'Lawrence and the chap who's supposed to be selling the picture, they've been pulling this trick all over the country, sir.'

The hotel told Gamblin that Lawrence had left without paying his bill.

The bank told Gamblin that he was virtually penniless.

Now, as he rode back to Newcastle, he blamed Emily as the one who had triggered the series of events that had culminated in his ruin. She had brought him to this by having him dismissed from his post as Nathaniel Franklin's agent.

His mood was murderous.

Chapter Fourteen

'So, this is where it happened?' Tom Peterson's light blue
eyes were cold this morning as his gaze roamed slowly
over the little ship's chandler that stood on the edge of the
river, with advertisements for oil and paint, canvas and
compasses. It had been built on the site of Sammy's
boarding-house although it did not project over the river.
The piles on which Sammy's house had stood still stuck
out of the water, the blackened timbers like rotten fangs.

'Yes, it was here,' Emily said low-voiced.

The chandler told Tom nothing. His gaze shifted to
Emily and he asked, 'What sort of place was this
Sammy's?'

'It was a boarding-house, mostly used by seamen
wanting a bed between paying off from one ship and
signing on in another.'

'It's not exactly the best part of the town,' Tom said. 'I gathered that from what Mr Franklin told me. It strikes me that it was little better than a brothel.'

Emily blushed but did not deny it and stared out over the river, its black, oily surface ripped white and boiling by a steamer plugging upstream with the tide.

'It beats me why she should have been in a place like that,' Tom said. 'Oh, I know she didn't have more than a couple o' bucks and she wasn't sure how the old man would treat her, but surely she would know he wouldn't turn his grandchild away.'

'I've thought about her a lot,' Emily said slowly. She could see now, with her mind's eye, the smiling girl in the portrait. 'She had lost her husband suddenly and theirs was a love match. Then she brought her little daughter two thousand miles, worrying about her welcome. I think she was tired and frightened and just wanted somewhere to hide. So she went into Sammy's for the night.'

Tom looked into her eyes. 'You really have thought about her.' And when she nodded he muttered, 'Well, it could be you're right.' But he was not convinced.

Emily shivered and he said, 'Say, we'd better move on. That wind off the river is a mite cold.'

Emily agreed willingly. But it was not the stiff breeze that affected her on this day of bright sunlight. She could picture the old house burning, the young girl with her daughter falling, ablaze, into the cold depths of the river. She could hear the hiss of the flames as they were snuffed out when the timbers plunged into the water, could see the smoke and steam rising . . .

Emily turned away and started the steep climb up the bank from the river. She was glad that Tom had already visited the graves of Marie and her daughter: Nathaniel Franklin had taken him to the churchyard that morning and Emily had been spared that melancholy errand. Her heart lightened as she led him on the next.

The offices of the *Sunderland Daily Echo* stood above the river and only a few minutes' walk away from the site of Sammy's house. Emily sat by Tom's side as they pored over the accounts of the disaster. '"All the residents perished in the flames or by drowning. Besides the proprietor, Mr Samuel Blenkinsop, there were five seamen and one woman with her child. This was Mrs Marie Leigh, daughter of Mr Nathaniel Franklin, shipowner and shipbuilder, with her daughter Emma,"' he muttered, finger tracing the words. He sat back in his chair and sighed. 'What an awful business. Nathaniel told me Marie had only small change in her purse. That would be why she was in a cheap lodging-house. But surely she must have known she could come to us – my family – for money. We were kin!'

'Perhaps she was proud – she was Mr Franklin's daughter, after all. She wouldn't borrow unless she desperately needed to. And maybe when she left America to come home she thought she had enough money to see her through and only found out later that she did not.' And then: 'She may have been robbed.'

'It's possible. I doubt if we'll ever know, now.' Tom stared at the black newsprint, brooding. Then he said, 'In some ways I regret coming here.' He gestured at the papers. 'Raking up all this again has hurt Mr Franklin. I could see that when he showed me the graves this morning. I don't know that it was such a good idea for me to move into his place. Every time he sees me he'll remember it all again.'

Emily reassured him firmly, 'It will be better for him if you're there, better than him sitting alone and grieving. You can cheer him. Tell him about Marie and her daughter, particularly the little girl. He had never seen her. You knew both of them, didn't you?'

Tom nodded slowly. 'That's right.'

'Tell him,' Emily said.

Tom parted from her with regret and thought a good deal about what she had said – and about her.

At dinner that evening Nathaniel introduced Tom to a broad-shouldered young man: 'This is Captain David Walsh. I think you may find each other congenial company.' The old man did not mention that he had decided against inviting Emily Jackson because he did not want more verbal sparring between her and David at his dinner table.

Tom did get on well with the young ship's captain. David talked of sailing east of Suez and Tom of ranching in the Midwest states of America. Bradley Carver and his mother, Clarice, were also there. Tom found Bradley interesting, an alert man of business, but decided Clarice was all cloying surface charm.

At one point the conversation turned, almost inevitably because of Tom's presence and pilgrimage, to Marie and her daughter. Tom remembered Emily's advice. 'The last time I saw them I was seven or eight years old. Vincent was touring with some play and Marie and Emma came to stay with my folks. Emma had been involved in a nasty accident not long before. A hairdresser dropped a pair of red-hot curling tongs on her shoulder, which left a V-shaped scar just on and below the collar-bone. She was still having this dressed and it must have been painful but it didn't bother her none. I was a wild kid but I always had a soft spot for her.' He saw Nathaniel listening intently, a smile on his lips, and went on, delving into his memory for odd anecdotes that might bring more cheer to the old man.

At the end of the evening, as Tom was about to go to his bed, Nathaniel thanked him. 'What you've told me has let me see Marie and her daughter as they were, not just as I had to imagine them. I find comfort in that. I'll not deny that when I first met you it brought back unhappy memories, but I'm very glad you came.'

The next day Tom sought out Emily at the Clipper. 'I took your advice and it seems to have worked. Nathaniel is happier now,' he told her.

'I'm glad.'

'It was an interesting evening. There was a Captain Walsh there, just come back from knocking about in the East and talking about ships and shipping. You should have been there.'

Emily smiled but inwardly disagreed.

He continued, 'I've been thinking things over and I've decided to stay on for a while.'

'Good!' Emily meant it. She liked this easy-going young man.

'It will give me time to look around here,' Tom elaborated. 'And maybe I'll take a trip to London for a few days. David Walsh is going down there to stay with the family of a young lady friend. He promised to show me the sights if I cared to go.'

Emily felt a twinge of disappointment.

When Tom Peterson returned from London he stayed on in Sunderland all that summer. He escorted Emily to balls and on frequent visits to the theatre. But all through those seemingly leisured days she was still intent on her business transactions, the Clipper and the shares she held in ships and the profits from them. In August she decided she was ready to buy a ship of her own.

Meanwhile, David courted Dulcie in Buckinghamshire and Kensington, where her father had rented a house for the summer season. He walked and talked and danced with her but again and again his thoughts returned to a girl on a swing.

In July Cora Worthy was carried off to hospital, her feeble protests silenced by pain. Her husband seized the opportunity to take a holiday and sailed to Hamburg. He stayed in the Hotel Salzburg for a week and found women and pleasure such as he had never known in the streets of that city. He returned regretfully, just in time for the funeral.

Florence Browning, née Hartley, lost the light in her life that summer when Harry died. She tried to pick up the pieces of her existence and put them together again but everywhere she went in London she was reminded of Harry. They had always been together. When autumn came she could not face the winter in that huge city without the one man who had meant everything to her. She remembered Nancy Bell's letter saying that Felix Ogden was dead and she decided she would go home, back to the place of her birth in Monkwearmouth.

Chapter Fifteen

Bradley Carver still lusted after Emily.

On a fine morning towards the end of the month he stood in the hall of the Franklin house and told his mother curtly, 'I will be home for lunch, possibly with Peterson and Miss Jackson – she will be at the station to bid Uncle Nathaniel farewell.'

Clarice looked around to make sure they could not be overheard. Nathaniel's worn leather suitcases, four of them, were ranged by the open door and the carriage waited at the foot of the steps. He was going to France again to spend the winter in St Raphael. When Clarice saw the hall was deserted she whispered, 'What do you want with that lass? She's nothing more than a jumped-up barmaid! In your position you could marry into the best of the county. I won't entertain her!'

Bradley's cold gaze was on the stairs, watching for his uncle, but now it slid to fix on Clarice: 'You'll do as you're told.'

Clarice shrank from the menace in his tone. 'You wouldn't harm your mother.' But it was a plea, not a statement. Clarice believed he would make her suffer for, and regret, any disobedience of his orders. She whispered this time out of fear, 'I'll see to it.'

Nathaniel came down the stairs then, slowly because he was reluctant to leave his home. Tom Peterson was with him, and the pair were chatting. They had grown close during the summer. Clarice summoned up a smile. 'I trust you will have a good journey, Nathaniel.' He would take her fear as sorrow at his leaving.

'I will write.' He kissed her and patted her arm. The footman had stowed the cases in the carriage and now the three men descended the steps and climbed in. The coachman cracked his whip, the horses wheeled away and set off down the drive.

Clarice waved her handkerchief and wondered if the old man would die this winter, if Bradley would inherit. She had always thought that would be the fulfilment of a dream but now she was uneasy.

'I will come to the station to see you off,' Emily had told Nathaniel, and she had risen early that morning because she had business to transact first.

She was at Silas Worthy's office on the stroke of eight.

Passing through the outer door she found that the desk once used by Cora had a new occupant. Behind the typewriter, which was still under its cover, sat a young woman, silver-blonde, in a thin cotton dress that strained over her full bosom, accentuated by her tightly corseted waist. She was peering into a small hand-mirror but at Emily's entrance she rose and simpered, 'Oh! You must be Miss Jackson.'

'Yes, I am.' Emily knew that Worthy's wife had died of cancer just two or three months ago. She was not impressed by this newcomer.

The girl was looking her over. 'You've got the Clipper, miss. That's right down by the river, isn't it?' she said, with an air of disparagement.

'It is.' Emily wondered what this had to do with her business.

'I live in Roker Avenue.' The blonde girl's simper was superior now.

Emily wondered if that comparison was intended to put her down. She was both amused and annoyed. 'You have your own house?' But she already knew the answer.

'I live with my auntie.'

'And you have just a room there.' Emily smiled. 'Never mind. I expect it's quite nice. Now, tell Mr Worthy I'm here. He knows I don't like to waste my time.'

The girl bounced up from behind her desk, opened the door to Worthy's office and announced sulkily, 'Miss Jackson to see you.'

As Emily entered the room she passed through a cloud of cheap perfume.

Silas Worthy stood up and extended a hand in greeting. 'Miss Jackson! Be seated, please.' He scurried around the desk to ease the chair under Emily. Then to the girl: 'Thank you, Violet. Let me have the papers, please.' He sat back in his chair and smirked at Emily. 'A proud day for you, Miss Jackson, now that you own a ship entirely. The *Margaret Glenn* is a fine, well-found vessel.'

Emily knew that, had paid to have the ship surveyed.

Worthy went on, 'And I have a cargo for her, coal for St Petersburg, and returning with pit props.'

Emily knew that, too, because she had pointed him towards the charter after she had talked with a colliery manager who had come to lunch at the Clipper. 'Yes, I know. The papers? I have another appointment this morning.'

'Yes, of course.' Worthy hurried out and Emily heard a muttered conversation, the words blurred by the part-closed door. But then came Violet's fractious whine: 'I don't know where you keep all these bits o' paper.'

Seconds later Worthy appeared, breathless but summoning up a smile. 'Here we are. All ready, only requiring your signature.'

But Emily read through the papers before she signed.

She walked out into the street as the owner of the *Margaret Glenn*. She paused a moment to smile up at the bright blue sky. Worthy had been right: it was a proud moment. But she had never liked him and today she thought she had detected a note of envy behind his congratulations. His smirk and his oily charm must always have been present in his manner, but suddenly they caused her to distrust him. Nor was she impressed by Violet. Perhaps she should seek another agent, but she had always found him efficient and fair with her. He deserved her loyalty.

She set off up the street, heading for the station. She had promised Nathaniel.

Silas Worthy called Violet into his office and brandished the papers. 'There y'are! All done!'

'There was no need for you to get at me like that because I couldn't find them,' Violet complained. 'I'm not going to be talked to like that. Not if you want me to be nice to you.'

'I was just a bit excited about the deal going through,' Silas excused himself. Now he slid an arm around Violet's waist and fondled her breast. 'How about if we go out tonight, and after . . .' he winked lewdly and bribed, 'You can buy a new dress. I'm expecting some more ships to come in before long, in a manner of speaking.'

Violet let his hands wander. 'What d'ye mean?' she asked.

'Some investments I've made. I always wanted to deal on the stock exchange – that's where the big money is – and now I can.' Cora would never have let him do it.

Violet disengaged his hands. 'You wait till tonight and give me the money for that dress.'

*   *   *

Emily saw the little group on the platform, Nathaniel at its centre with Tom Peterson, Bradley Carver – and David Walsh. She had time to conceal her surprise at his presence before she came up to them and the men parted to admit her. 'I'm glad you could come,' Nathaniel greeted her.

Emily smiled. 'I said I would.'

'But you had an important meeting.' Nathaniel knew all about it. She had told him of her plans.

'All done.'

'Satisfactorily?' Then Nathaniel laughed. 'I can see from your face that it was. Congratulations. You've done amazingly well for a young girl – or a man, for that matter.'

It was Emily's turn to laugh. 'Young? I'm twenty-five next May!'

'That's still young.' Nathaniel turned to the others. 'Emily has bought a ship of her own, not just a share but all of it.'

The three tall young men were all surprised, smiling down at her. She laughed. 'She's the *Margaret Glenn*, just a little coaster, though she does sail further afield. But she's not the *Mauretania*.' That huge liner was due to depart on her maiden voyage in a month or so.

'I've not heard of a woman shipowner before,' David said, not seeking to annoy her but just stating a fact.

Emily recalled his boyhood comment: 'Lasses don't own ships.' He had been dismissive of her dream then and, she decided, still was. Her smile stayed in place but it was brittle. 'There's a first time for everything. Do you object?'

'I don't think it's a suitable occupation for a woman,' David answered honestly.

'I suppose you'd prefer me to have stuck to skivvying, scrubbing floors and emptying slops!' Emily snapped. 'But you're entitled to your opinion, for what it's worth.'

David, remembering Nathaniel's presence, refused to be goaded. 'I hope you don't burn your fingers,' was all he said.

'I'll see to that,' said Emily. 'But I'm surprised to find you here, Captain Walsh. I thought you were otherwise engaged, in London or thereabouts.' Then she became aware of Nathaniel watching them unhappily, and was sorry.

David kept his temper in check. 'My leave is almost over and I'm seeking a command. I also wanted to see Mr Franklin before he left for France.'

'I'm glad all of you came.' Nathaniel reached up a hand to David's shoulder. 'You'll be looking for a captain for your ship, Emily,' he suggested. 'Why don't you take him on? You won't find a better.'

Suspecting a tart answer from Emily, David put in quickly, 'I think I may be already committed.'

'A pity,' said Nathaniel regretfully. It distressed him that these two friends of his could not get on together. He could not understand it.

Emily smiled bleakly at David. 'I'm sure I'll find someone.' She was declaring an armed truce because of Nathaniel.

Bradley Carver saw an opportunity to get closer to

Emily. 'I may know a man to suit you,' he said. 'A Captain Ruddock. He has commanded ships for Mr Franklin before now and I think he is seeking a berth at this moment. Maybe we can talk about it later.'

There was a slamming of carriage doors: the train would soon be pulling away. Nathaniel shook hands with the men, drew Emily to him to kiss her cheek and said softly, 'It's a pleasant life out there, but lonely. The winters seem long. I know you're busy but come to see me if you can.'

Emily heard the catch in his voice. 'I'll try. If I possibly can, I will come,' she promised.

He released her and climbed into the carriage but stood leaning out of the open window. The train eased away with a clanking of couplings and a hiss of steam, and they all watched until it rounded a curve in the track and Nathaniel was lost to sight.

They left the station together and David excused himself, wished them 'Good day,' and strode off along the high street. He told himself he was right to steer clear of Emily Jackson and wondered what the hell was wrong with the woman. He had given a straight answer about her owning ships, the answer most men would have given. He remembered the terrified women passengers when his ship was attacked by Chinese pirates. Was shipowning a profession for them? He could not imagine it.

He decided he and Emily Jackson would never get on. The sooner he was at sea and away from her, the better.

But still at the thought of her something stirred within him.

Emily hesitated only briefly before accepting Bradley's invitation to lunch. 'I will be able to tell you some more about Captain Ruddock,' he coaxed.

'Sure, take a couple of hours off, Emily. The Clipper will look after itself,' Tom urged.

Emily knew that it would. She had made certain that it ran like clockwork when she was absent. 'Oh, very well,' she said, and to Bradley, 'Thank you.'

The meal was a light-hearted affair, though Emily thought Clarice seemed on edge. In fact, Bradley's mother was afraid to anger her son, but Bradley put himself out to be charming and informative. He was good at his job and knew ships and shipping.

After lunch he offered to drive Emily back to the Clipper. She thanked him, then said, 'But I'm not going there yet. I have to visit my mother today – not for long, just to see that she's all right.'

'Why, of course, I'll take you,' Bradley insisted, and drove her in the Humber to the street of terraced houses where Ada had her two upstairs rooms.

'She refuses to move in with me. I've tried to persuade her but I can't,' Emily explained.

'I understand,' Bradley said. But he did not. He knew that thousands of people lived in narrow streets like this, of two up, two down houses, and they seemed happy, but he could not imagine anyone wanting to live there. As he sipped at the cup of strong tea Ada pressed on him, he lied, 'You have a nice home here, Mrs Jackson.'

'Aye.' She eyed him coolly. 'And I'll not leave till they carry me out. I've been here a lot o' years. I've got good neighbours either side of me, and Bridget Cassidy and her man downstairs. I'm content.' And before Emily left she whispered to her, 'I wouldn't trust that man.'

Bradley was still smiling when he drove Emily back to the Clipper. 'A wonderful old lady,' he lied again.

'She is,' said Emily, pleased.

As he handed her down from the Humber outside the Clipper he said, 'I'm planning a small dinner party soon. I'd be glad if you would come.'

Emily remembered her mother's words, but she knew the old woman sometimes took a dislike to people on sight so she discounted the warning. Wasn't Bradley Nathaniel's nephew? He was handsome, clever, and Emily liked him.

She smiled, 'I'd like that. Thank you.'

Bradley watched her walk away before he climbed back into the Humber and drove off. He coveted her body, wanting to despoil it – and to punish her for past slights. 'One day you'll weep and beg for mercy,' he whispered.

Hidden in a doorway, Digby Gamblin saw that look on Bradley's face and read its meaning. 'Not till I've done with her,' he swore.

The next day Emily met Captain Ruddock at Bradley's office. He was a stocky, weatherbeaten man in his fifties.

He said he had been sailing off the coast of Africa for some years. 'I had a lot of trouble with malaria and was ashore for a good while, then came home. But I'm fit now in these waters.' That was the story he had told Bradley. But Bradley knew the truth: a letter from an agent in Sierra Leone had informed him that the Captain had lost his last position through drunkenness and had been unable to get another. He had come home because in Britain his reputation was not known. Bradley was certain that Ruddock would wreck the *Margaret Glenn*.

Emily knew none of this, took to Ruddock at once and engaged him. 'Thank you, ma'am. I'll be glad to serve you.' Then he added, with a grin, 'There are a few chaps would like the job. You're being talked about as the lady owner.'

Emily blushed, and Bradley said, 'That's true. You're famous around here.'

'Nonsense.' Emily thought it might be true but wildly exaggerated. She found out later that it was not: when the *Margaret Glenn* sailed for St Petersburg on the 6 November the *Echo* gave several column inches to describing the ship, its cargo – and 'Miss Emily Jackson, who is becoming a well-known owner on this river'. Emily found that people were turning to stare at her in the street. She realised she had indeed become a local celebrity.

'Can I have a few minutes of your time to discuss business?' Silas Worthy asked her a week later in the Clipper when he called there for lunch.

'Of course.' Emily sat down at the table across from him. 'What is it?'

'I've found another ship for you,' said Worthy eagerly. 'She's at sea but due to berth here in a week or so and she will be put up for sale then. I strongly advise you to buy her.' He gave her some details of her size and seaworthiness.

Emily listened as he went on, listing the good points of the ship, but her mind was already made up. She was sure Worthy was offering her a bargain, but he was arguing from his point of view. She knew her own business best. 'Thank you, but no. I think I'm extended quite enough for the time being.' She had some capital in reserve, but not enough to buy this ship.

'If it's a matter of capital, I'm sure the banks would look favourably on a loan,' Worthy pressed her.

'So do I,' Emily replied drily, 'but I don't want one. I'm not buying another ship at present or for some time.' And she meant it.

Worthy saw that, and left the rest of his lunch uneaten. As he walked back to his office he cursed her for turning him down: the investments of which he had boasted to Violet had gone awry. He had lost a lot of the money earned and saved by the frugal Cora. If anyone would soon need a loan from the bank it was Silas Worthy. He told himself he would have to repair his fortune somehow . . . Violet was proving expensive, always wanting more new dresses.

In the quiet of the afternoon Emily had another visitor. The last lunch customers were leaving when a young woman of about Emily's age entered the Sitting Room.

She paused just inside the door, looking shyly across the almost empty room to where Emily was clearing and polishing the counter. She was fashionably dressed but all in black. Emily saw her and called, 'Can I help you?'

The girl came to her, saying, 'I'm looking for Miss Emily Jackson.'

'I'm Emily Jackson.' Surely this girl wasn't looking for work?

The young woman stared frankly at her, and Emily became uneasy. Then the girl said, 'Now I understand.'

'I don't,' said Emily.

'May I talk to you?'

'Of course.' Emily gestured to the chairs at a nearby table. 'Would you like a cup of tea?'

'Please.' She sank gracefully into a chair, took off her black silk gloves and laid them on the table.

'Jane! Can we have some tea, please?' Emily called, then joined the stranger at the table.

'You don't recognise me, of course,' the girl said.

'I – don't think so.' Emily studied the lovely young face before her. There was something about it that nudged at a chord of memory, but . . . 'No, I'm sorry.'

'I'm Catherine Wilkinson, née Rochester. I married Alastair.'

Alastair Wilkinson! Emily's mind flashed back over eight years to a summer ball and her last meeting with him. The details were lost in the past but she remembered he had sworn to seek revenge on her. Emily said, 'I remember now.' And the widow's weeds? She reached out to touch the sleeve of Catherine's black coat and asked gently, 'Not Alastair?'

Catherine nodded miserably. 'He died a month ago, of consumption.'

'Oh, my dear, I'm so sorry.' Emily took the other girl's hands in hers. Jane Kirby brought a tray, poured the tea and quietly went away.

'Alastair asked me to find you,' Catherine said, 'and it was quite easy, really. Jimmy Graham – he's a groom for Alastair's parents – knew all about you and told me I'd find you here. I didn't know what to expect but I see now why Alastair and you . . . May I be honest?'

'I think it's usually best.' Emily was bewildered.

'I was afraid I would find some girl who had tried to seduce him,' Catherine admitted. 'I can see now that that was quite wrong.'

'Yes,' Emily said. It was no time to argue over who had tried to seduce whom.

For the first time Catherine smiled. 'You're very understanding.' She opened her bag. 'When Alastair was dying he told me about you and the way he had treated you. He told me how you'd left him and why. He felt very badly about you and wanted to tell you how sorry he was for treating you as he did.'

'We were very young,' Emily said.

Catherine nodded. 'So I told him, but he wasn't consoled. He wanted to tell you, to apologise, but he was in a sanatorium in Switzerland and there was no time . . . no time. He asked that I should give you this. He thought it might make up for some of the harm he'd done.' Catherine took a breath. 'He had worried over this for a long time but he died at peace because this eased his conscience.' She held out a slip of paper and Emily took it, bemused. The cheque was made out to her for a sum that would pay for the ship Worthy wanted her to buy.

After some seconds of incredulity, Emily came to her senses and said, 'Thank you, but no.' She pushed the cheque into Catherine's open bag. 'I got over any harm Alastair did me years ago. I feel no bitterness and have no need for the money. I'm making my own way in the world. I suggest you give the money to a charity. Alastair can rest in peace.' She saw Catherine reach for her scrap of handkerchief and said, 'Excuse me a moment.'

Emily hid in her private living room behind the bar until she had composed herself again then wiped away her own tears. Once she had loved Alastair – or thought she did.

When she returned to Catherine she found her smiling. The young widow rose to her feet and said, 'Thank you. You've been very understanding. I'm glad I came. I didn't want to think it was Alastair's fault, though at heart I knew it was.'

She left then, in a smart motor-car driven by a uniformed chauffeur, and Emily waved to her from the door of the Clipper. Have you been a fool to turn down that money? she wondered. But she knew she had not. If she had taken it then it would have seemed that harm had been done, when it had not. She bore no grudge against Alastair, felt only sorrow for him and his young widow.

A week later, Emily bought a new dress for the dinner party at the Franklin house. She put it on in the evening, a silk gown that hugged her figure. She inspected herself in the mirror, whirled around on her toes so that the full skirt floated in a cartwheel around her. The décolletage was revealing but no more than was fashionable at the time. The small V-shaped scar showed on and below her collar-bone but only faintly. She wondered who else would be at the dinner party. Tom Peterson, of course . . .

Chapter Sixteen

NOVEMBER 1907. MONKWEARMOUTH.

Bradley Carver watched for Emily with hungry eyes. He had posed as cool and casual while he talked with his other guests in the drawing room, which looked out over the gravel drive up to the front of the house. He had told the servants to leave the curtains open and saw her cab as the horse came trotting into view. He strode down the steps to hand her down then escorted her into the house. 'May I?' He took her cape as she slipped it from her shoulders.

She smiled at him. 'Thank you.'

'Come and meet the others.'

Together they entered the drawing room and Emily saw eyes turn towards her. Clarice was smiling but hostile: there was a tightness about her lips as if she had tasted something sour. Perhaps it was because of the way the men looked at Emily. Bradley was smiling, and Tom Peterson was frankly admiring. Emily decided she had been right to change her mind and her dress at the last minute. She wore a silk gown that clung to her but it was buttoned to the neck. As she had looked in the mirror at herself in the new dress she had remembered Digby Gamblin and for some reason, some instinct, she shied away from the display of creamy bosom and instead donned this one, which she had bought a year ago. Tom Peterson and the other men saw a slender neck emerge from a lace collar but could not glimpse the faint V-shaped scar.

There was a third man: David Walsh bowed, unsmiling as he looked into her eyes, and held them for a long moment. She had not expected him – or this – and dropped her gaze with a catch of breath. She felt the blood rising to her cheeks and was angry with herself. Why did he have to look at her like that? She met his gaze again but now it was neutral.

'What a nice dress!' Clarice said. 'But I would have thought a lady of business would wear something more severe.'

Emily returned the glacial smile with an easy one of her own. 'Not this lady. I find it possible to conduct business without dressing in sackcloth and ashes.' She let her eyes rest briefly on Clarice's drab brown confection. Then she looked around at the men: 'But we aren't talking business tonight, are we?'

Tom and Bradley laughed and shook their heads.

However, they spoke of little other than ships and shipping as they sat at dinner. Tom Peterson asked, 'What news of that vessel of yours, the *Margaret Glenn*?'

'Lloyds report she's at St Petersburg,' Emily replied. 'She'll be discharging her cargo and loading another, if she hasn't already done so.'

The conversation flowed from there – except that David was silent. Emily was conscious of this and decided that he was in no mood to make up. Neither was she. The evening was a heady experience for her: now, added to her recent successes, she was listened to respectfully by these men as an equal, no longer patronised as just a pretty girl. She revelled in her confidence and sure grasp of her affairs.

Then Porteous, the butler, entered, bearing a salver that held an envelope. He offered it to Emily: 'A cable, ma'am. The boy took it to the Clipper but they told him to fetch it on here. He's waiting.'

Surprised and faintly uneasy, Emily picked up the envelope and ripped it open, unfolded and read the message inside. 'Do you wish to send a reply?' Bradley asked.

Emily was still trying to take in the import of the message but answered: 'No, thank you. Not now.'

Bradley nodded to Porteous. 'Give the boy twopence.'

'Yes, sir.' The butler left.

There was silence, then Emily looked up from the flimsy sheet. 'It's from Captain Ruddock of the *Margaret Glenn*. She's been in a collision in St Petersburg and the Russians have impounded her.'

They stared at her, shocked into silence. Emily caught a glimpse of satisfaction cross Clarice's face. It was gone in a moment, smoothed over with bland sympathy, but Emily had seen it.

'What will you do?' Tom Peterson asked.

Emily did not reply because she had no answer. Bradley said, 'First of all you must contact our embassy out there to act on your behalf.'

David Walsh broke his silence now, crisply: 'Whatever you decide, it will have to be done quickly.' And when he saw Emily's eyes on him he explained bluntly, 'St Petersburg will be iced in at any time from the middle of this month onwards. Any ship still there will not get out until the spring.'

Emily stared down at the cloth. The sudden news had taken her by surprise and she was unable to think. She heard Clarice say, with mock anxiety, 'What *can* you do, dear?' What could she? Her ship was more than a thousand miles away. If she had been lying here in the Wear or the Tyne then Emily would soon have acted but . . .

Emily saw the answer now and drew a breath. 'I shall go to St Petersburg.' She saw Bradley shake his head, sceptical, and Tom looked doubtful.

'What can you achieve by that?' Bradley asked.

'Even by fast packet and trains it will take you a week or more,' Tom said.

'I can talk to the people there face to face, as I cannot do while I am here. And I will go there directly in a ship of my own.'

Now Bradley was surprised. 'You have another ship?'

'I know where I can buy one tomorrow.'

He pursed his lips. 'Is it wise to buy in a hurry, especially when the *Margaret Glenn* may be iced in for the winter?'

'It would not be wise to sit here and do nothing,' replied Emily. She pushed back her chair. 'If you will excuse me, please? I have preparations to make.'

The men were on their feet. Bradley yanked at the silken cord hanging by the fireplace, which would set the bell jangling in the kitchen where the coachman waited. 'I'll call the carriage.'

Out in the hall Tom Peterson held Emily's cape so that she could slip into it. 'Do you speak Russian?' he murmured. And when Emily shook her head, he asked, 'Then will you take me along? My grandparents came from St Petersburg in 1848. Peterson is an anglicised form of their name. I learnt Russian from them.'

'That would be a great help,' Emily said gratefully.

She ran down the steps to the carriage where Bradley waited to hand her in. He had considered offering her a loan to help in this difficulty, thinking that it would put her under an obligation to him, give him an advantage, but decided against it. Better that she should lose everything, as he was sure she would. Then she would need him.

David climbed into the carriage and sat opposite her. The coachman cracked his whip and the carriage rolled away, swaying, down the drive.

Bradley and Tom Peterson turned back into the hall

where Clarice waited. Tom went on to the drawing room but Clarice detained Bradley with a hand on his sleeve. 'That young woman has got herself into serious trouble!' she hissed. 'A woman in business! Did you ever hear the like of it? She's running off to Russia, throwing good money after bad, and will land up with nothing. You'd do well to leave her alone.'

Bradley seized her wrist and the grip of his fingers made her whimper with pain. 'I know what I'm doing. Now, keep your mouth shut.' He went on into the drawing room, leaving her nursing her wrist with tears in her eyes. He smiled at Tom. 'Brandy?'

In the semi-darkness inside the coach Emily could see David's eyes, dark and brooding. He said, 'I'll skipper her for you.'

Emily began to refuse, but he stopped her. 'We have no time for fencing. You'll have a job finding a better captain than me – a hell of a job at short notice – and you have enough to do already. Have you got the money for this ship?'

Emily had not, and thought, If you'd kept that cheque offered by Catherine Wilkinson . . . 'I'm going to get a loan from the bank,' she answered angrily.

'With what security?'

'The Clipper,' she snapped.

'Will that cover the price of this ship?' David demanded. 'And how long will the bank take to decide? One week? Two?'

Emily knew the mortgage would neither be enough nor

in time. Angry at being driven into a corner, she said rashly, 'I'll find someone else to take shares in her.'

David stared at her impassively. 'Would you buy shares in a ship so that a young woman could sail her to Russia to try to recover another impounded there? That might sound like throwing good money after bad.'

'I'm going to do it – somehow,' Emily repeated stubbornly.

'Let me buy half and we'll share the profits,' David said. 'I can draw cash from the bank tomorrow. It will be quicker than hunting around for an investor to back you.'

Emily watched him, his eyes returning her stare, unblinking. She knew he was right about this. 'Very well.' The agreement was dragged out of her because his proposal made the venture possible. She had enough capital – just – to pay for her half of the ship. 'Thank you,' she added. Then she asked, 'Why are you doing this?'

He could not answer that entirely truthfully so he said, 'Nathaniel would want me to.'

Emily felt that odd twinge of disappointment again.

They did not speak again until he set her down outside the Clipper and said, 'I will meet you at Worthy's office first thing tomorrow. Goodnight.'

'Goodnight, Captain Walsh,' Emily replied, and closed the door on him. She stood with her back to it, listening to the carriage drive away, smiling. She'd had the last word, but now she felt relieved that David Walsh was going with her. He might annoy her but he had sailed the world. Emily had never been to sea, never travelled further than the outskirts of Sunderland and Hylton. This would be a giant step for her but she was determined to take it and glad to have the big man going with her.

Florence Browning got down from the train in Monk-wearmouth, handed her small case to a porter and asked, 'I haven't been here for over twenty years. Can you recommend some lodgings not too far away?'

'Aye, bonny lass.' He was a man of her age, his round face split by a wide grin. 'You'll see a few changes but the river's still there.' It would be, of course, and Florence smiled at the feeble joke. She followed him to where the cabs waited outside the station. He put her case into one and gave an address to the driver. When Florence tried to tip him he refused to take the threepenny piece: 'No, bonny lass. That's all right. He's taking you to Mrs Harris. She's a decent body, a widow who takes in two or three. You'll be fine with her. Tell her Geordie the porter sent you.'

Mrs Harris was welcoming: 'Come in, pet. Geordie's a canny lad.' She showed Florence to a neat, clean little room with the usual aspidistra. 'Come down when you've settled in and there'll be a bit of supper for you.'

Left alone, Florence thought that her homecoming was vastly different from her departure. She had left in fear for her life. Yet there had also been good times in Monkwear-mouth, out of the shadow of the evil Felix Ogden. It was too late for visiting old friends tonight. Tomorrow she would go to see Nancy Bell and they would have a long talk about times past when they had been young girls together.

After retiring to her bed Florence soon slept, tired by her journey up from London, but she woke in the night, crying out and threshing in the tangled sheets. Then she realised where she was and sat shivering, hugging herself. She had dreamt she was back on the quay where she had cowered in the darkness and seen a young woman drowned.

Emily met David as arranged – and to Worthy's delight. He was only too eager to push through the purchase of the ship as quickly as possible because he would get his commission sooner. He laid the ship's details before them. 'She's the *Sea Princess*, lying in the river now, ready for sea and whatever cargo you care to ship.'

'But she's forty years old,' Emily exclaimed.

Worthy shifted uneasily in his chair.

'That's why she's so cheap. You won't get the *Mauretania* for this sort of price.' The newly built giant liner like a huge hotel was 32,000 tons.

'I want a sound ship for my money or I keep it in my pocket,' David said crisply.

'She's been surveyed and she's sound, I promise you, and a bargain,' Worthy assured him. 'Her present owners want a quick sale to finance another purchase, so she could be yours before the day is out.'

David tossed the papers on to the desk and his gaze switched to Emily: 'I think this is the time to buy such a ship.'

She knew that he meant they did not have time to search the market, so she nodded agreement.

Worthy managed to muffle his sigh of relief. 'You'll need a master and a crew, though,' he said.

'I'll be her captain, and I'll find a crew at the shipping office this morning,' David said.

Worthy smirked. 'Of course.'

'Get her cheaper if you can but don't let that delay settlement,' Emily told him. She remembered to glance at David for his agreement because he was paying half the cost, and he nodded.

Within the hour they left Worthy's office. He would proceed with the mechanics of the purchase. 'I have business at the Clipper – but I want to see this ship,' Emily said.

'I must go to the shipping office,' David observed, 'but before that I'd like to look at the *Sea Princess* too.' He hailed a cab and they went together. As it bumped over the cobbles along the side of the river Emily wondered at this new mood of agreement between them. She stole a glance at the man sitting alongside her; he was gazing at the outside world, lost in thought. She wondered what he was thinking about. Her?

He turned towards her and she dropped her gaze hastily to her hands, folded in her lap, not wanting him to look into her eyes. 'She's certified seaworthy,' he said, 'but

I'd like to see her condition. We'll be living aboard her for two weeks or so.'

Emily had not thought of that: they would be sharing the cramped quarters provided for the ship's officers. She looked up at him and said, bravely and hopefully, 'I expect we'll fare well enough.'

'We'll have to.' David grinned, but before she could smile back at him, he had turned away again.

The horse was reined in and the cabbie called down from his seat, 'There y'are, skipper. The *Sea Princess*, lying alongside.'

They got down from the cab and stood on the quay. David paid the cabbie and told him to come back for them in half an hour. Meanwhile Emily looked to the river and saw the *Echo* offices standing high on the opposite shore. There she had sat with Tom Peterson and read of the awful death of Marie Leigh and her child. She could also see the rotten stumps of the piles where Sammy's boarding-house had stood – and Marie had died. She shivered and tore away her eyes to gaze instead at the ship lying at the quay.

The cab clattered away and David said ironically at her elbow, 'She certainly isn't the *Mauretania*. She's more like a ferry-boat.' Indeed, she was nearer the size of the little steamer that transported people across the river – she would look like a toy next to a liner.

'Oh dear.' Emily said. Besides being very small, the *Sea Princess* lay low in the water. Emily tried to picture her in a North Sea gale and her heart sank.

As if reading her thoughts, David mused, 'She's got nice lines, though. I think she might be a good ship in bad weather, though not very comfortable.' He walked up the narrow gangway and held out his hand to Emily, who followed cautiously. She had hardly set foot on the ship when a head poked up, seemingly out of the deck, right forward. A blunt-nosed stubbled face under a cloth cap peered at them. 'Are you the watchman?' David called.

The rest of the man came up now and Emily saw he was climbing out of a small hatch set in the lift of the forecastle head – Emily remembered Nathaniel explaining, 'That's the raised bit right at the front of the ship. The sailors sleep there.'

'Aye. That's me, Ben Danvers.' He was stocky and wore overalls with a blue jersey.

'We're the new owners. Are you looking to sign on?' David said.

Ben stared at him, incredulous. 'Me? Sail in this auld lass? No bloody fear! Begging your pardon, ma'am.'

'Why not?' David asked.

'The watter's nearly coming aboard her lying here in the river. At sea she'll be more like one o' them submarines than a ship. And she's forty years old.'

'She hasn't sunk in forty years; plenty of others have,' David pointed out.

'There's always got to be the first time,' Ben said gloomily. 'Did you want to look over her?'

They did, and saw the dark cavern that was the inside of the forecastle head, where Ben had a stove, an armchair and a book to while away the time. Two scuttles, their round glass faces just above the water, let in barely enough light to read, but a paraffin lamp hung from a hook in the deckhead ready for when night came.

Emily peered about. This is a miserable hole, she thought.

David caught her expression. 'This is normal. I lived in fo'c'sles like this for seven years before I moved to a cabin. Shall we move on there now?' He ushered her out into the daylight.

The bridge and wheelhouse were set right aft and the Captain's cabin was below it. It held a bunk, a chair and small desk; there was hardly room to turn around. Aft of the bridge were cabins for the engineers and the mate; they were even smaller. Emily was thoughtful when their tour of inspection was over because she could see that accommodation was going to present a problem.

Their cab was waiting and they bade farewell to the morose Ben. Then, on the quay, David said, 'She'll do.'

Emily hoped she would: her fortune depended on this ship. 'She's small,' she said doubtfully – and indeed she was, to cross the North Sea and run the length of the Baltic.

'She'll be big enough for us,' David assured her.

Emily wondered if the *Sea Princess* would be big enough for her and this sombre young giant to spend two weeks together. She would have to be.

'I'm going to take the ferry across the river to the shipping office to sign on a crew,' David said.

'And I have affairs to attend to. We'll meet again at Worthy's office this evening.' Emily smiled at him, and in return he touched his cap in a salute as he handed her up into the cab.

Emily's thoughts stayed with the tall, dark Captain Walsh. They had played as children on the swing, but even then they had argued. But there had been that single glance he had bestowed on her that evening at the Franklin house. It was gone in the blink of an eye but Emily had read its message. She was not sure how she felt about him . . . Yes, she was: he was nothing to her, nor she to him; he was aiding her now because of Nathaniel Franklin. She must forget David Walsh and consider her plight. If this reckless dash to St Petersburg failed she would be ruined – and a laughing stock to many like Clarice, who thought her a fool to involve herself in the shipping world, and like David Walsh, who did not consider it a fit profession for a woman. God knew, she had much to do before she set out.

She stared out of the window, contemplating her bleak prospects and mentally listing the tasks she had to complete before the *Sea Princess* sailed. She had to instruct the staff of the Clipper, pack a case or cases for two weeks – she would need warm clothing . . . Then she saw a blonde girl trudging heavily along the pavement, a woollen shawl around her shoulders.

Emily recognised an old friend and called on the cabbie to stop. 'Lily!' she cried. The girl turned her face up to the cab and Emily saw the tears on her cheeks. 'Lily! What's wrong?'

She jumped down, fumbled in her purse and paid off the cab – the Clipper was only round the next turning. She put her arms about Lily and the girl leant on her, let herself be comforted. 'Come round to the Clipper and we'll have a cup of tea,' Emily said. 'Then you can tell me all about it.' But she had already guessed that Lily was pregnant.

Her friend told her the rest over a cup of tea in the back room of the Clipper while Sadie Theakstone prepared lunches in the kitchen. 'Mr Wilkinson got a big new job in London and he sold up at Hylton. The new owner of the estate is bringing all his own people so my Jimmy is out of a job and we'll lose the house as well. My mam died this summer so we can't go to her. Jimmy has looked for a job here but it's nearly all shipyard work and he's always been with horses. We don't know which way to turn and I'm worried sick for the bairns.'

Emily thought about it for a while, stroking Lily's hand. 'I have to go out for a bit. You lie down on the couch and try to rest,' she said. She saw Lily settled and slipped into the bar.

Joe Kirby was serving there, a white apron round his waist, pulling pints of beer for men from the yards. His wife Jane was on duty in the Sitting Room, serving lunches. 'I have to go out again,' Emily told them. 'When I get back I'll tell you all what's going on and what I want you to do when I'm away.' Then she left them.

She had to walk past St Peter's Church and on as far as Dundas Street before she found a cab. Then she sat fretting over the time she was losing, but she had to help Lily.

She had been away for two hours when she finally returned to the Clipper. Sadie, Jane and Joe were tidying up after the lunchtime trade's departure and Emily found Lily asleep. She shook the girl gently until she woke. 'I've some good news for you,' she said. 'I've talked to a friend of mine, Billy Foster. He's the land agent for the Franklin estate and he has a job for Jimmy in the stables, and a house goes with it.'

'I canna believe it,' Lily said weakly.

'It's true.'

'Oh, Em! You're a marvel!' Lily burst into tears again.

Eventually Emily calmed her and sent her off to give the news to Jimmy. Then she told her staff about her proposed trip. 'Do you think you can manage?'

'We'll cope,' Sadie assured her, and Joe nodded in stolid agreement.

'I think you're awfully brave, going out there to those Russians,' Jane breathed, awed.

'I don't feel very brave,' Emily said drily. 'And I don't know when we're sailing so I'm going to pack now.' She was quick about it but it was evening when she descended to the bar again just in time for her appointment at Worthy's office. The bar was crowded and both Joe and Sadie were busy serving. Emily called to them, 'I'll be late back, some time after ten I expect.' They turned briefly from the bar to nod.

A light rain was falling, so Emily covered her head with

a shawl and set out for Worthy's offices. She hoped she would be late back because that would mean the sale of the ship had gone through. If it did not the meeting would break up early, to be resumed the next day. And every day counted. Her thoughts went to Captain Ruddock and the *Margaret Glenn*, doomed to spend the winter in the ice-bound harbour of St Petersburg if she failed.

And if she failed she would be ruined.

But she took it as a good omen when she left Worthy's office shortly after ten with Captain David Walsh. They were going to take on coal for the bunkers early the next day and then sail. Things were moving and she felt a rush of hope now they were owners of the *Sea Princess*.

'I'll walk back to the Clipper with you,' David said.

In her new-found confidence Emily shrugged off his offer. 'I'll be safe enough, thank you, Captain.'

'I remember a time when you were not.'

So did Emily.

'For my peace of mind — please?' he pressed, tactfully.

Emily remembered that she was to spend two weeks in this man's company and that he was her partner in a business venture. She decided it might be as well to try to continue the state of agreement. 'Very well,' she said, and so they set out.

Florence Browning had gone walking earlier that day, strolling down by the river, remembering times past. She paused on the quay where she had hidden all those years ago. There was the doorway that had sheltered her in fear, there the solitary gas lamp, though it was not lit in this afternoon light. For a moment she could imagine its hissing and its yellow light seen through the coiling mist. She could see murder done, too, and shut her eyes against it, but she still heard the cry of the child, pictured her standing alone and pathetic on the quay.

Florence shuddered, hugged her coat about her, and walked on. She passed the entrance to the cul-de-sac where the Clipper stood. At that moment a young woman emerged from the public house. Florence took note of her because evidently she was not a barmaid. She was fashionably and expensively dressed in a mustard-yellow tailored wool suit with embroidered revers, and a straw hat with a wide, turned-down brim. She was dark-haired and attractive. Florence wondered what she could be doing in the Clipper. Then the girl climbed into a cab and was driven away.

Florence went on to the house of her childhood friend, Nancy Bell, and got there just in time for tea. 'Why, Flo! It's lovely to see you after all these years.' Nancy put her arms around Florence and they both shed a few tears. They talked of days gone by, and had tea with Alec, Nancy's husband, then talked again. Late in the evening they were sipping at celebratory glasses of sherry when Nancy said sadly, 'I always remember when you went away. It was the anniversary of the Victoria Hall disaster and the night of that awful fire down by the river, when old Franklin lost his daughter and her little lass.'

Florence paused with the glass half-way to her lips. 'Fire? I never saw any fire. And Franklin's daughter? I never heard about that down in London.'

Nancy nodded. 'Oh, aye. You remember she'd fallen for this American chap, an actor, and the old man was against it so she ran off with this feller – Vincent Leigh he was called – and she married him? Well, he died over there in America and she came back. She got off a ship in the river and that first night she stopped in Sammy's – remember Sammy's boarding-house?'

Florence wrinkled her nose. 'Aye. What was she doing in a place like that?'

'God knows. Don't ask me. Anyway, it burned down that night with everybody in it but you must have been on the train by then, so you didn't see it.' Nancy's voice was hushed now. 'She was the only woman in there and I heard old Franklin could only identify them by their luggage and the rings she was wearing. They were that badly burned, both her and her little lass, Emma.'

'Emma?' The name came whispering down the years to Florence and she set down her glass. She had heard the woman on the quay call her child by that name just before she was drowned by her attackers. And afterwards Bert Jackson had come along . . .

Florence realised Nancy was staring at her and managed to smile. 'Sorry. Something else crossed my mind. Do you ever see anything of Bert Jackson?'

Nancy pursed her lips. 'Bert died years ago, but Ada was fine when I saw her last, just a few weeks back. Not to talk to – she was just getting on a tram as I was getting off – but she was looking well. Mind, she's well off now because that lass of hers is going up in the world. Ada had her late in life. She moved out of Monkwearmouth and across the river, and the next anybody knew she had this little lass, Emily. The girl's a licensee, would you believe? Keeps the Clipper now. A lot of the toffs go there for their dinners. *And* she's a shipowner! There was a bit in the *Echo* only the other day about how she had bought this ship, the *Margaret* something or other, and it was sailing to Russia.'

'I saw a young woman coming out of the Clipper today, dark, very smart lass,' Florence said.

Nancy nodded. 'That would be her: Emily Jackson.'

Florence could hear the voices in her head: The mother calling her child, 'Emma!' The mother who had been the Franklin girl, Marie but then married Vincent Leigh so the child's name was Emma Leigh, and Bert Jackson had misunderstood and called her Emily. And murder had been done – Florence was suddenly sure that whoever had died in Sammy's boarding-house it had not been the Franklin heiress.

'Are you *sure* you're all right?' Nancy was staring at her anxiously.

Florence was not all right. She was breathless at her discovery and on the point of blurting out what she knew. Then she became cautious. This was far more important to someone other than Nancy or herself. That person had to be told first. Florence stood up. 'I'm just a bit tired. It's time I was getting along. It's been a lovely evening, talking to you after all these years.'

'Aye, it has,' Nancy replied, and kissed her. 'And we'll be able to do it again now you've come home. Do you want my Alec to walk you back to your lodgings?'

Alec stood up. 'I'll fetch my coat.'

But Florence shook her head. 'No. I've nowt to be afraid of here, now, and Alec has to go to work in the morning.'

Florence wrapped her shawl over her head to keep off the rain and set off alone through the nearly empty streets. This was the evening of a working day and most people had gone to bed. She still had a trim figure and walked quickly, eager to find this Emily Jackson who was not Emily Jackson at all, to tell her that she was the grand-daughter of Nathaniel Franklin, one of the richest men on the river. She could see that river ahead of her now, at the bottom of the steep street down which she was descending. The water glistened black and oily under the gaslight, seen through the fine rain that was like the mist on that night so long ago. She might have stepped back twenty years. Florence shivered. Now on her right was the cul-de-sac, a place of deep shadows, and at the end of it the lit windows of the Clipper. She turned in and the darkness closed around her. Almost there . . .

A hand came from behind her to wrap itself around her mouth as Digby Gamblin stepped out of the doorway. He had been in the Clipper earlier, hidden in the crowd, when Emily had told Joe and Sadie, 'I'll be late back.' He had waited for her return as he had waited once before, but this time he would not fail. He would not try to have his way with her. He was there to make an end, had seen the beshawled figure stepping lightly, and pounced.

Now he said, voice cracking with hate and madness, 'You've destroyed me! Lost me my position and ruined me! Now you'll pay for it, you bitch!' And he sank the knife to the hilt into her back, again and again. The woman in his arms slumped like a sack of sand and he let her fall on to the wet cobbles. Only then did he see her face. He stared stupidly, jaw hanging loose, as it was borne in upon him that he had killed the wrong woman. He left her and ran.

As Gamblin burst out of the cul-de-sac he almost ran into Emily and David, but swerved and sped away, faster than he had since he was a youth twenty years before. In seconds the darkness had hidden him again.

'That was Gamblin, the man who attacked me years ago,' Emily said.

David stared into the darkness, listening to the fading beat of Gamblin's flying feet. 'What has he been up to?'

'Nothing good.' Emily was sure of that. She wondered if he had wrought some kind of mischief on the Clipper and quickened her pace. 'I haven't seen him for years. I thought he'd gone for good.' Now she could see the Clipper, which did not seem damaged, and she hurried on, David at her side. They almost fell over the body.

'Oh, my God, it's a woman,' David exclaimed.

Emily sank on to her knees. 'She's been stabbed.' She

could see the knife, its hilt and part of the blade projecting from the body.

David had gone to the door of the Clipper and now shouted inside, 'Fetch a light out here and quick! There's a woman hurt badly!'

'She's alive!' Emily called. Her head was bent close to the woman's and she could feel her breath and hear its rasp. She lifted her head as Joe Kirby came running with a lantern fetched from the cellar. Its light showed Emily's face smeared with the blood that oozed from the woman's mouth. And Florence's eyes were open.

She could remember all that had happened, all that was said. She did not understand it, except that some stranger had taken her for someone else. She was in pain and shock. All the light had gone out of her life when Harry died and she had only a feeble grasp on it now, but she recalled why she had come here and what she had to say to this girl, whom she had seen earlier coming out of the Clipper. She spoke in gasps: 'I was on the quay . . . that night. I watched. I was coming to tell you, Emi-ly, Emma . . .' Her head lolled, and the rasping stopped.

Emily felt for a pulse in the woman's neck but found none. 'She's gone.'

The men standing around her shook their heads. David asked, 'What did she say at the end?'

Emily shook her head, puzzled. 'She said she was coming to tell me something but she never said what it was. She knew my name but I don't remember seeing her before.'

'I remember Gamblin and he'll hang for this,' David said grimly.

In her bed that night, Emily wondered at the message from the woman who had died, and how she had known her. She remembered the choked words: 'I was coming to tell you, Emily.' Only she had gasped on the name so it came out: 'Emi-ly.'

Emily sighed. Now she would never know.

In Kimberley, South Africa, one-time seaman Fred Dinsdale decided to sell his team of oxen. He had made enough money to last him the rest of his days and it was time for him to retire and go home.

Chapter Seventeen

November 1907. Monkwearmouth.

Once into Church Street and away from the scene of his crime, Gamblin slowed to a walk so as not to attract attention. He was sane now, and frightened. He knew that with two witnesses to swear to his flight from the cul-de-sac he would be convicted and pay the maximum penalty. If he was caught the hangman's noose awaited him. He had to get away and knew of only one man who could help him.

At the Franklin house the gates were shut. He could have asked the gatekeeper to let him in – Darnley, the man he had put there, still held the post – but Gamblin would trust no one now, except the one man he had to trust. Then fortune smiled on him. The Humber Tourer came rolling down the drive with an overcoated figure at the wheel. Its horn blared and Darnley hurried out of the lodge to swing the gates wide open and stand with a finger to the peak of his cap. As the motor-car eased forward between the gates, the light from the windows of the lodge washed over it and revealed Bradley Carver, gloved and capped, at the wheel.

Gamblin guessed he would be heading towards the town, so he turned and ran back that way. In seconds the motor-car came puttering up behind him, he swung round into its path and waved frantically. The Humber slowed and halted with a squeal of brakes and Bradley bawled, irritated by this fool of a peasant, 'What the hell d'you think you're doing?' Then he recognised Gamblin in the light of the Humber's carbide lamps and his tone sharpened: 'What do you mean by coming here? What do you want?'

Gamblin clung to the Humber's bonnet for support. His flight and his fear had left him exhausted and he panted, 'You've got to help me. I killed a woman tonight. I went after that Emily Jackson—'

'*What?*' Bradley jumped down from the driving seat and strode round the bonnet of the motor-car to grab Gamblin by the collar. He was enraged but looked about him before he spoke to see if they could be overheard. 'You killed her?'

'No, I got the wrong one,' Gamblin muttered. 'Caught her outside the Clipper, was sure it was her, coming back at that time, but it was somebody I'd never seen before. I ran for it but as I came out o' the street that Emily Jackson saw me. She was with some big feller. They both got a good look at me. Two witnesses. No good me trying to get somebody to swear I wasn't there.'

'I won't,' Bradley said grimly.

Gamblin pulled himself out of Bradley's grasp. 'You'll have to help me! You and that lass together have ruined me. She got old Franklin to give me the sack but it was your fault in the beginning when you made me throw out her folks. I won't keep quiet, you won't frighten me into it.' Now he feared the law more than he did Bradley Carver. He added cunningly, 'If they take me I'll tell them everything: how you fiddled the Franklin job for me for the right price, how you told me to kick out old Jackson and his family – including Emily. How d'you think your uncle will treat you then? Keep you on as the boss of the Franklin yard and his ships? Not likely! It'll be *you* tossed out on the street! And what about her? I saw you looking at her when you brought her back to the Clipper the other day and I could read that look. But you won't bed Emily Jackson once I start talking!'

'*Shut up!*' Bradley hissed. 'I said I wouldn't swear to an alibi for you because we both know it would not be believed with two witnesses against you, but helping is another matter. I can and I will. I won't pretend we're friends but we've helped each other before and we need to stick together.'

'Aye? So what are you going to do?'

'Be quiet a minute.' Bradley thought for a few seconds, brain racing, sorting through alternatives, looking for the simple answer. Then he snapped his fingers: 'A ship. She's lying in the river now and sailing with the tide tonight, bound for Buenos Aires. I know her skipper and he'll take you without asking any questions.' He slapped Gamblin on the back. 'Come on! Get into my car and I'll take you there now.'

Gamblin obeyed, partly relieved but still fearing capture. When Bradley brought out a long motoring coat and cap from the back seat, Gamblin put them on without demur, glad of the disguise. Bradley turned up the collar and tweaked down the peak of the cap so Gamblin's features were hidden. 'That's better,' he said. 'Your own mother wouldn't recognise you now.' And no one would be able to swear that they had seen the fugitive in his Humber.

He drove it down into the town, across the bridge and through the narrow streets until Gamblin grabbed at his arm: 'This is the way back to the Clipper!'

'It's the road to the river that goes past the Clipper. We're going this way because that's where I'm going after I've got you aboard. Keep your head! No one would imagine you'd go back to the Clipper tonight after what you did. Just sit still.'

Gamblin complied, though he found it hard when the Humber rolled past the cul-de-sac that held the public house. There were several lights in the street where he had launched his attack and a small crowd with a policeman in helmet and cape keeping them at a distance. He glimpsed this in the second it took them to pass. Then the cul-de-sac was behind them and they were driving down to the quay.

Bradley stopped short of it, in a patch of deep shadow, and switched off the engine. 'We'll walk from here.'

He climbed down from the car, taking with him one of the battery torches that had come out in 1900. Bradley's was large and heavy. Gamblin came with him, saying, 'I'll need some money.'

Bradley took out his wallet, stripped it of the notes it held and handed them to Gamblin. 'There you are.' As Gamblin put away the money, Bradley automatically checked the torch. Its beam died as he switched it off. He remembered then that it didn't matter whether it worked or not.

'What's that for?' Gamblin asked.

'To signal the ship to send a boat for you.' Bradley led the way out on to the cobbled quay, Gamblin at his side and eager to be away, casting nervous glances behind him. The town hall clock struck midnight, the chimes tolling across the dark river.

The clock had been silent for some minutes when Bradley Carver returned alone from the river. He still had the torch but it was bent now. He would get rid of it elsewhere. He replaced the motoring coat and cap in the car and put the banknotes back in his wallet. Then he started the Humber and drove up to the Clipper. There, he pushed through the little crowd, and stared down at the blanket-covered body. 'What's happened here, Constable?' he asked.

The policeman saluted. He recognised Bradley Carver, manager of the Franklin affairs. 'A nasty murder, sir. A woman stabbed to death.'

'Good God!' Bradley said, in feigned horror. He passed into the Clipper and found Emily, expressed his sympathy for her awful experience, his congratulations on the purchase of the *Sea Princess* and his best wishes for her voyage.

Emily, her mind full of the strange woman's strange message, was touched by his concern. 'Thank you.' She reached out to squeeze his hand. 'I'll miss you. You've been a good friend.'

'Always,' Bradley promised, and kissed her fingers.

Driving home he thought that the day had gone well – and as he had predicted the previous evening. When Emily failed, as he knew she would, he would not lose financially because he had not put in any of his money. She, though, would be bankrupt, needing someone – and he would be there. He had noted the softness of her gaze when they parted. Earlier, when Gamblin had begun to confess his crime and Bradley had thought his victim had been Emily, he had known both rage and loss – but he had been angered by loss of his revenge.

Now he was sure that Emily, and vengeance, would be his.

Chapter Eighteen

November 1907. At sea and St Petersburg.

'Welcome to Russia,' Tom Peterson said drily.

Emily stood at his side in the lee of the wheelhouse of
the *Sea Princess* and screwed up her eyes against the snow
driving in on the wind. It was a bitterly cold morning, grey
sky over grey sea. Both were warmly wrapped in heavy
coats and gloves but they still felt the bone-biting cold.
Emily could see ahead the onion domes of the city of St
Petersburg. Her fate would be decided there. She had to
obtain the freedom of her ship held there – or face ruin.
She had set out with high hopes but as the days passed fear
had nibbled away that confidence because she had had too
much time in which to think about her predicament. She
felt very lonely.

During the first two days at sea she had sat out on a
deck-chair on the lee side with Tom for company, but

then the weather became bitterly cold and she was confined to her cabin or the tiny saloon where they all ate. She found this tiresome and dull, and prevailed upon Oldroyd, the dour Yorkshireman who was mate of the *Sea Princess*, to allow her to take the wheel. He was apprehensive of what the Captain would say, but remembered that this young woman was part-owner of the ship. He called down the voice-pipe to the cabin where David was resting, 'Miss Jackson wants to take the helm.'

After a startled silence, David replied, 'Well, keep an eye on her.'

Two hours later Emily relinquished the wheel, her arms and shoulders aching, but Oldroyd told the Captain, 'She did right well.' So Emily often stood a trick at the helm, although she was always supervised. For the rest, Tom Peterson was good company but David Walsh spent much of his time in the wheelhouse and the rest in his cabin. He joined them for meals but was taciturn. Emily told herself it did not matter to her how he behaved: they were only business partners.

She looked up at him now, where he stood squeezed into the little wheelhouse with the seaman at the helm. The rest of the space was filled by the Russian pilot, who was bearded and wrapped in huge oilskins, a fur cap on his head. David seemed to sense her gaze on him, glanced down at her, and his lips twitched in a faint smile. It was meant to be encouraging and drew a smile from Emily in return. But then his eyes went back to watching the ship's course.

'From the look of the weather it seems our Finnish friend may be proved right,' Tom said beside her.

Emily nodded. They had spoken to the Captain of a Finnish ship as they passed through the Kattegat, between Sweden and Denmark, into the Baltic. 'The ice will come early, I think,' he had bellowed morosely across the narrow neck of water separating the two ships. Now she replied to Tom, 'We'll have to get out earlier, then.' Her confidence had been eroded but not her determination.

But as they neared St Petersburg that determination was challenged again. Emily noticed an oddity in the water parted by the bow of the *Sea Princess*. 'You mean that soapy look?' Tom asked.

'Yes. Can you see it, too?'

'That's the onset of ice. My grandfather told me about it. The water is freezing into tiny crystals and later they'll join up together.'

The *Sea Princess* plodded on the long approach to the port and was nosed into a berth by a fussy tug, just a hundred yards from where the *Margaret Glenn* lay, tied up to the same quay. As soon as the *Sea Princess* was secured, Emily walked along the quay with Tom and David, treading through snow that had turned to slush. A big Russian sentry stood guard on the gangway of the *Margaret Glenn*, his long greatcoat almost covering his high boots, the bayonet fixed to his rifle standing above his fur hat. He barred their path when they tried to go aboard.

Emily was surrounded by the three tall men as Tom,

stumbling over a Russian word here and there, argued with the soldier. She had briefly lost that feeling of loneliness, absorbed now in what was going on. And David was at her side.

'It's no good,' said Tom disgustedly. 'He only knows one word – "No." He won't let us aboard.'

But then a voice hailed from the deck above them: 'Below! I'll come and talk to him!' A short, wiry man in reefer jacket over woollen jersey, wool trousers tucked into sea-boots, came hurrying down the gangway and introduced himself: 'Kilkenny, the mate. Miss Jackson! Lord, ma'am, it's good to see you but—' He broke off then to slap the sentry on the shoulder and bawl, 'All right, Ivan,' he waved at Emily and the two men, 'friends,' and tapped his own chest, 'With me!' Then, to clinch the matter, he pulled a bottle out of the pocket of the reefer jacket and passed it to the sentry. The Russian took a good swig, wiped his mouth on the back of his hand, then waved them on. As they followed Kilkenny up the gangway he stuffed the bottle back into his pocket and explained, 'Vodka. Oils the wheels.'

Now they were on the deck and David went straight to the foremast. A piece of paper was nailed there and he studied it. Then he looked down at Emily. 'It's in Russian but it's like notices I've seen before. I think it says the ship is not to move without the express permission of the Port Captain. Right, Tom?' He got a nod of agreement – Tom had also scanned the notice.

'That's what the lad from the embassy said,' Kilkenny

put in. 'He talks their lingo as if he was born to it. But come up into the saloon, Miss. It's a bit cold for you out here. I'll tell you all about it and make you a cup o' tea. The cook's ashore and getting drunk, I wouldn't be surprised.' They crowded into the little saloon, which was under the wheelhouse and warmed by a stove. They sat round the table while Kilkenny busied himself in the little galley, making tea that was brown, strong and sweetened with a dollop of condensed milk. He talked as he worked. 'The truth is, ma'am – and the skipper said I was to tell you the truth and no covering up – and I might as well tell it anyway for you'll soon hear it from others – there was a bit of bad luck to it but it was the fault of Captain Ruddock. We were easing out into the stream and I was at the wheel. The skipper said to me, "Cast off the tow." I said, "You'd better let me stay at the wheel, skipper." And he said, "I can steer my own ship when I want to, always could, always will. Do as you're told."'

Kilkenny sipped at his tea. 'So I went forrard, saw the men cast off the tow and the tug veered away. I was looking for the pilot we were supposed to pick up and I think the old man was as well. Then this steam yacht shot out of a gap between two ships and we ran into her – though we should ha' been able to take avoiding action. All it cost us was some paint but we stove in her side.'

He paused there and Emily said, 'I'd like to speak to Captain Ruddock. Where is he? When will he be back?'

Kilkenny sighed. 'He's in jail, ma'am. He'd been at the bottle. They could tell when they came aboard and there were witnesses who saw him at it. On the day we sailed he had a few glasses with some Russians he'd been drinking with while we were lying here, so they jailed him and impounded the ship. He told me to send that cable so I signed his name to it.' He was silent a moment then added sadly, 'I'm sorry it's bad news, ma'am.'

Again, Emily thought. First the ship being impounded, then the ice coming early, now her captain behind bars. It seemed the fates had taken against her, were intent on her destruction. But her first thought now was for her skipper: 'How is Captain Ruddock?'

'He's well enough now,' Kilkenny assured her. 'Has a cell to himself. The grub isn't what he's used to but as a seafaring man he's had worse. The same goes for the two fellers in hospital.'

'Which two?'

'Two of the lads were working up on the fo'c'sle. They were thrown off in the collision. One's got a broken leg and the other fractured his ankle. But, like I said, they're comfortable enough.'

The disasters were still piling up. When would they end? Emily wondered.

'That'll leave us short-handed when we sail,' David said savagely.

The remark and the set of his jaw cheered Emily. Her partner was not giving up. She was still not used to thinking of this tall, close-mouthed man as her partner, albeit in this one venture – they had been at odds for too long and would never see eye to eye, she was certain of that. But she was glad he was with her now.

They heard a clatter of feet on the ladder leading from the deck up to the saloon and Kilkenny yanked open the door. 'Ah! It's you, sir. Come on in.' He stood aside and a young man entered. He wore a heavy overcoat that seemed of better cut than those worn by the Russians. He was tall and pink-cheeked, and took off his fur hat as he stepped into the saloon. His eyes widened when he noticed Emily. 'This is the gentleman from the embassy – Mr Merridew,' Kilkenny said.

'Miss Jackson, isn't it?' Merridew beamed at her and held out his hand. 'I looked for you on the *Sea Princess* but they told me you'd come here. Jolly nice to meet you, ma'am, though it's an awful shame about the circumstances.' He shook her hand, then those of the others, and settled on the leather sofa beside Tom and David. 'The ambassador told me to give you every assistance. Do you know the situation here?'

'I've just told them,' Kilkenny said.

'I see.' Merridew's tone was neutral, as if he thought there might be more to the 'situation' than the mate knew. 'I may be able to add a little background information. In recent years there's been a lot of unrest in St Petersburg. They have a new parliament just sitting now, and hopefully that will improve matters, but I'm not sure. Then Russia lost the war with Japan, and there was that incident a couple of years ago when their fleet fired on our fishing-boats in the belief that they might be

Japanese. Relations are still a little strained between ourselves and the Russians.' He took a breath, then went on apologetically, 'Add to this that the yacht your ship rammed is the pride and joy of the Grand Duke Maximilian and you'll see why they're so angry about it. He really is very annoyed.'

'So they're having a dig at Ruddock and his ship because they're British,' Emily interpreted.

'Afraid so,' Merridew admitted sadly.

'So what can we do?' Emily asked.

'I'm afraid we just have to wait until they've cooled off a bit, but these things take time.'

That phrase 'cooled off' reminded Emily of the ice. They did not have time to wait. David made the point for her, biting off the words impatiently: 'In a few days' time we could all be iced in here for the winter. When ships aren't earning money they're losing it, and we could easily be ruined if we have to wait for the Russians to change their minds.'

'I do understand and I'm awfully sorry,' Merridew said. 'I assure you, the ambassador himself has talked to the Port Captain and the Grand Duke – the Captain takes his orders from the Grand Duke, of course – but he was unable to move them.'

Emily wondered if he had made her position clear. Had he said, 'Miss Jackson will be ruined if you do not release her ship'? 'You said you were to give us every assistance?' she asked.

'I am.' Merridew nodded firmly.

'Then you can take me to see Captain Ruddock.' Emily stood up. 'And then the Grand Duke.'

Merridew rose. 'Of course. Mind you, I can't promise we'll see Maximilian, but I'll try,' he said.

'I don't like the idea of you walking about here on your own,' David said.

Emily was nettled. 'I'm not a child, and I won't be on my own. Mr Merridew will be with me.'

'Miss Jackson will be quite safe, I promise you,' Merridew assured them.

David eyed him. 'I'll hold you to that. I have to see to some formalities – paperwork – and then ask our agents here if they can find us a cargo.' He shouldered out of the narrow doorway and started down the ladder to the deck.

'I want to look up some relatives of mine. Guess I'll see you all later,' Tom said, and to Merridew, 'You take good care of her.' Then he followed David down the ladder.

Emily smiled at Merridew. 'If you are quite ready?'

'Yes, of course, Miss Jackson.'

'You can call me Emily.'

His cheeks now were slightly pinker. 'Thank you – Emily.'

She turned to Kilkenny. 'Thank you for the tea.'

He put a finger to his brow in salute. 'You're welcome, ma'am.'

She descended the ladder and Merridew followed.

They saw Ruddock in a bare little room with a burly, bearded gaoler standing by. Ruddock was apologetic and shame-faced: 'I'm sorry to have caused you all this trouble, ma'am, sorry I lied to you and Mr Carver.'

Emily asked, 'Mr Carver?'

'I didn't tell him about my drinking, either,' Ruddock confessed. 'Ye see, ma'am, I started boozing a lot when I was out foreign and the finish of it was that I lost my last command for drunkenness. But I told Mr Carver, like I told you, that I'd been sick with the malaria. When you gave me the *Margaret Glenn*, I kept away from the bottle while we were at sea, but when we were lying here I got to talking to some fellers – Russkies but sailormen like meself – and they were at this vodka. I got into the habit of having a few with them and I did that the day I sailed. I suppose Kilkenny told you the rest. He's a good lad – no blame attaches to him – and if I'd listened to what he said I'd ha' been all right.' He waited, miserably, for her verdict.

'Thank you for being honest with me now, at any rate. Do you want for anything?' Emily said.

Ruddock had expected a tongue-lashing. 'Good o' you to take it like that, ma'am,' he muttered. 'No, I don't need anything, except maybe a book or two. But what about the ship? Are you going to get her out?'

Emily stood up. 'Her and you, I hope. And meanwhile Mr Merridew will find you some books, I'm sure.'

Outside in the streets covered with icy slush, Merridew said, 'He seemed more cheerful when we came away. I think that went quite well.'

'Yes.' But Emily knew she had now to honour that

promise, made on the spur of the moment to have Ruddock freed.

Their call on the Grand Duke Maximilian was less successful. They waited interminably in an anteroom in the ducal palace, which was high-ceilinged and lavishly furnished. A pallid, dark-suited secretary, who spoke English, finally came to ask their business with the Grand Duke. On learning it concerned the *Margaret Glenn* and Captain Ruddock, he flatly refused an interview and waved them away. Merridew argued heatedly but gained only a grudging half-promise: 'Maybe tomorrow.' Then they were ushered out. He sighed and apologised, 'I was afraid it would be like that.'

Emily turned up the collar of her coat against the cold. 'We'll try tomorrow.'

'I must tell you,' Merridew warned, 'that was only to put us off. Tomorrow will probably be the same.'

'We'll see about that,' Emily said determinedly. But she was not so brave inside.

Merridew entertained her to luncheon at the English club and introduced her to a number of British business-men trading in the city. She soon became the centre of a little group, the men clustering around the chair where she sat, coming at first out of curiosity then admiring. As she left on Merridew's arm she heard one say, 'Damned pretty girl. Charming,' but she reflected wryly that she had not succeeded in charming her way past the Grand Duke's secretary, let alone rescued her ship or Ruddock.

At Emily's request they visited the two injured seamen

in hospital and found them comfortable in body and able to travel, though not to work, and uneasy in their minds. 'When d'ye reckon we might get home, ma'am?'

'Soon,' Emily answered firmly. And told herself that she had again promised what she could see no way of delivering.

Merridew presented her with a fur hat and took her for a drive in a cab along the broad, two-mile stretch of the Nevsky Prospekt, the main street running right through the centre of the city. The cabbie was barrel-bodied in a peasant's wraparound coat that came down to his feet and the bulk of him served to shield his two passengers from the worst of the cold wind. Emily listened to Merridew's enthusiastic commentary but took in little: her mind was still churning over her problems.

In the late evening Merridew escorted her back to the *Sea Princess*. A paraffin lamp lit the head of the gangway and a seaman stood there on watch. 'I will be safe enough from here,' she told Merridew.

However, he was reluctant to leave her. 'Would you like me to pilot you around tomorrow? Or would you rather rest?'

Rest? Emily could have laughed hysterically, but she smiled again. 'I'd like that, and thank you for today. You were a great help.' She crossed the gangway to the deck of the *Sea Princess*, then turned and waved to him where he stood bareheaded on the quay. He flourished his hat and she turned away, wished the seaman on watch goodnight and climbed the ladder to the saloon.

David and Tom Peterson sat at the table and rose as she entered. Tom said, 'We were thinking of setting out to search for you. Have you had any luck?' He was the more obviously relieved to see her, but David had smiled briefly, eyes crinkling, when he saw her.

'No,' Emily replied. She sat down between them and related the events of her day.

'Not good,' Tom said gravely. 'I met those relatives of mine and they were as pleased to see me as a pup with two tails. They wanted me to stay with them tonight but I said I had to get back to – to the ship.' Emily noticed the momentary hesitation, guessed what he had been about to say, and looked down at the table. 'They told me a lot about the set-up here. Like that guy Merridew said, the Grand Duke is one of the people who run this town – this country, for that matter. They gave me a lot of gossip about all the high-ups and what they're up to – or alleged to be up to. Maximilian has a "friend", the Countess Leonie, and they grin when they say "friend". But at the end of it, the problem is still the same, the Grand Duke is the guy to get to.'

Emily was only too aware of that.

David yawned and stood up, his head brushing the deckhead. 'I think I've got a cargo for us.'

'That's marvellous,' Emily tried to enthuse.

David read her thoughts: 'But a cargo for the *Sea Princess* won't make up for the loss of the *Margaret Glenn*.' Then he added, 'And it isn't certain yet but I hope to confirm it tomorrow. Goodnight.'

The subdued little group broke up, and Emily turned into her bunk. Though leg-weary and worn out by the day and its frustrations, she lay awake for a long time, her worries chasing through her mind. When she finally slept it was to dream restlessly of running through snow, pursued by a monstrous Grand Duke who wielded a cabbie's whip, bellowing, 'No!'

Ada lay awake in her bedroom in Sunderland. She wondered if Emily was still in St Petersburg with those Russians. She told herself she mustn't worry, the doctor had said so: 'Your heart is weak. You must be careful and try not to worry.'

She had not told Emily when she had seen her briefly before she sailed. Nor had she ever told the girl of her origins. Ada had always flinched from that, in the beginning because she has feared that Emily might be taken to the orphanage but later because of the effect it might have on her to learn that she was a foundling. Ada still could not contemplate telling Emily to her face, but suppose . . .

She decided to write her a letter, telling Emily the truth and begging her forgiveness for keeping her in the dark.

The decision made, Ada was more at ease and finally slept.

Chapter Nineteen

The next morning Emily shivered, not from the cold, though that was sharp enough, but because thin ice was floating on the river Neva. She stood at the rail of the *Sea Princess*, looking out over the water, and Tom came to stand by her side. 'It doesn't look good,' he said heavily.

'No,' agreed Emily.

'That's called pancake ice,' he went on reluctantly. 'It forms in plates that join up to make a continuous sheet. When the sheet is thick enough, we won't be going anywhere.'

Emily stared down at the ice that threatened to lock her in. 'Thanks, Tom,' she said.

He glanced at her. There was colour in her cheeks from the breeze and she was smiling. 'What for?'

'For coming all this way to help. You could have found

better things to do.' Emily had learnt during those summer months that he was a very rich man.

'No, I couldn't.'

The thought came to Emily that if she was ruined by this adventure she could still live the life of a woman who was wealthy and loved. If that was what she wanted.

She turned away. 'I think it's time for breakfast.'

Nightingale, the cook, poked his bald head out of the little galley. 'Cap'n Walsh went ashore upwards of an hour ago.'

'Thank you.' David must be pursuing his cargo for the homeward run, Emily thought. But what about that already loaded aboard the *Margaret Glenn*? If she did not sail the pit props in her hold and stacked on her deck would have to be transferred to another vessel, doubtless at Emily's expense. She tried to push the thought from her mind and went into the warmth of the saloon for breakfast.

Before she and Tom had finished eating Merridew had come aboard. He accepted a cup of coffee from Nightingale. 'I hope we'll have better luck today,' he said.

The three went first to the office of the Port Captain but found him as intractable as before. He glared stonily ahead of him, answered, 'No,' to all their questions and dismissed them after a few minutes.

'We'll try the Grand Duke,' Merridew said.

They trailed Maximilian through that long day as he fulfilled his engagements. From his palace they followed him to the Admiralty, its white and yellow stone distinctive against the dark red of the other public buildings. Then they crossed the Neva by the bridge to the Sts Peter and Paul Cathedral, where he went to worship. Then he returned over the bridge to visit the Nicholas Military Academy on the other side of the city. Everywhere they went they sought an audience with him but without success. All the way they were fenced off by his escort of burly, bearded Cossacks and finally, back in his palace, forced to wait for an hour. Then they were told by the cold-eyed secretary that his master was receiving no one else that day. Merridew reasoned and Tom argued, both in Russian, and they wrung some further comments from the man but not admission to the Grand Duke. Eventually they were escorted out.

Merridew hailed a cab to take them back to the ship. As they rolled smoothly over the surface of the Nevsky Prospekt, then on to the cobbles where the *Sea Princess* lay, Emily asked, 'What did he say at the end?'

'That Maximilian was going to the theatre,' Merridew replied.

'Yeah. He'd finished work for the day because he was going to see Pavlova at the Marinsky,' Tom added.

Merridew explained tactfully, 'Pavlova is—'

'A ballerina,' Emily interrupted.

'Sorry. I wasn't sure . . .' Merridew tailed off.

Tom said, 'He got a bit sniffy when you asked if the Countess would be in the party.'

Merridew grinned, 'That was just to annoy him, to let him know he couldn't just walk over us, we could still get a dig in. You see, I knew very well that the Countess would be there. Maximilian is a widower and the Countess is a widow. She refuses to marry him because she won't be subject to court etiquette, but they – er – live as man and wife.'

Emily smiled at his embarrassment: 'I do know it goes on, Mr Merridew.'

They were at the ship and Merridew handed her down from the cab. 'Do you wish me to escort you again tomorrow?'

Emily was staring at the *Sea Princess*, then shifted her gaze to the *Margaret Glenn*. All she had was tied up in those ships. 'Never mind tomorrow,' she said. 'Can you change and call for me in half an hour? I want you to take me to the theatre.'

'Well, of course . . .' A bewildered Merridew stared after her as she crossed the gangway and went to her cabin.

Nevertheless, he was there, in evening dress, when Emily swept down the gangway again. Despite the cold she carried her coat over her arm because she had hurried down when she saw Merridew arrive in a cab. She wore a long, high-necked dress of white silk and lace that set off her dark beauty. She was glad she had brought that dress, had almost left it in her wardrobe at the Clipper. Now she saw its effect on Merridew, who was round-eyed. She smiled, 'Brrr! Will you help me on with this, please?' She held out the coat and he was quick to slip it on to her, slow to let it go. 'Thank you. Now I'm ready.' She switched her radiant smile from him to David and Tom, who were standing at the door of the saloon and peering down at her, admiring but bemused. She had given them no explanation, no hint of her plan. Merridew handed her up into the cab, which clattered away along the quay.

The Marinsky Theatre was full but Merridew had pulled strings and secured them seats in the stalls. As the orchestra was tuning up he murmured: 'There's the Grand Duke Maximilian in his box. The Countess Leonie is seated to his right and just behind his shoulder.'

At the end of the first act Merridew pulled another string. He wormed his way through the crowd in the foyer, past men in evening dress or ornate uniforms, and women in flowing, silken gowns with shoulders bare, glittering with jewels. He came to where the Countess sat sipping tea, and Emily, heart pounding — so much hung on this meeting — hissed at him, *'Leave us alone!'*

Then he was bowing and saying, 'May I present Miss Emily Jackson?'

The Countess, Emily saw, was in her thirties and a beauty, with lively eyes that could change in an instant from amusement to piercing interrogation. Now she smiled condescendingly. 'A young lady touring?' The words were addressed to Merridew in fluent though heavily accented English.

Emily answered, clearly and a little loudly, because she was nervous — and annoyed by the condescension: 'I am here on business.'

The finely arched brows of the Countess twitched upwards. 'Business?'

'If the Countess will excuse me?' Merridew put in.

'Of course.' She waved him away and tapped a spindle-legged chair by her side with her fan. 'Come and sit here.' And when Emily was seated: 'What business would that be?'

Emily answered, 'I am an innkeeper.'

The Countess laughed, 'So?'

'But I also learned the skills of shipowning. With the money I earned I bought a share in a ship. Now I own one and have a half-share in another.'

The Countess was impressed. 'And who owns the other half?'

'Her master, Captain David Walsh.' Emily saw no harm in divulging that.

Now the dark eyes were piercing. 'And is he your master?'

'No!' Emily replied quickly, blushing and furious with herself for it.

'Oho!' The Countess smiled. 'You won't admit but you don't need to. And you aren't being fair – everybody knows who is my man.' Her face softened at the thought of him, but then she added sardonically, 'And everyone talks about it.'

Emily took a breath and plunged in: 'I would like to talk about him.'

The eyes under the arched brows were wary now: 'Oh?' They switched away from Emily, because Merridew had returned to hover uncertainly. The Countess dismissed him impatiently: 'Later!' Then her gaze returned to Emily. It was steely now: 'What have you to say to Maximilian?'

'My two ships lie in the harbour here . . .' Emily began.

She returned to the *Sea Princess* very late, and found David and Tom in the saloon, curious to know what had happened, but she only said, 'The ballet was splendid and Pavlova was marvellous.' That was true enough: she would never forget Pavlova's ethereal elegance. The rest she would keep to herself. She saw no sense in raising hopes that might lead to disappointment. She gave them a Mona Lisa smile and retired to her cabin.

Next day Merridew took her sight-seeing, and they returned to the ship in the late afternoon. David and Tom had spent the day overseeing the loading of a cargo of timber into the hold of the *Sea Princess*. They met her on the quay, jubilant as they ran to the cab. 'We had a visit from the Port Captain just a half-hour ago!' Tom burst out. 'He came aboard all smiles and told us we were free to sail the *Margaret Glenn* whenever we wanted. He took the sentry away with him.'

'We slipped him a vodka or two and he told us the Grand Duke had had a change of heart,' David put in. 'He doesn't even want us to pay for the damage to his yacht. And Ruddock has been released with a ticking-off and he's aboard the *Margaret Glenn* now.' He put a big hand on Emily's shoulder and gazed down at her. 'You worked this, didn't you? How the hell did you do it?'

Emily laughed with relief and told them about the Countess, looking into David's eyes – stumbling on her words as the liquid fire ran through her. David's smile faded as he listened, realised their closeness. He released her and stood back: this girl was excited by the news, not by him. She had made it plain that he was not the man for her.

When she finished Emily had regained her composure. 'When can we sail?' she asked.

'This evening,' David replied.

The two ships cast off as the sun was setting and Merridew waved to them from the quay. Ruddock was in command of the *Margaret Glenn*, and the two injured seamen were aboard her. Tom had volunteered to ship as a hand for the voyage home to ease the undermanning, and had transferred his kit to her.

As the *Sea Princess* eased away from her berth a carriage came on to the quay, bouncing and swaying on the cobbles, to halt beside Merridew. A white-gloved footman handed down a slender woman who fluttered a scrap of a handkerchief. Emily, standing on the deck, snatched off the fur hat Merridew had given to her and waved it.

In the wheelhouse, David called down to her, 'Who's that?'

'The Countess,' Emily replied.

'He looks fine!' the woman on the quay called.

'What did she say?' David asked.

'She wished us good luck,' Emily lied.

The *Sea Princess* was out in the stream now, her stubby

bow pushing through the plates of ice. The *Margaret Glenn* was coming up astern of her. David said, 'We're just getting out in time but we shall still need all the luck we can get.'

Chapter Twenty

'She's blowing up rough!' David ran down the ladder from the wheelhouse into the saloon, ducking under the deckhead.

Emily, who had just emerged from her little hutch of a cabin, looked out at humping seas. 'So I see.' She was already bruised from being thrown about as she dressed while the ship pitched and rolled. The sky was leaden and low, the wind whipping spray from the crests of the waves – the windows of the saloon streamed with it. Emily could just see the *Margaret Glenn* labouring astern, the seas breaking over her forecastle. Tom Peterson was aboard her.

She tore her mind away from thoughts of him as David said, 'I've had the men rig lifelines along the deck but we don't want anybody out there who doesn't have to be.'

Emily looked forward to hours shut away in the saloon

and grimaced. 'I suppose we should think ourselves lucky,' she observed. All had gone well at first: they had made good time through the Baltic, despite floating ice and blizzards that reduced visibility to little more than the ship's length, but as they passed through the Skagerrak and into the North Sea, the weather had worsened dramatically.

'So far. We aren't home and dry yet.'

Nightingale poked his bald head out of the galley to say, 'I can't cook nothing in this weather. Bloody pans dance all over the stove. Got a pot o' tea, though, and a bit o' jam and bread.'

When David returned to the wheelhouse, Emily tried and failed to read as the *Sea Princess* rolled and bucketed. Instead she was busy with her thoughts as she planned ahead. Two ships were all very well, but they were small ships. If they were sold and she used her share of the proceeds to buy a bigger one, the costs would be less and the profits greater . . . She had enjoyed Tom Peterson's company all through the summer but had not allowed anything to develop beyond the bounds of friendship . . . David kept her at arm's length, and she knew that although he wanted her – she had seen it in his eyes – he had made up his mind about her and her choice of profession: this was a business partnership and there it would end.

'The *Margaret Glenn*'s signalling, skipper!' The hail came down to her from the wheelhouse as a distant siren blared, and Emily jerked back into the present. She peered out of the window of the saloon. Looking between the funnel belching smoke and the starboard side lifeboat, she could see signal flags flying on the ship labouring astern. She was further astern than she had been and Emily could see no bow-wave – the *Margaret Glenn* had stopped.

She climbed the ladder to the wheelhouse, clinging to the handrail as the ship rose and fell beneath her feet. Water had leaked into the wheelhouse – there was no keeping it out in this weather – and washed about under the gratings on which its occupants stood. Oldroyd was at the wheel and a seaman stood by the engine-room telegraph, both men in oilskins. David was in seaboots but wore only a reefer jacket. He was staring back at the flags flown by the *Margaret Glenn*, the bunting laid out flat on the wind, and now he said, 'Damn! She's flying NC – that's "In distress." Her engines have broken down.' He told Oldroyd, 'You're relieved. Simpson here can take her for a bit. You call all hands and rouse out the three-inch wire hawser. I'm going to pass her a tow.'

The mate pushed open the door of the wheelhouse, letting in the howling gale from outside and a shower of salt spray that stung Emily's face. Then the door slammed as Oldroyd let it go and she saw him drop down the ladder to the deck. He made his way forward to the forecastle, staggering over the rocking deck, hand to hand along the lifeline.

Emily did not need to ask if this was serious: David's face told her that. Tom Peterson, Ruddock and the crew were aboard the ship, which was now without power and at the mercy of the seas. 'Is there anything I can do?' she asked.

David was pulling on his oilskins. 'You can work the telegraph for Simpson to leave him free for the wheel. That's enough in this weather.' Emily remembered how her arms had ached when she had taken the wheel in a calm sea. David knotted a length of twine about the waist of his oilskins then grinned at her wryly. 'You can cross your fingers as well.'

Emily clung to the brass handles of the engine-room telegraph, ready to send any change of orders to the engineer below. Simpson stood at the wheel, a wiry little man, his legs braced as he fought to hold the ship on course. Emily saw David, with Oldroyd and the rest of the crew, out on the deck, laying out a towing hawser ready for use. He returned to the wheelhouse then to steer the *Sea Princess* in a wide circle to come up astern of the *Margaret Glenn* again then cross her bows. To do that he had to bring his ship broadside on to the seas and she heeled over as they pounded her. Emily held on to the telegraph for dear life and prayed like the rest of them.

Oldroyd threw overboard the small cask to which was fastened a light line. As the *Sea Princess* crossed ahead of the other ship the cask and line drifted down to wrap themselves around the blunt bow of the *Margaret Glenn*. Emily saw the tall figure of Tom Peterson in the bow with Kilkenny, hooking up the line and hauling it inboard. David turned the *Sea Princess* back on course again and shouted at Emily, 'Slow ahead!' She worked the handles of the telegraph. Then, as Simpson took the wheel from him, David said, 'Keep her head to the seas,' and was gone, leaping down the ladder to the deck to supervise the running out of the towing hawser. The ship was on a comparatively even keel again and her speed fell away, until she was just keeping station ahead of the *Margaret Glenn*.

The light line was hauled aboard the *Margaret Glenn* taking with it the towing hawser. Kilkenny waved, signalling that the hawser was made fast, and David raced up the ladder to the wheelhouse to take the helm again. The slack hawser – six hundred feet of it – tautened as the *Sea Princess* moved ahead. She began to feel the weight of the tow and checked for a second then eased ahead again, groaning under the pressure. David held the wheel, looked back at the tow, then ordered, 'Half ahead.'

Emily worked the telegraph again, and the ship's speed increased. 'That's enough,' he said. 'We'll hold her at that.' He handed over the helm to Simpson and said to Emily, 'You can leave Simpson to manage on his own for a bit. She's riding easier now, though I don't think we're out of trouble yet. You may as well go below and ask Nightingale if he can make some tea. We could all do with it.'

Emily realised that an hour had passed while they had fought the storm and taken the other ship in tow. She crossed the tilted gratings and cautiously descended the ladder to the saloon. She found Nightingale wedged in his galley with one foot against the base of the stove, the other on the opposite bulkhead. He held himself steady with one hand while holding a kettle on the stove with the other. 'I thought you'd all be wanting a drop and a bite, miss. I've made some sandwiches and the tea's just coming up.' The sandwiches were thick slabs of bread filled with corned beef, stacked in a square metal dish that was wedged in a corner of the cook's table. It had a rim to prevent plates sliding off in rough seas, which did not always work. The litter on the deck, awash with sea water, testified to that. It was a far cry from the kitchen of the Clipper but Emily had no complaint. She would have loved a mug of tea and a sandwich but would wait until the men had been fed. It was almost cosy in the galley after the sea-washed wheelhouse, and she saw her damp skirts steaming. But compared with David and the men out on deck . . . She shuddered.

Nightingale said, 'You take the sandwiches, miss, and I'll fetch the tea.' Emily had one foot on the bottom rung of the ladder and one hand on the handrail when the deck fell away under her. She swung by that one hand, legs flailing, to the side of the ladder, as Simpson hurtled backwards down the ladder from the wheelhouse, missing her by inches, and crashed to the deck. He lay inert, eyes closed. Emily released her hold on the handrail and went to aid him. At that instant the *Sea Princess* heeled right over to starboard and she was flung against the bulkhead to sprawl on the deck beside Simpson, water pouring down from the wheelhouse above and washing over her.

Emily gasped, winded, then realised that no one was at the helm. She struggled to her feet. Nightingale's face showed, dazed, in the door of the galley, and blood streaked his bald head where it had hit the deck. Emily was still holding the sandwich tin, now filled with water. She thrust it at him, saying, 'Look after Simpson!' then threw herself at the ladder again.

With the ship lying over on her starboard side, she had to claw her way up the ladder. In the wheelhouse she found the glass in the door on the port side had been smashed in by the sea and the wheel was spinning. She fought her way to it, grabbed it and peered out. David had said, 'Keep her head to the seas,' and Emily saw that the *Sea Princess* lay in a trough, the big waves curling over to crash down upon her. She winced and braced herself as she saw another coming now, lifting high above her, like a green glass wall, then smashing down on to the ship, which shuddered beneath her. She was up to her waist in water that tried to tear her from the wheel but she held on as the ship rose again and the water flooded away. Emily spun the wheel and the ship's head came round until she was thrusting into the breakers again. The *Sea Princess* was upright, still battered by the seas washing over her bow, but riding them. Then Emily wondered, heart plummeting, what had happened to David and the men out on deck.

She was answered almost immediately: David swung up the ladder on the port side and shouldered into the wheelhouse. He had lost his cap and his hair was plastered to his head. His face was pale under its black stubble and he stared at her in mixed relief and disbelief. 'Thank God! You're all right?'

Emily nodded and smiled weakly. He had not been

washed overboard, that was the main thing, but—'What about the men? And what happened?'

'We're all like drowned rats but nobody's hurt. That's one miracle. And what happened was that a big wave hit the *Margaret Glenn* and stopped her dead in her tracks. At the same time another hit us and threw us back and on to our side. But the tow didn't break and that was another miracle.' He looked astern and confirmed, 'She's still there. They're not having a smooth ride but they're afloat and with us.' He turned back to Emily. 'The third miracle was how you got up here to take the wheel. Where's Simpson?'

Emily told her story briefly and finished, 'I knew there was no one at the wheel so I came up here and took over.'

Now he was looking at her differently, Emily realised. She shivered and discovered she was soaked to the skin and her clothes clung to her, showing off every curve and line of her body.

David reached out to grip her by the shoulders and Emily shivered again, though this time not from the chill. He set her aside so that he could take the helm and said gently, 'You've done a marvellous job. Now go and change out of those wet clothes. Oldroyd will be up in a minute to take the helm and I will come down to see to Simpson.'

Emily picked her way down the ladder to the saloon, her legs shaking. In the wheelhouse she found Simpson sitting on the couch, dragged in there by Nightingale. He held his head in his hands but looked up as Emily entered.

He blinked at her and said thickly, 'I hear you took the wheel when I got knocked out, miss.' The source of his information, Nightingale, stood in the doorway of his galley, nodding his bloodied head.

Emily smiled. 'Yes, I did.'

'You did bloody well – begging your pardon, miss.'

She blushed at the sincerity of his praise. 'Thank you. How are you?'

'I'll be fine in a minute or two.'

Emily turned to Nightingale: 'You need to have your head seen to.'

'I must, to be out here in this lot when I could be sitting beside the fire at home,' the cook replied.

The two men guffawed, but then Nightingale said, 'Ah, well, the skipper does all the doctoring and he'll be down in a bit to see to the pair of us, I expect.'

Emily remembered the state of her dress now and went into her cabin. There she undressed and dried herself. She heard David come into the saloon, and his deep voice as he joked, 'What's wrong with you two shirkers?' Emily stood still, the towel held around her naked body.

She heard Simpson insist, 'I'm fit as a fiddle, skipper. Cookie gave me a mug o' tea and some grub. I can bear a hand wi' the rest of the lads.'

'You seem sound enough. No headache? If you get one, see me,' David replied.

'That Miss Jackson, she did bloody well,' Emily heard Simpson say.

'She did,' David agreed.

Emily felt herself blushing again and went on dressing.

Six hours later the storm eased and thereafter their passage was smooth. Twelve hours out from Sunderland, one of His Majesty's cruisers came alongside the *Sea Princess* to ask if they needed assistance. 'No, thank you,' David replied, and the cruiser went on her way, but wirelessed a report of their condition and expected time of landfall.

They towed the *Margaret Glenn* into the harbour at Sunderland in the dusk, the town sprinkled with gaslights. Crowds lined the quays to see them come in between the two piers. Both ships showed signs of their battering by the storm: the *Margaret Glenn* had shipped a great deal of water, with which her pumps could scarcely keep pace, and she lay low and listing in the river; the scars on the *Sea Princess* ranged from the smashed wheelhouse door to Nightingale's plastered head, with a number of buckled plates between.

Everyone aboard the two ships was worn out, but when they heard the cheering of the waiting crowds their hearts raced. David Walsh was at the helm and Emily beside him as tugs nudged the two ships into the quay where they lay one astern of the other. 'Ring down, "Finished with engines",' David said, and Emily swung the handles of the telegraph. The engines ceased their steady beat and the ship was still.

'Well, you did it,' David said, and Emily nodded, too full of emotion to speak. She had brought out her two ships from Russia and saved herself from ruin. The

crowds were still cheering and David said, 'That's for you
— and you deserve it.'

She preceded him down the ladder to the saloon,
which was deserted. Oldroyd and the cook had gone
ashore, as had the rest of the crew, and they had the ship
to themselves. Emily sensed his presence close behind her,
turned and found him standing over her. 'I couldn't have
done it without you,' she whispered. She had been near
exhaustion, but not now. It was as if some outside force
dictated her actions, and the blood was pulsing in her
veins, her heart thumping. She reached up to put her arms
around his neck, stood on tiptoe and kissed him. His arms
wrapped around her and he responded fiercely.

Tom Peterson had come from the *Margaret Glenn* to
offer his congratulations, but stood on the quay and
watched them up in the saloon. Then he turned and
walked away. As he had courted Emily all through that
summer, he had suspected that her heart lay elsewhere.
They had laughed together, she had not led him on, they
had been friends. He had hoped, believed, that they had
become closer during the voyage to St Petersburg, but
now he saw they had only spent more time together —
perforce. He had lost, and it was time he was gone.

In the saloon Emily clung to David, his body moulded
to hers as he lifted her. Then they were in his cabin. She
whispered, 'Wait,' uncertain.

He held her away from him, smiled, and said, 'Now
you've had enough of ships, will you marry me?'

'Enough?'

'You'll be ready to give up this shipowning business. Running the Clipper will take all your time.' He was still smiling.

'No.' Emily shook her head. 'I've not had enough nor am I selling up. I've planned what I want to do next.' And what she had intended to say to him stumbled from her now: 'I want to sell my shares in these ships and buy a bigger one.'

David released her, exasperated. 'Now you're being obstinate,' he said.

'I am not!' Emily stood straight.

'Yes, you are! It's not work for a woman. I've told you before. Did you ever hear of another woman shipowner?'

Emily pushed past him and out of his cabin. As she stormed away she threw back at him, 'And *I* told *you* there's a first time for everything.'

'It's time you saw sense and gave it up!' David shouted after her.

Emily was now on the ladder dropping down to the deck. 'Never!'

'You will one day and then you'll marry me!'

'Never! *Never!*' Emily ran down the gangway and off along the quay.

She returned to the Clipper, to be fêted by Joe and Jane Kirby, Sadie Theakstone and the men who packed the place shoulder to shoulder, to smile in return and join in the celebrations. And to go to her bed and weep.

While David Walsh told himself he'd been a bloody fool but now he could be free of the girl.

Chapter Twenty-One

'You could easily marry him. Many a girl would jump at the chance,' Emily told herself, but knew he was not for her.

Tom Peterson had come to the Clipper that morning to bid her farewell. The celebrations were over; Sadie and Joe were serving in the Sitting Room and the bar respectively. The tall young American came into the former and Emily sat down with him at a table. 'It's time I went home,' he said. 'I've checked out from the Franklin house — that Bradley Carver is a real nice guy, very hospitable. I'm not so sure about his mother. I get the feeling she says one thing and means another.'

Emily agreed with that. Bradley had come to the Clipper to welcome her home and praise her rescue of the *Margaret Glenn*. David Walsh had not appeared. Now she guessed why Tom Peterson was leaving and said, 'I'm sorry, Tom.'

He smiled lopsidedly. 'I wish you well.' Then he added, 'I still think there was something not right about the way Marie died. It's just a feeling, what we call a hunch.'

Emily thought there was no mystery, that it had been a tragedy that had left its mark on Nathaniel Franklin. She kissed Tom for the first and last time, and then he was gone.

His place was taken soon afterwards by David Walsh, who strode, cap in hand, to where Emily was helping Sadie in the Sitting Room and greeted her formally. 'Good morning. I think we have business to discuss.'

Emily sat with him at the table she had shared with Tom. David wasted no time: 'I've seen the dockyard about the repairs needed to the *Margaret Glenn*.'

Emily stiffened. 'I should have been consulted.'

David sighed. 'Yes, but their representative came to see me. He offered me a good price and we saved time and money by accepting it. Now will you agree?'

His exaggerated restraint angered Emily but she kept a hold on her tongue. 'Very well.'

'I've just talked to Worthy and he's going to seek cargoes for both ships as soon as they're seaworthy,' he went on.

Emily steeled herself. 'I'll buy your share of the *Sea Princess*,' she said.

'It's not for sale.' He had said he would marry this girl

one day. He thought there was little chance of that now but he was not going to cut the one tie between them.

'Now who's being stubborn?' Emily flared.

'I'm not. But you don't have the money. I had to buy half of that ship before you could sail for Russia.'

Reckless now, Emily said, 'I'll borrow it.'

'You'd saddle yourself with debt you'd never clear.' Then, shrewdly, David reminded her, 'You don't work that way.'

Emily sat silent for a while, staring down at her hands. Then in a low voice she said, 'I'll sell my half.'

Now David was still. She had made it clear that she wanted a clean break from him. 'All right. I'll sell my share,' he said, and as she stared, he added, 'Worthy will find a buyer for it.'

'Why have you changed your mind?' Emily demanded. 'I don't want any favours.'

'You're not getting any,' David replied curtly. 'Nor any explanation. That's my business. And you will find a new partner.'

'No. I want Worthy to sell my half-share of the *Sea Princess*, and the *Margaret Glenn*, so that I can buy one bigger vessel. The bigger the ship, the bigger the profit.'

'It doesn't always work like that but – I don't need to tell you.' He stood up. 'I think we're finished. I'll find another command. I've had offers already.' He grinned. 'The trip to Russia has been a good advertisement.'

Emily also stood, cold inside. *I think we're finished.*

Now he went on, 'I expect to be sailing soon so I'd be

glad if you would handle the paperwork for your sale and mine. We'll share the proceeds later. I'll write an authority for you to act for me and leave it with Worthy.'

Emily forced a smile. 'I'm glad you trust me.'

'I know my money is safe with you.'

He walked out, ducking under the lintel.

Emily watched him go, then returned to her work. Crying would have been easy but it would have to wait. She had the melancholy comfort of knowing she had been right in one thing: if she had relied on diplomacy in Russia she would never have recovered the *Margaret Glenn* before next spring – if then. But it seemed little consolation now.

We're finished.

Worthy was delighted when David Walsh called again. 'Of course, Captain!' He smirked. 'I will be glad to act for Miss Jackson and yourself in the sale of the ships.'

David did not like Worthy, but the man had a reputation for honesty and astute dealing. He did not know that Worthy's good name had been made by his wife, Cora, who was now dead.

As soon as David had left the office, Worthy went chuckling to put his arms around the bored and buxom Violet. 'I'll make a good commission on these sales,' he gloated.

'Oh, give over.' She pushed his hands away. 'I'm sick of this bloody typing and this bloody office. I wish we could get out o' the flaming place. You promised . . .'

Worthy beat a retreat. He had extracted several favours on the promise of a more expansive life for them when his investments paid off, but that had not happened. Violet was becoming impatient and he was increasingly worried about his financial position – or, rather, his debts.

'You've done marvellously!' Bradley Carver was in the Clipper later that morning, to repeat his congratulations. 'Everybody's talking about the girl who sailed to Russia and brought back her ship. You're famous!'

Emily contrived to smile. 'So I hear. But, really, I was very lucky.'

Bradley saw that she was unhappy about something and watched for a hint in their conversation as to the cause, but he was given none and did not probe in case he offended her. He had to play her like a fish. He had hoped that the Russian adventure would strip her of everything she had and drive her into his arms, but that had not happened. However, he would not give up, far from it. Her success had only made her – and her destruction – more desirable.

Two days later David sailed in his new command, and Emily was left alone.

Three hundred miles away, in London's East End, two men kicked in the door of an upstairs room and charged in. There was nobody to be seen in there but just to be sure they tipped over the table and the dishevelled bed.

The bigger man swore. 'Missed the bastard! The guv'nor won't be happy.'

'We'll get him,' the other snarled.

They left. If they had felt the grubby blankets they would have found them to be still warm from a body. Jaikie Nash stood in the yard below the window from which he had jumped. Ice lay on a puddle and he held his trousers, jacket and boots balled against his chest. Jesus Christ! he thought. I have to get out of this!

Chapter Twenty-Two

January 1908. Monkwearmouth.

'The winter drags . . .' That was the burden of the letter from Nathaniel Franklin in St Raphael in the South of France. Emily read it again and agreed. She sat in the living room behind the bar in the Clipper. A cheerful fire burned in the grate, but outside the window, flakes of snow flew thick and fast on the wind and clung wetly to the glass. The sky sat low, leaden and dark on the tops of the houses, each with its smoking chimney. Down on the river the men working in the shipyards moved cautiously, wary of losing their footing on ice and snow, and frozen by the wind driving in from the North Sea.

David is out there, Emily thought. She knew the name of his vessel and kept track of where he was by reading the shipping reports. He had not written and neither had she.

Emily told herself it was pointless because they could never be reconciled. She must forget him.

Her mother, Ada, was of the same opinion. She still lived in the same rooms on the other side of the Wear, refusing to leave for a better place or to come to the Clipper. Nevertheless, she had spent Christmas with Emily and noticed her unhappiness. 'What's the matter? There's something upset you. What is it? Is it a feller?' And seeing the twitch of Emily's lips: 'Aha! The bugger's let you down!' That came out triumphantly as she saw her guess was correct. But then she became worried: 'You're not expecting?'

'No!' Emily denied it but felt her face flaming, remembering the night in the saloon of the *Sea Princess*, when she almost . . .

'That's all right, then,' Ada said, relieved. 'If he's only walked out he could easily walk in again. And if he doesn't you can forget him. There are plenty more fish in the sea.'

Emily smiled now at the memory. But Christmas had not cheered her and afterwards Ada had gone home to Mrs Cassidy, who had the two rooms below hers, and all the other neighbours.

She took up Nathaniel's letter again: 'I find it very lonely here,' he had written. 'I know you are busy but if you could find time to visit me, for however short a time, you would be very welcome.' Emily peered out of the window again at the winter scene and decided she would go, for his sake – and hers. She had to get away.

She went to Worthy's office in a more buoyant mood,

cheered by the decision. He fawned on her, concealing his anxiety, fearing she had come to complain because he had not found buyers for the *Sea Princess* or the *Margaret Glenn*. 'I'm sure I'll be able to arrange transactions in the very near future. The stagnation in the shipping business at present . . .'

But Emily knew about that. 'I'm aware of the state of the market, Mr Worthy. I know I'll have to wait for a sale but I also know I'll be able to buy my next ship cheaper because of the state of the market. I came today to tell you I'm planning a holiday soon. I'm going away to the South of France for two weeks. You already have Captain Walsh's authority to act for him and I will now give you mine.'

When Emily had gone Worthy went out to where Violet sat pecking inexpertly at the typewriter with two fingers. 'We'll make a few quid out of this job,' he boasted. But not enough, he thought. He had lost too much money, was too much in debt, for one commission to save him. Absently he slid his arm round Violet and fondled her ample bosom.

'You're always pawing me!' She pushed his hand away irritably. 'This bloody job gets on my nerves. It's all right for her, stuck-up cow. She looks right through me as if I was dirt. But she's going to France. I wish I was. Anywhere to get out of this! I'd jump on a ship tomorrow.'

It was then that Worthy had the idea. It was a way for him to make a new start with Violet, and it was simple. Why hadn't he thought of it before? Beaming again, he reached out to her. 'What if I said we'd go abroad, get right away from here?'

She looked up at him, suspicious but hopeful. 'Where?'

'Hamburg, in Germany. The Hotel Salzburg. I know it.' He did not say how he knew it.

'Ooh! That sounds lovely,' Violet said. 'When?'

'Soon.' He was confident.

'Lock the door,' she said hoarsely.

That same day Emily booked her tickets to travel in forty-eight hours, which gave her time to pack and hand over the running of the Clipper to the Kirbys and Sadie while she was away. The following morning the sky had cleared and there was bright sunshine, though a bitterly cold wind knifed in from the sea. Emily had to go across the bridge into the town for some items of shopping, and it was outside the Victoria Hall that she met Lily. The slight blonde girl was heavily pregnant now and leaning on the arm of a brown-faced, stocky man in his fifties. She was her happy, perky self again: 'It's lovely living out on the Franklin estate. My Jimmy's getting on with that Billy Foster, the agent, like a house on fire.'

Emily laughed. 'I'm pleased to hear that.' But Lily's last phrase had caused a bell to toll in her mind. She shivered.

'This is Jimmy's uncle, come back from South Africa the day before yesterday.' Lily introduced him: 'Fred Dinsdale.' And to Fred: 'This is Emily Jackson, the lass I told you about that got Jimmy the job in the Franklin place.'

'Pleased to meet you, miss.' Fred shook Emily's hand and ducked his head over it in a little bow.

Lily had been eyeing Emily and now said, 'Did I see you shiver a minute ago? It's cold enough today, but are you sickening for something?'

'No. It's just what you said about a house on fire. It reminded me of another fire, the one just a year after the Victoria Hall disaster.' She nodded at the building across the street.

'That was an awful affair,' Fred said gravely. 'Nearly two hundred little bairns killed. Awful. But what was the fire you were talking about?'

'A boarding-house called Sammy's, down by the river,' Emily explained. 'It burned down on the first anniversary of the Hall tragedy.'

Fred frowned at her. 'Did it? I haven't been down that way since I got back but I supposed it would still be there. It burned down?'

'There were eight people in there and all died.'

'Hold on.' Fred's brow creased as he thought back. 'One man got out. I was in there earlier on that night but I left to join my ship. When I was coming out I met this feller, Jaikie Nash, coming in. He was with that Maggie he was married to, and her little lass. I wouldn't mistake them. They were up to owt, thieving, battery, owt for the price of a drink. And I saw Jaikie yesterday.'

Emily was trying to grapple with this, her mind whirling. 'Are you sure of the date? That you weren't in Sammy's the day before—'

'Aye!' Fred cut her off impatiently. 'It was the day I sailed. I'll always remember that, the sixteenth o' June. And there were bits in the paper about the Victoria Hall anniversary. I remember I was glad to be getting out because I wouldn't want to sleep under the same roof as those two. They'd steal your eyes today and come back for the sockets tomorrow.' He paused to catch his breath and then asked curiously, 'But what's so important about it now?'

'They found the bodies of six men, a woman and a child,' Emily explained dazedly.

'That's right.' Fred was certain. 'If a woman and bairn died in there it was Maggie and her brat.'

Emily believed him. So, she reasoned, Marie Leigh, daughter of Nathaniel, and his granddaughter had not died at Sammy's. Where had they gone? Why had their luggage been found at Sammy's – and why were Marie's rings on the fingers of the woman who had died there?

What should she do now?

'Where did you see this Jaikie?' Emily asked. 'I want to talk to him.'

Fred grinned. 'Ask the pollis. One o' them had his hand on Jaikie's collar, taking him in.'

Emily wandered aimlessly in Mowbray Park, which was almost deserted in the winter's cold, trying to come to terms with what she had learnt and decide how to act. Who could she talk to about this? Not Nathaniel, David or Tom Peterson. Though Tom's instinct seemed now to have been correct – there there *had* been something wrong with the presumed death of Marie Leigh. So who else? The answer was obvious: Nathaniel's nephew, his only relative as far as she knew, his manager and heir presumptive, Bradley Carver.

Emily found him immersed in work in the offices of the Franklin Line. He pushed back his chair, stood up and took both her hands in his. 'My dear Emily! A pleasant surprise!' He flashed a teasing grin. 'Or is this just business again?'

Emily settled in the chair he slid under her. 'Very important business, family business, your family.'

'Oh?' Bradley's smile did not flicker but inside he was wary.

Emily took a breath. 'Marie Leigh did not die in Sammy's boarding-house.'

'*Marie!*' For once Bradley was thrown off balance. 'What do you mean?'

'The woman killed at Sammy's was not Marie.' And as Bradley stared, Emily went on, 'It was a woman called Maggie with her little daughter. I've talked to a man who saw them go in that night.'

'But my uncle identified her.' Bradley objected.

'No!' Emily contradicted him. 'He told me he only identified her by her luggage and her rings. I think they were stolen by Maggie and her husband, Jaikie Nash. He was seen going into Sammy's with her that night, but he must have left because he was seen again in this town only a few days ago.' Then Emily told the full story. 'So you see what this might mean? Marie and her daughter might still

323

be alive. And the man who might tell us what happened to them is this Jaikie.'

Bradley saw that very well – and the implications for him. If either Marie or her daughter had survived, she would inherit the Franklin fortune – not he. But he had control of himself now, was thinking already how to deal with this threat. 'And this Jaikie was arrested by the police? Then they may have him still.' He leapt up from his desk. 'I'll go and have a word with this Mr Nash.'

'I'll come with you.' Emily was on her feet. 'I was going myself but I know your name will carry more weight with the police,' she explained.

Bradley had intended going alone but saw that she was determined to come with him and could think of no reason to stop her. 'Of course.' He opened the door for her.

The Humber waited outside and Bradley drove to the police station, where the sergeant at the desk said, 'Jaikie Nash? Aye, we had him, sir. He came up before the magistrate next morning, was fined five shillings for being drunk and disorderly and turned out.' But the sergeant had an address – and a warning: 'It's a bit rough down there, sir, not that they'd dare harm a lady and a gentleman like yourselves but you'll need to watch your pockets, and get somebody to keep an eye on your motor-car.'

They found the street and the small court leading off it where Jaikie Nash lived. They had to leave the Humber in the street in the care of a burly man in ragged dungarees. From there they walked through a short, noisome tunnel to reach the rubbish-strewn court, where ragged children swarmed watched by mothers at their open front doors. Jaikie Nash lived in one room off a passage, the bare boards of its floor like a drum sending their footsteps echoing up the stairwell, bringing heads to peer over the rickety banisters at the well-dressed strangers. Bradley banged on the door. 'Who is it?' a voice croaked hoarsely from within.

'Bradley Carver. I want to talk to Jaikie Nash.'

'He's not here.'

'The police said you were here, Mr Nash,' Bradley said.

'The pollis?' A note of surprise now.

'That's right.' And Bradley added, 'I'll pay you for some information.'

'What about?'

'I won't discuss my business out here for everyone to hear. Now, don't be a fool and let me in.'

There was a pause, then a key turned in the lock and the door opened. A narrow-faced, skinny rat of a man in his fifties peered out at them. Satisfied that the two outside meant him no harm, he mumbled, 'You'd better come in.' When he had closed the door behind them, he said, 'I've got to be careful. I was in trouble with some fellers down in Wapping and I thought they might ha' come after me.' His eyes shifted from Bradley to Emily and back again. 'What d'ye want, then?'

'You were in Sammy's boarding-house with a woman called Maggie on the night it burned down.'

Jaikie jerked as if he had been shot. 'I never!'

'There's no point in lying,' Bradley snapped. 'You were seen. We have a witness. You, Maggie and a child were in there. What was the child's name?'

'Tishy. She were Maggie's bairn,' Jaikie muttered.

'Not yours? Wasn't Maggie your wife?'

Jaikie shifted uncomfortably. 'No. She had the little lass already when I took up with her. Maggie took my name, Nash, because it looked more respectable.'

Bradley smiled pleasantly. 'That's understandable. And let me assure you that no harm will come to you. We only need information.' He took a handful of silver from his pocket and shook it in his palm so that Jaikie could see and hear it. Then he picked one shilling out of the pile and put it on the dirty top of the wobbly-legged table. 'You and Maggie had some clothes and other things belonging to a lady. How did you come by them?'

Jaikie's toothless mouth was working now and his eyes shifted, frightened. 'No! Not me! It was Maggie! She took the clothes! Aye, and the rings and the handbag! It was all her!'

Emily remembered the few coins found in Marie's purse. 'You took the money,' she said.

Jaikie's mouth opened and his head began to shake, but Bradley warned, 'The truth, mind, or we go to the police.'

'Aye, I took the money but that's all. Maggie had the rest and she did it. She saw the lass walking on the quay wi' just the bairn with her. It looked like she'd landed from a ship and took a wrong turning.'

Emily pictured Marie, straying on to the quay and

peering about her, alone but for the child at her side. She felt suddenly afraid of what was to come.

Jaikie was going on: 'Maggie said we could get the bag and the case off this lass but she fought, wadn't let go, and Maggie shoved her in the river and bashed her on the heid. She was floating face down but that was only her clothes keeping her up. When they got wet they'd take her down.' He paused to take a breath, eyes flicking from Bradley to Emily and back again. *'But that was Maggie! I didn't do owt!'*

Bradley put another shilling on the table: 'And then?'

Jaikie thought his plea had been accepted and breathed easier. 'We went to Sammy's. Maggie said she was going to have the clothes for her and Tishy. I went out for a drink. When I got back the place was afire.' His eyes were shifting again, but when Bradley did not challenge him, Jaikie went on, 'I thought the pollis might be looking for the stuff Maggie took off the lass and I didn't want them coming after me, so I went down to London. I've lived there ever since, only got back up here a few weeks ago.'

Bradley glanced at Emily. She was pale, seeing in her mind's eye the murder, the flight of the killers and the burning house. 'What happened to the child, the little girl?'

'I don't know.' Jaikie shrugged skinny shoulders. 'We saw this feller coming as if from Ballantyne's yard so we ran off. The little lass was all right, standing on the quay and bawling.'

Emily could picture that only too well and felt a surge

of pity for the child, who had just witnessed the drowning of her mother in the black water of the river.

Bradley took her arm. 'I think we've heard enough,' he said, and tossed a third shilling on to the table. He led Emily towards the door.

'You promised you wouldn't bring charges,' Jaikie whined.

'I'll keep my word, but shut your foul mouth and get out of the way,' Bradley snapped. He opened the door and left with Emily.

When the door closed behind them Jaikie locked it and listened to their departing footsteps on the bare boards of the passage. 'I reckon he could be a nasty piece of work,' he muttered to himself. Then he went to the table and scooped up the coins. 'Easy money. I could do wi' some more like that.'

When he heard a knock at the door, his grin broadened. 'They're back.' He hurried across to open it.

The big man outside seized Jaikie by the throat and walked him back into the room. The other man, as tall as the first but slimmer, followed, closing the door. He smiled unpleasantly at Jaikie, whose tongue protruded, the iron grip cutting off his air passage. 'We've had a hard time finding you, Jaikie, but here we are. You should never have split on the boss. The last thing he said before he went inside was: "Find that little rat Jaikie. He owes me for putting me in here." And now it's time to settle up.'

Jaikie never made a sound. The two men locked the door behind them when they left. It was two days before the local policeman, called by neighbours, broke in and found the body – and three shillings.

The car minder reported the visit of Bradley and Emily. Bradley told the police the truth, that they were trying to find the Franklin child – if she survived. 'Jaikie Nash was alive and well when we left him.'

Now Bradley paid the man in dungarees who had watched over the Humber and drove away with Emily at his side. 'We learnt most of the truth,' he said.

'He's a liar,' Emily said flatly.

'By nature,' Bradley agreed. 'And he shifted the blame on to Maggie. But I believe we now know what happened to Marie. I don't think we could get any more out of Jaikie.'

'No-o,' Emily agreed slowly, the image of the lone child still filling her mind, heartbreaking. 'The man who came from Ballantyne's yard, they saw him and ran. He must have seen the little girl. If we could trace him . . . We could ask at Ballantyne's.'

Bradley nodded but looked doubtful. 'Maybe he didn't work there, was just passing. I would have thought the yard would be shut at that time of night. And it was over twenty years ago. That's a long time to go back.'

'But it's worth it!' Emily insisted. 'We must try to find the girl, if she's alive.' Then she remembered: 'I'm leaving on a train tomorrow morning. Nathaniel wrote asking me to visit him and I'm going. Will you ask at Ballantyne's?'

'Of course,' Bradley assured her. 'If the girl is alive I'll find her.' He had already decided that. To the best of their knowledge the child *had* survived, though how and where was a mystery. He had to solve that mystery before anyone else did, because if the little girl – though she would be a grown woman now – was found and claimed her inheritance, Bradley would get nothing. There would be a bequest to him of some sort, of course, and doubtless he would keep his job running the Franklin Line and the shipyard, but that was all. The bulk of Nathaniel's fortune would go to the young woman. Was Bradley Carver to lose his birthright after twenty years of hard work? It was not to be thought of.

Emily was convinced that he would succeed if anyone could. And now she would tell Nathaniel the harrowing story of the death of his daughter, but with a message of hope – that he might still have a granddaughter.

'If she's alive I'll find her,' Bradley Carver said again, with grim determination. And he would deal with her.

Chapter Twenty-Three

JANUARY 1908. MONKWEARMOUTH.

'I'm sorry, but we can't tell you anything about who worked here at that time, Mr Carver.' The chief clerk in the office at Ballantyne's yard was smart and brisk but shook his neatly brushed head sadly. 'We had a fire about ten years back and lost all our records up to that date.'

Bradley Carver frowned. He had been at the station that morning to see Emily on to her train. 'Give Uncle Nathaniel my respects and best wishes,' he had said.

'I will. Thank you, Bradley,' called Emily, as the train pulled away. 'I'll see you in two weeks.'

Bradley thought that that would be ample time for his purpose – with a bit of luck. He had gone straight to Ballantyne's hoping to find out immediately the name of the man Jaikie had seen walk on to the quay that night twenty-four years ago, or at least be given a list of possibilities. Now he had to control his temper at this obstacle. He could have gone directly to the top, to old George Ballantyne, but he did not want to invest his search with too much importance. He did not want the matter to become public, fearing hoaxers claiming to be the heir. Worse still, that publicity might produce the genuine claimant before he could act. That would not do.

'You're sure you lost everything?' he pressed.

The chief clerk spread his hands. 'Every scrap of paper. I'm sorry, Mr Carver.'

It was then that one of the clerks working at the ranked desks behind him looked up. 'Excuse me,' he said, 'but what about Mr Goddard?'

The chief clerk pursed his lips. 'Indeed, he might be able to help. Goddard worked here for forty years, only retired a year back, and he had a wonderful memory. If anyone could tell you who would have been here at the time you're asking about, it's Goddard. Mind you, he can be difficult. He never talked much and I wouldn't be surprised if he kept his mouth shut now.'

Bradley thought that he could wring the truth out of Goddard if the old man tried to be awkward. He came away with the address and drove himself there. Goddard lived in one of a neat row of terraced cottages. This was a step up from the houses down by the river. There were no gardens and the front doors opened on to the street, but they were all shut. No children ran about barefoot and every window was covered with lace curtains, several of which twitched when the Humber drew up. The rap of the polished brass knocker echoed along the passage behind the door, but there was no answer. Then a grey-haired man, thin and frail, opened the front door of the next cottage and asked wheezily, 'Are you wanting Tommy Goddard? Because he's away.'

Bradley swore under his breath. 'When is he returning?'

'He's due back a week come Friday.'

That did not suit Bradley. 'Where is he?'

The old man shrugged. 'I don't know. He never speaks except when he goes off every now and again. Then he asks us to keep an eye on the place but never says where he's going. Gets shirty if you ask. I did. Just said, "Off somewhere nice, then?" And he told me, "None o' your business." So I told him, "No call to be bloody rude." But we still look after the place. You've got to help each other, neighbours. Even though he's a bad-tempered old bugger.'

'Thank you,' Bradley said. He turned to leave.

'Can I give him any message when he comes home?' the neighbour asked. 'That's if he'll listen – he doesn't most o' the time.'

Tell him he's a bloody nuisance, thought Bradley, but he said carelessly, 'No, thanks. It wasn't important.'

He returned to his office and his work. There was nothing he could do but wait for Tommy Goddard to return. He thought it was fortunate that Emily had decided to visit Nathaniel for two weeks. That gave him some leeway.

* * *

Emily made leisurely progress. She had never taken a holiday before, or ventured further than Sunderland and the Wilkinson house at Hylton, save for the voyage to St Petersburg. She wanted to relax and enjoy herself, recalling the old saying, 'All work and no play makes Jack a dull boy.' It applied to Jill, too. At the same time she reflected on how lucky she was: most women she knew had to be content with one week's holiday a year spent at home. She passed her first night in a London hotel and ate a lonely dinner, while covertly observing the staff at their work to see if she could pick up some tips for the Clipper.

The following two nights Emily slept in a hotel in Paris and in the day between saw some of the sights of the city. It was possible that David Walsh had sailed to some French port, she mused, but France was a large country. However, she turned to stare when she glimpsed a tall young man in a navy blue jacket, then told herself, 'Don't be a fool.'

Shadows lay on the hills behind the town as the train pulled in to St Raphael. Jenkins, the footman who always accompanied Nathaniel abroad, was there to greet her as she stepped down from the train: 'Nice to see you, miss.'

'And you,' replied Emily and asked, 'How is Mr Franklin?'

'Getting old before his time, miss, though he's perked up since he heard you were coming.' He busied himself with her luggage.

Nathaniel advanced towards them from where he had waited by his motor-car. It was a Darracq with its folding hood erected against the evening chill. Its big headlamps gleamed and Armand, the uniformed French chauffeur, held open the door. To Emily, Nathaniel seemed greyer, slower, and she felt a pang of pity for this man so aged by the loss of his family. She was also glad to be bringing him hope, and prayed that it was not premature.

'I'm a selfish old man to drag you all this way on a whim,' Nathaniel said with delight and contrition.

Emily laughed. 'My whim! I wanted to get away so I've accepted your invitation to take a holiday.'

'I'm glad.' Nathaniel took her arm. 'Come back to the villa and tell me all your news. The last I heard from you was a brief letter telling me you were off to Russia to rescue the *Margaret Glenn*.'

Emily related her adventure in the Baltic as Armand drove them through the town in the dusk, past the harbour, with its cluster of fishing-boats, and the casino. Nathaniel was delighted with her success, and said, 'So you and David made a good partnership.'

Emily managed to smile. 'Mutually profitable,' she answered neutrally. She headed off any further questioning on that subject as the Darracq wheeled into the courtyard of the pine-shaded villa. 'I have some news that's more important than my trip to St Petersburg. I'll tell you inside.'

They sat before a log fire in the cool of the evening. With the curtains open they could see the distant lights of St Tropez as they sipped aperitifs served to them by the white-jacketed François, who ran the house with his wife

Jeanne. Emily smiled at Nathaniel over the rim of her glass and said, 'I think you might have a grand-daughter . . .'

Nathaniel listened, incredulous at first, then horrified, intrigued and finally eager. At the end he whispered, 'I can't believe it!' Then he corrected himself: 'No! I believe it, though I find it incredible that after all these years I learn that the woman I identified was not my daughter. But I believe you. And my granddaughter is – alive!'

Emily warned, 'We don't know that. We still have to find her.'

'But we know of no reason why she should *not* be alive!' Nathaniel stood up creakily from his chair, but that was just the stiffness of old age. There was energy about him now. 'We must go home and look for her!' He paced back and forth restlessly. 'I must look up trains, ask François to pack my things—'

He stopped then, as he turned and saw Emily seated in her armchair, smiling at him uncertainly. 'But I'm for-getting about you! After persuading you to travel all this way to cheer me, I start talking of dragging you home again! I'm sorry. You must have your holiday.'

Emily laughed. 'I don't need a holiday that much!' But then she became serious: 'Don't you think it's early in the year for you to go back to Sunderland?'

Nathaniel shook his head vigorously. 'Not now! I'm going!' Emily knew that no one would change his mind. 'But you shall have your holiday first.'

They wrangled amiably for a minute or two then came

to an agreement: Emily would stay for three days, to relax and recover from her travelling, then they would return together to Sunderland.

They ate a leisurely dinner then sat and talked before the log fire. After a while Nathaniel realised he was doing all the talking and Emily was sitting silent and abstracted. 'Have you something on your mind?' he asked.

'No,' Emily answered quickly. But her smile was as quickly come and gone.

Nathaniel ignored the denial. 'Do you want to talk about it?'

'No, there's nothing, really.' But she would not look at him.

Suddenly his mind skipped back over twenty-odd years and he recalled a night when Marie had had a tiff with Vincent Leigh the man with whom she had run off. Marie had looked a little like the girl sitting opposite him now. He said nothing, but was sure that a man was responsible for Emily's abstraction. David Walsh, perhaps?

The next morning they sent a telegram to Bradley: BOTH COMING HOME THURSDAY. Emily sent another to Silas Worthy, giving the same information.

Silas Worthy went about his work happily. Now he did not have to wait for the best price he could get for the *Sea Princess* and the *Margaret Glenn*. He could take the first bids offered and had done so. The sales were going through. He read the telegram from Emily, was shocked at first, then calculated that he had enough time. He went out to where Violet stood at the window, prinking her hair. He stroked her haunches and told her, 'We'll be leaving Wednesday, so mind you're ready.' He had thought at one time that he might go alone because he would find all he wanted in Hamburg. But he could not leave Violet behind because she would tell the world. And he could not stay long in Hamburg: he would have to move on, change his identity and hide in Italy or Greece. First, though, he would sample the pleasures of the German city for a few days.

'My dress won't be done till Friday,' she complained.

'Then you'll have to leave it. We go on Wednesday.'

'It cost me well over a quid, nearly two.'

It had actually cost Worthy but he did not argue. 'I don't give a bugger. I'll be on that boat Wednesday. If you want to come with me you'll forget about that bloody dress and be there.'

Violet pouted sulkily but said no more. She saw he was having what she called 'one of his masterful turns'. They had started when he had told her they were going to the Hotel Salzburg in Hamburg. She wondered what had changed him.

He was already sensing the power money could bring and looking forward to having it.

The days slipped by. Increasingly frustrated by his enforced wait, Bradley Carver visited Goddard's cottage twice in case he had returned early. He did so surreptitiously, at night and without the Humber, which would have advertised his presence because few motor-cars were about. But Goddard did not return. Bradley came away cursing softly from his second visit on the Wednesday. It seemed certain the old clerk would not come home until Friday. Bradley was only too well aware that Emily and Nathaniel were on their way and would arrive on Thursday evening. Emily would want to know what he had learnt and he would have to tell her. Somehow he would have to make sure he kept ahead of her in the hunt for the heiress to the Franklin fortune.

And as Bradley brooded thus, Silas Worthy and Violet sat down to dinner aboard the ship carrying them to Hamburg.

'Marvellous to have you back, sir! And you, Emily, though I thought you would be staying longer.' Bradley was smiling and urbane when he met them at the station, with porters engaged to carry their luggage and Nathaniel's carriage waiting outside the station. 'You will have come home to follow our enquiries seeking your granddaughter, Uncle.'

'Nothing would keep me away.' Nathaniel showed no sign of weariness, despite the length of the journey. He looked ten years younger than when Bradley had last seen him. 'What have you discovered?'

Bradley became apologetic now, his regret real when he

said, 'Nothing, I'm afraid.' He explained the reason, finishing, 'Mr Goddard will return tomorrow afternoon and I'm going to see him then.'

'We'll go with you. Agreed, Emily?' Nathaniel said promptly.

'Please!'

'Of course.' Bradley could only agree.

Nathaniel's carriage delivered Emily to the Clipper and an excited welcome from Sadie and the Kirbys. The old man went on to his big house, and found he missed the girl who had been his companion this past week. She had been flushed and laughing when he left her, her melancholy forgotten for a while, or for ever, he hoped.

Emily unpacked then went early to bed, knowing that a full day awaited her tomorrow. She thought she owed it to David Walsh to tell him what progress had been made in disposing of the ship they owned jointly, the *Sea Princess*. She would visit Silas Worthy in the morning.

Emily found Worthy's office empty except for a grey-haired man, a caretaker in overalls, who was dumping files into a wheelbarrow. 'Worthy? He's gone,' he told a startled Emily. 'Gave his notice a few days ago. I'm getting the place cleared out for another tenant.'

Emily went to Worthy's house with a sickening feeling of apprehension. There was a sign in the window that read 'TO LET'. A neighbour told her, 'He went off in a cab on Wednesday morning, had two suitcases with him. I said,

'Off on holiday, Mr Worthy?" "Aye," he said. "A long one." And he laughed. Next thing, the landlord comes and puts that notice in the window.'

The manager at the bank where Worthy had his account told Emily that he had deposited two large sums from the sale of two ships. Then a few days later, on Wednesday morning, he had closed the account. 'He took it all in cash.'

Emily was numb with shock. She and David had given Worthy authority to act for them and he had taken full advantage of it. She was as ruined now as she would have been if the two ships had mouldered in the harbour of St Petersburg.

Chapter Twenty-Four

Penniless! Emily had lost all that she had worked for over the years since that bright, childish vision of owning ships. Those few who had heard of it had smiled – even laughed, as David Walsh had. But she had achieved it. And now? She would have to sell the Clipper to repay David. He had only invested his money in the *Sea Princess* to come to her rescue when the *Margaret Glenn* was impounded by the Russians. Then he had said, 'I'll trust you with my money.' Now she had lost it. She felt an awful responsibility for that. She had only the money in her personal account, which would tide her over for some weeks, but then . . . She had to support Ada, who could no longer work and had no pension. She felt sick.

'Are you feeling faint?' the bank manager asked. 'Some water, perhaps?' He hurried round his desk with the glass.

Emily realised she was drooping in the chair, hands to her face. She lowered them, straightened and said politely, 'Thank you. I'm fine, really.' But she took the glass and sipped.

She must inform the police, but what could they do? She could not tell them where Worthy was. The law would take its course but also its time. Meanwhile Worthy would be gone, taking her and David's money. He had destroyed her bright vision. Now anger came, sweeping through her like a flame. How dare he treat her like that? He had swindled her and David and, by God! she would make him pay.

Emily rose from the chair. 'I have urgent business to attend to. I'm sorry to have been a nuisance.' She left the office, the manager holding the door open with one hand, the glass with the other. Emily walked out of the bank determinedly and was gone. She had remembered Violet.

When Emily had first met Violet she had said, 'I live in Roker Avenue.' And: 'The house belongs to my aunt.' Emily recalled the snippets of conversation because she had been amused by the girl's snobbery at the time. That information might be useful now.

Roker Avenue was long but Emily did not think she needed to knock at every door. She started with a corner shop, 'Do you know a girl called Violet?' She asked the proprietor. He did not, and Emily moved on.

The fourth shop sold sweets, tobacco and newspapers. Its cramped interior was crowded with children on their way home from school for lunch. Because they had been

o school they all wore shoes or boots of some sort, if only
old and holed plimsolls, the canvas shoes that had first
come out thirty years earlier and were popular because
they were cheap. Just two were buying, the rest watching
hungrily as the woman behind the counter used a little
hammer to break toffee from a tray.

Emily put her question again. 'Would that be Violet
Tansey?' the woman asked. 'Big lass, fancies herself? Lives
with her aunt?'

'That sounds like her.'

The woman sniffed. 'I know Violet.' She wrapped
toffee in a scrap of newspaper and handed it to one of the
children: 'There y'are, lad. Give us your ha'penny.' She
dropped the coin in the drawer that served as a till and
took up the hammer again. 'Her aunt – that's Mrs
Gibbons – takes in lodgers. We deliver her papers. Third
house along on your right.'

'Thank you.' Emily handed over some coppers. 'Give
them a ha'porth each.' She left the crowded little shop
followed by a chorus of: 'Thank ye, missus.'

The house was one of a terrace, tall and narrow-
fronted, with a polished brass knocker. Emily tapped
firmly and seconds later she saw the lace curtains at the
bow window twitch. Another short wait and then the
door was opened. The woman was like the house, tall and
narrow. She looked down her long nose at Emily and
asked, 'Aye?'

'I'm looking for Violet Tansey. Does she live here?'
Emily smiled politely, hoping.

'Not now, she doesn't.' The woman's face tightened. 'Are you a friend of hers?'

'No. When did she leave?'

'The day afore yesterday she went off in a cab wi' this feller, but not till she'd said some terrible things to me. Said she was going, wouldn't tell me where but she wasn't coming back. My oath! I'll see she doesn't set foot in this house again.'

'Oh, I'm sorry.' Emily was because the tight face had loosened and she saw hurt there now. 'She treated you very badly. I suppose you're her aunt.'

'Aye.' Mrs Gibbons dabbed at her eyes with a scrap of handkerchief. 'You know her?'

'I've had dealings with her and I want to find her.'

'What's she done?'

Emily hesitated, then said diplomatically, 'Let's say I think she has something that belongs to me.'

'Oh, aye?' A sigh. 'Well, it doesn't come as a surprise. I thought she might turn out a bad lass, always thought it, but she was my brother's and when he died . . . His wife ran off wi' another feller so I suppose what's bred in the bone . . .'

While Mrs Gibbons rambled Emily thought. She knew she would not find Violet here, and her aunt did not know where she had gone, but . . . 'Can I see her room?' Emily asked. 'It's just that she might have left something to show where she's gone.'

'I don't see any harm in that.' Mrs Gibbons opened the door wider. 'I haven't cleared it out yet and it's just as she left it. I thought she might see the light and come back, and I've been that upset.'

The room was poky, clean but untidy, the bed unmade and odds and ends of clothing and papers littering the chest of drawers and the floor. Mrs Gibbons stood in the doorway, watching miserably as Emily sifted through the papers. There was a bill from a dressmaker. Emily's brow lifted. Violet had paid twenty-nine shillings and sixpence for a dress. That was a week's wages for a labourer in the shipyards, two or three times what Violet could earn in an office. The bill was endorsed: 'Paid'. Scrawled across its face were the words: 'To fwd'.

'May I take this?' Emily asked. 'The shop may know where she has gone.'

Mrs Gibbons shrugged. 'I shouldn't think it would be any use to anyone. So, aye, take it.' And as Emily left the house: 'My poor brother. He'll be turning in his grave.'

The dressmaker had a little shop off the high street and was imposing in black bombazine and tortoiseshell spectacles. She asked affectedly. 'Can I assist Moddom?'

Emily laid the bill on the counter: 'Have you sent this dress on yet?'

'Miss Tansey's gown? Not yet. It is finished but I have not posted it.' Then she looked over the spectacles and lectured, 'I cannot hand it to you. Miss Tansey insisted I forward it and she paid for the postage.'

Emily was annoyed by the woman's suspicion but relieved that she would soon have the information she wanted. 'I don't want it, but will you tell me where you have to send it, please?'

'I couldn't do that. It is a personal matter. I would need Miss Tansey's agreement before—'

Emily interrupted her: 'This will be a matter for the police. Will you tell me, or them when I bring them here?'

'The pollis?' Suddenly the refined accent had disappeared.

Emily rubbed it in: 'I intend to bring charges of theft and embezzlement.'

'Oh, very well.' A ledger was produced from under the counter and Emily noted the address then left the shop almost running. At the station she took a cab but not to the police.

Ten minutes later she was talking to Nathaniel Franklin, who had been about to sit down to lunch. 'I don't think the police can do anything – or, anyway, not in time. Worthy may move on very soon so I'm going to Hamburg.'

'Alone?' Nathaniel did not like the idea.

'Yes. I can deal with Worthy.' Emily was sure of that. 'It won't need force.'

'Let Bradley go with you,' Nathaniel urged.

In the background, Bradley nodded firmly but thought, Damn!

'No,' said Emily. 'You must find out about your granddaughter, and Bradley knows how to do that.'

'Very well,' Nathaniel agreed reluctantly.

Bradley mentally nodded his agreement: he wanted to

find the heiress, not waste his time trying to recover Emily Jackson's fortune. Anyway, the sooner she was ruined, the sooner he would break her.

'Is there anything I can do?' Nathaniel asked.

Emily hesitated. 'Worthy has taken David Walsh's money, too. I want to tell him, but while I know his ship was sighted off Gibraltar I don't know where she is now.'

'Write it out.' Nathaniel shoved pad and paper towards her. 'I'll find out from his owners.'

Emily wrote: 'WORTHY ABSCONDED WITH MONEY STAYING HOTEL SALZBURG HAMBURG. AM FOLLOWING.'

Nathaniel took it from her. 'I wish you luck and success. Take care, and let us know when you will be home again.'

When she had gone, Bradley seized an unexpected opportunity: 'I think it will be best if you see to sending that cable without delay and I will talk to this chap Goddard. He'll know you.' He grinned. 'Everyone does in this town. I think he will be scared of you and keep his mouth shut. Let me talk to him alone.'

While Nathaniel was eager to press on with the search for his granddaughter, he was also concerned for Emily and David. And there was truth in what Bradley had said. 'Very well,' he agreed, 'but let me know what he says as soon as you can.'

So Bradley went to see the elderly and obstinate Mr Goddard alone, but this time he drove the Humber. Goddard himself answered the door. He was bald, with grey sideboards and eyebrows, and glared. 'What the hell d'ye want? I've just got home. Can't a man have a bit o' peace and privacy?'

Bradley jingled a few coins. 'I need some information.'

Goddard's grey brows came down. 'You can keep your bloody money. I've enough o' my own, and I bloody well earned it.'

'I wasn't intending to bribe you, just indicating that I was prepared to pay for your help. The truth is, I'm making enquiries in connection with a small legacy and I need to find out which men might have been working at Ballantyne's over twenty years ago. To be precise, on the night of the sixteenth of June 1884. I asked at Ballantyne's but they have no records of that time. They suggested you might be able to help because you have an excellent memory.'

'More'n they could say,' Goddard growled. But he was flattered. Bradley thought contemptuously that it was probably the only talent the old man could boast about that might set him apart from, if not above, his fellow men. He was going on now: 'Aye, they had a fire. Lost everything. But 'eighty-four?' He frowned. 'The sixteenth of June, you say?'

'It was the first anniversary of the Victoria Hall calamity.'

But that did not help, either. Goddard shook his head. Then he saw the curtains move in the window next door and said loudly, 'Bloody nosy-parkers! Come in.' He opened the door wide, and as Bradley entered, he cackled, 'They'll be wondering tomorrow.' When Bradley looked at him questioningly, he explained, 'I'm off to Australia in the morning. My son's out there and I'm going to live with him and his wife. I've spent the last two weeks in London booking my passage. I only have to pack my gear tonight and then I'm off.'

Bradley smiled. 'Then I'm lucky to have caught you.' He meant it.

When they were in the little kitchen Goddard pointed to a chair. 'Sit down and give me a minute. I – I just have to put a few things away but I'll be thinking about what you want to know.' He disappeared into the room next door and pulled the door to behind him, but it was still open a crack. After a second or two Bradley tiptoed over to it and peered through. He could see half of the bed and Goddard lifting something from under it. The old man put a box on his bed, opened it and took out several books, glanced at them then replaced each volume. Finally he took out one and nodded as if satisfied. He fanned its pages then was still, reading. He put it back into the box and turned towards the door.

Bradley moved swiftly to his chair and was lounging there, legs crossed, when Goddard returned. 'I remember now. It came to me, clear as day. The sixteenth of June 1884. There was only the nightwatchman on duty and he sneaked out of the yard and went home to fetch his bait. He usually put his sandwiches in his pocket but that night he'd forgot. Somebody saw him outside o' the yard and reported him. He damn near got the sack. Then about a week after that he never turned in for work and we never

saw him again. Left without the two or three days' money
he was due!'

Bradley kept his voice casual as he said, 'That sounds
like the man I was asking about.' Then, admiringly, 'You
certainly have a marvellous memory!' To think that
Goddard's fabled feats of recall were based on a patiently
recorded series of diaries! But Bradley still waited for the
vital information: 'What was this man's name?'

Goddard was gratified. 'Bert Jackson,' he said.

The name was familiar. Now it was Bradley's turn to
sift through his memory. Bert Jackson . . . ? Then it came
to him.

Somehow he kept his face devoid of expression but his
lips felt like rubber as he said, 'Thank you. You've been
most helpful.' He took a florin from his pocket and put it
on the table. 'My client would wish you to have this.
Good day to you.'

Goddard saw him to the door and watched him drive
away in the Humber. Then he glared at the house next
door and said, 'Don't bother asking what he wanted. I'm
not telling you.' And then, under his breath, 'And I'll say
to hell with the lot of ye tomorrow.'

Bradley, his mind churning, now knew that Bert Jackson
had walked along the quay that night so long ago. Then he
and his wife had had a daughter. Bradley remembered
when he, David Walsh and the American, Peterson, had
all stood in the station to bid Nathaniel farewell on his

return to France. That had been last September and Emily had said she was twenty-four. So in 1884, when Bert Jackson had walked along the quay, when Marie was murdered, Emily would have been . . . He worked it out: between one and two years old.

He could not believe it. Could he have known this girl – could Nathaniel have known her – for so long and never realised? But then, he told himself, why should they? A lot of girls had been about one or two on that night.

He had to know and knew where to look, knew who could solve this mystery one way or the other.

He remembered the address, itched to go there at once, but knew it would be dangerous. In the street where Ada lived the wives would be gossiping at their front doors all the daylight hours and he would certainly be seen.

That evening Emily sailed from Newcastle in a ship bound for Hamburg. In the evening Bradley Carver, wearing an old overcoat and a scarf around his face, sought out the house where Ada lived. The front door was shut now but not bolted. He could see no light in the downstairs rooms, nor was there any in the passage or on the landing as he groped his way upstairs. He stood outside the kitchen in the darkness and listened. A glow showed through a crack at the foot of the poorly fitting door and he could hear a low crooning but no conversation. He tapped softly and a voice called, 'Come in, Bridget, if that's you.'

He pushed open the door and entered. He saw Ada sitting in an old armchair before the fire; there was no one else in the room. She stared at him, startled and suspicious, and he pulled down the scarf to show his smiling face because he did not care if she saw it. 'Remember me, Mrs Jackson? Bradley Carver. I came with your daughter one day.'

'Oh, aye.' Ada nodded, no longer wary or suspicious, but not welcoming, either. 'You'd better come in. Would you like a cup of tea?'

'No, thank you. I won't stay long.' Bradley crossed the little room in two strides to stand over her. 'I just want to talk about Emily. It must be nearly twenty-four years now since you took her in.'

'Aye . . .' Ada's mouth stayed open: she was frozen in shock after the admission had been tricked out of her.

Bradley knew that would not last. He reached out to seize her by the throat. 'Make a sound and I'll—' He squeezed to make his point. Ada's mouth was gaping, her eyes protruding, frightened. Bradley relaxed his grip to let her breathe but kept his hand in place. 'Did Bert bring the girl home?' Her head moved fractionally, nodding. 'Why did you keep her?'

A whisper: 'She was sent. A year to the day after my first bairn was lost in the Victoria Hall.'

'Why did you call her Emily?'

'She said that was her name.'

'She would.' Bradley had realised why, though Ada had not. 'Who have you told about this?'

'Nobody.'

'Have you written anything down?'

'No.'

But Bradley had seen the flicker in her eyes and knew she was lying. 'Where is it?'

'No, I haven't!'

'Tell me!' He tightened his grip and Ada's face contorted. He released her and repeated, 'Tell me!' But Ada lolled sideways in the chair and seemed to collapse inside herself, shrivelling before his eyes.

Bradley bent over her, his hand on her neck now seeking a pulse. He found none. Now he heard the front door open. He had listened for it since entering the house and it snapped him upright, alert. He had to get out. Ada was dead, and if he was found here—He glanced around the room, eyes hunting desperately for a likely hiding-place for Ada's record of the finding of Emily, but saw there could be dozens: a loose floorboard, in some cupboard, in her bedroom next door . . . It might be anywhere.

There were voices in the passage, a chorus of 'Goodnight', female voices and one male: 'Goodnight, Annie!' 'Goodnight, Bridget!' 'Goodnight . . . Goodnight . . .' Bradley knew Bridget was Mrs Cassidy, Ada's old friend. She might come up at any moment – her husband with her. He could wait no longer. He saw the old woman's purse on the mantelpiece, emptied it of its coins and thrust them into his pocket then dropped the purse on the floor where it would be found. It would appear that Ada had been killed for her money.

He stole out on to the landing and saw that there was light in the kitchen below but the door was shut. He ran, swift and silent, down the stairs and along the passage, his way lit by the glow coming from under the door of the ground-floor kitchen. He was checked for a moment because the front door was bolted now, but he eased it clear and passed through. No one saw him slip along the street in the shadows, a dark-coated, muffled figure.

Later, he told Nathaniel, 'Goddard could not remember that far back. One or two incidents, yes, but not details of who was working at Ballantyne's on a particular night.'

Nathaniel sat down suddenly, as if his legs had failed him. 'I suppose I was too optimistic, expecting to find her easily after all these years,' he said slowly. He looked up at Bradley. 'So what do you think we should do now?'

Bradley frowned. 'I don't think we should do anything in a hurry. Better to give it some thought. We don't want to rush into advertising, attracting a lot of publicity, because of the possibility of false claimants. I think we should wait a few days to see if we can come up with some bright ideas.'

Nathaniel sighed and agreed. 'We might as well wait until Emily comes home.'

Bradley winced, was already thinking of the next step. He decided it did not matter what Ada had written, establishing Emily Jackson as the heiress to the Franklin fortune if the girl could not claim it. Before, he had wanted to possess Emily. Now, he had to be rid of her.

Chapter Twenty-Five

A giant loomed over Emily and his hand came out of the night and seized her arm. She opened her mouth to scream but then saw the man's face in the light from the café: 'David!' His name burst from her in a puff of breath like smoke on the frosty air. He had a two-day stubble and was dressed in a tweed suit rather than uniform. They stood in the shadows at the side of the street, its surface covered by fresh snow. It laid a white carpet over the slush churned up by plodding walkers, wrapped up against the cold. Emily and David were outside the cones of light shed by the street lamps, and opposite the Hotel Salzburg. She had been about to cross to it, but now asked, 'How did you get here?'

'Train.' He led her towards the door of the café, a scant three long strides for him. 'When I got your cable I

decided there was no point in calling on the police becaus
Worthy might have disappeared before they could act
Better for us to strike while the iron is hot. I gather yo
came to the same decision.' Emily nodded. 'I received you
cable this morning when my ship berthed in Boulogne
The first mate will handle the discharging and loading and
we'll be lying there for another twenty-four hours anyway
I got here about an hour ago and I've been sitting in her
working out what to do and looking out for you.' Now
they were in the café and sitting at a little table in th
window. A waiter came, white apron to his knees and
black waistcoat. David ordered, '*Kaffee, bitte.*'

He watched the hotel through the window. When th
man had come with the coffee and gone, he said, 'I didn'
go into the place and ask for Worthy because if he finds
out someone's asking about him he'll be off like a shot
But I had a bit of luck. Half an hour ago a cab drove up
Worthy and his girl got in and off they went. Gone out to
dinner, I suppose.'

Emily felt as if a load had been lifted from her. She was
glad he was there. She had slept badly on the ship
worrying whether she would be in time to catch Worthy
and what she would do if she did come up with him. Her
boast to Nathaniel that she could handle the man seemed
hollow now. What could she do if he defied her? Would
the German police act to help a lone Englishwoman? Now
she, too, stared at the hotel across the street and asked
'Do you think we could get into his room?'

'I've walked past a couple of times, didn't stop because

didn't want to raise anybody's suspicions, but I saw enough. There's a porter on duty in the hall, hanging about in case he's needed, and a clerk sitting behind the reception desk. Anybody going in would have to pass him.'

'What about a diversion to distract them?' Emily suggested.

David grinned at her. 'That's exactly what I was thinking before you turned up, but I couldn't see how to work it on my own.'

'Suppose I pretended to faint in the foyer, off to one side, say, so they would have to move away from the desk and the stairs? Then you could slip past them and up to Worthy's room.'

David thought briefly, then shook his head. 'We don't know which one it is. If I started knocking on doors there would soon be uproar. That's the last thing we want. I don't know how we'd stand if the hotel called the police.'

They sat in gloomy silence for some minutes. Once Emily said drily, 'We could ambush him when he comes back.'

'It's a nice thought, but we don't want him. We want our money.' Then, a few minutes later, he said, 'Hold on. That's the porter. Is he coming here?' A man had emerged from the hotel, shrugging into a black jacket. Now he trotted across the street and David said, 'He *is* coming here. Out for a break, I expect. Hope he speaks English.'

The porter shoved his way through the door into the café. He was a man of forty or so, florid and portly with thick, upswept moustaches. He called to the waiter, '*Bier bitte!*' and made for what seemed to be his usual table.

David rose quickly and waved a hand: 'Will you join us, *mein Herr*?'

The porter accepted the invitation cheerfully. 'English, yes?' He shook hands with David and gave a little bow to Emily before he sat down. 'We get many English in the hotel. I speak all the time. Also, I work in English hotel many years, in London.'

The waiter brought his beer and he took a deep draught. David signalled for another then wasted no more time. 'There is an Englishman in the hotel now.'

The porter wiped foam from his moustaches. '*Ja.* There are five.'

'This one has a young lady with him,' Emily put in. She gestured with her hands to indicate the big-bosomed Violet – and caught David's surprised grin.

The porter sniggered lewdly, then coughed, embarrassed. '*Ja.* Herr Miller.'

So that was what he called himself. Emily glanced at David and he nodded. 'Herr Miller is my husband,' she said. 'He has run away with this girl. I want to go to their room and catch them. There is a back door?'

The porter stared at her. 'He is your husband?' He glanced at David. 'I thought . . .' His voice trailed away.

Emily could not meet David's gaze. She said, 'This is my brother. He has come to help me.'

'He left you? He is mad.' The porter tapped his head.

'But there is a back door.' He drained his second beer. '*Komm.*'

He led them across the street and down an alley at the side of the hotel. They descended stone steps and pushed through a door into a small cellar kitchen. White-clad cooks were busy over steaming pans set on a big range. They bawled greetings to the porter as he led Emily and David through. Then they were climbing uncarpeted service stairs until he stopped at a green-baize-covered door. He opened it and pointed. They saw a corridor, a narrow strip of worn carpet running down its centre to the head of the stairs at the end. Doors opened off on either side, all closed, all numbered. He pointed at one and said, 'Twenty-three.'

'Thank you.'

David dug in his pocket, but the porter pushed away his hand. '*Nein!* I do this for the lady.' He bowed to Emily again then left them.

They stood together, the green-baize door open an inch or so, just wide enough for them to see the door to room twenty-three. David stood behind Emily, looking over her head, his hands resting on her shoulders, his body against hers. Emily felt breathless, afraid to move, to face him. Then they heard wrangling voices and his grip tightened. Worthy said, 'Ah! You're never satisfied! You didn't want to eat in here but you didn't like where we went to. You're always moaning.'

'It's all right for you, going off every night and leaving me here on my own,' Violet replied discontentedly.

'Where do you get to? Business, you tell me, but what business?'

'Mine!' Worthy snapped back.

'And last night you said we'd be moving on today but this morning you changed your mind,' Violet went on. 'I'm fed up with this place.'

'We'll go when I'm ready!' Worthy burst out. 'Now shut up or I'll lay my hand across you!'

'You'll be sorry if you do,' Violet whined. But she said no more.

They appeared at the head of the stairs and David breathed, 'When they open the door.'

Worthy inserted the key, opened the door and led the way into the room. Violet followed him, then Emily and David were at her heels. As Violet turned to shut the door, Emily pushed her further into the room and David closed it. Worthy had turned and was gaping at the intruders. 'Here! What d'you want?' Violet squeaked. She wore an ornate flowered hat held on to her piled hair with long pins.

Emily pulled out one of the pins, levelled it at Violet's face and tried to look menacing. 'One peep out of you . . .' Violet squeaked again, then covered her mouth with her hands and peered wide-eyed over them at Emily.

David had seized Worthy. 'You should have moved on when Violet said. Where's the money?'

'It's in the safe, downstairs,' Worthy croaked.

But Emily had seen Violet's lashes flutter. 'He's lying,' she said. And now she was watching Worthy, whose waistcoat was stretched tight over his stomach.

'I'm taking my money, if I have to beat the life out of you,' David growled.

His expression frightened Worthy, who was shaking now but still claimed, 'It's in the safe.'

'It's round his middle in a money-belt,' Emily said.

Now Worthy fought, but he was helpless against David who found the belt under the waistcoat, ripped it off and threw it to Emily while he held Worthy one-handed. Emily made the frightened Violet lie face down on the floor, then opened every pocket on the belt. She found them packed with banknotes and gold sovereigns. She counted the contents swiftly. 'It seems to be all here,' she told David.

He released Worthy, who collapsed to sit on the edge of the bed, his head in his hands. 'Good enough,' said David. But he glared: 'I still think I should give you one or two to remember.'

Worthy shrank away, but then Emily asked, 'Have you any money of your own?' Worthy dug into his pocket and brought out a handful of marks. Violet shook her head. Emily transferred her gaze to David, who guessed at her unspoken question and nodded. Emily took out ten sovereigns and laid them on the bedside table. 'That should pay your bill here and your passages home.'

'Thank you,' Violet whispered. A second or two later, Silas Worthy echoed her. He looked up at Emily then averted his gaze, ashamed.

Emily and David departed as they had come, by the side door. As they came out of the alley into the street,

David glanced sideways at her. 'Would you really have stuck her with that hatpin?'

Emily laughed, almost hysterically, with relief. 'No! But it worked.' Then, two paces on, she looked up at him: 'Would you really have beaten the life out of him?'

He grinned down at her. 'It sounds like we're a pair.'

They laughed together but then Emily became serious: 'I'm taking the next boat home. What about you?'

'A train.' He hailed a passing cab. 'The first of several that will take me back to my ship. I should just be in time to sail her as planned.'

In the cab they were silent until Emily asked, 'Do you want to take your share of the money now?'

'No.'

'It's rather a lot,' she pointed out.

'My life savings. But it's as safe with you as with me. Bank it for me when you get home.'

His train was full and on the point of leaving, but he was first in a late rush of passengers. He found a seat in the middle of a coach as the others piled on behind him. He could not get back to the door because of the press of people in the corridor but stood at a little window to talk to Emily. Her mouth had drooped at the corners, but when he looked down at her, his head an arm's length above her, she smiled.

'We make a good team,' he said softly.

'Yes,' she murmured.

'I suppose you're going on with this shipowning business.' He was serious now.

Emily thought, Please! Don't let's fight. But she had to speak the truth: 'Yes.'

He said, 'I've never known anyone like you before. Those girls in London, and in the East . . .' The train shunted and started to move. Emily lifted a hand to wave but he reached down to grip it, pressed the palm to his mouth and kissed it.

'I'd take you as you are but you won't have me,' Emily said, the words wrenched out of her. 'You want me to change but that won't work.' He was snatched from her then as the train pulled away. Emily put the hand he had kissed to her mouth. She fancied she could still feel the roughness of his stubble against her palm. She told herself she would not cry.

But she did.

Chapter Twenty-Six

Bradley Carver had laid his trap. He had told the servants in the Franklin house: 'As you know, Mr Franklin is not well. I don't want him to receive any shocks, so all telegrams delivered to this house must come to me first.' Thus he ensured that he would know first when Emily Jackson planned to arrive in Sunderland. He would collect her from the station, telling her that he had found a clue to the whereabouts of Nathaniel's heiress. He had chosen a lonely place on the Durham road at which to stop.

But no telegram came from Emily until late one evening. Then it was brought to him, where he worked in his study, by Porteous, the butler. Bradley took it from the salver, 'Thank you.' It was addressed to Nathaniel and read: 'ARRIVED TOO LATE WILL GO STRAIGHT HOME.' It had been sent from Newcastle-on-Tyne. Bradley guessed

Emily would be at the Clipper even as he read it. He folded it and put it in his pocket. 'Thank you,' he said to Porteous. 'I don't think Mr Franklin should see this at present. I'll talk to him quietly later.'

When the butler had gone Bradley swore. His plan was in tatters and he had to act quickly. There would have to be an accident.

He drove down to the Clipper, parked the Humber outside and found Emily in her private living room behind the bar. Sadie Theakstone took him in, whispering tearfully, 'She's just had an awful shock. We've had to tell her about her mother being killed.'

'Yes. A terrible affair,' Bradley said gravely.

Emily sat in an armchair before the fire, her cheeks wet with tears. By her side stooped a dumpy little woman, red-cheeked and with grey hair showing beneath a black shawl. She had her arm around Emily's shoulders.

'I'm sorry you came home to such news,' Bradley said softly.

'Thank you,' said Emily. 'This is Bridget Cassidy, a neighbour of my mother. She came round to give me this.' She held up a cheap envelope.

'Aye,' Bridget said. 'Ada said to me: "Bridget, you've always been a good friend. If anything happens to me, I want you to give this to my bairn, my Emily." So I came over with it the day after it happened. The whole street was in an uproar. We've never had owt like that happen before. And he killed her for her few coppers! I hope the pollis gets the feller that did it.'

Bradley was sure they would not unless . . . His eyes were on the envelope and he could see that it was still sealed. Emily had not opened it.

Bridget went on, 'Well, Emily wasn't here that first day so I came over the next night, then yesterday and tonight I found her.'

Bradley thought she might be hanging on to find out what was in the envelope. He could not allow that. 'I'm sure we're all very grateful to you, Mrs Cassidy. However, I also have some news for Miss Jackson and I'd be grateful if you would excuse us.' He urged her out to where Sadie Theakstone and Joe Kirby were serving, handed them silver and told them, 'Mrs Cassidy has been very kind. Will you call a cab for her and give her a drop of something to keep out the cold?' He left Bridget relishing a glass of rum and went back to Emily.

She was picking sadly at the envelope and he laid his hand on hers, stopping her. 'I've just come from Nathaniel. He sent me to show you what we've found out about his granddaughter.'

Emily looked up at him with lacklustre eyes: 'Yes?'

'I can't tell you. I'll have to show you.'

'Now?' Emily was weary from travelling and heartbreak. The news of Ada's death had left her grief-stricken. She needed time to recover. 'Can't it wait until tomorrow?'

'It won't take more than a few minutes and Nathaniel was particularly keen that you should see it tonight.' He added cunningly, 'He hasn't been too well.'

'I thought he may have come home too early in the year,' Emily said worriedly. 'Can we go to see him later?'

'Of course.'

Emily put on her coat, glanced at the leather motoring coat he was wearing and saw that it glistened with moisture. 'Is it raining?'

'Just mist.'

'I'll put on a hat.' She pinned the wide-brimmed felt hat on her piled hair and secured it for riding in the Humber with a wisp of a chiffon scarf tied under her chin. 'I'm ready now.'

'You look very nice,' he said, and led her out to the Humber. Sadie, Joe and a bar full of men saw them go out together. Bradley knew he would have some explaining to do later but that could wait.

The Humber was open to the sky, its hood folded back, because he liked it that way. Anyway, it did not matter because it took less than a minute to drive down to the quay. Bradley stopped the Humber under the sole light. It would have suited his purpose better to have clung to the darkness but that might have made Emily suspicious, despite her preoccupation with her grief and her trust in him. He saw that he would have to wait because a shift had been working overtime in Ballantyne's yard and now the men were streaming out of the shipyard further along the quay. He could not see the yard from his seat in the car because the fog was drifting in from the sea, hanging over the river and hiding it. But the men were passing the Humber to climb the street leading up from the river and past the Clipper, their boots clattering on the cobbles. Bradley dared attempt nothing until they had gone.

He shifted restlessly, got down from the Humber and said, 'I won't be a minute.' He did not want to have to answer any questions. If he was evasive for too long the girl might become suspicious.

'What did you bring me to see?' Emily asked.

'I'll be able to show you soon.' He crossed the quay to look down at the river.

Emily watched him go, puzzled, but the shock of Worthy's theft, her dash across the North Sea, her parting from David and the death of her mother had combined to leave her stunned and apathetic. She remembered the envelope she held in her lap and opened it listlessly. She expected to read some last message of love from Ada and the sight of the familiar crabbed but now shaky script started the tears again. But then she became absorbed in Ada's last confession:

> My dear daughter because I always think of you as that but I have to tell you dear Emily that you are not my daughter. Bert found you on the quay by Ballantyne's yard, all by yourself in the fog, and he brought you home to me. It was a year to the day that I had lost my child in the tragick accident at the Victoria hall and I thought you had been sent to me by God because nobody claimed you. I was afraid if I reported you they would put you in the orphanage and I could not bear to think of that you were such a bonny loving little bairn. We called you Emily because you said that was your name. You didn't know a second

one. But I always knew in my heart that you were another woman's bairn. I thought she had left you on purpose so I saw no sin in keeping you. I've no way of knowing who she was but I owe it to you to tell you the truth. I can't bear to tell you to your face in case you hate me for deceiving you for all these years but I am leaving this with Bridget Cassidy and she will see you get it. I pray you will think kindly of a weak woman. God bless you. Ada Jackson.

Emily's tears were dry, her mind in chaos as facts and conclusions raced through her head like the jerky pictures on the silent screen. A year to the day after the Victoria Hall disaster. Bert had found her on the quay! She remembered that ten years ago, when she had set out to work for the Swindells, Bert had said, 'I wanted to do better than this for you. All those years ago I shouldn't have—' He had stopped then. Had he been about to say: 'I shouldn't have brought you home'? And Ada, when ill and delirious, saying: 'Emily was meant . . . was sent.' Emily had been the child Jaikie and Maggie had left weeping and alone after they had drowned her mother. The child had said her name was Emily – or had she? The woman who had died in Emily's arms outside the Clipper – Florence Browning – had said, 'I was on the quay that night. Emily . . . Emma.' She had been saying Emma Leigh. Somehow Florence had known.

Now Emily whispered it: 'Emma Leigh.' She was the daughter of Marie Leigh. She was Nathaniel Franklin's granddaughter. She had stood on this quay on a night like this with the tide lapping at the piles and the mist coiling in from the sea, swirling around the yellow light and lying wetly on her face. She shivered.

She was Nathaniel's heir and not Bradley Carver.

She raised her head, which had been bent over the letter, and looked for him at the edge of the quay but he had gone.

He had seen the last of the Ballantyne's men disappear from sight. Their voices and the clatter of their boots had faded to nothing. He had turned and seen Emily reading the letter. Now his hands clamped around her throat as he took her from behind . . .

Shock held Emily for some seconds and her brain ceased to function as she threshed in panic, but when he tried to bend her back over the seat she had to give in to his superior strength. Now she could see his face, twisted with hatred, above her. She reached up quickly with both hands, seized his ears and twisted savagely. His face contorted with pain and he released one hand from her throat to try to pry hers loose. He succeeded with one – and Emily dug her thumb into his eye. This time he gave an agonised cry and released the grip of his other hand to tear hers away. Emily rolled out of the car, taking great gulps of the night air and grabbing at the lamp-post for support.

He came after her, raging. Emily screamed, '*Help! Help!*' She swung around the lamp, keeping it between them, but that ploy did not delay him more than a second or two as he chased her round in the deadly game. He snatched at her once, yanked off the chiffon scarf and knocked her hat askew, then seized the collar of her coat but it tore away with a ripping of stitches. He tossed it aside, reached out a clawing hand and this time gripped her arm. He dragged her towards him and Emily hooked her free arm around the lamp-post to anchor herself. She was stretched between them and he gathered a handful of her dress, which showed through the torn coat, and ripped it from neck to hem. He glimpsed the gleam of flesh in the lamplight and Emily let go of the lamp to cover herself from him. She sobbed. All this time she had screamed, her voice thin and muffled in the mist, but no one came. Now he drew her in, inexorably. Drunk with rage and lust, he believed that now he could possess her *and* be rid of her.

In a heaven-sent flicker of memory Emily suddenly pictured the fear on Violet's face. She pulled the pin from her hat and jabbed it into Bradley Carver's face.

He screamed and let her go, felt for the pin and pulled it from his cheek with bloodied fingers. He threw it aside and started after her yet again. Emily knew she would not elude him or stop him again. This time he would murder her.

Then a great shadow leaped in and hurled Bradley away, to bounce off the bonnet of the Humber and sprawl in a filthy puddle. David Walsh's arms wrapped around Emily and he whispered, 'For God's sake, what has he done to you?'

'I'll be all right in a minute,' Emily whimpered, and even managed to smile.

Now there were voices in the street that ran down from the Clipper and the pounding of feet. Bradley Carver heard them, saw David, and knew that only one course was open to him now if he was to escape the noose that awaited him. David and Emily saw him run off along the quay to be lost in the darkness, tearing off his leather motoring coat as he went. David moved to go after him but Emily held on to him: 'Let him go! The police will deal with him.'

Hidden from his pursuers by the night, Bradley stripped to his drawers and made a package of his clothes and shoes, which he attached to himself with his braces. He lowered himself into the river, confident he could cross it because he was a strong swimmer. He shivered and gasped at the cold but he was well out in midstream when he heard the beat of engines.

The ship that emerged from the mist was black against the night, with a white moustache of foam where the water was split by the sharp bow. It loomed over him, the shadow of death, and he was swept along the ship's side, his screams for help unheard. Then, fighting desperately but vainly, he came to the stern and the propeller, just as the body of Marie Leigh had done so long ago, and his cries were silenced for ever.

Back on the quay, David held Emily and asked, 'Why did he attack you? Had he gone mad? I can't believe it of Bradley Carver.'

'I don't know, but I think he knew what he was doing,' Emily replied shakily.

David said, 'Thank God I came in time. I was hurrying all the way home from Boulogne. When we came to our mooring out in the river I got a couple of the men to row me ashore in one of the ship's boats. I was going to the Clipper but we couldn't see the quay in the fog and they put me ashore further downstream by Ballantyne's yard. It was only then that I heard you screaming.'

A group of men arrived now and one called, 'A lass came in the bar and said she could hear a woman screaming. Was that you, Emily?'

She answered them, voice still trembling, 'It was. Bradley Carver attacked me. He ran off towards Ballantyne's.'

There were startled exclamations of: 'Bradley Carver?' But then the leader called, 'We'll get after him, anyway.' They ran off along the quay.

'Are you sure you're all right?' David looked down at Emily seriously.

Was she? But before she could answer that Emily needed an answer to a question of her own. 'Why were you hurrying?'

He tightened his grip on her. 'I told you I'd never known anybody like you before. I wanted to know if that offer still stood, that you'd take me as I am. Because I'll take you as you are.'

Emily stood on tiptoe to kiss him and be kissed.

Later she said, 'You don't even know who I am.' And when he stared at her, she told him.

Chapter Twenty-Seven

A memorial service was held for Bradley Carver; his body had not been recovered. Bradley's mother, shocked, shamed and broken hearted over the loss of a son who had loved her once, retired to a residential home at Nathaniel's expense.

After the nightmares had been left in the past, Nathaniel hosted a spring ball in his house. He received his guests in the ballroom, an old man given a new lease of life and happiness. He stood under the portrait of his daughter Marie with his granddaughter, Emma Leigh, at his side. The resemblance between the two was plain. Now he saw why he had fancied he saw it that day he had walked into the Clipper and encountered Emily as a grown woman. But then, understandably, he had assumed it was only a chance resemblance. Emma's low-cut gown showed that V-shaped scar Tom Peterson had described. Now she was smiling radiantly, would always remember her beloved Ada, who had been so good to her and all that a mother should be, but her grieving was over.

When the band struck up for dancing, she circled the floor in the first waltz in the arms of David Walsh, his ring on her finger.